BACH'S PASSION

The Life of Johann Sebastian Bach

BACH'S PASSION

The Life of Johann Sebastian Bach

A Novel by RuthAnn Ridley

Packaged by WinePress Publishing, PO Box 428, Emumclaw, WA 98022. The views expressed or implied in this work do not necessarily reflect those of WinePress Publishing. Ultimate design, content, and editorial accuracy of this work are the responsibilities of the author.

ISBN 1-57921-170-4
Library of Congress Catalog Card Number: 98-89639

*To the teachers
who tended the flame of my passion for music*

Acknowledgments

First and foremost I acknowledge my husband Bob Ridley who listened to each new chapter and each new revision of *Bach's Passion* with genuine enthusiasm. His excitement about the project enabled me to finish the race.

To the readers who have been with me from the first rough draft—Renee and Todd Ellison, Monte and Linda Unger, and Renee Davis—thank you for your praise of what worked and your critique of what did not.

To gifted educator and visionary, Renee Ellison, I also owe the credit for the original idea. She was convinced that Bach's story needed to be told, and she convinced me that I had the gifts to do it.

Many hugs and kisses to my daughter Robin Ridley for the fun it has been to co-labor with you on this project. Your design for the book surpassed my expectations, and the equanimity of our teamwork was as satisfying as playing in a piano quintet.

Thanks to LMJ photographers for the author's photo. And thanks to the Colorado College music librarians who assisted us with issues of imagery copyright and public domain. We made many calls to Germany, New York City and Los Angeles. Our grateful thanks to those who responded.

I cannot conclude without thanking J.S. Bach for his profound music and for the monogram he designed for his seal ring crest. His design of mirror image initials introduces many sections of this book.

Table of Contents

BOOK ONE · · · *THE VISION*

Prelude
1 7 0 1

It was a dangerous time of history to be taking a walk. Louis XIV was warring against half of Europe, and mercenaries returning from the fronts were extending their pillaging to an innocent countryside.

People might have thought the young man a journeyman, sixteen years old and traveling the German roads, his extra pair of shoes dangling over his shoulder, his rucksack bulging. The traveler heard a rumble of hooves and wheels, and a carriage materialized over the rise in front of him. Some nobleman in a hurry. The young man edged off the road. Lipizzaner! And galloping so fast, you'd think it was the mail express—a glimpse of a red velvet interior, a wrinkled old baroness with a towering coiffure.

Dust caught at his throat and threw him into a spasm of coughing. His water skin was drained, and now his empty stomach heaved. He gritted his teeth. "Just tighten your belt, Trembler."

The youth regained the road with an air of determination and began whistling a tune he'd heard in Hamburg. What a city! The very air was commerce and cheer. He jingled the coins in his pocket and drew them out in his broad fist, checking one more time. Only two groschen! Well, it wouldn't hurt him to go a day without food. Where to spend the night was the bigger problem. Sleeping outdoors would be risky.

Rounding a curve, he spotted a copse of birch trees and detoured across the purple heath. The shade and the tumble of water welcomed him.

But he wasn't alone.

A burly man was sitting on a mound of rocks fishing. "Now you've done it with your infernal whistling!"

The youth sidled toward the brook, keeping an eye on the fisherman. The man cranked in his line. "Get your water."

The youth scrambled to the stream, dropped his rucksack on the rocks and cupped his big hands full of water. He drank, then threw some over his face. He could taste the sweat. He filled his water skin and, with a glance at the fisherman, collapsed on the grass.

The man had recast. He was staring, his black eyes luminous. "Come far?"

"From Hamburg."

"Ah, Hamburg!" The man's voice savored the name of the city like a sweet. "English ships, Dutch cargoes, cathedrals, music."

The youth bolted up."Yes, music! Have you ever heard the organ offerings at the Catherinakirche?"

The fisherman nodded. "Quite a virtuoso that Reincken! Then there's the Hamburg opera. You attended?"

"To the rue of my pocket book, yes. But it was the music at the church that held me."

The man continued to query him, listening so attentively to his answers that before long the youth was eagerly pouring out his story. He told the fisherman how, twice now, he'd taken summer trips from his school in Luneburg to hear Reincken play the organ, and how this summer Reincken had invited him to stay the week and had given him free organ lessons. "It will take me years to master all we spoke of: musica theorica, musica practica, suites, sonatas, melody in the Italian style. Have you seen the collection of manuscripts at the new Hamburg publishing house? I purchased a musical treatise this morning, a chance to study musica theorica at leisure."

The fisherman reeled in a small fish, dropped it into a pail, then threw out his line once more. "And what do you mean to do with all this learning?"

There was something about the way the fisherman asked the question. The man really wanted to know. The youth downed a cold swig of water, leaned back against a boulder and crossed his stocky legs. Shapes and sounds of glory passed through his mind, splendors trumpeting, voices chorusing, people being lifted to the heavens with the works he was going to write for cathedral organs and choirs. But there was more. "I think I am close to having the answer. It comes to me more clearly every day."

The fisherman probed, and the youth spilled out to him the heart of his aspirations and fears. Finally he dropped quiet.

The fisherman drew in his line. "I'm a musician myself," he said. And he began to talk of music and what it could do and what it had done and what it wasn't and what it was. And he said of the youth's dreams, "You must persevere."

Then, suddenly, he stood up. The youth gasped. The man was taller than anyone he had ever seen. Beneath his black traveling cloak, he was wearing a golden vest that matched the shine of his long hair.

"Try The Squire's Inn tonight," the man boomed, "in the next village."

Before the youth could explain that he had no money, the man swooped up his gear and strode away.

How long had it been since someone had taken him seriously? Not since the days of his father's tutelage. Music was a job, a way to make money, yes. But to him it was far more. Today was the first time anyone had encouraged him to pursue his dream of shaping truth with his composing.

"I want my music to help people get at the heart of life," he said out loud.

A crow cawed, and others joined in, swelling, then quieting, angry, then muttering, exclaiming, whistling. The youth laughed. He jumped up, opened his rucksack and drew out his violin. He would seek to capture the nature around him.

The violin sang. The youth stretched out the melody, questioning. The birds sang. The youth responded, weaving the violin tune more intricately, grasping for what he felt but could not yet articulate in his music.

But then he froze.

Rough voices from the road, coming closer!

He picked up a stick, backed into a chalky shelter of birches and waited, heart pounding. Men in red uniforms halted at the edge of the copse. Hessians! Stick ready, Sebastian backed toward the heath on the opposite side, watching the soldiers move toward the brook.

Then he was in the open again, snaking across the Luneburg heath toward the distant spires. He ran for a long time, then finally stopped. No one was following. Relieved, he walked on toward the village, slowly now, gasping for breath.

The sky was turning gold by the time he reached the town. And there it was—a white structure with window boxes of primroses and a calligraphied sign: The Squire's Inn. Smells of sausage soup and bread poured from an open door.

His stomach stormed. He jerked off his pack, and pulling off the boot that had been rubbing his heel, sat down on the step. Something slapped to the ground in front of him, then something else. A window ground shut over his head. He looked up but saw no one.

He leaned over the two silvery shapes. Herring heads! Might there be enough meat to roast? He picked one of them up and probed the slippery insides. His fingers felt something round and hard. He pulled it out. It couldn't be! He bit the object the way he'd seen his brother do. It was!

A golden ducat.

He searched the second head. Another ducat! In his hand he held two golden ducats. It was enough not only for a meal and lodging, but for another year of trips—home for Christmas, another trip to Celle, Hamburg, and maybe even Lubeck to see the mighty Buxtehude!

Why would anyone stuff herring heads with gold and toss them out the window?

He thought of the enigmatic fisherman in the copse. He remembered the petitions he'd placed before the Almighty concerning this particular trip, his uncertainties about the coming year, his failing funds. Surely the herring heads were meant especially for him.

The meal that night seemed the best he'd ever tasted and the path he'd chosen more Providence-affirmed than ever before.

Some men are driven. They are driven by hate or insufficiency. They are driven by greed or pride. Others are driven by gifting or commission or a synergism of both. History is made by such. Some of them think to make it. Others have no such thought. They are only, in the private spaces of their lives, doing what they have to do.

I

Noble Friends and Noble Foes
1 7 1 5

The three-note motif exploded through the chapel, then fled downward, stopping.

Nightmare figures rose in front of her, wraith-like, cloaked in black. Why was Sebastian playing this piece today of all days?

It was the middle of the morning, January 20, 1715. Barbara Bach, wife of Johann Sebastian Bach, was sitting with her two eldest children at the end of a back pew in the castle chapel of Weimar. She shuddered and looked up at the galleries lining the sides of the gold-hued chapel. The princes and baronesses were as still as the green and gold columns behind which they sat. What did they think of the music? Barbara wondered. What did the clergy think, the Lutheran dignitaries from all over Germany? What was Duke Wilhelm thinking? She couldn't imagine how anyone, even someone who hated frivolity as much as the Grand Duke, could be pleased at having his birthday ceremonies launched in such a macabre way.

On and on the organ thundered, filling every empty thought and space in the chapel. Sebastian had written this work, a toccata and fugue in the key of D minor, two years earlier—an effort, he said, to deal with the heartbreak of losing their twins. Why would he take the risk of playing such inappropriate music at a time when pleasing his employer was so important? Had he had another conflict with Duke Wilhelm? Or another premonition?

Barbara felt a quiver of anger toward her husband for being so complex. Then she felt guilty about her anger. *I do love my husband. Yes, I love him far too much.*

The fugue rushed at last to its end, and Sebastian moved to take up the viola in the Kapelle. The music struck up again, this time a quartet of soft, undulating strings, calling people to prepare for the opening chorale.

The people in the pews around them—other court musicians' families, royal chamberlains, kitchen maids, pages and lackeys—shifted in their seats. Barbara scanned the gold-scrolled pipes of the organ. Built into a small room in the ceiling, the organ was set against a mural of angels and clouds, as though it floated in heaven itself. An appropriate setting for Sebastian Bach. Barbara thought of her husband's broad, oval face, the way it had looked this morning at breakfast. His dark eyebrows had been pulled down over his black eyes. His fluted lips had been uncertain, his ample jaw set into severity.

There were so many things about her husband she didn't understand—his bond to the Invisible Being, his drivenness, his generosity, the way he seemed to be forever doing the most imprudent things.

What she did understand about her husband was that he was brilliant. All he needed was a groschen of a chance and he would accomplish things men had never accomplished before. She was convinced of it.

Sitting beside her in his gray satin best, five-year-old Friedemann began swinging his square-heeled shoes across the floor. *Click-scrape, click, click-scrape.* Barbara laid her hand on his leg to still the rocking muscles, and Friedemann screwed up his mouth in a pout. She silenced his rebellion with a look. Birthday services weren't as strictly quiet as regular services, but Barbara didn't want Friedemann to feel too free. He had it in him to make a commotion.

She bent to pick up the purple embroidered bag sitting on the floor in front of her. Her family called it her miracle bag, as filled with provision and surprise as the herrings Sebastian loved to tell about finding on that trip when he was sixteen.

Barbara drew a small, brown book out of her bag and opened it on Friedemann's lap. Then she settled in for the long service: hymns, versicles, responses, prayers, speeches extolling the Duke, a sermon, more prayers, music, then Duke Wilhelm marching out with his retinue of black-robed clergy. Finally the service was over.

Barbara arranged the drape of her blue taffeta dress to cover the bulge of her stomach—five months it was now—and reached for Friedemann's hand. She stepped into the aisle, nodding to the cellist's wife, who glided ahead of her, then turned to give her seven-year-old daughter Dorothea an encouraging smile. The little girl was struggling to maneuver the bustle of her new green satin dress through the pews.

When the three Bachs reached the door at the back of the chapel they stopped to wait for Sebastian. The silk pastels and exotic perfumes of the aristocracy were flowing along in the hall behind them like a fleet of bannered ships.

Everyone was going to the Grand Parlor for the presentations and birthday festivities.

"I much enjoy the harpsichord *ordres* of that French composer," someone said, "Couperin, I think his name is."

"Couperin!" a bass voice scoffed. "The man has feathers in his skull! Now that toccata of Bach's today, *c'est fantastique!*—there's something worth heeding."

Barbara strained to hear.

"You jest! Why, if I were Duke Wilhelm and Bach my Konzertmeister, I'd have him horsewhipped. Is that the kind of beginning you'd like for your birthday celebration, Leopold? It's no wonder Wilhelm hasn't promoted him to Kapellmeister."

"I didn't say Bach was a puppet." The other man's voice was deep and mellifluous. "Such willingness to risk has great merit, to my way of thinking."

"Methinks you think too much, Leopold," a woman said.

There was laughter and a change of subject.

Barbara turned back toward the chapel to see Sebastian coming toward her. He looked heart-stoppingly fine today in the wig she liked best—the long honey-blond one—and his red and gold uniform. With one big hand, he hugged a sheaf of manuscripts to his chest, and with the other he cradled a viola d'amour. A lute swung from his shoulder by a strap.

At age thirty, he was broad shouldered with a heaviness of the square solid sort, and the force of the way he moved belied his short stature. It came to her suddenly that the court musician's uniform, which had originally been that of a Hussar soldier, suited Sebastian as much as the idea of being seated in the heavenlies. Sebastian's instruments are his weapons, thought Barbara, weapons against mediocrity.

Today the tension in his big jaw made him look angry. But as he drew closer, Barbara realized it wasn't anger. His black eyes were roiling with anguish. Whatever could be wrong?

He stopped so close to her, she thought he would drop everything and embrace her right there.

"Your gypsy eyes gleam in that stunning dress, wife," he teased. But his eyes did not smile.

"What is it?" she asked.

Sebastian shook his head.

Friedemann was tugging at Sebastian's coat. "The bow, Father."

Sebastian placed the D-shaped bow in Friedemann's hands and watched while the boy trimmed it of its loose strings. "You may carry it if you wish."

Friedemann's narrow face brightened. The instrument was his favorite, a twelve-stringed instrument possessing a luminous tone that could rend your heart.

Barbara tried again, "The toccata! Sebastian. Why?"

A tall nobleman in a silver coat interrupted them. "My highest commendation for your music today, Konzertmeister."

The voice was the one she'd just overheard.

"Ah, Prince Leopold!" Sebastian bowed low. "I consider such words from you a great honor, a great honor."

Prince Leopold's cobalt eyes danced. "And I would wish to honor you more. Have you considered my offer? The Kapellmeister position at Cothen awaits you."

Barbara was startled, but Sebastian only smiled. "Duke Wilhelm is a hard taskmaster, Your Excellency."

The Prince bowed low and strode away. A bevy of duchesses flocked to him, scolding, the feathers in their wigs bouncing with indignation. They're probably telling him he should remember his rank and not treat court servants as equals, thought Barbara. Prince Leopold of Anhalt-Cothen was an unusual man. Oh how wonderful working for him would be! But leaving Wilhelm would not be easy.

According to the law of every city-state and electorate in Germany, Sebastian's relationship to the Duke was as binding as that of landlord and serf. Rulers often threw their servants into prison for something as minor as dressing inappropriately in their presence. Sebastian had been in the Duke's employ for eight years, and so far he'd escaped this kind of discipline—but it was always a possibility.

Sebastian hurried his family down the hall lined with paintings that were rich with the color and emotion of the Italian baroque, and on into the Grand Parlour. He seated the three of them near the Kapelle, then left to ready his musicians for the polonaise.

Barbara let her eye roam about the pilastered room. The wall to her right was covered with gold-framed art. Under it stood a decorated platform, and at a diagonal to the platform, the traditional group of singers and instruments called the Kapelle. Violinists, violists and cellists were sitting in twirl-legged chairs. Singers were standing. Sebastian sat a little apart from the others in the position of first violinist. She could see his profile clearly—his long, straight nose; his tendency to fullness under the chin; his body bent over the arranging of his scores.

The nobility milled about her. Many were conversing in French—the men flattering and the women flirting with swoops and flutters of their fans.

Some of the men wore Adonis wigs, long and flowing. Others wore the cauliflower style, and a few, the new buckled wig with horizontal curls above the ears. The women moved through the Parlour in their pinks, blues and greens, like beautiful creatures in an enchanted tale. There was some jostling and bickering as they proceeded to arrange themselves in lines according to rank.

The presentations, which Sebastian hated, were always Barbara's favorite part of royal ceremonies. Sebastian struck up a polonaise, then softened the Kapelle at the first announcing. Barbara inched her chair to the left, stretching to see through the line in front of her. The first presentation was a countess from Saxony. Her shelved skirts were fashioned in cream silk with red-and-gold-painted flowers. They were at least eight feet wide.

Next came a Duke and Duchess from Wittenburg, then a prince from Jena. Each presented gifts to Duke Wilhelm. The Grand Duke stood in the center of the platform with a row of scholars and clergy. One of them was a member of the Leipzig town council, an influential man named Adolf Georg Kirkman.

"Prince Leopold of Anhalt-Cothen!" the herald announced. The prince started toward the dais alone. He was tall and lithe in his silver coat and white breeches. Young-looking and rosy-complected, he possessed eyebrows that were almost invisible and blue eyes alive as the sea is alive, and as deep. Duke Wilhelm stood waiting, his small frame overerect, his shoulders engulfed by a set of red-brown furs. What a contrast! For all his simplicity, Prince Leopold exuded a level of royalty that outshone that of the Grand Duke as surely as silver outshines crockery.

The Duke's underlip curled beneath his great nose when he accepted the Prince's gift. His smile looked dangerously close to a sneer.

And then it happened. August marched into the Parlour, his corpulent figure taking up almost as much room as the Countess's shelved skirts, and headed straight for the dais, ignoring all courtesies.

The Duke's face went red with fury.

But Barbara had to smile. August's new court suit was red with gold embroidery, his vest an outrageous purple and green. He looked like a Chinese emperor.

August was the oldest nephew of Duke Wilhelm.

He and his younger brother Ernst lived with their mother Mariana in the Red Castle, the smaller of the two castles on the royal grounds. Duke Wilhelm valued Ernst, but he abhorred August. The Duke was rigidly religious and sought to control everyone around him.

August was irreligious and accepting to the point of overindulgence.

He loved good music, and he had a good heart; but his penchant for pleasure perpetually got him into trouble.

Last July August had engaged traveling players who had celebrated so voraciously at the Red Castle that they ended in a drunken brawl. To Wilhelm's mind, it was the crowning insult. He'd issued an edict saying no one in his employ was to cultivate August's company or visit the Red Castle, on pain of fine.

The edict had incensed Sebastian. He had been friends with August and Ernst for years. He ignored the edict and continued his musical evenings at the Red Castle. Then one Saturday last November, it all came to a head.

Sebastian had just returned home from a rehearsal and had gone straight to the music room when Barbara heard the clatter of a carriage and the shout of a coachman drawing horses to a stop.

She walked into the hall, where Friedemann was leaning in the open doorway.

The five-year-old smiled his slow smile. "At least something's happening today, Mama. It's Duke Wilhelm."

Barbara tensed and bustled into the music room.

Black-buckled shoe planted on the harpsichord bench, elbow on his knee, Sebastian was glaring at an official-looking letter. "I received it this morning," he said.

She scanned it. "A summons! Didn't you go?"

Sebastian's face was tight under his everyday wig, his coal eyes sparked with fire. "I did not!"

Barbara struggled to keep from taking the hardness of his tone personally. She knew his gentleness—always he was gentle with her personally. But certain issues made him appear hard.

The outside creaks and whinnies of the coach and horses became the inside clank of military regalia in the hall, and suddenly Duke Wilhelm was standing in their music room doorway. He wore his red-and-gold-medallioned uniform, complete with sword and tricornered hat. He must have come straight from drilling his grenadiers. And there was no mistaking the rage in his eyes.

Sebastian buttoned his black coat and threw back his shoulders.

Barbara placed the summons on the harpsichord and stepped back.

Duke Wilhelm marched toward Sebastian, skimmed the document off the harpsichord and shook it in Sebastian's face. "How dare you ignore my summons!"

"I have paid the fines you required. With all due respect, another discussion seemed a waste of time."

"What is and is not a waste of your time is *mine* to decide!"

The Duke jabbed his finger into Sebastian's chest. "Your disobedience filters down into the ranks. I will have no one, absolutely no one in my service associating with August. He is a reprobate, a disgrace to the church and a disgrace to the royal name. You are forbidden to enter the Red Castle again."

The Duke's knobby nose was quivering in his small face. His voice rose to a shriek as he continued jabbing his finger into Sebastian's chest.

Sebastian planted his fists on his hips and began railing at Wilhelm nose to nose. "August and I have been friends since before I came to Weimar. Is a man to be there for his friend only if the friend measures up to his standards?"

Wilhelm tried to retreat, but Sebastian dogged him. He shook a big fist in the Duke's face. "Have you ever taken time to notice the artistry in August's soul?"

The Duke clenched his teeth and held up his hand to ward Sebastian off. Sebastian whirled around and began pounding a path back and forth between the harpsichord and the door. "I try to speak with your pious divines, your doting librettists, your seminary scholars; and the majority of the time, I uncover nothing but pride. I have yet to find one of them who has the humility of the man you call reprobate."

Sebastian flung his arm, palm upward. "All men and women are reprobate. We slip. We err at every turn. It is part of being human."

Barbara stepped forward. "Herr Bach."

Sebastian put his hand to his forehead.

Barbara held her breath. One never knew what Sebastian might say when faced with something he thought unfair.

"I have one more thing that must be said."

"How dare you—!" roared the Duke.

Sebastian plunged on. "A lack of compassion in devout men has often made it difficult for the faltering to believe. I would not wound my friend more."

Silence. And in the silence, tension and anger.

The Duke's orange-brown eyes darted with offense. Finally he spoke. "If you want the Weimar Kapellmeister position, if you want my help in getting your music into Lutheran churches, you must cease all converse with August."

He turned and stalked out of the house.

Barbara and Sebastian stayed up late that night discussing the confrontation. In the hope of a higher good, Sebastian decided to abide by the Duke's edict. At least for a time.

A draft as cold as snow touched Barbara's shoulders and neck, bringing her back to the Duke's birthday celebration. The Kapelle was no longer playing, and the outside doors of the Grand Parlour had been flung open. Flying bits of snow breathed frost through the room as the crowd moved back, murmuring, wondering. Then suddenly a woman in a fur-lined surtout burst into the room. She ran wailing toward the dais. It was Ernst's mother Duchess Mariana. With her was a leather-coated courier. There were whispers and indrawn breaths.

Dorothea abandoned her seat to stand by Barbara. "Mama, what's wrong?"

Barbara took her hand.

Mariana was kneeling in front of Duke Wilhelm now, her hood thrown back from her gray-streaked hair. The courier approached Duke Wilhelm. They conferred. Then, rattling a paper scroll, the courier faced the audience.

"With boundless regret and lament," he read, "with a grief the whole kingdom will be bound to share, her Most Excellent Highness the Duchess Mariana Ernst announces the untimely death of her youngest son the Serene Duke Johann Ernst."

Barbara gasped, and Duchess Mariana exploded into a wild sobbing.

The courier continued, "Duke Ernst, nephew of the Grand Duke Wilhelm and brother of Duke August, was seized by a fever two days out of

Italy and henceforth lapsed into a coma from which he never revived. His body awaits burial. Therewith, let the kingdom of Weimar commemorate his life and death by declaring itself in a state of mourning."

Barbara's eyes began to fill. Dorothea was sobbing and clutching at Barbara's hand. Then August's voice pierced the air with his own lament. All else was silence. The murmurs and deprecations of the very rich who care for nothing but appearances were, for once, stilled. The young Duke Ernst had been much loved.

Hard working, intellectual and a lover of God, he had been Sebastian's favorite pupil. Barbara could almost see Ernst now: small and agile; short brown hair; tan face lit up in a smile.

He'd so often remained in the Bach home for a game of hombre after his music lesson, followed by dinner and discussion, that the children thought of him as part of the family. And his music! Hazel eyes flashing over his virtuosic violin, he would play with every parcel of his being. He had coveted excellence and worship with an intensity so like Sebastian's that they had become more than mentor and disciple. Sebastian had thought of Ernst—how Wilhelm would have rebuked him if he'd known—as a beloved son.

When Barbara could repress her tears enough to see through the blur, she realized that Sebastian was no longer in his seat. Duke Wilhelm had ended the festivities, so with the children trailing behind her, Barbara wandered worriedly through the crowd, out into the hall and down the stairs. She couldn't find Sebastian anywhere. She and the children walked home alone.

2

Before the courier had finished his announcement, Sebastian was stumbling through the shocked crowd, clutching his violin and a folio of music. He squeezed his way through the press with half-blinded eyes and emerged into the hall. The strife in his mind, with the cacophony of noise and sham and sudden stabbing pain, had become intolerable. He had to be alone. He reeled through the corridors, plunged through the chapel doors and fell before the altar.

He remembered the day when Ernst had coughed so much during his violin lesson that he'd been unable to play a note. Soon afterward, the young duke's physician prescribed a rest-cure in Italy. The letters from both Ernst and Mariana were encouraging. They had all hoped and prayed for a miracle, and they thought it had been granted.

"Why?" he demanded. Then softly, "God, where are you? How can you? Why, with all our prayers?"

But he could hear nothing except the swirl of the morning service about him, honoring the Duke with obsequious platitudes. Even now he knew that Duke Wilhelm would be quoting some scripture to Duchess Mariana and commanding her to remember who she was.

He must flee this place. He would go to the Red Castle. He took the back stairs to the organ two at a time, snatched up his greatcoat and muffler and hurried down the hall to the winding staircase. The shocked quiet in the Grand Parlour had become a low rumble—three hundred courtiers and burghers crowded into that place, and now this heart-rending news.

"You there, Bach!" Wilhelm's secretary was tapping down the hallway toward the stairs.

Sebastian bolted to the bottom of the stairway, veered to the right, then back to the left.

"The Grand Duke is calling for you, Bach. You will pay for this." The secretary was right behind him.

Sebastian ducked down a narrow corridor and into a broom closet. The secretary clattered by. Sebastian waited. Wilhelm would be thinking of his position and wanting music to restore order and dignity. Well, let them figure it out, Sebastian thought. Lorenz can manage it. I have taught my apprentice well.

Sebastian believed in duty, yes, he believed in it with a passion. But there were times when the duty entailed in serving royalty was so consuming that the space within him lost its room, lost its hearing, and he had to break away from his employer's demands to find sanity and peace. There could be no music, no true music, coming from him until he wrestled with death and wrestled with it alone.

When he could hear the tap of the secretary's footsteps no longer, he strode back the way he had come, then passed through the side door of the castle and out into the snowy cold.

At the Red Castle the chamberlain let him in without a word. He pointed in the direction of the small drawing room.

When Sebastian walked into the room, everything stopped. Already the vigil had begun. A chambermaid was draping the windows in black, and an old woman sat weeping beside the bier. The slight figure of his pupil and friend, Johann Ernst, lay above her on a black-swathed table. The boyish fingers that had played the violin first like a spirit, then like a saint and then like a sage lay across his chest.

His small, square face was hollow and unspirited, his bright hazel eyes covered with hateful coins. Position meant nothing in the end.

Sebastian dropped to his knees. He spoke through clenched teeth.

"I rebuke you, Death; how dare you wrest from us year after year the ones we hold most dear. You would not stop at the taking of my mother's life or my father's, or the taking of the breath of life from the twins Barbara and I prized beyond possession. You would continue your ravaging and wrest life away at its prime. You would bring a whole kingdom to despair."

The beginning of the toccata and fugue thundered through his mind. He had felt it, known from the moment he wakened this morning that something terrible was going to happen. He had prayed, and even as he'd played the toccata, he'd tried to hope. But it had been in vain.

A lackey tiptoed in with a mammoth candle stand and set it at the head of the bier. A page followed, set a white candle in the stand and lit it, shielding the flame. He stood with his head bowed for a minute, glanced at Sebastian, nodded and left.

Then Joanna, a maidservant who had been with Duchess Mariana since the Duchess was a little girl, hobbled in. Immediately, she came to Sebastian. He rose. She placed her hand on his arm. Her rheumy eyes were filled with compassion.

Sebastian bent his head on the old maid's shoulder and sobbed. Together they wept, the woman at her vigil joining loudly with them. Sorrow was not a private emotion but part of the common life of a town. There would be sufficient weeping today for even the most demanding of spirits.

There was a clamor in the atrium—a woman's voice protesting, argument and shouting, then boots echoing across marble. Clothes and hair disheveled, patrician features contorted, Duchess Mariana charged into the room. She knocked over the candle and began tearing at the black drapings on the windows. "He needs the sun," she cried.

She threw herself on Ernst's body while August hurried to right the candle. A crowd gathered behind them. "Mother," August pleaded, " if we do not do this properly, Uncle Wilhelm will take Ernst from us."

The back of the Duchess's hand slapped like the crack of a whip across August's face. He staggered, and she bent to whisper into Ernst's dead ear. "My son, my dearest. No one will take you from me. Oh, that the sun might see him. He will revive. I will take him back to Italy. Fetch the carriage. Bundle him. He must be bled again. Yes, yes, I will fetch your violin."

A black-cloaked physician emerged from the crowd, opened his bag and drew out a vial. "This will help Your Highness."

Mariana flung her hand against the vial. It cracked and splattered across the floor.

The old maidservant appeared at her elbow. "Honored Duchess, listen to your Joanna. Take what the good Dr. Graun gives you. The sleep will help, and when you wake you will know what you must do."

Finally Mariana agreed. As they guided her out, Sebastian stepped from the shadows. "August!"

August stumbled toward him, bursting into tears. Sebastian clapped his hands on his friend's shoulders.

Together they wept until they exhausted themselves. Too soon the chamberlain entered to warn Sebastian that Wilhelm's marshall was outside asking if they had seen Konzertmeister Bach.

August took Sebastian's elbow and guided him out the opposite way.

When Sebastian stepped outside, he could see the red-coated figure of the marshall and two grenadiers at the front entrance of the Red Castle. The marshall was sending his grenadiers, one to the left and one to the right. Sebastian headed for the royal gardens.

He tromped past the stark stemmed rose garden, the cherubimed fountain, now dotted with snow, and deep into the gardens to his favorite spot—the copse near the ruins. He stepped beneath the canopy of fir trees.

Instantly, relief fell upon him. The curve and bend of branches were like tresses, mothering. At last he was alone.

Wilhelm would insist that Ernst's body be transferred to the Wilhelmsburg, Sebastian was sure of it. The Duke would not tolerate even a hint of Catholic or pagan custom, no prayers for the dead or seeking to propitiate the spirit, and no caparisoned horses or hired mourners following the hearse. But Ernst deserved the finest of commemorative services. Surely Wilhelm would not deny him that.

These last few days everyone had been concerned about the change in the weather. They had wondered why Ernst and his mother had been so determined to arrive in time for the birthday festivities. Now all seemed shattered and useless, like the vial Mariana had broken across the floor. The day had fragmented like the whole of last year. There had been apprehension, celebration and the ever elusive attempt to worship. There had been frustration and life-wrenching loss, anger and a need for change. Nothing seemed right about living in Weimar any more. Sebastian found himself composing to express his personal feelings far too often. He was sick of the spirit of show. Yes, as he walked under the stretch and tower of trees, he saw it: his real work was almost at a standstill. He waited, clearing his mind to silence with the discipline he had learned to practice at will. He listened. He asked. He waited. And finally there opened up within him a steadiness of being and of Being With. At the center of him, it was no bigger than the flame of Ernst's candle, but it possessed the strength of Rock and anchoring. He was ready to go home.

The walk home was long and benumbing, the day drawing to a close. Sebastian hitched his muffler to cover his nose against the snow. With the dark of the growing night and the need for mourning, Wilhelm would set aside his determination to find his truant Konzertmeister, at least for a while. He would not shirk his duty to honor his royal dead.

When Sebastian finally reached home, Barbara was at the door before he had a chance to knock. Her heart-shaped face was flushed, her dark eyes questioning. He stood looking at her, silent. She raised a hand against the flying snow and smiled. "Lord have mercy, husband, look at you."

She drew him into the warmth of the hall and whisked the snow off the shoulders of his greatcoat and hat.

Before he knew it, he was sitting in the rocking chair in the kitchen, feet rubbed till they tingled and hurt, a quilt tucked across his lap and his cold fingers wrapped around a steaming cup of tea.

Barbara sat on the stool in front of his rocking chair and laid her hand on his knee.

Sebastian took her warm hand and pressed it against his chest. "I'm sick of death, wife."

"We have to make our peace with it."

He grimaced. Her words were his own—words he had used to try to soothe her after the death of their twins.

"Did you go to the Red Castle?" she asked.

"How could I not? Mariana is wild with her own grief, and Wilhelm is stone. August needs someone."

She looked at him, long and deep and lovingly, then placed her small hands on his cold cheeks, drew her thumbs beneath his eyes and leaned to kiss him.

He encircled her small frame in his big arm and pulled her close. He kissed her fiercely. He drew into him her solace. She was as warm as embers, and as alive.

When he finally let her go, she patted his face and adjusted her apron. He laughed and leaned back to enjoy the spectacle of his beautiful and precise wife. Barbara knelt to wipe up a spill, rose, dropped the cook spoon in its jug and selected two blue-and-white bowls from the rack on the wall. Then she uncovered the fresh strudel waiting on the cart, sliced two squares and measured a fourth cup of cream over each.

Together they ate and sipped the pungent tea—silent when they needed to be and speaking when they wanted. But rest had only begun to sift into their spirits when tumult thundered over them again. They were snuffing out the candles and preparing to go upstairs when a courier arrived with a summons from August. Duchess Mariana had tried to throw herself from the castle wall.

Immediately Sebastian heaved his wet greatcoat off its peg and began tugging on his boots. Barbara swirled back into the kitchen and emerged in minutes with her bag. "Some soothing teas and draughts from the herb closet. I'll go ask Lorenz to sleep near the children while we're gone."

The carriage August had provided for them careened through the town, past rows of half-timbered, peaked roofed houses, past the library and then—with a noise like porcelain breaking—out onto the cobblestones of the market square.

They could see the columned Rathaus at the far end of the square, and next to it, the barred windows of the detention hall. A lamp flared behind one of the windows, and a man's scream ripped the covering of the night. Barbara clutched at Sebastian's arm. He reached across her and unfastened the velvet curtain to drop it across the window. Then he took her cold hand in both of his and rubbed it in his big grip. He appreciated her stoicism right now. She knew when one must choose mercy over practicality.

But she would have had doubts already about whether they should be breaking the Duke's edict again.

"For Ernst's commemorative service, I shall use the concerto he wrote last Christmas," he said.

"You are certain Wilhelm will give you the responsibility? What about young Drese?"

"Even Duke Wilhelm wouldn't bend so low! Drese! His works are as shallow as a milk saucer. Mediocrity at its worst! The spirit of a man must be probed, caught up, spoken. Every juxtaposition of word with note and rhythm with tune elevates or diminishes the man who writes and the man who hears. No, Duke Wilhelm will ask me to do it, and I will be ready with a service that will honor my friend's life in the manner he deserves."

The horses' hooves struck wood, echoing. They were crossing the bridge that led to the castle grounds. They swept past the sentinel and around the edge of the sporting pond. The carriage lurched to a stop. In an instant the footman was opening the coach door, and lackeys and chambermaids were rushing from the Red Castle to whisk them inside. They hurried up three flights of stairs, turned into a broad hallway and proceeded toward the carved doors of the Duchess's suite.

Before they could reach them, the doors burst open, and Dr. Graun and his black bag catapulted into the hall. A glass crashed to the floor behind him, and Mariana's voice screamed, "Liar, death-monger!"

Spider-like, the physician crouched to pick up his black tricorner, jammed it on his head, then shoved past them, cursing. A series of thumps came from inside, a man's yelp, and more glass shattering against the wall. Then August shot out of the room in his nightgown. His mother's expletives tortured the air.

He screwed up his pouched face and jammed his hands to his ears.

Then he saw Sebastian and Barbara and groaned with relief. He explained how they'd found his mother on the wall in her nightclothes and how it had taken several men to get her down.

"I brought my lute," said Sebastian. "Could you have someone fetch the clavichord?"

August sniffled and nodded his leonine head. Then he disappeared down the hall.

The scent of wood smoke and laudanum came strong from Mariana's room. Barbara moved toward the doors, and like the blast from a fowling piece, a vase flew out of the room, and with it, a litany of curses.

Sebastian leapt to pull Barbara out of the doorway. "She doesn't know it's you," he said.

He guided Barbara to sit with him on the red couch behind the door, then drew his lute from its bag. He picked at the cold strings, adjusting the pegs until each of the eleven courses was tuned to perfection. At first he strummed randomly. Then it came to him, "Jesu, Joy of Man's Desiring." Mariana had always like that.

He played it simply at first; then, in and around the trumpet-like melody, commenced a weaving of triplets, soft and flowing.

He tiptoed, still playing, to the open door. Mariana was lying with her back to him, a tiny white-clad figure in a massive bed of state. Barbara moved to stand by his side for a minute, then crept toward the bed. She laid her hand on Mariana's shoulder. "It's Barbara, Mariana."

The Duchess bolted up, hugged Barbara to her, and began moaning and rocking.

Careful not to jar the flow of music, Sebastian entered the room. Soon August appeared, hugging the portable clavichord. Sebastian nodded to his friend, and August picked his way fearfully across the Turkish rug and set the clavichord on a table in front of Sebastian. Sebastian wound the lute melody to a close and switched to the clavichord. His strong fingers sank into the downward striking, relishing the smoothness of the keys, lifting the well-known words of the ancient chorales with harmonies and figures to fit the meaning of the text. On he played into fugues and canons and dances, gentled so as to lift but not jar.

The Duchess unclenched her fists and closed her eyes. August was sitting in an armchair in front of the fireplace, head thrown back, a touch of smile on his lips. Barbara sat motionless on the edge of the bed, eyes lifted. Her face glowed. Sebastian was glad to see it, glad to know his sacred music could touch her. It didn't always. On he played. And at last the Duchess lay back.

Barbara convinced her to take a tea she'd stirred up, and when Mariana's breathing grew deep, Barbara whispered to Sebastian that she wanted to stay for a while. "Why don't you find a place to rest?"

Sebastian nodded. He headed straight for the study Ernst had furnished for him on the second floor. There he stoked the fire in the tiny fireplace and lay down on the couch. Immediately he fell asleep. When he woke, it was still dark.

A tune was humming through his head.

He hurried up and sat at the desk, taking a sheaf of manuscript paper from the middle drawer and dipping a quill in the inkpot. The pen scratched across the paper in the night silence with Sebastian humming as he wrote. He did his best composing in the early morning.

When Barbara called to him from the door, he jumped. She smiled. "Your hair looks like a sweater that's been knitted and unraveled piece by piece." Sebastian ran his fingers through his short brown hair. "But in your face," she continued, "there is peace. The artist has something that others do not: he takes what is and creates beauty. He makes something out of his problems."

She fell silent for a moment, then, seeing his muffler and gloves on the couch, gathered them up. "Dawn will come soon."

They hurried to wake August, which was no easy task. Then the postilion and coachman had to be found and the horses harnessed. By the time their carriage crossed the wooden bridge, there was light at the horizon. On they drove, making such a clamor Sebastian was certain the whole town would soon know of their misdemeanor. Back through the market square they clattered, past the tall, half-timbered houses awakening for the day, and at last, into their quiet street.

But this morning it wasn't quiet. A wagon occupied by a man in irons and a guard stood in front of their house. Beside the wagon, pounding on their door with a cudgel, was the town bailiff.

He had a warrant for Sebastian's arrest.

It was the Age of Science and Invention, the era of the telescope, the thermometer and the pendulum clock. The world of literature was rich with the genius of Shakespeare, Milton, Cervantes and Racine. John Bunyan's Pilgrim's Progress *was well known, and Daniel Defoe's* Robinson Crusoe *would soon be circulating. It was the age of the Enlightenment, an age of paradox when men were expected to exercise freedom of thought along with respectful obedience to authority. It was the age of the sovereign right of kings with Louis XIV declaring, "I am the State," Peter the Great touring France and Germany and Frederick William establishing himself as the founder of Prussia. The Golden Age of Art—with Rembrandt painting profoundly of daily life and piety, Rubens decorating palaces of kings and Velasquez capturing the glory that was Spain— was drawing to a close. And the Golden Age of Music was about to dawn.*

2

Beginnings
1 6 9 9 – 1 7 1 5

The cell door slammed behind Sebastian, and he threw the chamber pot the guard had shoved at him to clatter against the wall.

"Quit your cranking," someone yelled from across the corridor. "We're trying to sleep."

"It's that fiddle player Wilhelm was lambasting to the bailiff the other day."

"A fop of a musician, eh? He'll not make it in here for a week."

"Probably used to boiled custard and lamb."

"Hey, what you in for, Trembler?"

"Probably wrote a dance Wilhelm didn't like. You know how the Duke hates dancing."

"Well, I say this fellow should entertain us. Serve him right for waking us up. Sing us a tune. Pay for your keep!"

Sebastian couldn't help being amused. Well, they wouldn't like his paltry baritone, that's for sure. He reared his head back and let out the rooster crow his children liked best.

The men guffawed. "That the best you can do? No wonder the Duke's locking you up! How long you in for?"

Sebastian smiled. Maybe I belong in here with these outlaws, he thought.

Uncle Martin was always calling me subversive. He rubbed at his wrists where the manacles had chafed, massaging back the circulation and flexing his long fingers. It was difficult to believe Wilhelm would pursue this kind of petty vengeance at such a time. But here he was.

He jerked off his greatcoat, tossed it across the end of the cot, and emptied his spacious pockets: manuscript sheets—the fugue of this morning and the first five pages of Ernst's concerto; a piece of graphite; a tuning fork; a pair of reading glasses; three thalers and a few groschen; some hard candy August had slipped him as they left the Red Castle; a piece of strudel wrapped in a handkerchief; another handkerchief Barbara had given him, carefully folded. He laid it all out across the end of the bed. "Well, here we are, just you and me, no wife, no lute. How shall we get on?"

Sebastian sat down on the hard cot. Pain stabbed through his head. Would this last visit to the Red Castle prove the undoing of his vision, all his carefully thought out plans? What would he say to Duke Wilhelm when he saw him? How would he convince him to listen to his view of things, to release him and give him the kind of support he needed?

Duke Wilhelm had a reputation throughout Germany for being a pious and magnanimous ruler. Theological schools from Leipzig to Halle were the grateful recipients of his grants. He was also a patron of the arts. It was this combination of a passion for the arts and what Sebastian had thought was true spirituality that had convinced him to move his family to Weimar. He'd thought that at last he'd found a patron who would enable his creative work. But, far from being kindred spirits, they'd turned out to disagree on practically everything.

Sebastian's mind began to tug at him, like a tiger tossing him every which way.

"Slow down," he muttered to himself. "Focus." He massaged the soreness in his temples and rubbed the muscles along his jaw. He took a deep breath, let it out, then took another. He'd been pushing himself too hard for too long.

Gradually, his thoughts slowed. One thing at a time. The cell: the floors were gray and white stone, the walls some kind of brick. The space was no more than six feet square, the cot the only furnishing except the chamber pot. There was a tiny window above his head. Still no sun.

He thought of Ernst's stone face. Confound it! I must have music. He picked up the sheaf of manuscript paper and scanned the first page of Ernst's concerto. It was written entirely in Ernst's hand. Sebastian smiled.

I could never get him to keep the notes stark. Ernst always would add flourishes that made the manuscript difficult to read.

He began pacing the cell, conducting his student's composition and playing it mentally. Violas here, shimmering. Trumpets now, sforzando! The violin solo. All the way to the end, Sebastian conducted, performed and interpreted the work. He changed chord structures in his head and wrote the polyphony truer and truer to the intent of Ernst's inspired theme. His student's instincts had been excellent, but there was always room for improvement.

Sebastian felt better after he conducted the last measure of the piece. Ernst's spirit was alive. The joy of being able to share in the rhythms of men's minds long after they are gone—capacious minds like Palestrina and Pachelbel and the young Duke Ernst! Music made life rich.

It was one of the essentials of bounteous living.

Almost as essential as food, he mused. His stomach rumbled, and Sebastian decided he'd not save the strudel any longer. He seized the pastry and stuffed it down, his taste buds watering with appreciation. But the pastry was gone in less time than it took to say "counterpoint and canon," and he was still hungry. What he wouldn't give for some of Barbara's incomparable oatmeal right now—smooth and creamy, with a hint of spice, maybe some apples and honey. The prisoners hadn't seemed very enthusiastic about the victuals here.

How would he manage?

Sebastian wrapped his muffler tighter around his neck and rubbed his hands, trying to keep warm. Five paces, then turn, five paces, then turn. Whatever happened, he knew he wasn't sorry about yesterday.

What a solace it had been to him to be able to comfort Mariana! If one had bread, one did not refuse to give it to a friend who was hungry. What a dishonorable deed it would have been, in truth, if he had known he had the power to help Mariana in her hour of grief but had failed to do so. That's why he'd been given the gift of music—for comfort, hope and the apprehension of truth.

Truth was what had compelled him to play the toccata yesterday morning. He'd sensed that the truth of the day would be best embodied in that macabre work, and he'd been right.

What a difficult taskmaster truth was! How often it had gotten him into trouble: the truth of caring, the truth of fairness and justice, the truth of a man's calling!

He was motivated by it even as a boy, when he spent all those months secretly copying the masters.

He was fourteen years old. It was the autumn of 1699, and he sat at a rickety table with moonlight falling in shafts across his work. Shivering with the autumn cold, he rubbed at the ache above his eyes, forcing himself to continue the scurrying of his quill.

A candle would have helped, but it was too risky. If his brother Christoph discovered him working at this forbidden task at three in the morning—no, he was afraid to think what might happen.

He had been working for six months and now had only two more pages to go—a measure of sixteenth notes, a rest here and here. On and on he wrote, the notes moving in and out of his vision, blurry, then clear, then blurry.

He was oblivious to the German world that lay outside his window, the world of provincial Thuringia, Bavaria, the Palatinate, the electorates of Saxony and Brandenburg and thousands of city-states ruled by petty princes (who were) seeking to enlarge their power.

Sebastian was consumed with only one reality, the reality that he had to study the music of these masters despite the fact that his brother Christoph had refused him the use of his personal volume. Here were composers Sebastian could learn from, and copying Christoph's book note for note, making his own volume, was the only way.

Sebastian pressed on. At last he reached the ending line—the fugue theme entering once again, the resolution! Sebastian wrote *FINE* under the last chord, then squinted at his manuscript, checking for mistakes. He slid his chair back from the table and sighed. "At last," he whispered, "a chance to study master composers in detail. My own book! I'll bind it the way Father taught me."

He flipped through the pages of thick rag paper, the big, square notes dancing, alive in his mind. If only he could try this Pachelbel piece on the harpsichord right now. Not a good idea. It would wake the whole house.

His eyes swept the garret room: the green bedstead, the chest and box-bench and the plain deal floor. His sister-in-law Maria Dorothea did all she could to keep him from feeling like the orphan he was. He had no four-poster and no curtains to hang over his bottle-glass window, but she supplied him faithfully with linens and stockings stitched by her own hand.

His brother Christoph, however, did little to make him feel welcome. Never, since the day their father Ambrosius died, had Christoph let Sebastian forget how much he owed him: a room of his own in Christoph's house in Ohrdruf, food, clothes, shelter, and lessons at the harpsichord, clavichord and organ—all of the claviers.

Sebastian smoothed his hand across the leather cover of Christoph's book. He remembered something he'd overheard his father tell a fellow musician. "Christoph's music has no soul, I'm afraid. But Sebastian! There is genius in him. If he offers it back to God, it will serve him well."

Sebastian wondered if Christoph might be jealous. Perhaps that was the reason he'd denied him the book. If Sebastian conquered works at age fourteen that Christoph couldn't master until he was twenty, perhaps that was it.

Sebastian wrapped a frayed cravat around his hand-ruled manuscript, tucked it under his pillow, then tiptoed down the stairs with Christoph's volume one more time. Wraith-like in his nightshirt, he glided across the landing near his oldest brother's bedroom. Christoph's voice!

Sebastian halted, muscles tensed, breath tight. Finally, Christoph stopped his sleep-muttering, and the house grew still. Sebastian shuddered. It would feel good to have these clandestine evenings done with. Compelled though he was, he couldn't shake the feeling of being a thief.

He crept on, down the last section of stairs and into the music room, where the harpsichord stood like a giant wing pinned to the wall. This was his favorite spot in the house, at the keyboard next to the window. He'd spent many hours of happy practice here—not so happy these days, though.

Sebastian traced his fingers across the glass-smooth keys of the harpsichord, then moved on to the corner cupboard. Slipping the book through the latticed doors of the cupboard for the last time, he left the room.

A few minutes later he tumbled into the warmth of his featherbed. He drifted, then slept.

He was late to breakfast the next morning and thought the meal would never end. Eager to escape to the music room to try out his new pieces, Sebastian would have to hide his excitement until Christoph was gone. He quieted baby Gottfried while Maria finished breakfast, forced himself still during Christoph's sanctimonious blessing, and accepted Christoph's long list of Saturday chores without flinching.

During breakfast Christoph was harsher than usual. He insisted Maria return upstairs with three-year-old Juditha and dress her properly for the meal; and when his apprentices queried him about the morning rehearsal, he cut them short. Perhaps the Count's visit to the service tomorrow morning was unnerving him. As Hoforganist of the only Lutheran church in Ohrdruf, it was essential Christoph please the ruling nobility.

When Christoph finally left for rehearsal, Sebastian sprinted through his downstairs chores, then hurried to his room to finish his Latin conjugations. He raced through the assignment, willing himself to the end but deploring every minute of it. He could understand the need for arithmetic and a smattering of rhetoric. And theology? Yes, he reveled in the study of the life and beliefs of Martin Luther. But Latin? Dry as century-old legumes.

He looked out the window at the line of green hills and forests on the outskirts of Ohrdruf, then down at the vegetable garden. Maria had begun gathering the last of the beans, and Juditha was tagging behind. With a swirl of her brown dress, his sister-in-law turned to look up at the garret window. She lifted her hand, waved it in the direction of the music room in shooing motions and turned back to her harvesting. She was in his confidence. "Just check on Gottfried from time to time," she'd said. "Christoph will be gone all morning."

Sebastian scrambled for his manuscript and skipped down the stairs to the music room. Past the box-like clavichord, the bass viols readied for the afternoon's rehearsal, and on to the harpsichord . . . A quick adjusting of the bench . . . His hard-won manuscript open to the first piece . . . He began.

Soon Sebastian's long fingers were racing over the keys—steel pricked rapids, smooth, then stumbling. No, that fingering won't work. Try . . . yes, the thumb! The use of the thumb was an invention of Sebastian's. Christoph scoffed at it, but Sebastian refused to abandon the experiment. Instead of using eight fingers alone, as was the custom, he was practicing including the thumbs. He rehearsed the technique, working the thumbs smooth and lever-like under his palms.

Chimes from the hall clock broke into his mood. An hour gone already. He got up, walked into the hall, and listened to the still and creak of the house. Then he peeked into the kitchen where six-month-old Gottfried was sleeping in his cradle. His full name was Johann Bernhard Gottfried Bach. A long name for a being no bigger than a viola. The baby was still as a portrait, his carrot curls in twists around his chubby face. Maria's sausage-bean soup was simmering on the stove. Sebastian sampled the spicy soup, then rushed back to the music room.

Fortunately, Christoph's rehearsal was longer than usual today. Sebastian plunged into a piece by Froberger, then moved on to the next composer. He played on and on, tapping his foot and singing in his clear soprano voice. In this weaving, melodied place, he fit. He forgot about baby Gottfried. He forgot about the rest of his chores. He didn't hear the alerting of the clock, the slamming of the front door or the footsteps behind him.

Suddenly, a huge hand materialized in front of him. It tore his music off the harpsichord and sent the pages crashing to the floor. It was Christoph. His colorless mouth was working under his long nose. "What is this foolishness?"

Sebastian scrambled to gather the pages. "Please, Christoph!"

But Christoph ripped them from him, pivoted toward the fireplace, and with two long strides, flung the manuscript onto the burning pile.

Frantic, Sebastian lunged to retrieve his treasure, but Christoph grabbed his arm, twisting.

"Please, sir, you don't understand!"

"What I understand is your disobedience. I said you were not ready for those works."

"But I've mastered all the music you've given me. I worked so hard on that copy. You've no right."

Pain burned through Sebastian's arm as Christoph flung him to the floor and stood over him, a mass of a man hovering like a vulture. "You're a fanatic," he roared. "Arrogant, wicked—after all I've done for you!"

The boiling inside of Sebastian would stay inside no longer. He sprung to his feet. "I hate you, Christoph! You're petty and mean!"

Christoph reared back, his arm high above his head, his fist clenched.

"Christoph, no!" It was Maria.

Christoph dropped his arm, then thrust it pointing in the direction of the stairs. "To your room, to stay."

Sebastian marched past Maria—his head held high, his back straight—and out into the hall. He stormed the stairs two at a time, turned the knob of his door, then kicked it to crash like thunder against the garret wall. In a second he was across the room throwing an arm across the table, sweeping Latin book, conjugations, ink, pens and music to the floor.

"I hope the music gives off a stench tomorrow, and the Count fires Christoph," he muttered. Then louder. "I hope he gets the pox and dies."

Clenching his teeth at the hate-filled words, Sebastian began to pace the room. If there were only some way he could get out of Ohrdruf. If his father were alive, he could tell him what to do. He would understand. Jakob would too. But his father was only a memory, and his brother Jakob wouldn't be home from his apprenticeship until Christmas. Sebastian was a prisoner in Christoph's home, dependent on his oldest brother until Christoph considered him ready for an apprenticeship.

"All that work for nothing," Sebastian cried. And his thoughts whirred and beat and tormented him until he could take it no longer. Finally he let the sobbing come.

For days afterward, he woke each morning feeling bereft. The loss of the manuscript was like the loss of a friend. He sulked. He took long walks. He wrote fugues in his head, rebelling against Christoph's command not to waste his time on unassigned exercises. He swiped the organ key from where he'd seen Christoph secret it and practiced the church organ when Christoph was out of town.

In the end his conflicts with Christoph resulted in good. Christoph's frustration over Sebastian's willfulness caused him to cast about for a way to be rid of him sooner than he had planned. When the school choirmaster recommended a school in Luneburg where Sebastian might secure a scholarship, Christoph leapt at the suggestion. Within a year Sebastian was traveling the strange country of Northern Germany with its Frenchified cities, its heaths and lowlands and its intriguing ports.

Sebastian would always remember the three years he spent in Luneburg the way a person remembers the glow of a first love. The time at the Michelsschule provided him invaluable opportunities to accompany the Symphoniac Chorus and master the mechanics of the organ. These years also anchored him scholastically. Then there were the journeys every summer to Hamburg and Celle. He attended operas, studied organ under Reincken and heard the newest in French music.

Not until several years later, however, did he decide what precise goal he would take for his composing.

2

The sound of a racing horse and carriage brought Sebastian back to the present.

He heard shouting outside the detention hall, doors slamming, and feet thundering up the stairs in his direction.

"What! You've got him down here with these rascals?"

It was August. "This is fool's work. By the eleven's! The rats are as big as swine!"

The door clanked open, and there was August, dressed in black cloak and breeches with a feather bouncing in his mammoth hat. He tossed his bags and parcels on the cot. "This is a preposterous turn of events; when I tell Mother . . ."

"Don't tell her," said Sebastian. "It will only make her worse."

August grimaced. "I thought, well, you know what kind of influence *I* have over Wilhelm."

August plopped down on the cot. "I *have* managed *some* help for you. Sustenance!" He grinned and fell to tearing open the parcels.

There was a link of warm sausages, a huge tankard of coffee with mugs, several brotchen and other breads, cherry preserves, a tin of walnuts and a nice cheese. Together they ate, joking a little, avoiding the subject of Ernst.

"Have you spoken to Barbara?" asked Sebastian.

"I will whisk by on my way home. Tell her you're alive. By the gods, she's a fine woman, Bach. How have you merited her?"

The guard was pounding on the door. "Your ten minutes are up."

Grumbling something about not being given his royal due, August gathered his wrappings and left.

Sebastian spread another roll with preserves and thought about what a fine woman Barbara was indeed and how close he'd come to not marrying her! He cringed at the memory of the alternative.

When he took his first real job as Hoforganist in Arnstadt, he discovered that he had cousins in the city. One of them was Barbara, no longer a spindly eight-year-old, but a young woman, and as comely as a willow tree. He'd been courting her several months when the superintendent of the Arnstadt Church Council summoned him. "We believe it would behoove you to take some time away. You are provoking too many altercations in your Kapelle rehearsals. Some travel and study would, perhaps, be beneficial. We have apprised Herr Buxtehude of your abilities and your possible visit to Lubeck. Go. Learn from him. You have a month's leave."

Sebastian was twenty years old. It was October, the best time of the year for traveling, and he'd just been handed an opportunity to hear Buxtehude's famous Evening Vespers at last! Sebastian was ecstatic.

But Barbara was upset. "Lubeck? That's two hundred miles away. So much could happen. Duke August was expecting us to come to the concert he's playing with his brother next week, and there's the Bach family reunion Uncle Martin's planning. I was going to surprise you with a picnic as soon as the leaves were at their peak: roast lamb and strudels, the way your mother made them. I was making a new blue dress, and I had the place all picked out, a perfect hill, out in the countryside. This is the best time of year for picnicking! Oh, Sebastian, please don't go!"

Sebastian was touched, but he was also frustrated. He took Barbara's face in his hands and kissed her black eyebrows. "Sweetheart, I will miss you. But you need to trust me and let me go. The artist must travel. He must have room or he dies."

At last she assented, and he promised a correspondence that he knew would be as difficult for him as coaxing a fire out of wet kindling. He loved Barbara very much, but he hated writing letters. If only he could compose fugues and send them instead. His truest communication was always in his music.

He bid Barbara good-bye, then hurried to the marketplace to buy one of those mahogany-handled walking sticks he'd been admiring.

By dawn the next morning he was traveling the road north to Lubeck.

How he loved the open road! He relished hitching rides in wagons and carts and traveling the river whenever possible. The swifter the river and the stranger his companions, the better. When he traveled, everything was grist for his creative mill. He never knew when some jocund melody might reveal itself to him. He'd known it to happen in the midst of a storm on a river and in a post wagon surrounded by talk.

This journey he made in record time. It only took ten days.

It was Friday, the last week in October, when he arrived. The sun was setting, and he couldn't believe his good fortune when he encountered a clergyman who said Buxtehude would be beginning his Friday rehearsal within the hour.

Soon Sebastian slipped into the back of a splendid Gothic cathedral. Some church buildings encouraged chatter with your neighbor. Others compelled you to silence. The arched ceilings of this church lifted his spirit into spaciousness.

He loved the way the flames of the candles fluttered like architecture against the walls. He loved the mystery of the dark, stretching, side aisles, the majesty of the columns and the intricately crafted capitals.

The Kapelle members were beginning to take their seats. Sebastian turned around to see. The organ was situated in the balcony in the back. He decided a seat in the side gallery would better suit his purposes.

Huffing from the dash up the back stairs, Sebastian selected a seat in the empty gallery. That must be Herr Buxtehude opening the organ, he thought. The old musician was as round as an acorn squash, and his yellow-gray hair looked as though a gale had torn through it. He seemed unsteady, tentative as he struggled onto the bench. But once seated, he selected his stops with a confident flourish and raised his right arm. Every whisper was stilled, every instrument readied. On his downbeat, a fanfare broke through the sanctuary.

Sebastian was riveted.

The acoustics were perfect. He could hear every nuance of dynamic. There were trumpets, fugal horns, trombones, kettledrums, bassoons that sounded the way bassoons were supposed to sound and at least forty string players and voices.

The boys' soprano section was better than any he had heard in Luneburg; and the organ rumbled power. Here was something wholly German and wholly spiritual.

After the rehearsal, Sebastian began jotting notes. How did Buxtehude achieve . . . He must ask him . . . That last melody . . .

"Who's this pilfering my ideas?" a voice demanded.

Startled, Sebastian looked up into the old eyes of Dietrich Buxtehude himself.

The old organist clamped Sebastian's shoulder in a bruising grip and scrutinized his face, his clothes, and his notes. The nostrils of the ancient's big nose flared. Suddenly he began coughing and gasping for breath.

Concerned, Sebastian jumped up.

But Buxtehude raised a hand to ward him off, swigged something from a vial, then advanced on Sebastian again. "I see old Heinrich Bach in your face and in your thinking." He shook a forefinger at him.

"If you are his nephew, I will tolerate your stealing. But, . . ."

Reminding himself that he too was a Hoforganist of a significant church and not a school boy anymore, Sebastian buttoned his coat tightly across his middle and bowed. "You have seen the likeness to my uncle correctly, Herr Buxtehude. I am Johann Sebastian Bach, and I am in awe of what you are doing with German church music. I have much to learn from you."

Buxtehude's flabby jowl relaxed. Amusement flickered in his eyes.

"And you shall, Bach, you shall. Come!"

Sebastian gritted his teeth against the pain as Buxtehude gripped his forearm and propelled him in the direction of the stairs. Soon they emerged into the hall, where he introduced him to his daughter, Margreta.

She had to be the most unappealing woman Sebastian had ever seen. Her face was pocked and her nose large, like her father's, with nostrils that flared. Like a gray mouse that knows its only hope is to stay hidden, she mumbled, "Good evening," curtsied, then picked up a bag of music and crept into place behind them.

As they strolled toward Buxtehude's home, Sebastian hammered the musician with questions about the evening rehearsal.

"Wait a minute there, son," Buxtehude croaked. "You forget that I am an old man. I need quiet before retiring. Did you not see my trembling and the way I lean over my cane? Old age has made me frail."

Sebastian was sure he heard Margreta stifle a laugh.

Her father continued, "We will not speak of my techniques anymore tonight."

At first Sebastian feared he had offended the old sage, but in the next breath, Buxtehude was assuring him that they would have plenty of time together. He even insisted Sebastian lodge with them, since the inns were full.

The next day, Sebastian attended one of Buxtehude's student gatherings. Young men who had traveled from as far away as Bavaria to learn from the master played their compositions and asked for criticism. After only two days, Buxtehude began tutoring Sebastian privately.

On the fifth day, Sebastian was sitting in a pew in the cathedral listening to a particularly poignant aria. It was scripture woven into a personal plea. "I long for Thee, my heart, my satisfaction, and Thou for me. To know Thee, to journey with Thee. In Thee alone I love, with Thee alone I live."

It came to Sebastian like light that was pure fire. His soul was blinded to all else but the summons. He knew his destiny. He would write a new and deeply personal music for the Lutheran liturgy, one that would woo a person into the love of the Divine Bridegroom.

It would be a music that would bend each unique personality in the appropriate repentance, lift it in praise, manifest to it the personal God. It would inspire all to seek and to find. It would be enough music for the whole five-year-cycle of scripture, prayer and creed. It would be a music that would cause the hearer to feel, to see, to understand—a high art music for the liturgy that would move people to an experience of their Maker.

He spilled out his revelation to Herr Buxtehude that evening, and the ancient's jowl shook like jelly with his nodding. "You will do, Bach. You will do."

Sebastian hurried to his room, inked up his favorite quill and wrote it all out in a letter to Barbara.

"Given the scope of the direction I have now for my studies here in Lubeck," he wrote, " I will need to stay longer than the month allotted. I must mine the knowledge available as diligently as if my livelihood, our livelihood, depended on it, and it may. Please try to understand."

The next day Herr Buxtehude revealed his true intentions. He wanted Sebastian for a successor—and a son-in-law.

3

That evening a fellow student explained the situation. "Herr Buxtehude offered his position to George Frederick Handel last spring. The problem is that if you accept the position you have to marry the daughter."

Sebastian was appalled. Marry the daughter? Why must a man always pay his dues in blood to get a decent position in a church? Margreta Buxtehude was thirty years old to Sebastian's twenty, and compared to Barbara, she was as alive as a wooden door.

Herr Buxtehude primed Sebastian, explaining to him that his daughter might not be an Esther, but that her deferential spirit would make her a good wife. "Love is not always," he said, "the best criteria for a good marriage."

As Sebastian brooded on it, crisscrossing the streets of Lubeck, ice wind stinging his face, he became less and less certain of what he should do. Buxtehude had forged such a powerful reputation for the music at the Marienkirche that church musicians all over Germany looked to his services as a model. Buxtehude's successor would inherit Buxtehude's prestige. It would be the perfect position from which to disseminate a new music for the liturgy.

After an hour of walking, Sebastian's hands and feet were growing numb, and his mind was still in chaos. A carriage stopped. A richly dressed woman with a motherly look offered him a ride, but he refused. He couldn't return to Herr Buxtehude's home without achieving an equilibrium of some kind. Buxtehude's offer had taken Sebastian completely by surprise. If he stayed now, it would be tantamount to saying yes.

Or would it? Sebastian wasn't ready to leave. His days were filled with performances, master lessons and musical discussions. Mealtimes were a concert of ideas from every angle imaginable. Each musician threw out both his conceptual and his technical dilemmas, and Buxtehude never failed to slice through every irrelevance and open up the core. When Sebastian compared his musical milieu at home to the one here, he realized that in Arnstadt he'd been like a peasant existing on nothing but gruel. Here in Lubeck, every day was a festival, an offering of the richest of fare.

He and the other students wrote canon puzzles for each other, laughing and working together in a boon of camaraderie. If he didn't have his notepad with him when ideas and questions came, he would rush home and spend hours jotting down bits of knowledge.

All his note-taking was decorated with new theme techniques and melodies to accompany biblical texts. Best of all, he was learning how to sculpt music to evoke the emotion of the words—word-painting, it was called. He must learn all he could.

Even though the thought of marrying Margreta was reprehensible, Sebastian knew he must not rush his decision. True, he and Barbara were considering marriage, but nothing had been settled as yet.

He would bide his time.

Two weeks later he received a letter from Barbara. "Change the face of the German worship service, Sebastian? There is plenty of music out there without your having to rewrite the whole liturgy. Hasn't Buxtehude written enough on biblical themes to fill volumes? It's not that I don't believe in you; you can make the simplest melody so profound that it bears hearing a thousand times. But really, dear, you mustn't waste your good humor on a thankless striving to better the church. You will turn into some kind of Luther or Hus, and I would not lose my boisterous Sebastian for the world. Do rethink and come home soon."

Incredulous, Sebastian stared at Barbara's beautiful script. It hurt him that she could so easily brush away an idea that fit him as perfectly as a child fits inside its mother's womb.

Does she not care whether people understand the truth? he wondered. Do I really know her? Some would say cousins shouldn't marry, even three times removed as we are. We fell in love so unexpectedly.

Am I making a mistake?

He shuffled out of his room, folding and refolding the letter. Margreta was polishing the dining room table. The room was elegant, the wall decorated with gilded carvings and a cartel clock. Margreta's French desk stood in an alcove, and a red and bronze musician's chair with tucked-in legs and a music stand waited by the window.

Buxtehude makes a fine livelihood, thought Sebastian. "Fraulein," he said out loud. "I need your opinion."

Margreta looked up, startled. Tendrils of auburn hair fell from her mobcap. He'd never seen her in anything but gray or brown, but today she wore mauve with a touch of lace at the collar. Her figure would actually be quite nice if it weren't for her hips. They bulged out like lifeboats.

"Do you require something, Herr Bach. Candles, perhaps?" Margreta's voice was soft as feathers.

Impatient with her predilection for acting like a servant, Sebastian shook his head. "What would you say if I told you I would like to write a new music for every Sunday and feast day, with the purpose of guiding people into an experience of the Creator?"

"You speak of the vision you apprehended while listening to my father's music?"

"Herr Buxtehude told you."

She avoided his eyes. "I'm afraid I was listening when you spoke to him."

Sebastian laughed. "A curious woman! Well, curiosity is not without its merits."

She colored and sneezed.

Sebastian proffered his handkerchief, and she wielded it like a grease rag across her nose. Then she peered up at him. Her eyes were troubled. "Forgive me, I . . ."

He willed himself not to stare at the redness of her great nose. "So what do you think?"

"Oh, Herr Bach!" She sounded close to tears. "You must think me unbearably boring and ugly. My feminine graces are few." She twisted away.

Sebastian was stung. Had he been unkind to Margreta the two months he'd been living in her home? No, it was worse. He had treated her as though she didn't exist. Whisking a white rose from the arrangement on the dining room table, he lay his hand on her shoulder and offered it to her. "You are like this rose, Margreta, tightly closed, fearful to reveal who you are. Beauty resides in every soul."

He was saying it to himself, as much as to her. She rolled the rose in her hand. A gust of air blew through the room, and Sebastian caught the scent of her perfume. Lavender?

She still avoided his eyes. Sebastian had an idea. "Have you heard the new ballade that's been wending its way through the city this week?"

Margreta shook her head.

He winked. "I will play it for you."

Laying Barbara's letter down, Sebastian began whistling the tune, slapping accompanying rhythms on the smooth surfaced table.

Margreta smiled. Encouraged, Sebastian abandoned all caution. He beat his hands across his chest and legs, blew through his knuckles, and ended his improvisation by bonging like a chime.

Her laughter rose like leaves rustling in the wind, and he guided her to sit beside him on the sofa.

"Now, Fraulein Margreta, tell me your opinion of my schemes. Am I being arrogant to think I can revolutionize the liturgy? Is it even needful?"

Margreta sniffed and fingered her hair.

"I . . .," she cleared her throat again.

Finally she looked him straight in the eye. Her words came in a rush, "I think it is the most wonderful thing I've heard any young musician who's come through here say. They always try to impress Father, and he always sees through them. Most of them don't really care that much about the heavenlies, they just want prestige, and a good church position is one of the surer ways to do it. I think," she caressed the rose in her hands, breathed in its scent with a little smile and finished furiously, "frankly, you are the most real, most sensitive man I've ever met. I applaud your vision, and I admire you with all my heart."

With that she bolted out of the room.

Sebastian sat stunned. There was something to this ungainly woman.

Now Sebastian was even more confused. Not knowing what to reply to Barbara's letter, he didn't reply at all. January arrived and still he was no closer to a decision. He didn't want to encourage Margreta too much, so he limited their encounters to family meals and an occasional walk. He explained to her that he was seeking guidance, and she accepted that, remaining in the background.

Two more months passed, and Sebastian was still unearthing gems from Buxtehude's cache of knowledge. Every night Sebastian stayed up late composing, employing every new idea. He played the viola in Buxtehude's Kapelle and sometimes even took Buxtehude's place at the organ.

He sent no message to his church employers about his long delay.

He didn't know what to say. The only person he corresponded with regularly was Duke August. Sebastian had met August while working as a lackey violinist in Weimar, waiting for his first organist job.

August was one person he could count on not to give him advice.

Then in early February, he received a letter from Barbara. He smoothed his hand over the beautiful script. "It has been so long since you've written," she wrote. "Perhaps my last letter has made you doubt. I too have doubts—that I am not worthy of you, that my struggles with the Invisible Being are too deep, that your lofty goal (and it *is* lofty, deserving of your gift) needs a companion more worthy than I."

To Sebastian's horror she wrote on, saying that she was refusing his proposal of marriage. She had had another offer.

Sebastian was not prepared for the emotions that pounded through him. He was angry at the man who dared propose to Barbara. He was jealous, and he was also, unexpectedly, afraid. Barbara's humility wooed him, as did the remembrance of her beauty: the shining black hair, the slender figure, her breasts small and rounded, her shoulders just broad enough for her to be able to wear any garment beautifully. Her nose was Grecian and her black-fringed eyes brown with glints of green. Some would say the size of her mouth was too generous, but her kisses!

He thought of how she looked when she was engrossed in conversation—the green sparks in her eyes, the repeated little uplift of her chin. If I lose Barbara, he thought, I will have lost the whole world.

Within an hour, he'd packed his bag and was hurrying to tell Margreta and Buxtehude about his decision. Grateful to find them together, he said what, now, he knew he must say—that his place was in Arnstadt, that his promises must be kept, that love and obligation must be obeyed.

Buxtehude walked him to the door.

"We are disappointed," the old man said. "You are certain?"

Sebastian looked over his mentor's shoulder at Margreta, who sat on the couch, head bowed, arms tensed. Sebastian sighed and sought Buxtehude's eyes, pleading silently for understanding. "Beyond a doubt."

"Well then!" The ancient slapped him on the back and cleared his throat. "It is best that you go. We are not without God's help."

Sebastian started home, confident that as surely as provision had come for him through the ducats in the herring four years before, provision would also come for Margreta.

He strode home toward Thuringia and Arnstadt, hopeful about his future and at peace.

In his prison cell in Weimar, Sebastian began strumming the lute August had left with him. God knows, he thought. Wait we may have to, agonize, but He works things out in time. August's hearty provisions and Sebastian's lack of sleep began to work on his body. His strumming slowed. His eyes drooped, and, lute cradled against his chest, he lay back and slept.

In the summer of 1715 Louis XIV was on his deathbed. He sent for his son and gave him his counsel: "Do not imitate the taste I have had for buildings nor my delight in war. Try, on the contrary, to keep the peace with your neighbours . . . try to relieve your peoples, which I have been unhappy enough not to be able to do."[1]

From the beginning of Bach's (Last Judgment) Cantata #70 "we hear the tumult motif to denote the end of the world. The urgency imparted by the nervous tone of the music and the staccato vocal exclamations make this one of Bach's greatest choruses."[2]

3

The Great Wait

1 7 1 5 — 1 7 1 7

When Barbara and Sebastian returned from the Red Castle that morning to find the bailiff waiting, Barbara felt as if an army had marched upon her and left her with nothing but fear. The guard roughed Sebastian into the wagon, and it lurched and rumbled away while Barbara watched, mind reeling, limbs mute.

The front door flew open. "Zounds! Is that Herr Bach in the bailiff's wagon?" Sebastian's twenty-two-year-old apprentice, Lorenz, was still in his nightshirt and cap, a "w" ridged between his blonde eyebrows, mouth working in his long face.

"Yes," she said. "What we dread has fallen upon us." She let Lorenz lead her into the house, scarce knowing what she was doing. He told her he'd be back in a minute and galloped up the stairs. She stood in the hall. Everything was cold and still. Mechanically, she walked into the kitchen and began stoking the fire in the oven—coffee pot, water.

Lorenz huffed into the kitchen. He'd thrown a brown vest over his nightshirt and an old pair of black breeches. His perpetually startled eyes looked concerned. "You must rest, Frau Barbara."

"You will be hungry," she said.

She started to slice some bread, then bent over the loaf weeping.

"Now, now, you—oh dear! You really must sit down."

Barbara dropped into the kitchen chair, and Lorenz slumped his tall frame into the chair next to her. "So, what happened? You and Herr Bach went to the Red Castle. . . ."

Barbara poured out the events of the night before: the fears she had had about their going, the magic Sebastian had wrought for Mariana with his music, the rush to get home before dawn, and then. . .

"Zounds! The arrest! One never gets bored living with Herr Bach."

Barbara shook her head. "I've always feared something like this would happen. I've known Sebastian to provoke duels and almost come to blows over improper executions at rehearsals. He could be in prison for months over last night's kind of disobedience. What am I going to do?" She broke down again.

Lorenz touched her hand. "We don't know that Herr Bach is in jail. The Duke may have only taken him to the Wilhelmsburg."

Barbara found a handkerchief in her bag and wiped at her tears. "Freedom is so important to Sebastian. I broke our engagement once because of it."

Lorenz's eyebrows arched up, and she wished she hadn't confided that bit of information.

At age thirty-one it pleasured her to be able to attract a man's notice, but Lorenz was in love with her, and she knew she must tread a fine line.

The aroma of coffee swirled toward them. Lorenz insisted she let him pour. She let him bang about looking for cups and spoons, her mind journeying back to those days when she'd tried to convince Sebastian she cared nothing for him. She'd learned of Margreta Buxtehude through August, and the hurt had been marrow deep. But she'd forged a plan. She would say "yes" to Manfred.

When Sebastian returned from Buxtehude's tutelage, she had refused to see him. She ignored his messages and gifts and let him know she was spending her evenings with Manfred. But every Sunday she had gone to church and listened to Sebastian's organ music. It was majestic and tinged with longing. She would watch him from her pew—his strong shoulders and arms, his broad chest, and those black diamond eyes that sometimes caught hers—and she knew that she would never stop loving him.

That's what she had feared—the indelibility of her love, the intensity of it. She would always love him more than he loved her.

It had taken only one encounter with Sebastian for her defenses to break down. In the marketplace, among the fruits and flowers, he had poured out his contrition.

An hour later they were eating melon on a bench hidden by lilac bushes and sealing their engagement with a kiss. The way of a man with a maid! That was one biblical saying Barbara understood.

The clink of a cup interrupted her reverie. Lorenz was pouring her coffee into a porcelain cup that she used only for company. He clanked the sugar bowl on the table, and it toppled. A sheet of sugar poured into her lap.

She jumped up. He apologized profusely. He scrambled to find the broom.

Barbara sipped at the hot coffee. "Never mind. Pour yourself some coffee and sit down."

"Would you like me to go to the detention hall and see if Herr Bach is there?"

"Let's wait. Surely the Duke will send word."

By the time Barbara finished her second cup of coffee, she felt better. She hurried upstairs, peeled off the sticky clothes she'd slept in and stepped into a fresh chemise and skirt. The baby was growing large within her. She unpinned her black hair, brushed it, and coiled it up with a blue hair-lace.

After checking on the children and finding all three still sleeping, she descended the stairs once more and set the oatmeal to simmer. She lit several candles across the kitchen window sill, brushed across the hall to light the candelabra in the music room where Lorenz was practicing, then lit the candles in the niche beneath the staircase. Candles always made her feel better.

These were strawberry-scented. They touched the dank air with spring.

The children soon woke. They lingered over breakfast with Barbara giving them only a hint of Sebastian's troubles. When she positioned seven-year-old Dorothea in front of the glass where they did their hair, Dorothea began asking questions. Barbara tried to explain Sebastian's predicament in a way that wouldn't frighten the sensitive little girl. She brushed Dorothea's fine brown hair until it shone, then braided it with a ribbon laced through, bright blue like her own.

"He'll probably be home before the day is over, " Barbara said.

"Really, Mama?"

"Really."

But in her heart, Barbara was not at all sure. The day was a crazy quilt of worrying and working and waiting and being disappointed and thinking and trying not to think. When she let her mind float, it conjured up frightful images: Sebastian being flogged; Sebastian in a dungeon with murderers; Sebastian falling ill in a frigid cell. She had to stay busy.

She nailed a black wreath to their door in honor of Ernst, then set Emmanuel at her feet with a pile of spoons while she and Dorothea began preparations for their usual Sunday dinner: roast mutton and pike, peas, carrots, cabbage and potatoes, a variety of Barbara's specialty breads and preserves, and a torte. She would work as though tomorrow would be a normal Sunday: a good dinner after church, then a quiet afternoon, punctuated with soft music and prayers. She and Dorothea would work on their stitchery in the parlour while Sebastian and Lorenz read from the Bible and Friedemann worked on his catechism. And tomorrow night Sebastian would attend communion at the Stadtkirche. He never missed it. "Please God," she prayed, "let it be."

On they worked till noon. They kneaded and shaped the Sunday brotchen, rubbed the mutton with spices, and threw the leftovers into a pot for tonight's soup. Every hour seemed pasted on the morning like pain. Barbara's back ached. Her abdomen pulled. For the baby's sake, she would have to rest soon. Why didn't anybody send word?

A knock at the door! It was the square-faced courier from the Red Castle.

"A message from His Excellency Duke August Ernst. Duke August sends his greetings."

Barbara motioned him in.

"Duke August has visited with Herr Bach in the detention hall," he continued.

"Herr Bach is well, but there is as yet no news of what awaits him."

"That is all?"

"His Excellency is appalled at the turn of events, but he fears there is nothing he can do."

The courier regarded Barbara with sympathy. His concern undid her. She turned away, sobbing. Dorothea began crying also, and then Emmanuel. Only Friedemann remained calm.

"Do you think Papa will have to stay in jail for a long time?" he asked the courier. "I've heard fearful stories."

"Don't think of it," said the courier. "It will not help."

Barbara fought down the panic. What would help? Mariana! "Wait here," she said.

She hurried past Lorenz into the music room. Quickly, she penned a message to the Duchess. Barbara felt bad about asking for the Duchess's help when Mariana was so depleted by her own grief, but she was growing desperate.

The courier agreed to get the note to the Duchess within the hour, and not long after he left, Baron von Lyncker's carriage rumbled up to their door. A courtier who often sang in the Kapelle, the Baron was a friend of Sebastian's. At first Barbara thought he might be bringing Sebastian home, but no, he was bringing condolences for the death of young Ernst.

When she told him about Sebastian's imprisonment, his dark face turned shocked. "The ruler before Wilhelm threw a lutanist into jail for cavorting with a maidservant and forgot about him for five years," he said. "I must see what I can do."

Barbara watched the Baron's carriage lurch down the street. Five years! Her anxiety was becoming so intense, it felt like a wound. Baron von Lyncker wouldn't be any help. He was a minor nobleman who possessed too little land and too many leanings toward Catholicism. Duke Wilhelm wouldn't give his opinion a second thought.

She tried to nap while Lorenz watched the children, but every time she drifted off, worry wrestled her up from the depths. She made her decision. "Lorenz, if you will go to the post station and hire a chaise, I'll pack a valise for Sebastian and dress the children for the drive."

Lorenz was out the door in a minute.

She packed warm clothes for Sebastian, then set Emmanuel in her lap and tugged black woolen stockings and breeches over his plump legs. After all the children were dressed, they waited. Barbara tried to read to them, but couldn't. She went downstairs to stir the soup. She peered out the window. The streets were deserted. Everyone was in mourning. Upstairs again, she found the boys bickering and Dorothea crying.

Then they heard the front door bang open, snow-packed boots pound and stomp, and men's voices!

"It's Papa!" Friedemann cried. He scrambled down the stairs with everyone else clattering after him. Sebastian was home.

2

The whole family was on top of Sebastian before he could hang up his coat—laughing, crying, asking questions and hugging and kissing him until he could scarcely get his breath. Yes, Duchess Mariana sent a note to the Duke, and yes, there were rats, and the noon meal was a hateful, watery gruel. They celebrated with what Sebastian announced to be the tastiest, chewiest cabbage and sausage soup known to man. "Good food is the best earthly antidote for soul-weariness," he declared.

After the meal he played the children's favorite gigue. Sometimes, Lorenz spelled him at the harpsichord, and they danced until they collapsed with laughter and exhaustion.

In bed that night he told Barbara the details of his day. Duchess Mariana had indeed sent a message to the Duke. Baron von Lyncker had acted as courier, and about 4:30 that afternoon, the Duke himself had entered Sebastian's cell. He said he'd only wanted to make Sebastian take notice. If it had been Sebastian's first offense, he would have done nothing. The Duke meant to honor Ernst properly, and he knew Ernst would not have wanted Sebastian in jail.

"Baron von Lyncker happened by the detention hall just in time to bring me home," said Sebastian. "We passed the post station, saw Lorenz paying the postmaster for your chaise and stopped him just in time. We rode home together."

"And what about Ernst's service?" asked Barbara.

"That's the one dissonant note. Wilhelm has asked someone from Halle to plan the music for Ernst's service, an old teacher."

"Did you tell him you wanted to use Ernst's concerto?"

Sebastian felt suddenly exhausted. "Yes. He rebuked me. Said I was in no position to be trying to push ideas on my Sovereign when he'd already made the decision."

"Did that not anger you?"

"Of course. But he'd just told me that if my Sunday service music measures up to his expectations the next few months, and if I desist with my rebellions, he will recommend my liturgical music to the Lutheran hierarchy. What could I say?"

"Ernst would have wanted you."

Sebastian stretched out in the bed beside her and traced his finger along the smoothness of her cheekbone. "The question is, do you?"

Barbara snuggled closer to him. "If you only knew. All day I wrestled with the fear that it might be months before you would be back home, months before I could be with you like this again." She kissed his bare chest, then his neck, then his chin.

He threw his arm about her, pulling the warmth of her closer, covering her lips with his, exploring, meeting, asking, answering. Her lips were soft as fleece, and they were alive. He forgot everything else but this world, his world, their world of passion and of joy.

For a while Sebastian thought he and the Duke might be able to mend the breach between them after all, but one Sunday in March he accepted an invitation to play in Halle at that Liebfrauenkirche without asking the Duke.

Sebastian left for Halle on Saturday, and early the next morning, old Drese, Wilhelm's official Kapellmeister, fell ill. Normally, young Drese would have taken the Sunday service, but he was in Leipzig visiting relatives.

Lorenz had to direct the music for Wilhelm's services without any preparation.

When Sebastian returned, he and the Duke had words.

Barbara suggested that he should apologize to the Duke. But Sebastian saw no reason to apologize when he'd done nothing wrong. Canon and counterpoint! he thought. I'll be asking permission to make love to my wife at this rate.

Sebastian began brooding over all the Sundays during these last eight years when he'd written the music for the Weimar Chapel services, rehearsed the Kapelle and then conducted and played the organ for the service.

All because old Drese was too infirm to do his work properly. The ancient musician hadn't composed anything for years.

Sebastian might not have the official title of Kapellmeister or even Assistant Kapellmeister. That was Young Drese. But the work of the Kapellmeister was usually what Sebastian did. At first he hadn't minded it. He was just glad to be working for someone who supported art music in the church. But after a while, the unfairness of his position had begun to gall. His only hope was that when old Drese died, the Kapellmeister position would finally be his.

May came, and with it, Barbara's time. She gave birth to a boy. They named him Johann Gottfried Bernhard Bach and sent invitations to their friends to join them at the baby's christening.

It was the third Sunday in May. Sebastian stood in front of the Stadtkirche altar, listening to the gently singing organ. Barbara was beside him holding the baby. He stirred, cried a little and Barbara shushed him, rocking back and forth. She looked at Sebastian, the joy that had been there ever since the baby's birth sparking green in her dark eyes. Little Bernhard had carrot-colored hair and fat cheeks. Sebastian was as proud of him as though he were his first.

Across from them stood Barbara's sister Catherina. She wore brown muslin, and her broad bosom and hips exuded a comfortable motherliness that, though she had never married, she played out daily in her work with orphans. It was good to see her again.

Beside Catherina stood Sebastian's nephew, Gottfried, with his mother Maria. But no Christoph. The rift between Sebastian and his oldest brother remained. Would it ever be mended? Sebastian had had no problem maintaining a bond with Gottfried all these years. But then, who would? There was congeniality written all over his nephew's freckled face.

The stately Pastor Elimar from Muhlhausen stood next to Maria, and next to the pastor stood Lorenz, stiff as a pole in his black coat and cauliflower wig. Baron von Lyncker stood on the other side of Sebastian with several others from Weimar. August would have been there, but he was courting Prince Leopold's sister Elinor, and today was her birthday. Elinor was a tiny, fun-loving woman whom they had met only twice, but Barbara already considered her a friend.

Sebastian looked up at the soaring arches of the Gothic church. Such an edifice always made him feel the greatness of the Above and relegate to the background, at least for a while, his own concerns. The altarpiece had been designed by Luther's friend, Lucas Cranach. The artist was known for his portraits and engravings, as well as for works such as this that honored the saints. Cranach had also created work with mythological themes. In these, it was said, there was always a hint of humor.

Sebastian wished he could see them.

The music changed as the Stadtkirche pastor approached the altar. The christening ritual began.

After the service, they celebrated with a picnic outside Weimar. Everyone else seemed to have the same idea. The Bachs rolled along in the cart they'd hired, their friends following past couples and families, all laughing, letting their horses go at a gentle pace. The hills were a chorus of tiny suns.

"Over there," said Catherina. Barbara and Catherina had traveled out the day before and set up a tent to reserve the spot Barbara liked best—a rolling area near a wood.

The women busied themselves laying out food while the men talked. Sebastian asked Gottfried if they'd heard from Jakob. "Mother had a letter last week. He's back in Sweden with his king."

"It's a relief to know he's out of Turkey," said Sebastian. "Where my brother gets his allegiance to Sweden I'm not sure."

"Mother says both of you have always been adventurous," said Gottfried. "Your brother just plays it out on the edge of a battlefield instead of at home."

Sebastian thought about that for a minute, remembering his years in Ohrdruf with Maria and Christoph. "Yes, well, still, an oboist for Karl XII's army! I'll never forget my shock the day he told us he'd enlisted."

"Sounds like Jakob is a man of the times," said Pastor Elimar. "We scarce know what it means to be German these days, what with our larger states letting out their soldiers for hire as a matter of course.

"I've a friend from Bavaria who actually fought on France's side at Heidelberg. When he realized Louis meant to burn the city, he almost deserted. He still has nightmares about the destruction of the bridge."

"Every bit of that beauty, gone! All because of the French king's determination to gain glory for himself!"

"The supreme right of kings! Some would say he wielded the hand of God."

"Whoa!" Gottfried was almost knocked over by a streak up the hill and a whoop.

"Ride, Gottfeed!" It was Emmanuel.

Gottfried set Emmanuel on his shoulders and galloped down the hill, red hair flying.

The men followed the sixteen-year-old and his cousin toward the tent. The scent of the earth was rich and musty, the air bracing. The laughter and squeals of the children skipped across the hills. They were delirious with the feel of freedom.

Maria was walking up from the chaise with a bottle of wine she'd brought from Ohrdruf. "Looks as though you will be acquiring some help with the children," she said to Sebastian.

"Then Christoph has assented to Gottfried's taking his apprenticeship with me?"

Maria's auburn hair had bands of gray in it now, but her figure was still trim and her practical no-nonsense manner the same. Sebastian would ever be grateful to his sister-in-law for her kindness during those years under Christoph's roof.

She tucked her arm into Sebastian's. "Your virtuosity at the keyboard is becoming a byword, even in our area. Christoph has all but assented. Perhaps Gottfried can join you next spring!"

Catherina called for them to come fill their plates, and Sebastian and Lorenz hurried to be first in line.

Barbara was arranging strawberries and cheeses on a pewter plate while Catherina added slices of roast beef to a platter of meats.

Sebastian piled a heap of reddish brown slices onto a plate. "Sausage," Sebastian said to Lorenz, "the kind you like, hot as embers."

"And is Duke Wilhelm hot or cold for your church cantatas these days, brother-in-law?" Catherina's brown-bonneted head was tilted, her query as direct as a man's.

"That is the question," Sebastian answered.

"Zounds, that is on the upright!" said Lorenz. "Duke Wilhelm had no word of commendation for the cantata we performed last Sunday, and it was one of Herr Bach's best."

"He has had no word for me at all since last February," Sebastian growled, "not for my music at least. Plenty of word about everything else. Rebuked me for speaking to August on the street, reprimanded me for not insisting Barbara take her weekly test on the sermon the day after the baby was born. The list is endless."

"The aristocracy is accustomed to doing the thinking for their subjects," said Pastor Elimar.

"Johann Sebastian Bach not think? It's a contradiction of terms," said Catherina.

"Which is why I believe," continued Pastor Elimar, "Sebastian is having so much difficulty gaining Duke Wilhelm's support. Why, when I think of all the initiative you wielded when you were in Muhlhausen! The village churches are still benefiting from the new perspectives you gave them on worship.

"Your confidence can be intimidating, though. It offends Wilhelm, I'm sure. He expects you to forsake your independence and pride and trust your future to your Sovereign."

"And what would be wrong with that, Sebastian?" Catherina asked.

"I'll tell you what's wrong with it. It's a simple matter of justice. The laborer is worthy of his hire. I am doing the work of Kapellmeister already and have been doing it variously for eight years. It is ridiculous to have to grovel to purchase a title I have already earned."

"Everyone recognizes the superior quality of your work," Baron von

Lyncker said.

"When Drese's son Johann composes for the services, the Kapelle can barely get through his music without choking."

"You see, Catherina?" said Sebastian. "What kind of man propagates such mediocrity in God's service?

"If Wilhelm had no choice, had not the musical resources in his establishment to offer up the best, that would be one matter. Konzertmeister Bach! I'm sick of the humiliation. My apprentice has all the skill necessary for the proper work of the position. I've a good mind to just let him have it."

Lorenz swung around, his tankard sloshing wine on Barbara's tablecloth.

"Lord, have mercy!" Barbara leaned over with a cloth to blot at the wine.

Lorenz's bean-shaped face was quivering.

"My regrets, Frau Barbara. I've done it again."

Barbara reached to squeeze Lorenz's hand.

"Never mind."

Sebastian watched all this with only half of his attention. His mind was roiling with frustration.

After they had eaten, Barbara retired to nurse the baby in the tent, and Lorenz and the Baron left with Gottfried and the children to see to the horses. They were talking of taking a ramble through the countryside.

Catherina asked Sebastian to walk with her a ways. The sounds of nearby picnickers had quieted, some napping and others walking along the paths at a leisured pace. Sebastian and his sister-in-law strolled near the edge of a rustling wood, the sun warm upon their heads. Her coronet of braids made her look like a matriarch.

Sebastian asked for news of Uncle Martin.

"Adding to his library as always," said Catherina, "and still involved on both the church and town councils. Our discussions are always stimulating. I am fortunate to have such a guardian."

"And he to have such a housekeeper."

"But tell me your views on the supreme right of kings."

Sebastian shook his head. "My views on that are as various and as contradictory as the ways of a woman, sister."

She raised her eyebrows.

"With the exception of my supremely steadfast and objective sister-in-law, of course. All I mean is that I wonder if it is in men to understand most women. And so I wonder if it is in me to understand the rule we are given to obey the king. I believe it, and yet I do not. Look at what obedience to Louis XIV has accomplished in Europe. Widespread destruction and an enmity between Germany and France that I fear will never be mended. And besides all this, I hear Louis lies ill and begins to repent of his ambitions."

"And yet your situation is not so severe."

"Meaning?"

Catherina eyed him. Her mouth and chin that were so like his own were set, her brown eyes demanding. "Meaning: having a title withheld from you is not the same as being commanded to destroy a city. Why is it so important that you possess this title right now? Why not simply serve? Why not rather be defrauded? Sometimes timing is all."

Sebastian heard what she was saying, but everything in him rose up against it. Yes, he was proud. He knew it. He also knew that pride was no virtue. "I am what I am," he shrugged. "Besides, without the title, the Lutheran clergy will pay no attention to my music."

"How can you be so certain?" Catherina asked.

"It's the way things work."

"And the Almighty cannot change such workings?"

Sebastian looked at Catherina with a sudden feeling of sadness. "Such submission is not in me. Not now, Catherina. Someday, perhaps. But now it is impossible. Try to understand." He turned and walked away.

3

It was two years before Kapellmeister Drese finally died. The day after the death, Sebastian rose at 6:00 A.M. as usual and sloshed water in the washbasin. He meditated on Drese's death and the lingering of it. The old musician had been an invalid for twenty years, and the last year he'd not been able to rise from his bed. A living death, it seemed to Sebastian—not to be able to work, trapped in one room. Scrubbing his face and arms with some of Barbara's herb soap, he wondered what it would be like to experience such a lingering. The thought of death would be sweet then. Yes, he was sure he would long for it.

Drese's mind had fled too this last year. It took only one visit after the senility set in for Sebastian to decide he would never visit Drese again. Now Sebastian wished he had. So many emotions mixed up in the situation of that man! One thing about Duke Wilhelm, when he finally decided to commit himself to an employee, he did right by him. Many rulers would have interrupted the old musician's salary long ago and left him to his own devices.

Sebastian slipped his cotton shift over his head, then pulled on his breeches. Next came his long vest. He tugged on his white stockings, stretched them over his black rolling breeches, then folded them down to make a two-inch cuff. Hesitating over the three black coats lined up in his wardrobe, he chose the one with the bronze buttons, nicer than his everyday. Then he slipped into his bronze-buckled shoes. The square-heeled fashion suited him well, perfect for maneuvering the pedal keyboard.

He swirled his powder mantle about his shoulders, jerked his wig off its hook, shaking the surplus powder out of it, and fitted it over his short brown hair. Someday he would shave his head, as so many did. Make life simpler.

He worked at the wig a little, cleaning his brows with a powder knife. Then he examined himself in Barbara's full-length glass. He shook his head at his reflection. "You scoundrel. You will curry favor with Wilhelm right now in spite of your so-called convictions."

The Duke would be announcing his choice for Kapellmeister at the end of the month, and one never knew when Wilhelm might appear at a rehearsal. Sebastian was in the process of writing a new cantata for Sunday. It would be one of his best, he thought, assuring him of the appointment.

The day unfolded much as any other: devotionals and breakfast with the family, ending with a chorale—Gottfried was living with them now, and his tenor was a pleasant addition to Barbara's alto and Lorenz's bass—practice at the castle organ for two hours, section rehearsals with Gottfried and Lorenz assisting, then individual work with soloists.

At 11:00 A.M. Sebastian ambled outside bearing a parcel of Barbara's meat pies and some fresh cherries. He tore off his wig and stuffed it into his pocket. On difficult days he found himself imagining his wig to be the source of his plague. Binding his mind and body, it was a picture of the censure that had been hampering his composing.

He found a quiet bench near the cherubimed fountain in the park and breathed in the scent of early roses. Tulips, so popular now, were planted in triangles encircling the green around the fountain. Blue hyacinths bordered the bottom of each triangle. Sebastian knelt to touch the miniature petals, frilly and pliant, each blue petal a wisp of perfect.

How did God do it?

A melody leapt into his mind. Sebastian jotted it on his pad. It brought back memories of the mood he'd experienced under Buxtehude's Evening Vespers those days in Lubeck before his marriage. His mentor had inspired him to work on word-painting, the use of melodies and harmonies that expressed the emotions of the text. Yes, this tune was lifting, hopeful, exactly what he needed. Now he could finish the cantata.

He munched on his tarts. Seasoned with curry, they were as delicious as anything he'd ever tasted at a royal board. He felt happier than he'd felt in a long time. If a person created as a result of only what was in him, as some said, with no outside influence affecting the flow, why was it that he'd not been able to write worship music for six months now? Only the organ music had come. He wanted to think that like any craftsman who knew his craft, he could hammer out whatever work was required, whenever it was required. But it didn't always happen that way. Not with his standards, at least.

He supposed that sometimes creative work came as a result of opposition—if a person learned not to feel the stings, if by some inner strength he was enabled to block it all out. He'd had that experience before. Such works wrought in the furnace, he suspected, would be the more profound.

The fact was, though, that during the last two years he'd felt Duke Wilhelm's disapproval so strongly that he'd drudged around like a workhorse tethered to a cart.

It had taken this fresh possibility of receiving the Kapellmeister title to free up his creative energy. What did that energy consist of?

Inspiration? Ego? Hope? Pride?

Who knew? For whatever reasons, it was a fact that at the age of thirty-two, he required a signpost, an affirmation of a proper title before he could continue his ordained work.

4

At noon, Sebastian attended the weekly meeting the Duke required of his employees. There Duke Wilhelm disseminated information about the guests who would be arriving that week and the schedule of events. He also announced any penalties for infractions of rules. Sebastian had escaped reproach in these meetings for two weeks now. Probably a record.

After the noon meeting, Sebastian met with Salomon Franck, the librettist he had chosen for his cantata. Franck was especially slow this week. Would he finish the libretto in time for the Kapelle to rehearse the words with the music? The anxiety was always there.

Back at the castle chapel, Sebastian summoned Lorenz from his organ practice and set him to repairing a kettledrum. Gottfried he took with him to walk through the innards of the organ. They worked together repairing faulty linkages. Then, before going home to his afternoon roster of students, he returned to the organ to practice some more.

Ensconced at the organ high in the ceiling of the castle chapel, Sebastian fingered the marble smooth stops. Which ones would work best for the prelude to Sunday's cantata? Perhaps the Gedackt, the Mixture? Yes, for the pedals he would try the thirty-two-foot Gross Untersat and perhaps the Posaune.

He played through the prelude, penned in a change, replayed it, then crossed out the whole page with two big slashes. He selected another stop for a reedier effect and plunged into an idea that had come to him. His fingers flew. His feet followed. Take the theme this way, expand it, invert it. Pedal point right here. Good! He rewrote the section quickly and played it again. How he loved this perfecting, this working it over and over to get it just right! He loved immersing himself in the craft, adding color, movement and architecture.

He paused, leaving the organ silent. Voices drifted up. "You have my condolences." It was Duke Wilhelm, standing near the altar with young Drese.

Johann Drese bowed low, then rose slowly, whisking a handkerchief to his eyes. "We are bereft. My sister sits beside father's casket weeping all the day and will not take food."

Young Drese's gushing tone was almost impossible to bear, something about relatives coming, his father's emaciated face. The fellow whisked off his tricorner and bowed to Wilhelm again.

"Oh, Grand Duke, we are grateful beyond . . ."

Sebastian rolled his eyes. Not only could he not attend to young Drese, he couldn't attend to his own practice. The mere presence of the simpleton cast him into an irritable mood.

The Duke was dismissing Drese. He urged him to the organ to practice for Evening Vespers. Drese bowed again, his frame frozen in the shape of a comma while Wilhelm exited through the backdoor.

Disgusted, Sebastian turned back to his music and played the last section of his work again.

"I congratulate you, Bach."

Sebastian jumped. Drese was standing no more than two feet from him. For a man slain with grief, he had vaulted up the stairs with suspicious speed. His swarthy face looked ridiculous under his long Adonis wig.

"On what do you congratulate me?" Sebastian asked.

"On your organ fantasy last Sunday. I could not have done as well."

"Hmm!" Sebastian's mind was on a phrase that didn't quite work. He rewrote it, then played it once more. When he was satisfied with it, he stacked his music and swiveled down from the bench. Johann Drese's face was the color of beets. He pounded his fist on the bench. "I will not tolerate the way you treat me. You think to steal the title that is my rightful inheritance. But you will see!"

Sebastian wedged a violin that needed restringing under his arm, then strode past Drese. "You may have the organ for the rest of the day."

As Sebastian hurried down the stairs, Drese's words chased after him. "I may have it? I may have it? It is my right!"

Sebastian spent the rest of the week agonizing over the Sunday cantata. He spread pieces of manuscript all over the music room floor, slotting and re-slotting chorale tunes between arias and choruses, working the whole of the thirty-minute cantata like a puzzle. At the end of the cantata, he'd penned in his usual "Soli Deo Gloria,"—"To God Alone Be the Glory." But today, as he reviewed the work and realized how many spots were faulty, he wrote a new plea above the first chorus: "Jesu, Juva"—"Jesus, Help Me!"

He'd decided to use a melody from Handel's first opera *Almira* and adapt it for his own uses. Would Duke Wilhelm notice and be displeased? Composers were in the habit of borrowing from each other, but it was possible Wilhelm might castigate him for using a secular melody. The question at bottom, of course, was not what Duke Wilhelm thought of using secular melodies, but what the melody did for the work.

The librettist presented him the libretto in time for Kapelle rehearsal Friday morning, but Sebastian didn't complete his own revisions until Friday afternoon. He remained up all night copying parts with Lorenz and Gottfried. The Kapelle would only have one day to rehearse the work in its final form.

Sunday morning arrived. Sebastian was waiting nervously at the organ. This was the day and performance that could determine his future. At last the Prelude was executed and the routine hymns and responses done. It was time. Stops selected, left hand ready on the bottom keyboard, Sebastian raised his arm to command the attention of the three curved rows of singers and instrumentalists. He took a deep breath and gave the downbeat.

The voices rang out in staccato cries, shouting, "Watch, pray, pray, watch!" The orchestra backed the voices, following Sebastian's lead, the mood exactly as he desired, tense with tumult.

Then came the bass solo—a chant-like recitative accompanied by woodwinds, trumpet and strings. The music seethed with fear, then joy, then fear and joy again. An alto aria, a tenor recitative, and a soprano solo painting a sound-image of Jesus in heaven. At the end of the hope-filled aria, Sebastian flung open the swell pedal, signaling the congregation to join in the familiar chorale "Rejoice Greatly, O My Soul! God is calling you out of your valley of tears into His eternity."

The chorale died away, and immediately, Sebastian brought in the crash of trumpets with full orchestra, the depiction of the world falling into ruins. There were outbursts of Luther's hymn, "Now Rejoice, Dear Christians," and at last, the congregation and choir sang together, "My Jesus I Do

Not Leave."

The chapel fell into silence. Nobody moved. His own soul challenged, Sebastian waited, then began the music for the pre-sermon meditation.

When the service was over, Sebastian vacated the loft earlier than usual. He needed to store some instruments, and he was tired. Home was all he could think of, the refreshment of family and food.

He was arranging music and instruments in a downstairs cabinet when he heard voices in the hallway. "I was deeply affected by your Konzertmeister's depiction of the last judgment today, Wilhelm."

It sounded like one of the visiting clergy. Yes, it was Clergyman Kirkman from Leipzig.

"You must see to it that Bach's music finds a wider audience. Publishing, perhaps?"

Duke Wilhelm's voice sounded agitated.

"Works in print would only increase his pride."

"His pride may be warranted," Kirkman said. "His musical instincts are superb."

"The man is a rebel," Duke Wilhelm scoffed. "I've been trying to mold him for years, and I see little progress. Such a spirit will never be used by God, I can tell you that. I advise you to shun his music until he learns obedience."

"Then you do not plan to award him the Kapellmeister title?"

"I do not. Young Drese will suffice. Bach will continue to write much of my music, of course. I am not so obtuse as to fail to appreciate his gift, but the Kapellmeister title will not be his."

The voices faded.

Mechanically, Sebastian closed and latched the cabinet. He stood there for a minute, unable to believe what he'd just heard. How could Wilhelm be so unjust? How could God allow this thing to happen? He felt the anger rising. He banged his fist into the cabinet. The tears welled up hot. There he stayed for a long time, breathing hard in the shadows, listening to the voices of the everyday above him, wondering, what next?

He was quiet at the noonday meal. Barbara finished before anyone else. She ate so little. He watched her, deftly wielding her knitting needles while the conversation undulated about her. Lorenz analyzed the performance. Gottfried spoke of another time when he'd encountered the Leipzig man who'd read the gospel. Friedemann said he'd seen Prince Leopold sneak into a back seat in the middle of the service. The prince had been a regular visitor to Weimar ever since his sister Elinor's marriage to August a year ago.

Occasionally, Barbara looked up from her knitting with that excited little jerk of her chin that was so endearing. She commented, "Prince Leopold is pursuing Sebastian like a hound on the trail of a rabbit. He will have you for his Kapellmeister, dear. Elinor was hoping Leopold would be here. She was stunned with your cantata, as was I!"

Later that afternoon, when they were alone, Sebastian told Barbara what he'd overheard.

Her brown eyes widened, then clouded. "Wilhelm doesn't deserve you."

"Shall we accept the position in Cothen then?" Sebastian asked. "Leopold's offer has been official ever since August's wedding."

Barbara looked away for a moment, pensive.

He took one of her small hands and rubbed her warm palm with his thumb. "Yes, take some time to think about it. Uprooting is always difficult for you."

To his surprise, she suddenly smiled. "We shall accept the Kapellmeister position from Leopold, and you shall also accept that challenge the Elector's Konzertmeister has been urging upon you—travel to Dresden in September."

Green was sparking in her eyes. She was genuinely enthusiastic. "You will win a victory for Germany with your brilliant improvisations, and we will move to Cothen. You need new vistas."

Sebastian took her chin in his hand and kissed her. The warmth in her lips, the responsiveness, meant so much to him in so many ways. She was shade in heat and safety in war. What would he do without her?

Eighteenth-century society delighted in contests of skill between musical giants—
a famous example is the one between Handel and Domenico Scarlatti in Rome.

"(Bach's) works for clavier and organ will remain . . . the higher school of
organists and clavier players, just as he himself, as a practicing artist, was the
highest model for organists and clavier players."[1]

4

Prince of Claviers
1717

Four months later, Sebastian was traveling to Dresden with Prince Leopold and August. The carriage trundled through the leaf smells of autumn, the breeze touching Sebastian alive. Fall was his favorite time of year.

The conversation in Leopold's carriage was as refreshing as the crisp air. The young man who sat across from Sebastian was reading a philosophical journal and bursting into some exclamation every once in a while that plunged them all into discussion. His name was Picander.

August was wedged in beside Sebastian; the monocled Duke Kober sat next to August, and across from Duke Kober sat Prince Leopold and his violinist Spiess.

"By the roods," Picander was saying to the Prince, "you've not read Leibniz, Excellency? You must." Picander had the broad shoulders and chest of an athlete. As he leaned forward and turned his head in the Prince's direction, the wooden cross about his neck swung back and forth.

"Isn't Leibniz the philosopher who invented calculus?" asked Sebastian.

The blonde youth nodded. "And fathered the Academy of Science in Berlin. My tutor's mentor.

"Scientific methods are being applied not only to chemistry and biology, but also to politics and even biblical criticism. Leibniz's ability to influence the Prussian Elector toward this new university is significant. These are exciting times."

August circled out a podgy hand, "And do you study astronomy, Picander?"

Before the youth could answer, Duke Kober cried, "It is my passion!"

Kober adjusted his monocle and launched into a diatribe about his newest telescope.

Sebastian chuckled to himself. This was the fifth time Kober had said this in as many days, and every day it was a different passion. Duke Kober was a friend of Leopold's, a courtier from Cothen.

To better hear Kober, Picander leaned closer to Spiess.

Spiess elbowed him away. Intent on Kober's description of what he was discovering with his new telescope, Picander ignored the slight, allowing the edge of his journal to cover part of the score Spiess was studying. Spiess shoved the journal away and cursed.

Picander drew back and grinned at the violinist. "You must make allowances, fellow. Space is not something to be expected when one's on the road."

Spiess glared at him, his small eyes angry in his lantern-shaped face. Sebastian began to wonder if it might come to blows. But Spiess simply shrugged and returned to studying his score. The little man was a cranky old bird, but he was reported to be one of the finest string players in the land.

Picander was a gifted poet whom Leopold had met in Berlin. The young man had already written several successful librettos. But he was interested in science, philosophy, history, and the other arts also. How refreshing it was to be in the company of men who understood the times! Thuringia was island-like, isolated—almost immune to what was happening in the Europe around it. To be with men who were conversant with thinkers and artists like Descartes, Milton, Rembrandt, Newton and Leibniz was stimulating to Sebastian. It met a deep need within him that he'd almost forgotten was there.

As Leopold took the lead and guided the discussion into the organic view of the universe versus the mechanical, Sebastian let the rocking of the carriage and the flow of the countryside lull him. The places of still green beneath stands of trees were splotched with red and yellow. The autumn daylight was tinged with brown.

It wasn't long before Prince Leopold noticed the beauty of the terrain and called for the coachmen to stop. The Prince leapt out, motioning them all to follow. But Sebastian hung back. Soon he would be meeting the French Court Organist. In a duel of wit and fingers, he and the Frenchman would exhibit their individual skills at the keyboard. It was Sebastian's responsibility to win, and thereby, prove the superiority of German musicianship.

His traveling companions sought the brook, but Sebastian meandered alone, watching a flock of ravens. They settled, flew up wind slides, then settled again in the tops of trees. He listened to their caws and clicks and trills and thought of the days of his early boyhood in Eisenach—concertizing with the perambulating choir and stopping to rest in a park, running at the ravens with the other boys when the choirmaster wasn't looking, throwing rocks, feeling guilty.

In Eisenach he could never escape Wartburg castle, high on its cone-shaped hill. Martin Luther's shelter in the early 1500s, the castle had seemed alive to him, like a conscience, inspecting and warning.

It was Duke Wilhelm's castle that inspected him these days, even in his absences it seemed. Four different times since young Drese's appointment, Sebastian had petitioned Wilhelm for release from his Weimar job, but the Duke always refused. As a court servant, Sebastian was locked into the laws of the land.

An employee could not leave one court for another without a written release from his current employer. Prince Leopold had already begun paying Sebastian the Cothen Kapellmeister's salary, but Sebastian could make music for the Prince only on surreptitious trips.

Wilhelm knew Sebastian was traveling to Dresden to engage the Frenchman Marchand in a contest of musical skill, but Wilhelm didn't know he was traveling with Prince Leopold.

Sometimes Sebastian thought he would suffocate in the Weimar atmosphere. He hoped that if he won the favor of influential Saxon aristocracy by dueling successfully with the French Court Organist, Wilhelm would be more willing to consider his desires.

Would he win the contest? He must. Sebastian thought of the letter he'd received from Marchand in answer to his challenge. The French never seemed to fail in the ability to make a German's blood boil.

Sebastian buttoned his coat fiercely across the middle. He could hear his traveling companions' voices rising and lowering. August was sitting on a great rock, listening to Picander and Leopold discuss monads and self-determinism.

Sebastian ran his hand along the rough bark of the birches and savored the earthy smells. The area had been mowed, the trees trimmed and benches set—a resting place for travelers. Barbara would love it here, he thought. The guilt he couldn't quite shake over leaving her pricked at him like a bur. She always had difficulty sleeping when he was gone, and the problems she'd had carrying this current baby made extra rest essential. She was three months along and wanted this baby desperately. She was hoping it would be a girl.

All Barbara had said when he expressed his concern about leaving her alone was that Gottfried was excellent with anything that might need to be repaired and that the midwife was alerted. She urged him to put his mind to his performance. But when he kissed her good-bye, her eyes pooled with tears.

Sebastian patted the manuscripts in his coat pocket: a lullaby he was writing for Barbara and a Handel overture he'd been wanting to study. Five days out of Weimar and already his mind was bristling with new possibilities.

On the road behind them the traffic was increasing: barons, merchants, Catholic divines and university men clipping along in heated discussion.

Ahead he could see the cloud-capped towers of Dresden. This was his first glimpse of the celebrated city. It was the capital city of the electorate of Saxony, ruled by August the Strong. Like Hamburg, Leipzig and Frankfurt, Dresden was one of those rare commodities, a German city that was in touch with the rest of the world. Prince Leopold visited it as often as possible.

As they approached the city through the gardens of August the Strong, the Prince pointed out the Elector's chateau. It was elaborate, but also striking in its good taste.

Within the hour they were driving through the statuaried entrance of Count Flemming's estate, down the poplar-lined driveway and past stone cottages carved with gargoyles.

Above the jangle of the horses's livery, the lantern-faced violinist spoke directly to Sebastian for the first time. "What about it, Bach? Do you think you can best this fellow Marchand? The Frenchman is lauded everywhere I travel. His credentials as French Court organist are impeccable. He heaps up fame with every performance. The variety of what he offers, his experiments with new styles—to think that you think you can best such a man!? Well, you either have an abominable amount of talent or an abominable amount of pride."

The violinist fell silent as abruptly as he'd begun. Sebastian felt defensive and a little angry. He started to say something but decided it would be best not to. Better to bide his time, let his performance be his answer. When he moved to Cothen, Spiess would be his first violinist. It was paramount that Sebastian have his good will.

Picander's pale brown eyes were wide with interest. "What do they say about Marchand's improvisation skills?"

"Konzertmeister Volumier informs me that, thus far, no German has dared to challenge Marchand," Sebastian answered, "and of course, I have on hand what the mighty Frenchman writes about himself."

"I couldn't believe you didn't tear the infernal letter to pieces," said August.

August mimicked Marchand in an effeminate voice, twirling his hand like a fop, "These tournaments are a good way to make a name for yourself—if you do not lose, that is. I have many to my credit, my good man. You have reason to fear a thorough trouncing."

Everyone in the carriage roared. "Arrogant Frenchmen—spineless Catholic—heads must roll—it must be a victory, Bach!"

"The man has no idea who he is dealing with," said August. "Sebastian was born improvising."

Spiess eyed Sebastian doubtfully.

"You have not heard the art of improvisation until you've heard it from Bach," Leopold assured his violinist. "Cothen has contracted someone to learn from, as has France."

They could see the castle at the end of the drive. Sebastian's blood began to pump. His fingers tingled at the thought of the puzzles that would soon be set for him. Performing always enlivened him. He amazed himself sometimes with the ideas that whirled into his mind and ear and flowed out through his fingers when the challenge of an audience awaited. Improvisation was like a game to him, as delightful as a round of backgammon.

The coach slowed, gliding around a wide curve, and the driver shouted the horses to a halt. Sebastian leaned out the window to see several gilded carriages lined up ahead of them. Servants and courtiers streamed out the front doors. Prince Leopold seemed to know everyone.

Within fifteen minutes, Sebastian was in his room. He washed his sweaty face in the basin and stretched on his honey-blonde wig.

Then he drew on his silver-buckled shoes and shook out his new black coat. Barbara had summoned a tailor to stitch it for him in velvet. Warming his fingers in his woolen gloves, he leaned to peer at his broad face in the glass.

His cheeks were flushed, his eyes bright. His hands were shaking a little, but such nervousness always subsided the minute he began playing. He considered it a good sign, a building up of energy to be tapped into in the performance ahead.

Their host, Count Flemming, and Volumier, who was the Elector's Konzertmeister and the one who had suggested the contest, were downstairs waiting for him with guests, as was Louis Marchand. Volumier had requested that Sebastian give them a preview of his skills.

Downstairs again, his footsteps echoed across the multicolored floor. Voices drifted out of the Grand Parlour, shifting high and low, masculine and feminine.

Sebastian stopped in the open doorway, and immediately, a man wearing an Adonis wig rose from a circle of flounced and coifed nobility and hurried toward him.

It was Konzertmeister Volumier. Sebastian remembered him from the Halle concert last year. "A thousand welcomes, Konzertmeister Bach. Let me present you."

Volumier guided Sebastian across the room toward the guests who were gathered near a harpsichord. Sebastian scanned the faces, wondering which was Louis Marchand. His eyes settled on a tall man who had arrogance carved into his face.

Volumier presented the elderly Count Flemming, who was hosting the contest, then arced his arm toward the other side of the circle: "The French Court Organist Louis Marchand."

The arrogant man uncrossed his blue-silked legs, slowly unfolded his frame and inclined his head.

Sebastian inclined his. Their eyes locked.

Volumier cleared his throat. "I have heard Johann Sebastian Bach perform on a variety of claviers. You will find him a formidable foe."

Marchand's voice was smooth and malicious, "You are the most current in a long line of family musicians I understand."

Sebastian nodded, "I am quite proud of my family heritage."

"As you should be!" Marchand's heavy gray eyes flitted over Sebastian like a feline sizing up its prey. "A heritage of talented family members enables a man where he cannot make it on his own. Now, we in France have begun to choose vocations suited to our individual natures. We set the standard for the rest of the world in every area, whereas Germany. . ." He paused. There were indrawn breaths. "But enough!" he hurried on. "I must hear a sampling of your repertoire."

The Frenchman sank coolly to his seat, crossed his arms and waited.

Sebastian felt as though kindling had been set to burn an inch from his face. Englishmen were glaring. Germans were tapping their fingers on their chairs. French guests looked nervous, if amused.

Sebastian whirled toward Volumier, "At your leave, I will play."

The women began fluttering their fans and whispering excitedly, and some of the group broke into applause. Sebastian strode toward the double-manualed harpsichord, tested the instrument with a soft swift scale, adjusted the bench until it was perfectly aligned with the keyboard, then launched like a fury into his newest fugue. He threw all his emotion into the music, made it crash and flow, swift and full of mood.

The audience loved it.

"My Lady has a theme for you." It was a courtier at the back of the parlour. He stood beside a stately woman whose skirts took up an abominable amount of room.

"The Electress," Volumier whispered.

The courtier hummed a four-measure tune. Sebastian closed his eyes, thinking the melody to himself and analyzing its structure.

Flipping out a couple of stops, he stepped his fingers into the keys, feeling out the melody, working it first as a round-like canon. Then he opened the exactness into a freer fugue, harmonizing it and varying it, modulating it into different keys. The melody grew and sang, more and more complex, and with each new complexity came a fresh round of applause. Sebastian lived the music.

Finally, he brought the improvisation to a close and asked for another theme. He glanced in Marchand's direction. The expression on the Frenchman's face could only be described as hate.

When Sebastian finished enlarging the second theme, the audience clapped wildly and called for more. But Sebastian declined and sat beside Count Flemming. On the other side of the room, August was grinning like a chimpanzee, and Prince Leopold was nodding his head. His cheeks were flushed with pride. Even Spiess was nodding approval.

A maid offered Sebastian coffee. Sebastian stirred in three cubes of sugar and sipped the hot brew while Konzertmeister Volumier explained the order of tomorrow's contest. It would begin at nine the next morning.

The Elector was hoping to attend, as was his Kapellmeister and some foreign ministers from France and Poland.

Marchand was leaning back in his chair, pretending to study the mural on the ceiling.

Count Flemming had risen, one hand on his hip, the other hitching up his pants with the air of one who is accustomed to wielding authority. "Germany is impatient. We have given you a taste of our standards, Marchand. You will now give us a taste of yours."

Marchand glanced at the ringleted woman next to him and ran his finger under his cravat. "My journey has wearied me. Our lodgings await, and the confectioner who travels with us has prepared a repast of congenial food. My companion faints from the rigors of the journey. Tomorrow, my good people, tomorrow."

The Frenchman strolled out of the room without looking back, the woman mincing along beside him.

The next morning Sebastian woke early, full of anticipation. Would he make his reputation today and further honor Germany, or would he lose both his own honor and that of his country? He entered the aristocracy-filled salon ten minutes before the hour.

Leopold and his cohorts, along with August and his wife, Elinor, who had joined him in the night, were sitting near the harpsichord.

Count Flemming and Volumier sat further back on the aisle, and most of the same duchesses and countesses he'd seen yesterday had returned. Today, however, they all had escorts. The electress was there, not the Elector, though. Other new faces. But where was Marchand?

Sebastian took a seat beside Volumier and waited. One minute to the hour, five minutes after the hour, fifteen minutes, thirty. Sebastian grew restless. Must a man wait interminably for true reckoning in every situation? he wondered. Where could Marchand be? Had the man mistaken the time?

Finally, Count Flemming sent a courier to Marchand's lodging. When the courier returned, he was alone. The Count conferred with him, then marched back into the room, looking agitated. He whispered something to Volumier, who took the floor.

"Monsieur Marchand left town early this morning by express mail coach."

The buzz in the room grew into a clamor. "And how do you interpret this action?" someone demanded.

"What else," said Volumier, "but Marchand's certainty that he was doomed to lose the contest? He could not face the odds."

Everyone expressed their consensus. Yes. The Frenchman surely concluded after yesterday that he had not the slightest chance of winning over so musical and ordered a mind as Johann Sebastian Bach's.

"Our champion must play for us," someone cried. "Germany has won by default."

2

Sebastian spent the rest of the morning playing for them. The elite audience gave him theme after theme. They set him puzzles other musicians had failed to unravel. He went at them all with a passion, experiencing again and again his mind unfolding in ways that surprised even him.

Finally, he launched into a recital of some of his recent compositions. His fingers flew faster and faster over the dancing keys, broadening at last into three mighty chords of resolution. Applause roared through the room; then, like the pulse of timpani, a chant—"Prince of Claviers, Prince of Claviers! Bach is the Prince of Claviers." It began as a single voice and rose to a chorus of acclaim.

Astounded, Sebastian stood, then turned toward the rising audience. He bowed once, twice, three times. Still they chanted, "Bach is the Prince of Claviers!"

At last he had found a place.

When the tumult finally quieted, half the nobles in the room abandoned their seats and sailed toward him.

A coterie of French duchesses flirted at him with their fans and pronounced him brilliant.

August pounded him on the back, his pouched, red face crinkling with glee. "You old rascal! Wield your magic at the keyboard when men of sense are listening, and you vindicate the whole of Germany!"

One by one the nobles courted him: "The arrogance of that Marchand! I knew you would best him! The French court organist so intimidated he couldn't bring himself to face you! It's too delightful!"

Konzertmeister Volumier presented him to the Electress who honored him with a shower of praise and an invitation to court, and Leopold introduced him to aristocrats from Berlin, Frankfurt and Nuremberg.

And so the rest of the day continued. Gone was the condescension Sebastian had grown used to when he was companying with nobility. Surely now the doors would open for him—markets for the instrumental works he was planning to write for Prince Leopold and eventually for his church music. It was destined to happen, he was sure. The only question was, When?

The next morning Sebastian ambled through Count Flemming's gardens alone.

Wild roses danced pink and red over trellises. Fountains and ponds sprayed and rippled, and the scent of sage grew stronger as the sun rose higher. Sebastian wandered off the paths through the crisp mounds of leaves and rolled his triumph about in his mind like a piece of hard candy he wished never would dissolve. Success had a fine palate.

At noon, he joined his traveling companions for the midday meal. The five men, plus another Leopold had invited, were already seated in the garden gazebo. Coifed in a white frizzed tie-wig, Leopold was calling for attention in his deep silk voice, tapping his glass with a fork.

August was draining a bowl of soup like a hungry bear while Spiess tried to convince him that Telemann's new trumpet concertos were better than Vivaldi's. Louis Marceaux, a French painter Leopold had met in Paris, was sitting between Kober and Picander nibbling meat tarts. Kober was trying to explain the thermometer to him in French.

Leopold's bid for attention continued.

Sebastian sank into a chair next to Picander, relishing the bell sound of fork against crystal. The perfect touch of percussion for Barbara's lullaby! He must get it on paper this afternoon. Tomorrow they would be leaving for home, and writing was impossible on the pocked German roads.

A manservant was maneuvering a first course tray between Sebastian's and Picander's elbows, and a plump serving girl stood ready with wine .

"We have a fine choice today, Konzertmeister Bach." The servant was bowing so low Sebastian feared he would plunge his nose into the soup.

"And a variety of libations, Your Honor, " the girl said.

Even the servants were being more solicitous. This little thing was a pretty sort—filled out neckline, a fluff of blonde hair framing her rosy cheeks.

Picander was staring at the girl's bosom. He raised his heavy eyebrows at Sebastian with a lascivious grin. The poet had the kind of good looks and masculinity that made some women swoon.

Sebastian suppressed a smile and forced his thoughts away from the maid to the dishes on the manservant's tray. He selected a turtle bisque, took the bowl in both hands and downed the creamy concoction. Wiping his chin with one hand, he stuffed bread in his mouth with the other and winked at August across the table. They had challenged each other to a contest as to who could eat the most at any meal.

Suddenly, Leopold flung his fork down with a clang and sat to sip his wine. Everyone looked up, silent at last. Sebastian wondered if Leopold was angry. Wilhelm would not have tolerated such disregard.

But Leopold was not Wilhelm. His blue eyes gleamed with amusement.

"Gentleman! We are extending our stay. Tomorrow we tour the new Zwinger Gallery. Again, Louis, you will find your countrymen challenged by German offerings."

"Nothing will ever exceed the genius of Versailles," cried the French painter. "It is the best of architecture, art galleries, landscaping—the best of everything!"

A word storm burst over the table, and again Leopold had difficulty quieting them down.

"We are your friends, " the prince said to Louis. "Your *sprezzatura* forsakes you in your passion."

Louis sighed at this reminder of the nonchalant attitude that was supposed to be part of an aristocrat's bearing.

"But then," continued Leopold, "it has forsaken all of us. And what is life without passion?"

Everyone laughed, and Leopold continued his announcement. "The Elector proffers his greetings and his apologies, Kapellmeister," he said to Sebastian. "The Polish ferment required his attention, and he was not able to witness your victory. But the Electress apprised him of your skill, and he wishes to honor you by offering you and your companions the unfettered use of his library—and an invitation to attend a Shakespearean play in his private theater."

Wooden cross dancing about his neck, Picander jumped to his feet and clanked his beer mug against August's, "To Hamlet, to Othello! It is beyond my greatest hopes! We shall attend, Your Majesty?"

Leopold laughed. "We shall attend, stay three extra days, perhaps more."

"Volumier speaks hopefully of the opera to be held over the weekend," Spiess said. "Add a few more days, and we could have that privilege also. Telemann is to be down from Frankfurt."

Sebastian sank into his own world, his emotions dueling between concern for Barbara and elation at the possibility of several days of feasting on art. Dresden! With no other purpose but delving into the culture of the city and discussing it with thinking men. And Telemann! George Phillip Telemann: cosmopolitan musician, violinist, prolific German composer and old friend. There had been a time when he and the composer had been so close that Telemann had consented to be Emmanuel's godfather. How good it would be to see the man!

If they stayed in Dresden longer than they'd planned, however, Barbara would be concerned and Duke Wilhelm upset. Not that he cared anymore about Wilhelm, but Barbara could lose the baby from anxiety and exhaustion. Family! The dilemma was always there.

An artist needed travel; he needed new places and images, new sounds and shapes. Not that he had as much problem with ideas as many composers seemed to, but away from Weimar, inspiration always came upon him like new birth.

What a joy to wake in the morning and gaze on buildings and scenery different from his everyday! And now Leopold was offering him even more than he'd hoped.

Sebastian leaned back in his chair. Prince Leopold's face was shining like the face of Moses when he descended from Sinai. Elinor had told Barbara that if a friend admired a painting, Leopold would send it as a gift to him by post. If a tenant enjoyed flowers, Leopold would leave a crate of carnation plants on his doorstep. As court musician to Leopold, Sebastian's monthly wage would be higher than under Duke Wilhelm, and the Duke was the wealthier of the two.

"Money is to be spent," Leopold would shrug. "None of this hoarding and scraping over groschens for me. Use it to learn, to live, to enjoy what the Maker has given. We have only a few years on this earth, and once they are gone, we can never retrieve them. Money, on the other hand, can always be replenished."

Elinor said that if Leopold required more funds, he would sell a morgan of forest or breed more horses for the market.

Certainly, he saved thousands a year by turning away the hawkers of damasks and brocades who would deck him in a new suit every week. The Prince's code for attire was simplicity. Sebastian admired him for it.

Watching the Prince's animated face, Sebastian decided he would trust God for Barbara's welfare and treat the extended stay like the gracious gift his Prince intended. He would give himself to the leap and flame of ideas. He would let loose every artistic question hammering in him while he had a chance to hear from educated men. He'd not had such an opportunity since the days of Lubeck and Buxtehude.

3

The next day was sunny, excellent for enjoying the fountains and outdoor statuary of the Zwinger. The buildings were only half finished, but the long pavilions and domes were already stunning. The Zwinger was planned on a rectangle, meant to provide orangeries where trees could winter, as well as a frame for court festivities.

They entered through the *Kronentor,* the crown-gate, and soon Leopold and the others were stopping to admire a row of emerging wall fountains. Sebastian wandered off by himself. He stepped inside one of the buildings and strode the length of the pavilion, losing himself in the sweep of the Baroque architecture. The building didn't have the dramatic power of a Gothic cathedral with its steep arches and flying buttresses, but something about the stretching on and on of the pavilion and then the emerging into the domed cupola gripped him.

When, however, he exited the building and pivoted to look at the columns, he almost swore.

The mammoth pillars swarmed with birds, swords, fruit and satyrs posturing. Sebastian knew that many would either admire the columns or pass them by without a second thought. But they affected him like steel striking flint.

Sebastian shouted to the approaching August, "Look at these monstrosities! Empty virtuosity!"

His arms like flailing ship booms, Sebastian stormed around the columns. "This sculptor is posturing like his imbecile satyrs. What could Popellman have been thinking? He's let some lackey ruin the genius of his design."

August cocked his head to the side, considering the columns. "People tire of heavy dictums, Sebastian."

"It is true." Leopold drew up beside them.

"Is that what it's come to?" asked Sebastian. "Artists sinking to the level of popular taste? We should be stretching the mind of the populace, not aiming at its median intellect!"

Mounting the steps with the others not far behind, Louis interrupted, "And so, Herr Bach, you do not like the Italian sculptor's columns? I would introduce you to a new thinking, the French painter Watteau."

In his green and blue waistcoat, yellow breeches, flowing wig and embroidered cravat, Louis looked like a peacock strutting among a cluster of ravens.

Picander was climbing the steps with a book tucked under his arm. "Show us this Watteau's works."

Louis waved everyone in behind him.

Sebastian followed them back into the Zwinger, forcing himself to bite back his frustration at the lengths artists will go to please the whims of men. Footsteps echoing, they passed painting after painting, until Louis halted in front of a large canvas. It was a country idyll, crowded with people and romancing.

"Jean Antoine Watteau." Louis' tone was reverent.

Sebastian had to admit the colors were riveting. They had a shimmering, iridescent quality about them unlike anything he had ever seen.

Louis flanked the painting and began pointing examples. "Watteau misses no detail of beauty in anything. In a tree, in the details of a woman's face, in the hands of a lutanist. You see it in the background as well as the foreground."

It was an extremely sensual painting. Watteau has genius, Sebastian thought. And yet. . .

Louis stepped back and fanned his hands in a slow arc across the painting. "Watteau captures the fleeting nature of life. He challenges us to take our pleasures seriously, since they will soon be out of reach."

"I hear his work is at the heart of the new Rococo Movement," Picander said.

"Watteau is only thirty-four years old," Kober said, "and a consumptive."

Louis nodded. "He would seize life while he can."

"The painting has a charm," Leopold said. "The question is, is charm all art is about?"

The group stood discussing while August lumbered on to the next painting. Sebastian followed.

August swept an arm toward a row of dark-hued paintings. "Rembrandt," he said, "not the uplift of Watteau."

Sebastian was silent. He'd heard of the Dutchman's prowess, but this was his first glimpse of his original paintings.

There were portraits, Bible scenes, everyday scenes—not the shimmering color of Watteau, but a use of light and shadow that was dramatic. The works gripped him, calmed him, drew him. He studied each painting, each face, then moved to the next and the next. He saw innermost feeling in Rembrandt's faces, humanness even in the Bible characters, but also something else. A divine spark?

"Charm, August?" he prompted his friend.

"No, not charm. They disturb me."

"Disturbing, perhaps, but something to engage the whole being. I suspect there will always be more to discover in a work by Rembrandt."

"Unlike Watteau?"

Sebastian snorted.

"Rococo! People want ditties and pleasures, and they want them now. I fear the trend, especially in music."

"Mediocrity!"

"Right you are, my friend, mediocrity!"

In the Elector's library that afternoon, Sebastian was accosted by an elaborate copy of Handel's *Water Music Suite*. It was displayed on an easel at the end of the stacks.

Premiered only this summer, Sebastian thought, and already Handel's composition is featured in August the Strong's library. Jealousy snaked through him.

"Got something burning under your fingernails?" Picander's voice startled him.

"How does Handel do it?" Sebastian whispered. "I work till my fingers cramp, and I can't even get my own employer to give me proper support."

Picander began flipping through the volume. "Handel knows how to appease, how to work the possibilities."

Sebastian shook his head. "It is not in me."

Humming quietly, Picander continued to turn the pages. Finally, he closed the volume, his handsome features pensive. "Handel has no family either. I have decided not to marry."

"Counterpoint and canon!" exclaimed Sebastian. "That will be difficult for a man of your vitality."

"Be that as it may."

A few minutes later, Sebastian took a seat at the windowed end of a long table near Prince Leopold. He opened Handel's *Water Suite* on the table in front of the Prince. They talked a little, then Leopold stood and dropped his arm across Sebastian's shoulders. "I hope to provide many opportunities for you in Cothen that have been kept from you in your current position. All in good time, Kapellmeister."

Leopold joined Louis and Picander at the other end of the table, but Sebastian stayed where he was. Kapellmeister—would it really happen? Would Wilhelm ever allow him to leave Weimar? Would there be trouble? What of publication? What of using his keyboard virtuosity more widely, with the specific goal of gaining a wider audience for his compositions?

As Sebastian worked that afternoon amid the comforting smells of leather and print, letting his mind turn to this and that, analyzing Handel's orchestration techniques and reviewing yesterday's victory and the truest longings in him, the truth of things emerged. It came clear to him that his reaction to Handel was more than jealousy of a successful peer. It was the realization that his victory over Marchand meant nothing. Composing is my life, he thought. Not performing. Prince of Claviers! He looked at the title he'd scrolled across his notepad, and with two slashes crossed it out. Ridiculous!

Mind cleared, he passed the rest of the day in contented study.

4

The next afternoon the group attended a musical Mass. Sebastian decided to walk back to his lodgings alone. He freed himself from his wig, which had been growing tighter by the minute, deposited it in his rucksack, wrestled on an old pair of boots and tramped the banks of the River Elbe. The heat of the day was beginning to dissipate. A breeze was blowing over him from the water.

He swiveled to look at the spires behind him, then turned toward the bridge ahead with a sense of exaltation. As much as he loved the company of men like Leopold and Picander, he must have time alone.

He approached the bridge—a score of white arches across the blue of the rippling Elbe. The structure had a rhythm about it, and a grace. Architecture, music, sculpture, painting, and he suspected, all the other arts, rose in the creator's mind and developed under his hand according to many of the same principles. The arts were blood brothers.

Besides music, architecture intrigued Sebastian the most. Like music, architecture had its line and flow, its supporting structures, its rise and fall, its moods and ornamentation.

Some thinkers called architecture frozen music. If that were true, mused Sebastian, then music was flowing architecture.

That night after a light meal, Sebastian retired. Relishing the sense of space, he poured water into his wash basin and rubbed his tired feet on the Persian carpet. Here there were no accounts to deal with, no children's arguments to resolve, and no sounds but the soft thrum of crickets outside his window. He let his mind float over the last two days: the shimmer in Watteau's people and landscapes, Handel's orchestrations, the lines of the white bridge against the river.

He slept.

At midnight, he woke wide-eyed with clarity. He seized the tinderbox on the night table and relit the candelabra. Why not use the harpsichord as a solo instrument with the orchestra? It had never been done, but it was a simple manner of inverting, moving what was typically a background instrument to the foreground of the musical landscape. He must build the proper architecture for the work, experiment with structures that wouldn't overpower the harpsichord. A percussive keyboard instrument with a penetrating tone was what was needed. The organ builder Silbermann was experimenting with something he was calling a pianoforte.

Yes, I will write a concerto for clavier! thought Sebastian. Harpsichord for now. Pianoforte when it is perfected.

He slid a piece of manuscript paper off the brick-high stack on the table across the room and began to write. He composed straight through the night.

The next morning, Prince Leopold announced they would be staying the rest of the week in order to attend the opera. Anxiety sliced through Sebastian. He would be arriving home eight days late instead of three. Barbara would be frantic with worry, and he didn't have the money to hire a courier.

"A good 'Landesvater' considered it to be (his) duty . . . 'to teach his subjects even against their will how to order their domestic affairs, or, as (one prince) expressed the ideal again with unconscious humour, 'to make them, whether they liked it or not, into free, opulent and law-abiding citizens.'"[1]

"Bach is the only great composer known to have undergone arrest by the authorities."[2]

5

Confinement
1 7 1 7

In Weimar four days later, Barbara flung off her bedcovers and began rummaging in her wardrobe for a chemise that would not bind. She couldn't tolerate the midwife's prescribed idleness any longer. It was difficult enough to leave so many things undone without the added torment of Sebastian's failure to return home when he'd said he would. The fact that he was a day late worried her, but it also made her resentful. The mixture was painful. She was afraid that some dire mishap had come upon him on his way home. She knew her husband well, however, and suspected he might have become so involved in Dresden culture that he'd failed to consider how anxious she would be if he delayed his return.

She scolded herself as she worked deftly down the dress hooks at the back of her neck. You know how much Sebastian needs this time away. Think of his needs instead of your own. Resentment never does anyone any good, least of all yourself. German roads are unpredictable. And Sebastian is not on his own. He's probably made a phenomenal showing against Marchand and been pressed to stay longer than expected. Yes, I'm sure that's it, she thought. Sebastian has won the contest, and the Elector is parading him about town.

Barbara tied her hair back with a red ribbon and smiled at her reflection in the glass. "Your husband loves you," she said out loud. "If he could have sent word, he would have."

Feeling better, Barbara threw a shawl about her shoulders and began descending the stairs. Just as she reached the bottom of the stairway, Gottfried emerged from the music room, harpsichord strings draped over his shoulder.

"Aunt Barbara! You're not supposed to be up."

"I'm going to the market, nephew. I will lose the baby out of worry and boredom if I don't get out of this house."

Lorenz appeared in the doorway. "You must at least take Dorothea with you."

"Perhaps." She found Dorothea outside sitting under the apple tree. From her place at the backdoor, Barbara watched her, thinking how, in that moment, her daughter reminded her of her husband. Gray skirts spread about her, the nine-year-old was sketching the apples that lay in the grass. She touched one and rolled it, head aslant. Then she continued her work, the soft scrubbing of the charcoal on the tablet the only sound in the autumn afternoon.

Barbara couldn't bring herself to disturb her.

Soon, basket on one arm, Barbara was clipping along the street, breathing in the crispness of the air, relishing the feel of her skirt as it swished against her legs.

She hated being cooped up. She loved the variety in the Thuringian skies!

Today, gray-white clouds were shelving diagonally in front of her. Above them white cotton ones mounded, spliced with bright blue. They were towering and blackening behind her, but that she ignored. She concentrated on maneuvering the crowded streets. Sebastian might be nearing home even now, she thought. Duke Wilhelm's environs—Ettersberg, the mill town of Ilmanueu and the rest of the rolling countryside around Weimar—were considered quite safe. Wilhelm visited them often and assigned rustic bailiffs to oversee. But Dresden was so far away, and as capable a ruler as August the Strong was said to be, the influx of foreigners had to make for more peril upon the road.

She pushed on, marveling more and more at the crowd. There were too many children in the market for it to be an ordinary Saturday. When she reached the edge of the square, she saw the mole-faced fruit vendor make a scramble beneath his counter.

"Missy!" he called. "Look what I've got you today!" He thrust up a ribboned basket of fruit.

Barbara hurried toward the stall and fingered the fuzzy peaches in the basket. "Dates too," she laughed. "You are a man of resource, Hans!"

She nibbled at one of the tough, sweet fruits.

A group of children romped nearby, their mothers chatting leisurely with friends.

"What's happening today?" she asked.

"The carnival's coming, Missy. They are due any minute. And a powerful large troupe they are too: actors, egg dancers, jesters, tightrope walkers, tumblers, maybe even a bear."

"Wilhelm has permitted this?"

Hans' warty nose twitched. "Nary a chance. These troupes are a lawless bunch. Duke August, I'd expect."

Barbara laughed. "He's in Dresden. Do you really suppose they've a bear? I've heard horrifying stories about how these troupes treat their animals."

But Hans just nodded and danced a fragrant pineapple under her nose. "From Prince Friedrich's orangeries. Ten groschen, Missy?"

"Zounds! Ten groschen, and you patronize this usurer!" Barbara turned to see Lorenz standing behind her. He was rubbing at his long chin and grinning.

"I will bring him down," she said. "Don't worry."

Lorenz's amused eyes turned tender, then embarrassed. He thrust her miracle bag toward her. "You forgot your money."

"Lorenz, you know I always transfer it to my indispensable when I go to market."

"I did need some graphite," he said, "and yes, I was worried about you."

Barbara sighed, "I am well."

She took the bag, then turned to bargain with Hans for the fruit. By the time they had agreed on a reasonable price, Lorenz was on the other side of the street, deep in discussion with a friend from the Kapelle. Just as well. It really was time Sebastian and she moved on. Lorenz needed to make his own life.

Barbara pressed on to the next stall. She bargained for three large cabbages, some squash, onions and potatoes, and stashed them in her basket. The basket felt heavier and heavier as she trudged toward the apothecary. In front of the baker's, a group of young women and children were tossing nosegays. A crier was jostling through the street throwing coins.

The commotion made Barbara's head throb. The crowd was thickening, and inch by inch, she struggled through it, barely noticing the drops of rain.

She had almost reached the curb when it happened. A streak of light cracked the heavens. Thunder boomed and echoed. Rain poured in sheets.

Dogs and children and horses and women scattered.

Barbara stooped to retrieve the vegetables that had fallen from her basket. She heard the rumble of hooves and a shriek. The wagon was so close she could see the bear. The cage teetered. She bent to the sharp cramping in her abdomen. Then something crashed into her, and she fell.

That night Barbara woke shivering in her bed. A nightmare? Surely!

Then she noticed her clothes on the chair. The skirt was spotted with blood. She shut her eyes. Pain cramped through her abdomen.

A large hand caught hold of hers, warming it.

"Sebastian?" she cried. But no, Lorenz was gazing down at her, his shirt rumpled and stained, the worry ridge creased between his eyes. Gently, she pulled her hand away.

Gottfried entered the room and sat down on her bed, running his hand through his red hair. "Lorenz saved your life," he said. "Many were plowed down by that runaway wagon. One child is still unconscious."

Barbara drew in her breath—again the pain.

Someone was placing wet cloths on her forehead and stroking her stomach. "It's all right," the midwife soothed. "Breathe."

Barbara came up panting from the pain. "The baby?"

"It's too soon to know."

2

To Sebastian's shame, the days in Dresden rolled along with so much festivity and stimulation that he found himself forgetting Barbara for hours at a time. Back and forth he would vacillate between delight in performances and conversations that fed a starving part of him, worry over Barbara, and guilt that he didn't worry or pray more than he did. How much prayer was enough prayer anyway?

Thursday, he performed for the Elector and Electress in the drawing room of the royal palace. Friday, they attended a Shakespeare play. Each night he worked on his harpsichord concerto with an inspiration like fire. The muse upon him this strongly was rare. Ideas he always had, but bringing them to fruition normally took months of the plodding perseverance that was his strength. This was different.

In the silence, he heard the unhearable, the melodies sounding and interweaving with flashing scales and resolutions, the strings playing off the flow of the harpsichord. The whole of each of the work's parts was upon him in flashes as ecstatic as sexual passion. It was for this that he was made.

The opera Saturday night was an eighteenth-century diva's nightmare. It was an hour and a half siege of vicious fruit throwing—pulp-soft plums and rotten oranges pelting headdresses and skirts. Finally, the players dropped the curtain in the middle of the last act.

It was Spiess who spotted Telemann first. "There," he pointed, "near that card table." Leopold's group angled their way around the sofas and tables on the ground floor, and Sebastian grabbed Telemann's arm as it swung back to throw a last orange at the curtain.

Telemann pivoted, his cipher of a mouth pruned into a frown.

"Sebastian Bach!"

"Old friend! Prince Leopold wishes you to join us."

Telemann threw out his twig-like arms as though Sebastian had offered him the world.

"I can think of nothing I'd rather do. My jaunt this trip has been a lonely"—he cast a look at the stage—"and a disappointing one."

The group mazed their way through the crowd and out of the opera house. Leopold scurried them into a nearby coffee establishment, and against a background of Polish bagpipes and fiddles, Leopold and Spiess hammered

Telemann with questions about his Konzertmeister work in Frankfurt. Soon the talk turned to the situation of the artist who either chose or was forced to stay in Germany.

Booted feet propped up on the table, Picander tapped his book.

"If taken to their ultimate conclusion, Leibniz's tenets could be revolutionary for artists who find themselves hampered by century-old traditions. Leibniz hypothesized the universe is made up of monads, each self-contained, the soul being the most pertinent example.

"Since the soul is self-contained, all it needs for positive action and growth is found within itself. Some feel the upshot of this philosophy is the belief that the surest way to happiness and societal order is for each man, apart from class demands or family expectations, to pursue his unique interests and gifts, working diligently toward becoming all he senses he can be."

"Hard work accomplishes all," Sebastian nodded. "Yes, it accomplishes all."

"And the freedom for such?" Telemann leaned forward, "Where does freedom find place in a feudal society such as ours? We are hedged in by class at every turn. Even in the free cities."

"Freedom is the power to act," Leopold said.

"To have the courage to seize life while we can," added Louis.

"If you are talking of self-determinism being similar to Watteau's approach to naturalism, that is something worth discussing," Telemann's genial personality took the reins, the humor that made him so popular with audiences transforming his prude of a mouth into the tool of a jester.

At each flip and turn of the conversation—from Picander's thoughts on how naturalism aids self-determinism to Louis' stumbling explanations of Cartesianism—Telemann elucidated the value of each person's contribution, even August's, who was growing more drunk by the minute.

"The natural, the organic," August shouted, lifting his tankard of beer. "I could live by it!" He grabbed at the skirt of a passing cock maid.

The maid jerked away. Her tray teetered, and tankards and bowls of soup clattered to the floor. The coffee shop proprietor yelled at the girl. The girl threw a curse at August, and August shrugged his mountainous shoulders.

He and Elinor had been married for a year and a half. Duchess Mariana was living in Italy, and Elinor was now the mistress of the Red Castle. Elinor was good for August, loving him for his qualities and humoring him in his faults. Sebastian could see changes in his friend, but if he and his wife were apart for too long, August's insatiable libido always reared its gargoyle head. Sebastian was relieved when Elinor's footman appeared.

"Duchess Elinor has arrived," the footman said, " to convey His Excellency Duke August back to his lodgings."

Soon afterward, the group decided to adjourn. Sebastian invited Telemann and Picander to his lodgings for a smoke.

As soon as they arrived, they rid themselves of their wigs and their shoes, exclaiming over the thickness of the Persian carpet. "Not the usual lodgings for a musician," Telemann said.

Sebastian was proud to be able to offer comfortable chairs and even a bottle of French wine, compliments of Count Flemming. They settled in with their pipes.

Telemann wanted to know about his godson Emmanuel. "Four-years-old, right? Is he musical?"

Sebastian nodded. "He loves to listen to Friedemann's violin practice. He hums and plucks about and definitely has an affinity for numbers. He also has his father's figure." Sebastian patted his generous stomach. They laughed.

Picander, it happened, was writing a libretto for one of Telemann's operas.

The poet soon had Telemann explaining his desire to create a public music as excellent as that heard in the courts. "Concerts in the town halls and on the streets for the burger and serf," explained Telemann.

When Sebastian explained his own goal, a worship music that would draw people personally into the profundities of the Divine, both men shook their heads.

"Why must a man's goal be so ponderous?" asked Telemann. "Does man not bear burdens enough without the music he hears also weighing him down?"

Picander considered. "But if that, Bach, is what is deepest in your soul, you cannot escape it and have any kind of happiness. It is your fate."

After the men left, Sebastian repacked his bag and stretched out in the luxurious bed for the last time. The more he listened to Picander's reasoning, the more intrigued he became with the way the man's mind worked. He was constrained by few boundaries, and because of it, dealt freshly and freely with every new topic. He was, in the new sense of the word, a seeker of truth.

And how good it was to converse with men whose drivenness to create was as strong as his own!

As hard as Barbara tried and as dear as he held her, she never seemed to be able to understand that time to create was as essential for her husband as time to eat.

3

Sebastian arrived home on Friday of the next week, eight days later than he had originally planned.

He dropped his bags on the front step when he heard children's laughter in the back. He hurried around the house.

"Papa!" Friedemann and Emmanuel were on him in a flash, whooping and jumping. Friedemann was shouting something about a tightrope walker, and Emmanuel was punching at him when Dorothea's face appeared above him.

Sebastian struggled up from the tumble. "Your mother?"

"In bed," Dorothea's eyes brimmed with tears. "We were so worried."

He put his arm around his daughter's narrow shoulders, then looked up to see Gottfried in the doorway. He was holding Bernhard, and his blue eyes were flat in his freckled face.

"She lost the baby, Uncle."

Sebastian's heart began hammering. He pushed past his nephew. "Let her be all right," he whispered.

Barbara was sitting up in bed wearing her white muslin wrap. Her dark hair was ragged, her face a tomb.

"You are here," was all she said.

He sat on the edge of the bed and reached for her hand. It was limp as rope, and cold. "Tell me."

Like a figure on a clock face, she turned slowly toward him. There were black circles under her eyes.

He leaned to kiss her, but she turned her head. He sat back. The baby things she'd been embroidering were spread across the bed like lost children. She scooped up one of the blankets and nestled it against her cheek. Her hair fell across her face. She stared up at Sebastian with a pleading look in her eyes. She folded and smoothed the blanket and reached for a tiny gown.

Sebastian touched her hair, but she flung up a small hand and began carefully folding the garment.

Sebastian spun away from the bed, opened the shutters and stood gazing at the neighborhood children playing in the street. He listened to the child laughter woven into the under-rhythm of the creak of the bed. Barbara was reaching for garment after garment.

"I waited," she finally said. "I prayed, I hoped. I knew that if you would just walk in the door, the pains would stop. But you didn't."

He stepped toward her. "It was only to be three extra days. The Elector . . ."

"You won?" She looked up at him, new interest in her eyes.

"I won," he said.

"Prince of Claviers, they called me. Can you imagine?" He tried to smile.

"Prince?! It suits you. I must prepare you a feast. We will invite Baron von Lynker and August and Elinor, perhaps even Catherina. Yes, I would like to see Catherina."

Lorenz appeared in the doorway with a tray, "The midwife sent soup."

He set the tray of onion-scented brew on the bed table and promptly sent a bowl of potpourri flying to the floor. Mumbling apologies, he scooped up the scented petals and backed away.

Barbara didn't seem to notice.

"At first I was worried," she said, "so worried I couldn't stay in this room any longer, wondering what had happened to you, worrying about the baby."

She stopped.

Sebastian wondered if he should ask her what happened? He needed to know everything, but—

"She went to the marketplace," Lorenz offered. "It stormed. There was a carnival troupe, and a wagon broke its chain."

"One that housed a bear," Barbara said. "I was in its path, and Lorenz saved me; but," her voice sounded weary, "no one was able to save the baby."

The apprentice was shifting his tall frame from foot to foot.

"I am in your debt, " said Sebastian.

Lorenz dipped his head and left.

The silence lengthened, the pall palpable—regret, despair, blame, Barbara's emotions, his—poison spidering through the room.

Would it have made a difference if I'd returned on time? Sebastian wondered. Should I have made a greater effort? Was all that inspiration and encouragement a villainous affair?

Mercifully, Barbara broke the silence. "It never felt normal, though—this pregnancy. I should have expected . . . Oh, husband, I wish I didn't need you so."

Sebastian knelt beside her bed. "It is only proper for you to need me, as I need you."

"Do you, Sebastian?" Her wide eyes probed his. "I bled and cramped and vomited. Time was nothing, evaporating, surfacing, like the ceaseless shapes and shapelessness of clouds. I prayed, but I could find no peace. Is death like that? The darkness tugs at you, and it has no face."

Sebastian reached for her hand, and this time Barbara let it rest in his. "Then the midwife said . . . oh, Sebastian, she said it was over. The baby was gone forever."

Sebastian clasped her hand tighter, feeling the loss of this child for the first time. He had lost a child, too, another one—someone near and dear.

"No!" he said. "She is *not* gone forever. Always remember that. Not forever."

She beat on his head with fists like leaves. She asked his pardon for her weakness. She wept. Then finally, in a whisper so low, he had to feel her breath to hear it, "Oh, why weren't you here, my love, why weren't you here?"

He wrapped his arms around her, fighting back his own tears, pulling her, quivering, to him, holding his beloved while she wept.

Barbara woke before dawn the next morning, having slept better than she had slept for two weeks. Sebastian's body was warm and comforting beside her. She propped up on her elbow and touched his forehead—the eyebrows like darts, the piercing eyes now shut and dancing beneath his lids. She touched his nose and started to trace his full lips, but he turned over. He would be weary from his journey. She would let him sleep.

Rising, she wiggled her feet into the warmth of fur slippers and slipped into her wrap. She shuffled to the window and pulled back the curtains. Dark lingered over the town like a worldwide cloud.

She waited. Soon a trail of light traced its way timidly along the horizon. She rubbed her eyes. They ached from weeping. Her legs trembled. She would eat better now that Sebastian was home, gain her strength back.

She scuffed across the hall to check on the children: Bernhard in his trundle bed, Dorothea in the ruffle-necked flannel she'd made her, seven-year-old Friedemann, his light brown hair falling across his long cheek, and Emmanuel, his covers twisted in knots. She covered Emmanuel with an extra blanket, shoveled up the wrap on the floor and hung it on its nail above the bed. Then she opened the shutters. The golden east was stretching its arms.

She tiptoed back across the hall and dropped into her rocking chair. The stack of baby garments stood waiting on top of the chest, waiting to be put away, out of sight, buried. This baby had had no burial. The tears welled up in her eyes. She closed them. She shouldn't have blamed Sebastian last night. Never, never did she want him to feel burdened by her need. Women had their own loads to carry, and as much as they might long for their husbands to share them, the reality was that it should never be. At least she didn't think so.

From strength to strength, she told herself. Iron in my will, the way my father taught me.

It is possible. I will begin walking again today, to the gardens down the street and back, and perhaps this afternoon I'll even try that new recipe for sweetmeats.

She opened her eyes. A glow was spreading behind the houses across the street. They were silhouettes against the sky. Then silently, the magic happened again. The light shimmered and burst into rose. An eye blink later, the sky was white.

Barbara lived that day remembering the sunrise. She must hold on to every minute of mercy—the strength to get out of bed, the joy of the times when Sebastian was there for her. Sebastian was thirty-two and she was thirty-three. They had been married for ten years. Who knew how many more years they had? Life could be cut short so unexpectedly. She would cherish every happy moment—they were miniature daybreaks she must hold onto to keep out the night.

5

Duke Wilhelm summoned Sebastian not two hours after his return.

"You failed to tell me you were traveling to Dresden with Prince Leopold!" Wilhelm said.

Sebastian, who was standing in front of the Duke's desk in the royal library, raised his eyebrows but said nothing.

Wilhelm shook his finger at him. "The man is an infidel! He studies Leibniz and Descartes. What about this intent of yours to write music for the liturgy, Bach? There will be no opportunity to do this under Prince Leopold. Calvinists do not tolerate art music in the church, and Leopold abides by that edict, though I doubt he himself believes much of anything."

Sebastian wanted to defend the Prince, but again he said nothing.

Wilhelm looked up at him and sighed. "August tells me they are calling you the Prince of Claviers."

Sebastian grinned, "Ridiculous, but pleasant to feel I've represented Germany well."

For a minute he thought Wilhelm was going to commend him.

But the Duke seemed to think better of it. He pursed his thin lips under his knobby nose, slid a brochure off a stack of papers and thrust it at Sebastian. It was a theological brochure on obedience to authority.

"You will understand that all the decisions I make on behalf of my employees I make for the good of their souls. You need not to ask me for your release to Prince Leopold again. You will remain in Weimar."

Sebastian refused to let Wilhelm's obstinacy discourage him. During the next weeks, he proceeded as though he were leaving Weimar within the month. He delegated almost all the Kapelle work to Lorenz, and since he wouldn't have an organ in Cothen, he concentrated his energies on perfecting his organ compositions. He was discouraged about his progress, however, especially on the devotional chorales he envisioned for the organ. Every attempt seemed trite.

God did not seem near.

Three weeks after his return from Dresden, he was hurrying home from the Red Castle on a Saturday afternoon. Through the palace grounds he wound, past the royal gardens and snow-clumped park and on through the wide streets of the market.

He couldn't remember it being so cold, not in November. The tips of his fingers throbbed, and the air seemed rigid—a block of ice you could almost touch. Sebastian's mind, however, was liquid, his anger seething above and around the swirl of fugues and harmonies he'd been practicing with August and Baron von Lynker.

He nodded to Baker Schmitt, who was shoveling snow in front of his shop, and strode on, watching for treacherous ice. He turned the corner and quickened his steps. He would freeze to death if he didn't get out of the cold, unless anger could prevent death by freezing. His anger was certainly heated enough right now!

A half-hour ago he'd been improvising with August and the Baron when a courier from the Duke interrupted them. The man had spouted off the usual fines for being at the Red Castle and had ended with a command for Sebastian to appear at the Wilhelmsburg within the hour. The Duke needed two hours of lute music to entertain unexpected visitors. Rococo, he'd said, something light.

Sebastian banged the snow off his boots at his doorstep. "The Duke will go wanting," he swore out loud, "at least of this musician's services. He has never expected me to entertain with facile dinner music, and I refuse to begin now."

He twisted at the door handle, to no avail. "Blast this infernal latch!"

He beat on the door. Lorenz let him in.

Sebastian shoved past him. "Tell Gottfried the latch needs fixing. What has he been doing anyway?"

Lorenz gave him an odd look, but Sebastian hurried on into the music room where a student awaited him. He thought later that things might have developed differently if he had mentioned the Duke's new summons to Lorenz or Barbara.

His wife and apprentice would have reasoned with him, reminded him that concessions would be necessary if he expected Wilhelm to yield. But Sebastian didn't mention the summons to either of them, and halfway into his afternoon of teaching, the bailiff burst into his house with three guards.

They jerked him up from the harpsichord bench where he was demonstrating a three-voice fugue, shouted to Barbara that she had five minutes to get some things together for her husband's imprisonment, and cuffed his hands so tightly he gasped at the pain. The Grand Duke had had enough insubordination, the bailiff said. This time it was prison until Sebastian agreed to stay in Weimar and do whatever his Sovereign required.

At first they placed Sebastian in a cell as tiny as a closet, no furniture and only a slit for a window. He stared through the slit at the slice of outdoors: an occasional horse and rider, a dog, a woman struggling through the snow with a parcel. He turned away from the view, and suddenly the walls seemed to squeeze the breath from him. Whirling back to the slit, he pressed his nose into it, breathing deeply and reciting the Lord's Prayer. He quoted portions of the Psalms and the catechism and was just beginning to feel calm when the door clanged open. A burly guard jerked Sebastian's hands behind him and wrapped a chain tightly, roughly, about his wrists.

He shoved him into the hall, "Follow me."

Down the narrow stone stairs the guard clipped ahead of him, so fast that once Sebastian lost his balance, stumbled and fell. The ancient cold of the stone seeped into him.

"Hurry it up!" the guard shouted.

Sebastian struggled up and continued on.

Finally, they reached the ground floor. The guard led him to a corner cell. He unlocked it with a clack of keys, loosing Sebastian's hands, then pushing him in and clanging the door shut behind him. Sebastian breathed a sigh of relief. This cell was much bigger. There was a cot, a small table and a wooden chair, a decent-sized window and a chamber pot.

Here at least he could breathe, and perhaps work.

Later, the guard brought the bag Barbara had packed for him, and soon a snaggle-toothed trustee slid supper through the slit at the bottom of the door: hard black bread and a piece of salt pork.

Sebastian spent a troubled night, the straw of the mattress pricking at him, the cold seeming to get colder no matter how many layers of clothes he bundled on.

Barbara came to see him the next afternoon. She sat on the cot holding his hand. "I brought your books and an extra blanket. Duke Wilhelm sent word this morning that I might bring whatever you wished for your comfort: chairs, blankets, rugs, clothes, books, manuscripts. I'm not sure whether to be glad or fearful."

"One does wonder what such generosity portends about the length of my imprisonment."

"Surely there is some compromise the two of you could reach?"

"One compromise with Wilhelm will simply mean more later."

Barbara thought a minute. "If only the Duke could conceive of it as the will of God for him to withdraw from your life. He would be enabling an artist to more fully pursue his divine gift. Why can't he see that?"

Sebastian sighed. "The problem is that Wilhelm is just as stubborn as I am. I begin to wonder if I've met my match."

Over the course of the next week, Gottfried and the children helped Barbara transfer Sebastian's favorite black leather chair, a fresh down mattress, a brazier, a candelabra and candles, two wool rugs, more blankets, his lute and a host of manuscripts and writing equipment. Barbara also secured permission for Friedemann and Emmanuel to come twice a week for violin and arithmetic lessons.

August visited as often as he could evade Wilhelm's spies. He brought news of his and Elinor's plans to buy peacocks for the royal gardens. They had also acquired a black Persian cat and two poodles.

When August visited, he always smuggled in a cheese or a bundle of fritters. For this Sebastian was grateful. The one thing Wilhelm had forbidden him in his cell was meals from home. His daily food rations were the same as the most notorious criminal in the detention hall: two pieces of hard black bread with salt pork, a bowl of gruel, and occasionally, a serving of fetid cabbage soup.

The only bright place in Sebastian's days were visits from family and friends. He could feel no stirring, even when he tried to compose. In fact, for the first time in his life, he couldn't compose.

He was wrestling with a profound depression.

There are many kinds of prisons, he thought: the prison of class—if you're born in a lower strata you're expected to bow and scrape; the prison of marriage—for as much as he appreciated Barbara, there were moments when he longed to be free like Handel, free to travel, to study wherever he wished at his leisure and not have to explain. Then there were the prisons of one's own character, or lack of it: the prison of drivenness, the prison of a bitter spirit, the prison of an unpliable will. Would Wilhelm be able in good conscience to hold him indefinitely? Was Prince Leopold attempting to do anything to help? August had mentioned nothing to that effect. Sebastian stared up at the sky through his window. God touched, embraced, encompassed the universe, and here he was, the supposed servant of that God, trapped like a rat in a snare.

6

Sebastian had been in the detention hall for two weeks when Barbara made her decision. She would go to Duke Wilhelm's levy on Thursday and present her view of her husband's case. Many praised the Duke for the way he conducted these forums. Any Weimar subject, be he serf or nobleman, could present himself outside the state bedchamber on any given Thursday and be assured of a hearing.

When she visited Sebastian early Thursday morning and rehearsed with him what she planned to do, he urged her not to. "You will only open yourself to the Duke's abuse. You know how he feels about women who are too bold."

"I must try, Sebastian. Please give me your blessing."

Sebastian agreed.

It took her twenty minutes to walk from the prison to the Wilhelmsburg. She reviewed her plan. She would speak to the Duke of her husband's daily leading of family devotions, of his unerring attendance at monthly communion, and of the way he drilled the children on the catechism. She would tell him of what she had learned from her father about how the artist/craftsman needed to have his employer express belief in him continually.

Father—bushy mustache, laughing green eyes—Johann Michael Bach, an excellent musician, in the tradition of the long line of talented Bachs. He'd had a shining tenor voice, a competent hand at the organ and a talent for graceful composition. But his Church Council's criticism had so discouraged him that he had finally quit composing and limited himself to performing other men's works. If only the council had considered something besides their pietistic rigidities and listened to what her father had hoped to do for the worship services. But no. And what beauty had the world lost because of it?

It was Sebastian's genius to forge compendiums, explorations of forms that were comprehensive and concise. After he exhausted a field, he needed to press on to new climes. She would mention that to the Duke also. And last of all, she would tell him that though Sebastian might seem prideful at times, underneath was a genuine humility. He believed his gift to be no more than that, a gift. His compulsion was only to be all God meant him to be.

When she arrived at the castle, she took a seat on a bench filled with petitioners just outside the state bedchamber. One by one, those waiting with her were summoned, until it was late afternoon and she was the only one left.

The spectacled secretary finally opened the door. She jumped up. But the secretary threw out a hand of dismissal. "The levy is over. You will have to return next week."

"Can you not intercede for me?" she asked. "All I need is a few minutes."

The man's eyes passed like brushes over her. His smile was lecherous.

Barbara forced herself to look straight into his eyes and return his smile. "I would be in your debt."

He took her arm, his touch groping and repulsive. But he led her through the door and across the room to the mahogany desk where the Duke sat writing.

Barbara dropped a deep curtsy and waited. The Duke dipped his head, frowning.

"Proceed."

Barbara took a deep breath and began. She was fine for a few minutes, but then the fact that the Duke was writing the whole time she was speaking began to unnerve her.

She stumbled and fell silent.

Wilhelm looked up at her. There was contempt in his orange-brown eyes. He resumed his writing.

Heart pounding, she checked her notes and finished her planned points.

Impulsively, she ended, "Please, Your Excellency, for Sebastian's sake, for his family's sake, be merciful and free my husband. Prince Leopold may not wait forever."

The last was a mistake.

Duke Wilhelm threw down his pen with such a violent sweep of his arm that his pot of writing implements clattered to the floor. "I have heard enough. When Bach decides to stay in my employ, I will release him. Show this woman out, Franz."

Barbara whirled and fled before the secretary could reach her. She went straight to the Red Castle.

Elinor dispatched a courier with a message for her brother the moment Barbara finished her tale. Four days later, the Prince arrived on horseback and called for the Bach family to join in deliberations. Dressed in a long blue coat, knee boots and a buff vest and breeches, the prince laid out sheets of lists on the oval table around which his sister Elinor, his brother-in-law August, his secretary and Barbara and Gottfried sat.

"As Elinor has probably told you, I have been in Berlin and have known nothing of Sebastian's plight," said Leopold. "We must act quickly. I am sending letters to relatives in Halle and Weissenfels. I may even be able to secure some help from one of the professors at Berlin University."

Elinor's small round face lit up. "And what about the influential divines Father knew? Friar Maslem will help. I'm sure of it."

"Ah yes, Friar Maslem." Leopold indicated the addition to his secretary.

"Here we have a list of nobles in Dresden who have honored Sebastian. I will explain to them my need for Sebastian's incomparable talents and outline the dealings of the Grand Duke with his Konzertmeister.

"I am asking each noble to write to Wilhelm and urge him to release Sebastian. Wilhelm will have no recourse if he is to maintain his reputation as a reasonable man."

Barbara's eyes welled with tears.

Elinor reached over and squeezed her hand, and Barbara breathed a thank you. She felt light for the first time in weeks. To think that she and Sebastian should count such royalty their friends! An hour later, Barbara, Gottfried and the children were drinking wassail with the royal family and enjoying a skate on the pond.

Interlude One

Sebastian felt suspended in time. The solitude was plunging into him, probing a place he hadn't known was there.

Shadows shifted, floated. Light pierced above him at unexpected intervals. But mostly, all was gray and confused. There was no music, just the screech of iron doors and the eternal click of keys.

He was roiling in and through. There were layers, the first trenched and winding. A wagon rolled upon it, its axle intractable, wheeling the same trench day after day. No! He swore. I will slowly die. I must have change. I must have freedom, the power to act.

And yet . . . another layer. Uncertainty.

Did the Almighty approve his current acts? The question hung there for eons. Then the gray space blurred like an old manuscript torn around the edges. Red whirred through the blur. It was the sound of a violin playing furiously and out of tune. So much anger: against mediocrity, against injustice, against the walls that closed him in.

The layers peeled away like papers in a dust storm, and then, he heard a dissonance. It was the sound of a long bitterness—over the loss of his father, the death of the twins, the cutting short of the life of Ernst, the death of their unborn child, and now what looked like the loss of his future hopes.

His voice slapped like a razor strap against the night.

"I have every right to be bitter. The God I understood was not one who destroyed promise and hope. Not one who would give joy only to take it away. Not one who would punish a man for desiring a position where he could pursue the gifts divinely given."

Sebastian circled and ranted until he saw for the first time that for years now he'd been wondering whether God might not be, after all, like the Grand Duke: A Sovereign bent on rules, and taking nothing else into account, a Sovereign God whose only desire was to hedge His people in.

Sebastian questioned, accused and clung, until at last his speech became dialogue. The Other was there. Around him? Within him? He wasn't sure, but the Presence was real. The Voice was silent and gentle. It was scored deep with love and understanding. But it was also firm.

"Who are you to question me? Know only this, that I author no pain, but I redeem. I AM—the God who turns curses into blessings."

Gradually, in Sebastian's understanding there formed a knowing beyond all knowing that the pulse of His God was a love so much greater than anything he'd ever experienced that no human love would ever be able to touch it.

He basked in the fire of that ineffable love, and the image of the law-ranting Sovereign was burned away.

And then the music came, page after page of devotional chorales for the organ— for Advent, for the days of the New Year, for Lent.

Here Sebastian rested, no longer in the gray but in the greenest of places, aware— at a distance—of the rush and swirl of nations, but knowing that here in this quiet music place lay his destiny. And it was a destiny no man could take away.

He wrote his chorales in a diminutive book he sewed with his own hand, its title Orgelbuchlein, *its inscription: "In the Praise of the Almighty's Will, and for my Neighbor's Greater Skill."*

BOOK TWO · · · *THE PATRON*

The same year Bach was imprisoned in Weimar, twenty-three-year-old Voltaire was imprisoned in the Bastille. His crime was writing satirical verses that ridiculed the government. His imprisonment lasted eleven months.

The combination of Prince Leopold's passion for pure instrumental music and Sebastian's own hunger to learn and to perfect drew unsuspected compositional powers from Bach. He experimented with innovations, producing massive effects and rhythms of unimpeded vitality.

6

Hope
1 7 1 7

Prince Leopold's letters did their work, and on the second day of December. the bailiff surprised Sebastian by flinging open his cell door and announcing he was free to go. The official's squint eyes were suspicious in his mottled face. "I don't know how you've managed it, Bach, but the Grand Duke has changed his mind. He is releasing you from his service."

In a moment Sebastian's whole family was crowding into his cell.

With hugs and chatter, Barbara, Gottfried and the children helped him gather his things, then waltzed him down the dank stone halls and out into the street. The fanfare of trumpets broke over him the same moment as the brightness of the sun. Lorenz was directing an ensemble on the street, part of an entourage only August could have assembled.

There were horses festooned with bells and feathers, several gilt carriages and even a juggler juggling eggs.

The day was spring-like. The sudden shift had come in night winds from the south. It was the first time Sebastian had felt warm in weeks. With one arm wrapped around Barbara's slim waist and the other hefting a wiggling Bernhard, Sebastian stood listening as the trumpet fanfare dissolved into a dance. The rejoicing within him was like the rejoicing of Easter.

August herded them all to the Red Castle, where they feasted and danced, then Sebastian begged leave to return home. How he ached for the solace of his own roof! He wanted to give thanks with his family around his own table; he wanted to surround himself with his children and learn how they had grown; he wanted to be alone with his wife.

He spent the next morning making himself presentable and gathering his thoughts, then he practiced the harpsichord and gave Friedemann a violin lesson.

The seven-year-old ended his sarabande with a sound from his bow that was part saw and part squeak. Friedemann grimaced, "I need a better violin."

"You need to practice," Sebastian said. "Talent without work is useless."

When Lorenz returned from his day at the castle, he reported that Wilhelm was in a villainous mood. "This day is not one I would repeat! Nobles the Grand Duke respects have had harsh words for him over you, Herr Bach. And Wilhelm does not take rebuke well. He was not pleased at my involvement in your celebration yesterday. Zounds! That is an understatement."

Sebastian had trained this young man for eight years, and he was proud of the results. He placed his hands on Lorenz's shoulders. "It will aid you to continue to call to remembrance the solidness of your own musicianship. You will make Wilhelm a fine Konzertmeister, yes, a fine Konzertmeister."

Lorenz showed Sebastian his plan for the chapel services for the next year, and Sebastian was pleased. His apprentice was composing some of his own feast cantatas and drawing in works from other composers, but he was also including many of Sebastian's works on the appropriate days of the liturgy. Sebastian had a long way to go to his goal of providing new music for every service in the five-year cycle, but with Lorenz using some of his cantatas, the upgrading of the Weimar liturgy would remain intact.

Feeling like Moses hurrying the Israelites to leave Egypt before the Pharaoh changed his mind, Sebastian launched everyone into packing. He was appalled at how much they had accumulated. "I think we should give half of our goods to the poor, " he said.

Barbara looked up from her packing. "What should we give away?"

Her chin tilted in merry little jerks. "The dozen goose down comforters you purchased at that fire sale, your voluminous books of sermons, or, yes, how about that keg of French wine?"

"That's unjust, woman!

You're picking my favorite commodities."

"Ah then, shall we give away your second harpsichord or perhaps your collection of lutes?"

"Enough, dear, enough. Let's take a hundred wagons if we need to, and all your linens and tankards and cream pitchers and pewter plates." He tweaked her nose, and pulled her to him. The comfort of the feel of her! He stroked her hair, and she tightened her arms about him.

The strength in them made him feel ready for anything. They stood that way for a long time.

It took them two days to pack. Lorenz helped when he could, but his free hours were few. Gottfried, however, had such a knack for practical things that he made up for Lorenz's absence. He built rolling boards for heavy furniture and took the initiative to disassemble tables and cupboards and purchase rope and padding to secure each load. He organized the children to help and made it seem like play.

Everyone was delighted that he was moving to Cothen with them.

The night before their departure, August and Elinor arrived with a leaving present. Sebastian was weary. He and his family, aided by the three lackeys Leopold had sent that morning with horses and wagons, had accomplished two weeks of packing in two days. August began reliving their good times and rambling on about how much he would miss being able to make music together. Sebastian hated long good-byes.

Out of the corner of his eye, he could see Lorenz on the doorstep talking to Barbara.

She looked down, then speaking in soft, serious tones, made a sweeping gesture with her small hands. In a moment she dropped quiet. Lorenz closed his eyes. Barbara turned from him, and Sebastian wondered at the bleakness in his apprentice's face. August continued his reminiscing, and with the barest of nods to Sebastian, Lorenz shouldered his bags and left.

A courier woke them the next morning with a package for Gottfried. They were all sitting on a rug of hemp in the stripped kitchen, eating bread dripping with honey.

Sebastian savored the sticky sweetness while Gottfried read the note inside the package and presented the rest of the contents to Barbara.

"Mother wants you to have her newest good-luck calendar."

Barbara flipped through the art prints and dates. "Maria does me honor."

"She sends her congratulations on the new position," Gottfried said to Sebastian.

"And is there word from Christoph?"

"My father is a poor letter writer."

Of that Sebastian was aware. Not even when he was in school in Luneburg had Christoph written, only Maria. But being a poor letter writer was not the difficulty.

The difficulty was that he had never forgiven Sebastian for copying that forbidden book. Would they ever be reconciled? Such hostilities in a family did not bode well.

He shook off the dark feelings and began loading last-minute things, not the least of which were three picnic baskets full of cheeses and rolls, dried fruits and wursts of all shapes and sizes. Barbara handed him a warming tankard full of coffee, and Sebastian boosted Dorothea into the wagon. "It's like going on a picnic," she said.

"A picnic that won't end for six days. That's gotta be more than a hundred hours!" exclaimed Emmanuel.

Sebastian and Gottfried checked to be sure the other drivers were ready. Then they clambered into the wagon, and Gottfried clucked to the horses. They were on their way.

"What did we bring to eat?" asked Friedemann.

Feeling suddenly mischievous, Sebastian belted out a song about bratwurst and coffee. In the age-old tradition of the Bach's, Gottfried joined in, improvising a quodlibet about his preference for brown eggs and strudel. Barbara caught up the tune, and then Dorothea and Friedemann. All the way through the town of Weimar and out into the foothills the Bach family rolled, six wagons strong, chorusing at the top of their voices.

As they neared their destination at the end of the first day, Barbara called Sebastian's attention to the sunset. The clouds were long and pink, merging and remerging. They watched in silence, lulled by the steady clop and rumble of horses and wheels.

Barbara leaned against him. "It seems a portent to me, of good things to come."

Sebastian was silent.

He felt her head move on his shoulder. He could imagine the question in her eyes.

Being in between places made one more objective. The past lay behind them, literally, and the future lay ahead. He'd felt so ecstatic when he first learned of his release. There he was in prison, waiting and learning in the wait. He'd almost given up the hope of being Leopold's Kapellmeister. Having the reality of the longed-for position finally materialize had seemed an infinite brightness. But this morning a shadow had returned, and now as he looked ahead—

"What is it?" Barbara's voice was anxious.

Sebastian rubbed his forehead. "Just weariness. I see the inn up ahead." He forced himself to smile at her. "We have arrived."

Sebastian's foreboding left him with a good night's sleep, and the rest of the journey was filled with merriment and anticipation. They left the hilly terrain of Duke Wilhelm's environs on the third day and continued through flatter terrain. The road routed them through Leipzig, one of the major trading centers of Germany. It was known throughout Europe as the "Little Paris." Sebastian decided to diverge from the route the others were taking along the outer edges of the city and travel straight through the center of Leipzig. The children could use some excitement.

The gigantic market square was crowded with stalls trafficked by buyers and sellers in foreign garb. There were Dutchmen sporting pantaloons and pointed hats, and Russians wearing colorful tunics and boots laced up the calves with thongs. A Venetian was singing an aria in a pocket of space decorated with tapestries and a fringe-cushioned chair. People were bargaining at top voice.

Barbara convinced Sebastian to let her and Emmanuel trek their way through the crowd to buy bread and kuchen, and when they returned, Emmanuel's face was plastered with crumbs, and Barbara's bag was bulging. "I've never seen such a selection," she said, "and the prices were irresistible."

They drove down tree-lined avenues that led to imposing buildings— the structures of Leipzig University, several fine churches, a public library and two walled-in estates.

As the wagon rolled on through the Small Thomas Gate, they found themselves skirting a park with towering trees. Couples were beginning the afternoon promenade.

It reminded Sebastian of Dresden, " I wonder what it would be like to live here."

"Is that a possibility?" Barbara asked.

"There's the Cantorship of the Thomasschule."

"Father speaks of it," said Gottfried. "Musical scholarships for boys?"

"Yes, and for the Cantor, the chance to compose for the city's churches and," Sebastian raised his eyebrows, "a considerable amount of prestige."

2

Around noon on the sixth day of their journey, one of Leopold's drivers took the lead. Soon they were entering the gates of Cothen and drawing up in front of a three-story house with a red-gabled roof. It was their new home. Barbara was the first one in the door.

No matter where Sebastian was that first hour, the children were like popcorn bursting in upon him with every new discovery. Friedemann was excited about the outside stair to the attic rooms, Dorothea about the nook off the kitchen. Sebastian watched Barbara as she skated her hand over the golden wood cabinets and gasped at the marvel of the ceramic stove. It was good to see her so happy.

With the help of Leopold's men, Sebastian and Gottfried were able to unload everything and assemble the beds before the early winter setting of the sun.

After the evening meal, Sebastian began tuning his best harpsichord. He had to tune it every day, even in normal situations, and six days of bumping about on German roads had turned the task into a nightmare. He struck the tuning fork again and again and twisted the hand-sized tuning hammer, straining, listening, adjusting. He would need to requill the whole instrument before long. Gottfried would be good help.

Finally, the work was finished, and against the quiet of the night, when everyone else had fallen into an exhausted sleep, Sebastian began honing ideas for Prince Leopold's birthday cantata. Leopold wanted to see it tomorrow morning, and the work was barely begun.

Prince Leopold's coach roared up to the new Bach home the next morning. The coachman jumped down from his stoop, flung open the door, and the Prince leaned out to help Sebastian into the carriage.

The Prince's smile fairly danced under his frizz of light brown hair. "At last I've hooked you, *mon ami.*"

They cantered through the treeless streets of the town, the royal gardens, and then the domes and towers of Leopold's medieval castle loomed ahead of them.

Sebastian felt as though he'd been plunged into a fantastical world, caught up in a story with endless possibilities. Joy leaped up in him, unsolicited, unexpected—a holy laughter that had an energy of its own.

Inside, Prince Leopold sped him through the echoing atrium, and up the stairs to the second floor rooms. "So much of this fortress is unlivable," he said. "Most of our resources have gone into reshaping the west wing. And here is my favorite chamber."

The room was circular—built into one of the towers—the ceiling high and coved. The walls were lined with bookcases full of books, larger volumes on the bottom in descending heights toward the ceiling. Hung in pleasing fashion around the window facing the moat were a pan pipe, a folk harp, a circular trumpet, and a child's violin. A clavichord was nestled under the window. Leaning against it was an ornate bass viol, and next to the viol, a standing globe of the world.

Behind the sitting area where Leopold bid him make himself comfortable was an elegantly carved desk made of the native oak *wohnstube*. It was stocked with pens and brushes, several standing volumes of violin music, and a sheaf of drawing paper. Leaning against the desk was a deep-hued violin, and to the side, an oil portrait of a black Arabian horse.

Sebastian scanned the titles of the books. There were rows of philosophical journals, thick tomes by Spinoza, Leibniz and Descartes; the omnipresent *Manners for Children*, in several different publications—even Erasmus' original work, it looked like; French plays and novels; English writers like Milton, Shakespeare and even the new writer DeFoe.

Leopold sipped on the tea a mobcapped maid presented him. "I'm experimenting with some of the English customs," he explained. "Morning without tea is not to be thought of on the island."

He noticed Sebastian's interest in his books. "My grandfather started the library, mostly John Calvin's works at first. Mother enlarged the theological sections, and Father accumulated works on horticulture." He indicated the volumes behind Sebastian.

"I spent a year at Berlin university. It was like opening the mysteries of heaven. Not that I had that much in the university itself of the new philosophies, but I did spend a considerable amount of time in the coffee houses consorting with men who read. I used to be hounded at every turn by a set of mind that hampered my living with incessant fear that I would not prove good enough to be one of the elect. These days the mind can be free, free to explore the universe within and without, and by such empiricism, free to discover truth. 'What a piece of work is man!'"

Blue eyes lambent, the Prince fell silent.

With a swish of pouring tea and the click of cups and spoons, the maid continued her preparations. Sebastian waited. Where did Leopold's faith rest? In man? He thought of the tales he'd heard of Michelangelo's *David*. The artist had decided to sculpt the youthful David in the process of making a decision he knew would change his life, a youth who possessed the ability inherent in every man, according to Michelangelo's beliefs, to perform what seemed impossible, if he only had the will. The *Moses* had a similar message: a human being in his prime, who had the strength and wisdom to form a nation. The Renaissance, the glory of man, where did the balance of truth really lie? The atmosphere in Cothen was going to be something he'd experienced until now only on journeys.

"If father hadn't died," Leopold continued. "I would have extended my stay in England and returned to another year of university in Berlin. I attempt to make up for it by expanding my library and inviting scholars here."

Sebastian took the cup the maid offered him and stirred in four cubes of sugar. His eye fell once more on the painting of the horse.

"Mandolin," Leopold explained. "He died last year. I am training his foal."

"The breadth of your interests astounds me."

Leopold looked amused, "A tiger, my mind. It bandies me about. There are many times I long to still it."

He leaned forward. "I want to learn music thoroughly. The majority of my music study in Berlin was on the bass viol, but I prefer the violin. I'd like to take my violin technique as far as possible, vocalize daily and learn to play the clavier. I want to create a musical haven, a place where people can come almost any day of the week and find good music discussed and performed. My particular interest, as you know, is instrumental forms, specifically suites for strings and woodwinds. There is not enough good music available, and it has long been my desire to offer patronage to a German composer who can create music of all textures for the orchestra."

Leopold laid out his schedule: an "Exercitium Musicum" every Saturday, with regular guests from the nobility who would come from nearby estates or the University of Halle; an unofficial musical evening every Wednesday for members of the court; a Kapelle rehearsal every day but Sunday, with daily lessons for himself and certain members of the Kapelle.

"I also desire that you perform some of your original compositions and improvisations during noon meals. We will prove to all environs that you truly are the Prince of Claviers."

Four times a year, Leopold would spare no expense. He would send invitations all over Germany inviting guests to a week of concerts, cotillions, dramas and royal cuisine.

He placed a hand on Sebastian's shoulder. "The music must be the very best. Your music, Sebastian! Original and superb! Now let's see what you've done on my birthday cantata. We've only three more days."

Sebastian drew the work he had done the night before out of his folio and began laying the separate pieces on the floor: some standard arias and choruses he thought he might use with adjustments, a prelude he'd composed for one of Wilhelm's hunting cantatas, and a lively dance written by Heinrich Bach.

"We must have something new also," Leopold said. "At least a third of my birthday music must be new and entirely instrumental. I have assembled trumpeters, woodwind and string players who can sight-read anything you put before them."

Ah, Sebastian thought. Excellent sight-readers mean excellent musicians. He begged leave. "I need some time to think how best to accomplish what you desire."

"First, you must help me with this piece."

The Prince played a page of a Vivaldi violin concerto, then asked for critique.

"You will find," said Sebastian, "a lift of the elbow that keeps your bowing arm level will give you a more vibrant tone."

Leopold tried it and drew a squawk out of his instrument. "It will need practice."

"Always, Sovereign. Music is no vocation for the sluggard."

Sebastian spent the next hour walking briskly to warm himself against the growing cold. He might have been overwhelmed if he hadn't been starved for so long for a patron who believed in him—and, he realized, a patron who had a musical vision far-reaching enough to capture his own imagination and zeal. True, his personal vision was in a different realm. Yet he could feel his creative energies rise to the Prince's challenge.

He jotted ideas for the musical evenings on Saturdays, then spent the rest of the time planning the next few days. For the birthday cantata, he would need at least fifteen minutes of new music and individual copies of all the parts.

If he had a good flautist, he might be able to use that sprightly melody he'd thought of on the journey, perhaps for a badinerie. He could incorporate the dance into a complete suite later. The harpsichord concerto wasn't finished yet, but if he had good improvisers in the Kapelle, he could give them the figured bass for one movement. It would be something new on the spot.

The next three days were going to be so pressured that he would be needing his nephew's help almost all the time. Barbara's need for Gottfried would be pressing also. He felt bad about monopolizing Gottfried's time at this juncture, but he saw no help for it.

At the end of the hour, Sebastian stood outside the doors of Leopold's orchestral hall. His first encounter with his new Kapelle. How would they respond to him? Would they be like-minded? Or would there be problems?

Would *he* be what they expected? Would *they* be what he expected and hoped for? He drew in his stomach, wishing now he'd worn a coat that wasn't quite so tight. He adjusted his wig one more time, tucked his leather folio under his arm and strode through the door.

The hall was long and domed with tall French windows and several large chandeliers. At the western end of the room, a Kapelle of about twenty-five members sat waiting.

Someone began a welcoming applause.

Encouraged, Sebastian hurried toward them. He sat down at the harpsichord. "Let us get right to work."

"Introductions are proper, Herr Bach." Spiess had risen to his feet.

Sebastian sighed. How he hated the long-winded vacuousness of the customs of civility. When he was ready to begin, he was ready to begin, but this man's favor had not been easily won. "Speak, friend."

The lantern-faced violinist spoke, as always, in the manner of one racing through a breviary. "I welcome you, Kapellmeister Johann Sebastian Bach, on behalf of the reigning prince of Anhalt-Cothen, His Most Serene Highness Prince Leopold's Kapelle— I have provided a list of names according to present seatings—I have informed everyone of your qualifications and of your performance in Dresden. "They wish me to tell you they are committed to working hard—I believe you will be pleased."

With a gasping sound, like that of a man who has just run up a flight of stairs. Spiess presented the list to Sebastian.

Sebastian traced his finger down the list of names. He scanned the faces of the waiting musicians—blonde German demeanors; dark Italian ones; a cellist who was so large he took up two places; a sandy-haired bassoonist who looked wary; five singers in the back, two of them women who stood tall and tense; and Leopold, who was taking his place at the end, taller than any of them. Sebastian wondered what it would be like to have his Sovereign in his Kapelle. Well, he thought, we shall see.

Sebastian grew more pleased with every hour that passed during that first rehearsal. The Kapelle's sight-reading was virtuosic. The vocalists were a joy—with Leopold's bass no exception—and though his own violin prowess was nothing to scoff at, Spiess led the string section with an authority Sebastian could not have matched. The sauce on the fritter was the bassoonist: he wielded a tone Sebastian had had access to only in his dreams.

3

Sebastian arrived home before dark and found a surprise waiting for him. There in his new study, a massive volume open in his lap, one arm on the back of a chair and the other on the desk, was George Phillip Telemann.

"Counterpoint and canon!" Sebastian cried. "Where in all the environs have you come from?"

Telemann flung out his arms with a shrug of his shoulders. "Been visiting Handel in Halle, remembered Prince Leopold's invitation to attend his birthday celebration. Decided it wasn't worth the hurry home to suffer in an inn tonight. Where did you get this commentary? No volumes of the new philosophies? This book is as old as Methuselah."

The tiredness in Telemann's eyes gave the lie to his effort at joviality.

"You must stay with us tonight."

Barbara brushed in to set up candles. "You must. We've an extra bed in Gottfried's room."

Telemann shook his head. "It is impossible to be ready for hospitality the day after a move."

"With Gottfried's help, we've done it. I declare, that young man can nail things together with nothing but his hands. He's got every piece of furniture assembled and repaired where needed, and every brazier in place. You must at least stay tonight and sample my borsch."

After Telemann was settled, Sebastian relaxed in the kitchen with a strong cup of coffee while Barbara piled a bowl with sour cream.

"So things are going well?" he asked.

"Overall, I am pleased. Except . . ." she paused, "except, we can't find the crate that held my best kitchenware."

She dabbed her handkerchief at her eyes and began dicing the cabbage with quick metallic thuds.

"Perhaps it is still in one of Leopold's wagons."

"Perhaps."

After the evening meal, they all retired to the music room. Warmed by steaming cups of chocolate and a crackling fire, the children clamored for Sebastian to tell them a story. Telemann was sitting at the harpsichord with his arm around Emmanuel. "Ah, comes forth the storyteller in the musician!"

"But not the herring story, Papa," Friedemann said. "Even Bernhard could tell that one."

"The duel, Papa," Dorothea pleaded.

"Tell us the story about the duel."

Sebastian leaned back and lit up his pipe. "It all began when I accepted my first Hoforganist job. No sooner had I arrived in Arnstadt, than I discovered that a beautiful cousin was living in the same city. Her name was Maria Barbara. She had black hair that fell in ringlets around her heart-shaped face. And she had a sister named Catherina.

"We often attended concerts and festivals together. Of course, I was always longing for some minute alone with the beautiful Maria Barbara, but Catherina would adhere to us, like a wicked stepsister, I thought at the time.

"I was only twenty and liked to think I would have been something of a bard if I had lived in days of old—an exceedingly romantic bard, if only given a chance to once be alone with a woman who was truly beautiful. Of course, I did not know Aunt Catherina as I know her now.

"Well, while I, the swashbuckling new maestro whom everyone in the city was lauding, bemoaned this state of affairs, I was also having a most lamentable run-in with one of my so-called musicians, a ruffian of about my age who made a sound upon his old bassoon that was like the mewling of a cat in heat."

Telemann snorted. Barbara touched Sebastian's arm. "The children, dear."

But Sebastian was feeling adventurous. He swept an upturned palm toward his listeners. The fire flickered across their faces, conjuring for Sebastian that aura of hope and fantasy he'd felt earlier that morning—bright faces, thoughtful faces, mischievous and expectant, intrigued and amused.

"You must understand how severe the case was," he continued. "The sound this fellow forced from his bassoon was destructive to the well-being of all who heard, and I could not in good conscience let it continue to spoil the atmosphere of the church. One Saturday afternoon while we were attempting a rehearsal, I told this Geyersbach what I thought of him and his bassoon, and I minced no words; and by all that is holy in music, like a bolt out of the blue, he sprung to his feet and struck a fist straight in the direction of my nose.

"Now you have to realize that this Geyersbach was half again as tall as I and had muscles that bulged like fortresses. However, due to the excellent fencing training I'd had in Luneburg, I was quick to duck and feint, and was preparing to place a blow to his jaw when the pastor walked in.

"He insisted I dismiss the rehearsal. In fact, I considered it just as well. I could do a better job playing the entire service on the organ alone than I could trying to make up for that constant bleating from the Kapelle. I informed the pastor I intended to do just that.

"I was an arrogant rascal in those days, and you must remember, boys," Sebastian pointed the stem of his pipe at Friedemann, Emmanuel and little Bernhard, "that no matter how gifted you are, arrogance can get you into a pile of trouble."

"I liked what you called the ruffian," Emmanuel said. *"Zippelfagottist."*

"A nanny-goat bassoonist?" Telemann asked. "You didn't!"

Sebastian wished he could deny it. Now it seemed that surely he could have come up with something more abrasive. Bassoons offered much interest when played with finesse, but let an incompetent get hold of one, and you were in the pit.

"As Providence would have it," Sebastian continued, "a week later I stopped by Uncle Martin's to pick up the enchanting Maria Barbara"—he wriggled his eyebrows at Barbara— "and the dastardly Catherina. They were to accompany me to a concert where I would be playing at the castle on the edge of the city.

"Uncle Martin greeted me with fortuitous news. Catherina had fallen ill, and Barbara and I were allowed to go to the concert alone. I can still see the way your mother looked that day. She was standing on the walk in a green silk dress with red roses blooming behind her.

"I took her arm, sure that heaven had fallen upon me, and we began to walk through the streets of the town. Her dress swished like the sound of a gentle tide. Her white hand on my arm was like snow and fire."

"And her perfume Papa, Mama's perfume," Dorothea said.

"Yes, she wore the scent of lavender, and it traveled with her like the fragrance of a hundred harems—delicate, tantalizing, mysterious.

"Ah, the magic of that summer afternoon. The sky was blue; the sun was warm, and my heart beat so loudly, I was sure she would hear.

"I thought the concert would never end. The harpsichord continuo I was locked into was as dry as century-old legumes. My plan was to sweep Barbara out directly after the finale, not loiter the way I often did on such occasions.

"But Duke August and Ernst were upon us before I could scarce take my lady's arm.

"I was forced to introduce them. August bent over Barbara's hand, kissing it and muttering pleasantries for so long that the heat in me boiled into a jealousy I knew was going to erupt if something didn't happen soon. That something was young Ernst. Only ten years old he was at the time, but the maturity! I could feel Ernst's gaze upon me as the heat inside me grew. Then of a sudden, he burst into speech.

"'Brother,' he said, 'Father calls us from across the room. Now! he says, we must come now.'

"But I saw their honorable father nowhere, and I had heard no call. Ernst winked as he and August left, and from that moment I held the young noble in high esteem."

Sadness welled up in Sebastian. He blinked back the tears.

"Ernst was a unique young man," Barbara said.

Dorothea sniffed, and Friedemann jerked his head toward the fire.

Sebastian jumped back into his tale.

"The doorman at the castle entrance was an acquaintance. He stopped me in the atrium and told me to watch my back. 'There's a fellow,' he said, 'who's been asking about you, and he doesn't look friendly.'

"I patted the sword that accompanied my court uniform and promptly forgot his warning. I strolled with Maria Barbara through an archway of oaks along the footpath into town. We talked of music and family and dreams.

"We laughed. Ah, the bell sound of her laughter. As we approached the marketplace, the sky prismed peach and lavender above the houses.

"The wind stirred smells of sausages and flowers. The vendors were closing up their stalls. The square was emptying. Across the way, I saw some rough-looking fellows loitering.

"We circled the maze of stalls, and I began to be as enamoured of this young lady's mind as I was with her form. I asked one of the vendors if he would oblige me by letting me buy some flowers. He had them all stored away in a cart, but he pulled out a couple of carnations and thrust them at me, glancing furtively across the square. All I thought of was how perfectly the red carnations matched my companion's lips."

Sebastian stood up and began moving about. "On we strolled. I was oblivious to the darkening of the sky, oblivious to any other sound but her voice. Maria Barbara Bach had woven her magic spell.

"Like a dam breaking, the trouble flung itself upon us without warning: a gang-shout, the pounding of feet, and suddenly, a giant figure in front of us swinging a weapon. I flung out an arm to protect Barbara.

"'I'll teach you to insult me in public!' the giant said. It was that bungler of a bassoonist Geyersbach.

"'Don't be a fool,'" I said.

"'And what would you be, Herr Know-It-All? A coward? Yes, I think that's it, don't you, men?'

"The ire in me arose, and I gripped the cold metal of my sword. His gang of men pressed around us chortling and coughing out obscenities. I signaled Barbara away.

"Geyersbach shouted at me. 'I demand an apology for your insolent remarks!'

"He advanced, raising above his head a stick the size of a fence post. His muscles bulged, his face contorted.

"'I made no such remarks!' I countered.

"'You insulted my bassoon, and anyone who insults my bassoon insults me. You dirty dog?'

"He hurled himself upon me, his weapon slicing down. I ducked and drew my sword."

Sebastian circled his sword arm forward, illustrating the postures. He plunged. He thrust.

"I'd caught the ruffian by surprise. He struggled to regain his balance. Wildly, he hit at my sword with his stick. I forced him to drop it, then lunged at the opening. His fist smashed into my nose. We fell.

"My head struck the cobblestones. My sword clanged to the ground. Then a shout ripped through the air. I saw someone dragging Geyersbach away, heard feet racing after them.

"Then Barbara was beside me lifting my head. She pressed her lace handkerchief against my nose. Blood spread across it. And at the same moment a voice shouted above me. 'What roguery is this, you blackguards?'

"I struggled to a sitting position, the salt taste of blood trickling into my mouth, and I found myself staring into the black-helmeted face of a watchman. He held a cudgel in one hand and my sword in the other.

"What a state of affairs I'd got myself into. I knew now that the Church Council would hear of the duel and I would be given a reprimand or something worse. I was preparing to make some angry retort to the official when Barbara touched my arm and began explaining for me. She probably prevented my spending the night in jail.

"When the watchman finally departed, my stomach heaved, but Maria Barbara possessed the knowledge of an angel. 'Take deep breaths,' she said. Then she wet her handkerchief in the market fountain and pushed it under my lip, instructing me to press upward to stop the bleeding. She knotted her shawl about my shoulders, and when I thought I was able, I stood. The night reeled.

"I'll never forget those next two hours. Barbara walked me to my rooms, and there she applied poultices, stirred up soothing teas, and made sure I stayed awake. 'Head injuries,' she said, 'must be watched.'

"I told her I was worried what the congregation would think when they saw me at the organ the next day with a black eye. The most incredible green glints sparkled in her eyes. As she puttered about my room, straightening and stirring up more tea, she was singing in a most pleasing contralto voice.

"We talked about how so many seemed to think art was unimportant. Her father used to worry, she said, about something he'd once overheard a friend say. 'Music, hah, what use is it? All it does is fill in the spaces. Now give me a cobbler or a blacksmith or a baker. Those are vocations worth fretting over.'

"It came to me to say then that you could talk of flowers that way too, and trees. All they did was fill in the spaces. And what would the world be without them? She understood.

"Before she left, she reached across me for her shawl. Her shoulder brushed mine, and I could restrain myself no longer. I threw my arms around her and kissed her. Her mouth was like stirring warm velvet. It was the most wondrous kiss I had ever experienced, and this beautiful woman was also kissing me!"

Barbara interrupted. "I was not. You had your arms so tight about me, I couldn't move."

"Now dear, a man knows."

Barbara sighed in amused exasperation.

"You must tell the rest of it."

"Must I? Well, unfortunately, the kiss was extremely short. The beautiful Maria Barbara wrenched herself to her feet, whipped her shawl about her, and in a tone full of fury, asked me what I was thinking.

"'How can a man be expected to resist such a woman?' I replied. 'It's all your fault.'

"But she denied any responsibility and was out the door before I knew what was happening. I had fallen irreparably, irremediably, hopelessly in love."

Everyone clapped, and Sebastian basked in the incomparable feeling of having performed to an audience that turned out to be more than pleased.

With that wild-haired look he got when he'd been concentrating, Gottfried jumped up to heap more kindling on the fire, Friedemann swooped up Bernhard in a jig and Dorothea knelt in front of her mother chattering.

Telemann watched them all, his arm still around Emmanuel, but his face, for once, unmasked. On it, Sebastian saw despair.

During Johann Sebastian Bach's first years in Cöthen, England declared war on Spain, Prussia made school attendance compulsory and Handel became Kapellmeister to the Duke of Chandos.

"*He could hear the thunders of Johann Sebastian Bach's oceanic soul: the winds and storms . . . the people's intoxicated with joy, fury, or pain . . . he could hear the roaring fountainhead of thoughts, passions, and musical forms . . . of visions—pastoral, epic, or apocalyptic—that were contained within the narrow frame of the small-statured cantor from Thuringia.*"[1]

7

Immersed
1 7 1 7 — 1 7 1 9

Barbara opened the door the next morning to a yowling kitten. Its gray tail drooped, its side was splotched with blood, and its green eyes looked up at her with such expectancy that all she could think of was how much it needed her. Poor thing! It had probably been abandoned by some heartless rogue and then gotten itself into a tussle with a bramble bush or something worse. She scooped the kitten up, rubbed its velvety ears till it relaxed a little, then poured it a saucer of milk.

Bernhard squealed and scrambled down from his stool to squat beside it. She looked down at the auburn curls of her youngest. He'd been as alive as a kitten himself ever since they arrived at their new home. But then, all the children were excited, as was she.

The house was a dream—a kitchen on the second floor with a nice-sized scullery below it; four bedrooms; a sitting room as well as a parlour, the parlour at last being the size they really needed for a music room; alcoves and nooks for reading or practicing; a narrow work space off the music room where Sebastian could repair instruments; and instead of the old style *Erkers* built out from the wall, flat-framed windows lent an air of nobility to the whole establishment. There were apple trees, cherry trees, and evergreens in both the front yard and the back.

An ancient oak extended a limb almost the girth of its trunk across the front of the house, and Gottfried and Friedemann were discussing building a tree house. Gone was the feeling of being crowded that she'd so hated in Weimar. Once again she had a place to live where she could reach out and touch the solace of nature at any moment.

Her first project after breakfast was to make the kitchen more workable. She rummaged through a box of assorted woods—spindles, old chair legs, slabs scrolled with gingerbread—some beautiful pieces, actually. She examined each of them, smoothing her hand over the turns and crevices. They were like sculpture, she thought; you couldn't resist touching them. Now this piece might be exactly what she needed. Yes, a varnished spool. She would wrap a length of linen towel about it and fasten it to the cabinet, hang it vertically. It would drop in folds and be out of the way.

The kitten rallied well with a nap and some ointment from Barbara's bag. After setting the older children to tasks, Barbara worked happily through the day with Bernhard and the kitten following her from room to room. Sebastian's study had a large window, for which she was pleased. Far too often, he worked with abominable light.

She would hang the best lamps she could find above the desk and space candles and candelabras at different heights around the walls.

From the music room she could hear Phillip Telemann giving Emmanuel a harpsichord lesson. Emmanuel was laughing at the sound of his godfather's tinkling dance. He attempted the melody, and Telemann cajoled, showing him note by note. They laughed and talked and altogether seemed to be having a good time.

As Barbara breezed up the stairs to the children's rooms, she thought how Emmanuel had begged and begged for Sebastian to begin teaching him the harpsichord, but Sebastian insisted it was too early.

For the noon meal, Barbara dipped up borsch from the dilapidated kettle, the only large vessel she'd been able to find, and served her family and guest.

Telemann slurped his soup with appreciation "I marvel at your efficiency and resourcefulness, Frau Bach. "Such fine meals at such a chaotic moment in your life."

She wondered if he noticed the crack in his bowl. "I wish I could set you a more elegant table."

Gottfried offered his bowl for another helping. "Who cares about elegance?"

"Lord have mercy, you eat like a rabbit on the run."

Gottfried grinned. "That old soup kettle won't take many more mendings."

The worry Barbara had been able to relegate to the back of her mind during her flurry of morning creativity returned. The copper soup kettle Uncle Martin had given her as a wedding gift, her grandmother's Christmas bundt pans, the pewter pitchers, bowls and plates she'd been collecting since she was a girl—it looked as if all of them were lost. If the crate had been transported to the castle in one of the wagons, she was certain it would have been returned by now. Had they left the box in Weimar? Perhaps it had not been properly secured and had fallen off the wagon during their journey. Or maybe it had been stolen during one of their stops.

She mustn't dwell on it.

"I'm sure your wife sets a lovely table," she said to Telemann.

Telemann's eyes glazed, and for a minute the only sound was the clinking of the children's spoons. His small mouth pursed. "She doesn't enjoy it. Tries to find servants we can trust."

Telemann's first wife had died in childbirth, and he had remarried only three years ago. Sebastian told her last night that he'd heard unsettling rumors about this second wife. And none of Telemann's children thus far had survived infancy.

"Might I have your permission to take Emmanuel with me to Sebastian's afternoon rehearsal?" Telemann asked. "I'll not have another chance. I leave before dawn in the morning."

Emmanuel's black eyes grew big as griddle cakes, "Please, Mama!"

She agreed.

Sebastian didn't return from the castle until after the evening meal. He immediately closeted himself in his study.

When the children were all settled, Barbara snuggled on her fur slippers and padded down the winding staircase. Sebastian beckoned her from his desk. His broad face looked as excited as Emmanuel's had at the noon meal. It was the end of the day, and she was exhausted; but Sebastian had only begun.

"The cantata must be going well," she said.

"Yes." He glanced at the manuscript in his hands and then back up at her with a little frown. "I have neglected to tell you that I must travel to Leipzig after the Prince's birthday celebration to inspect an organ. A long-standing commitment."

Barbara was surprised. "Leipzig!"

"It is the organ at the University church, and therefore an opportunity to meet important people and make my work known. And even if it weren't, integrity forbids I break such a commitment if it is at all possible to fulfill."

Barbara's eyes welled with tears as she thought of the weeks she'd had to spend without him during the last few months. She hadn't expected him to be leaving home until next summer at least.

"I have an idea," he said. "The Prince tells me of a year-around stall in Leipzig where they stock excellent pieces of pewter and copper. Make me a list of the items you've lost."

Still she fought back the tears. He flung the manuscript aside, strode toward her and wrapped his arms tightly about her. Relaxing against the comfort of his body, she let the tears roll down her cheeks. After a moment, he smoothed his big thumb down the traces of tears and kissed her nose with a warm peck.

She gave him a weak smile, "I will make a *long* list."

Gottfried entered the study with his pouch of nails. "Your pardon!" He started to leave.

"Come in, come in. I'm ready for you to begin copying parts."

"So much work in so short a time. An exception?" Gottfried asked.

"I cannot relieve your mind on that point. But it's a whole new world. I have renewed my study of the French stylized dances—Lully and Fischer's in particular. The French overture has infinite possibilities. By all that is holy, I believe I'm more excited than the Prince."

"Your worship music?"

"I'll scarcely have time to think about it, much less work on it."

"But Lorenz says your sacred music is more profound than anything he's ever experienced. It is greatly needed." It was a long speech for Gottfried.

"Ah, nephew. You do not need to remind me. I know, I know. But what can I do?"

Barbara returned to their bedroom. Like a rock in a riverbed that was forever going dry, her desperate need for her husband would keep reappearing. She blew out the candle and wrapped the quilt tightly about her, but still she felt cold.

Four days later, she stood in the pre-dawn, looking at the calendar where she'd marked the day of Sebastian's departure. December 15. The picture on Maria's calendar was a field of snow against a purple night, with angels, a castle and a painted frame of golden scroll. Barbara sighed and bent to sniff the scent given off by the Christmas candle she'd just lit. She'd managed a cedar fragrance in her last session of candle-making.

Sebastian stumbled into the kitchen in his morning fog and downed the coffee and bratwurst she'd prepared for him.

Then he gave her a crushing embrace and was off to catch the post wagon for Leipzig. Barbara watched him stride away, head down, greatcoat flying behind him. The wind swirled snow about him like smoke.

She lingered in the doorway. The road to Leipzig was not a bad road, as German roads went, but the journey would take at least two days, and horses could get bogged down on any road in a heavy snow.

Bernhard was struggling with the gray fluff of a kitten. She was determined to get out. Barbara snatched the creature up, held the squirming body firmly against her own and heaved the door shut against the cold.

Better put some salve on that wound while she was thinking of it.

2

Sebastian considered the Leipzig trip a necessity only, and a pressure.

He would rather not have broken the momentum of his work for Leopold. But there were compensations, his encounter with Picander for one. They'd met in one of the many Leipzig bookstores. Picander called it fate, Sebastian, providence.

Sebastian returned home on December 20, loaded with bundles. He slipped into the house, gratefully dropping his load just inside the door. Evergreens decorated the bannister, and the scent of ginger cookies spiced the air.

"Merry Christmas," he roared.

From the music room and the scullery and the upstairs kitchen, everyone streamed to meet him. Dorothea and Barbara were wearing their white aprons and Gottfried, a sprig of holly on his undress.

The evening meal was festive. Candles flickered in the Advent wreath centered on the table. The children chattered, wondering what Christmas would bring and having great difficulty keeping secrets. Sebastian suspected they were tooling a leather music folio for him for Christmas.

"Mama burnt her foot because of that old pot," Emmanuel said.

"What's this?"

"Oh, that great old pot slipped, the handle is only half there, you know, and the soup had been boiling. The water scalded my foot, but my salve is working upon it. How I'm looking forward to finding out what you've brought me from Leipzig!"

Sebastian hesitated. What was he going to tell her? Gottfried rescued him with a question about the Christmas cotillion.

That night in their bedroom Sebastian changed into his dressing gown and nightcap while Barbara set the bricks to warm over the brazier.

How she kept her figure! The sight of her unfettered form never failed to cause the passion to rise within him. As she stood up, he caught her around the waist and kissed the back of her neck. But when he turned her toward him, she stepped back. "Could we talk first?"

"Of course. Let me get my pipe."

He secured his pipe and tamper from the nightstand, along with the pouch of tobacco August had given him as a leaving present. Then, settled on the box bench at the end of their bed, he opened the pouch, felt the tobacco's roughness between his fingers and began filling his pipe. He patted it until he got it to the right firmness, then lit it with a spill from the brazier.

His first draw—ah! just right. He tamped down the loose coals and puffed again. The smoke curled up with a hickory nut smell.

Barbara was sitting in her rocking chair in front of him sorting through her mending.

"So what did you think of the organ at the Pauliner-Kirche?" she asked.

Her long black hair lay in curls against the white of her bedgown. So lovely, he thought.

"Some problems with coarseness in voicing the lowest pipes, trombone and trumpet basses particularly. A low window behind the organ that could cause weather damage, a somewhat heavy touch. But given what he had to work with, Scheibe did an excellent job, yes, an excellent job. Fine construction of pipes, wind chests and roller boards."

He fell silent, and Barbara waited. Sebastian was remembering when he'd worked as a bellows blower in Ohrdruf, sitting inside the organ's walls and studying its workings. Later, he'd explored the innards of the pipe organs in Luneburg, then the four-manual organ in Hamburg with its sixty speaking stops. The mechanics of the organ had always intrigued him. And now many considered him an expert in organ assessment and repair. It was a way to make extra money and meet people of influence, although he feared he'd made a bad impression this time.

Sebastian puffed on his pipe. "I had a discussion with the University Hoforganist that has my mind in a turmoil. The man rebuked my interest in secular forms. He implied it was pagan for me to spend time composing purely instrumental music."

Barbara lifted Friedemann's shirt from her basket and examined the tear in the elbow. "What do you think?"

"I think people are determined to make God as small as they are. What are they afraid of? We learn the earth circles around the sun instead of vice versa; we start to explore the workings of the body and discover and tabulate the precision of the movements of the cosmos, and church men begin foaming at the mouth like rabid dogs."

Sebastian abandoned his seat and began pacing back and forth. "They're terrorized that if a man broadens his mind, if he lets it dwell on new discoveries and new forms, if he learns in fields that aren't specifically religious, he'll turn apostate. What did God mean anyway when he gave us the command to take dominion over the earth? Now that is a question

I would like to explore."

Barbara grabbed his outflung hand and drew it to her cheek.

Sebastian looked down at her. "The universe has no scripture attached. What do you think? Can my orchestral suites glorify God only if I attach words?"

"Husband, how can we know these things? You must sit down and relax."

He jerked the belt of his wrap tight across his middle and sat down, trying to calm himself with his pipe.

Barbara was sorting through her button box—a soft clinking sound, metal against metal, wood against gem. "Did they pay you well for the organ inspection?"

"Tolerably." He studied his pipe. He might as well get it over with. "I must apologize. I have come home empty-handed."

"The bundles?"

Sebastian couldn't bring himself to look at her. "I was on my way to purchase everything on your list when I encountered Picander. He gave me a tour of the bookstores of the city and got me so engrossed that before I knew it I'd spent practically all the inspection fee on study music and books. You should see what I found: Corelli, Frescobaldi, Albioni, and even something new by Reincken!"

Barbara's eyes widened with hurt. "You promised," she whispered. "Everything has been so chaotic in the kitchen. I burned the cookies. The Christmas cake ran over. The scalding from the old soup pot has me fearful about using it anymore. When will we have another chance to purchase the kitchenware we need?"

Sebastian assured her that he would think of something. But she didn't seem to be listening. She pushed the needle in and out of the button she was sewing, faster and faster. He rose to plump up the pillows and turn down the covers. He could hear the quick snipping of her scissors.

He moved to rub her neck, "Come now sweetheart, I truly am sorry. I will make it right. Let me hold you, and you will feel better."

"I can't be with you like that, not tonight. You will have to give me time."

He circled in front of her and bent to take her face in his hands.

But her glance was sharp as needles. She was hurt, but she was also angry. He strode toward the door, grabbed the frigid knob, then turned back once more. But she didn't look up.

It was the first time she had ever refused him.

3

This year Sebastian didn't have to worry about music for Advent services. He was relieved.

Fortunately, Prince Leopold's father had allowed the establishing of a Lutheran church in Cothen, despite his Calvinist persuasion—the Agnuskirche. It was there the Bachs attended services on Sundays. There was much animosity between the city's Calvinist and Lutheran contingents, but Sebastian refused to get involved.

He did writhe, however, under the shallowness of the Agnuskirche's music. Over and over again, he sat under the liturgy, planning what he would have done differently: what prelude he would have played instead of the overused ones the Hoforganist seemed to invariably choose, or how this chorale or that could have been better harmonized to communicate the proper emotion. Such facileness Sebastian considered an affront to God. But it was not his place to interfere in this church's worship. The door that was open to him right now lay elsewhere, in the realm of pure music, not in the depiction of words.

By the time February arrived, Sebastian felt well established in Leopold's court. One Wednesday afternoon Sebastian and the Prince were clipping down the stairs to the orchestral hall surrounded by several courtiers. Sebastian had just finished giving Leopold a violin lesson. The Prince's technique was developing rapidly.

"And so, Excellency, how does the training of your foal progress?" Sebastian asked.

"A bit slow with the bad weather we've been having, but Bandit and I are friends."

"You miss riding?"

"With all the new music you've given me to learn, I am content with the season. The joys of perfecting! How right you are about it. Every skill has unimagined deeps."

Leopold wore his favorite silver coat and breeches.

A young courtier in a red brocade vest walked on the other side of the Prince. "So, Your Highness, what musical feast is in store for us today?"

"Kapellmeister?"

"We will try a suite that shows off His Excellency's fine bassoonist."

"Ah, a tricky sound, a bassoon. Humorous, one normally thinks."

The bright-faced Fraulein clinging to the courtier's arm looked interested. "I'm not sure I've ever heard a bassoonist featured."

"Reeds lend a hearty timbre that have the sound of Germany if used properly."

"Yes! If you'd heard the way Sebastian uses reeds when he plays the organ," said Leopold, "you'd understand."

Leopold's chamberlain scurried ahead to swing open the double doors to the hall. Just as he did so, a new guest joined the group, a man with a jutting brow who wore tall leather boots and a pigtail. Sebastian was sure he'd seen him somewhere before. The Prince was welcoming him when Sebastian left to ready the Kapelle.

Square-heeled shoes echoing on the polished floor, Sebastian hurried to the harpsichord at the end of the domed hall.

Spiess was already in his seat practicing. One did appreciate the punctuality of the cranky little man. And Schmidt, yes, there he was bowing away on his cello. "A beautiful sound, Schmidt." The big man glanced up, nodded, and continued his playing without a break in the sensuous lines.

As Sebastian lifted the lid of the harpsichord, he wondered why the cello had never been considered a solo instrument. What possibilities might lie in that direction!

Gottfried arrived, passed out the new parts, and seated himself in the viola section.

The sandy-haired bassoonist scanned his part and groaned. Sebastian was always having to encourage the insecure young bassoonist. "It is within your reach, Gustav, it is within your reach."

When everyone had arrived, Prince Leopold took his place in the violin section. Everyone's whispering stopped. Even the handful of courtiers who had drawn up sofas to listen were silent. Prince Leopold always made it clear that once they were in the hall, guests were to listen to the creating of fine music, not to discuss the fashions of the day.

"Three pieces to rehearse," Sebastian announced from the harpsichord. "We'll start with the new C major suite. The gavotte needs a military texture; the forlane is in triple meter, very quick and lively."

They plunged into the music.

For two hours, Sebastian worked them as mercilessly as a trainer grooms athletes for games. He drilled the bassoonist where he stumbled; he appealed to the two oboists and the bassoonist to listen, listen to one another, blend their sounds, bring the melody out here, diminish there, attack each note just so; trumpets, sing, dance, listen; strings brilliant, now extending.

At the end of the two-hour rehearsal, the Prince invited Sebastian to join him and his guests for discussion. Thirty minutes later, Leopold's scholars were all gathered in his circular chamber. They sat with their coffee, wine, pates and cheeses, surrounded by Leopold's shelves of books, engaged in lively discussion. The group of ten included the young courtier in the red vest, Duke Kober, Spiess and the man with the jutting brow.

Leopold's old Hausmarchall was waxing strong. "Germany, I'm not sure there is such a thing. The wars have made us wary. We are now concerned only with our home environs. We are so various. Think of the light-hearted Bavarian and the smooth-tongued Saxon, the Frenchified Rhinelander and the somber Prussian. And the dialects! You can scarcely understand anyone in the town next door much less in the Hanseatic cities!"

"But a German spirit, a German character? I think yes," said Sebastian.

Duke Kober set his monocle to his eye and peered at Sebastian. "A universal language is what is needed."

"A German music that captures the German character," said Sebastian. "You will find it in some church music, but scarcely at all in our court music. We borrow from France, from Italy."

The old Hausmarchall pointed a knobby finger at him, "And yet, you use French forms for your orchestral suites."

"And Italian ideas for your concertos."

"Only a place to begin. The French move away from baroque textures, and the Italians spend their energies creating new opera tunes. I would exploit contrapuntal techniques to the limit."

"Yes! There is solidness in good counterpoint. The determination to work it out feels German."

"And surely orderliness is highly characteristic of the German?"

"As is piety," said Spiess.

"Perhaps," said the man with the jutting brow. "But what sort of piety are we alluding to? May there not be different definitions?

"Some of us in Prussia seek to organize our government to increase unity. We desire a new piety in which the individual desires to work toward the economic and cultural growth of the nation as a whole."

The next hour was taken up with discussions of Friedrich Wilhelm's goals in Prussia and England's disagreements with Spain. As they were adjourning to the common hall for the Wednesday night banquet, Prince Leopold introduced his Prussian guest to Sebastian. His name was Christian Ludwig. He was the Margrave of Brandenburg.

The Margrave bowed. "I was pleased to be among those who heard you play in Dresden last August."

That was it. Sebastian had seen the noble come in the morning of the contest with Marchand.

"After your victory," Leopold explained, "the Margrave asked me if you possessed the *savoir-faire* for composing for the orchestra that you do for improvising on the clavier. I told him that you write compendiums for every medium, that you walk about composing string fugues on invisible tablatures in your head, that you hum appoggiaturas and semi-quavers under your breath when birdsong even hints itself in our midst, that if any maestro had the ability to compose for any amalgamation, be it oboe da caccia, pomposa, zither, bagpipe, sheephorn, windmill, balustrade, gaglioni, or ocean tide, it would be you."

Sebastian grinned. Then he chuckled. Then he laughed. The button at his middle sprang loose, and still laughing, he bent to rescue it.

When he rose, the Margrave's face had relaxed into a smile. "I see you are a man of humor, and if honest also, tell me in truth if Leopold is exaggerating?"

"Well, I've not yet considered a concerto for balustrade, but I have begun experimenting with different textures—the harpsichord as a soloist against the orchestra, some new ideas utilizing the oboe, and a concerto for double violins."

The Margrave's eyebrows shot into his hair. "With Spiess and Leopold at the violins! Now that is something I would like to hear! May I have a preview this fortnight?"

"The concerto, as yet, is only in my head."

"Well, then, I must needs make the journey to Cothen again when the work is ready to be performed."

Sebastian spent the rest of the evening at the castle, feeling elated and a little smug. Yet another noble interested in his works and this one from the burgeoning state of Prussia.

And so Sebastian's days went. Never had a patron made him feel so affirmed. At night he composed furiously at his desk, and in the day he reveled in the enthusiasm of his Kapelle and the perspicacity of Leopold's guests. He wasn't home much, but he thought Barbara understood. By way of a resourceful peddler of Leopold's acquaintance, they'd managed to purchase Barbara's kitchenware soon after Christmas. Then with Sebastian's encouragement, she had used the alcove off the upstairs kitchen to create her own sewing closet. She had bustled about happily, furnishing it with curio cabinet, cherub candle holders, her father's portrait, a small writing desk, and a wide shelf she had Gottfried hinge to the wall for a cutting board. These private spaces for women were becoming more and more acceptable. Sebastian saw much possibility for good in it, not only a space to create but also an opportunity to meditate on eternal things.

4

Spring came with the surprise of red and yellow tulips blooming in the round side beds and stems of fragrant lavender under the front windows. But as Sebastian hurried home from the castle, he scarcely noticed the riot of color. He was late again for his student teaching.

Barbara met him at the door. There was reproach in her eyes.

"I know," Sebastian said. "I'm late again."

"Fortunately, a lackey brought word that your next student is ill. But Andreas! I've never seen a boy so nervous," she said. "He's been waiting an hour."

"The Prince desired instruction on a difficult passage."

Barbara looked as though she were going to say something else, but suddenly she drew in her breath, whirled and ran to the scullery.

Hmm! Sebastian thought. Andreas was standing in the music room doorway fidgeting.

"Come, let's get to it," said Sebastian.

He wondered if he should have canceled his lessons today. He had so much to do tonight. The Double Violin Concerto pressed him most. The first movement was almost finished, but the second eluded him. Every work had its own time, he knew that. If he pushed too much, the result would not be pleasing. But too long a wait might cause the Margrave to lose his enthusiasm.

He was also composing a cello suite for Schmidt. And he couldn't get by without practicing tonight. Tomorrow he would be performing the harpsichord concerto for the second time, this time to a bevy of guests from all over Saxony. The last thing he wanted to do was teach Andreas Breitkopf.

Andreas opened his composition book.

His pudgy face looked nebulous and indistinct. He squirmed on the bench.

"The definition of counterpoint, Andreas."

The boy fidgeted some more.

"Andreas! We've been working on this for three weeks."

"I—my tutor has been giving me so much work lately."

"All right, all right. We will learn it together then. 'Counterpoint. The art of adding a related but different melody . . . to a basic melody . . . in accordance with harmony.' Repeat after me."

He drilled the boy on the definition, then set him a counterpoint exercise. "Write a two-measure melody; then skip to the next staff and write the same melody two measures over, then down to the next staff and write the same melody four measures over."

When Andreas, with much squirming and blotting, had accomplished this, Sebastian instructed him to write counterpoint under the melodies when he got home—away from the keyboard.

"Now your finger exercises."

Andreas began playing the exercises. He was making the same mistakes he had at the last lesson.

Sebastian clenched his teeth with exasperation. "The thumb! Why aren't you using your thumb?"

"My other teacher . . ."

"The only sensible thing is to use the thumb."

Andreas tried again and struck more wrong notes. Sebastian's impatience roiled.

He jumped up and walked away, making an effort to let the boy finish the page, but it was too abominable. He swung around and slammed his hand on the bench with such force that Andreas sprung off it like a scared rabbit.

Sebastian slid onto the bench and attacked the keys. "Play it this way. Listen, Andreas! This phrase soft, this one loud, this staccato, popping every single note with identical precision. And here the thumbs move back and forth, in and out, smooth as hinges. Listen to yourself when you play. Smooth, steady, rhythmic."

Andreas was blinking back tears. Sebastian ignored them, slapping the exercise book shut and thrusting it at him. "Work, Andreas! I want the fingering perfect next time and the speed tripled."

Andreas stuffed his books into his folio while Sebastian flipped through the copy of Handel's *English Suites* that lay open on the mantel. He heard his pupil shuffle out, then Barbara's voice. She came to stand in the doorway.

"I deal with music all day at the castle, " Sebastian said, "and I'm fine. Then a half-hour with a student like this, and I've a horrendous headache." He was justifying himself, he knew.

Bernhard and Emmanuel scampered into the room. Emmanuel plopped down at the harpsichord, and Barbara picked up Bernhard.

"Everyone can't be a prodigy," she said.

"If you live, you work. If you love God, you do everything at the highest level of competency possible."

Barbara set Bernhard down with a jolt. Her fists flew to her hips, her elbows angling out like brown wings on a mother bird. "What does he know about such things? How can you expect him to write counterpoint and play those exercises as well as you can? He's only a little boy."

"I have no patience for students who don't practice. Anyone can try."

He saw no softening in Barbara's eyes.

"Diligence is all," he said.

"Is it? Is that what you really believe? Diligence is all? I'm not sure I agree."

She began walking away. He followed her.

"I need your patience," he said. "My work at the castle has been overwhelming."

"Others need your patience, and a little of your time."

"Stop that infernal plunking, Emmanuel," Sebastian shouted. "Haven't I told you to wait until I can instruct you properly?"

He turned back to Barbara, "Try to understand!"

Her lip started to tremble, but Emmanuel interrupted them with his slate of figures. "I can't work this problem."

Sebastian extended his hand, "Let me see, son."

Emmanuel hugged the slate to his chest, "Mama will help me."

Barbara knelt to look, and Sebastian watched them murmur over the calculations. He felt angry, hurt, confused and misunderstood. He wrenched his vest off the hall tree. "I'm returning to the castle. I'll be late getting home."

5

Later, Sebastian looked back at that altercation and realized that if he had had more time, or if he'd taken the time instead of trying to please Leopold's every whim, if he'd treated the Prince as though he were a man instead of a demigod, he would have seen what was happening to his marriage. He would have realized that the strain between him and Barbara was something far more profound than a lack of empathy over how difficult it was for him to teach ungifted students. Sebastian felt bad about the way he had vented his abominable anger upon her. She didn't deserve it, but he didn't see how he could make any changes at this particular time. So what he did was buy Barbara a gift—a pair of ruby combs for her hair.

She was wearing them the day she told him about the baby. He and Gottfried were in the workroom, experimenting with ideas for a lute-harpsichord. Sebastian could hear music for the lute that was almost impossible to play upon it, and the Prince had agreed that the ability to get a lute sound from a keyboard would be worth whatever time it took to perfect the invention.

"The plectrum at this angle, perhaps," said Gottfried. "The hinge forward."

They had secured an ordinary lute to a workbench and were experimenting with ways to depress the strings between frets while plucking them in the manner of a harpsichord. A short keyboard would control the whole apparatus.

"Now, stretch the wire down."

The wire cut through Sebastian's palms.

"I've spread an afternoon repast under the oak tree," Barbara said from the door. "I need to talk to you."

"Can it wait?"

"Please, this is important."

Guilt stung at Sebastian, then resentment. She waited. He hated the feel of her hovering, then hated himself for feeling that way. He wound the wire around its bolt, steadying his hand, taking it slowly, refusing to be rushed. When the wire was tethered, he took a deep breath, and by some grace, left Gottfried to finish. He followed Barbara outside.

When she told him, things began to fit. Another baby. Why hadn't he suspected? Of a sudden, his wife seemed infinitely precious. "Do you think you're strong enough to have another child?"

She shrugged. "There is this, though: I'm more excited about this baby than I've ever been before."

He threw back his head and laughed, "That's what you said last time, sweetheart."

She laughed too. "Did I? Well, I love being the mother of your children."

The green flicks sparked in her eyes. The rubies glistened in her black hair. He bent to kiss her. He must try to do better by her. Music wasn't all.

During the remaining months of her pregnancy, through the summer and the fall, Barbara went about singing lullabies in her husky alto and knitting sweaters and caps.

She never complained, but Sebastian could tell she often felt ill.

Her time came in mid-November. The labor lasted longer than the midwife expected it to, but there were no serious difficulties. And the baby was a fairy child. His hair was curly and blond, his face pixie-like, and his eyes the color of violets. They held you.

They decided to christen him Leopold August.

August and Elinor arrived for the christening ceremonies after Christmas. August looked like an amiable elephant in his looped-fringe velvet. How good it was to see him!

After the ceremonies, they relaxed together in the music room. August and Sebastian smoked their pipes while the women snipped and stitched at the new point d'Angleterre lace.

"When will you do me the honor of singing alto in my Kapelle?" August asked Barbara. "I now have musicians who answer only to me. Wilhelm and I have no dealings at all." He laughed as though it were a jest.

"And the quadrilles and card-playing do go on and on," said Elinor, squeezing her husband's trunk of an arm. "But I think I would not have it otherwise. Even the new theater has been fortuitous. Duchess Mariana has returned from Italy and found some zest for life upon the boards."

"And is Lorenz faring well with the Duke?" asked Sebastian.

"Wilhelm has no complaints that I know of. You trained Lorenz well."

Barbara looked up from her stitching. "Is Lorenz well?"

"He is to be married this summer," Elinor answered.

Sebastian saw surprise in Barbara's face. Quickly, she looked down.

Elinor continued, "Lorenz told me it is a marriage his family has hoped for for a long time. The daughter of a benefactor of his father's. If you ask me, though, Lorenz seems none too happy about the prospect."

The comment made Sebastian think of Margreta Buxtehude. Eventually, she had married an organist named Christian Schiefferdecker.

"A man I admired once told me that some of the best marriages do not commence for reasons of love," Sebastian said.

Barbara bent her head closer to her work, and Elinor seemed at a loss for words.

August was looking from Elinor to Barbara to Sebastian. He stood up. "You must show me this lute-harpsichord."

That Sebastian did willingly, and August loved the way it played. They spent so much time trying new music together that Barbara was already snuffing out the candles when Sebastian entered their bedroom.

That night they made love for the first time since the baby's birth. He'd almost forgotten the woman scent of her flesh. Had she ever wanted Lorenz? he wondered. The thought of it made him urgent. He encased his wife in his arms, kissing her until she gasped for breath.

But she pulled him more tightly to her, and his mind, his will and his emotions whirled in darkness, in light, in love, in need as powerful as a thunderous sea.

She was beautiful and giving and all his own.

"Until the 18th century people were helpless in the face of disease. Death claimed its regular tribute of infants."[1]

"The famous D Minor Concerto for Two Violins and Orchestra *is one of the happiest products of Bach's . . . genius. . . . In the second movement he reveals his incomparable ability to endow the {fugue} with intensely felt emotion."*[2]

8

Hauntings

1 7 1 9 — 1 7 2 0

It seemed to Barbara that the days of her recovery from Leo's birth would never end. She was always exhausted, and her appetite was poor.

It used to be that the highlight of her day was when Sebastian returned home. But he missed supper often now and sometimes even failed to return until after she had retired.

The burden of the children's education and discipline fell upon her more heavily than it had in the days of Weimar. Emmanuel was eager to learn and was especially partial to her, as second sons often were, but he was also stubborn and so intense that he wore her out. The only time she really felt happy was when she was alone with baby Leo. The baby's laughter came as easily as wind chimes at the touch of breeze. His violet eyes grew luminous when she sang to him, and when she ceased, they turned troubled.

She was his slave.

Spring came at last, and Barbara welcomed it with the fervor of a bride. Leo had survived the winter and the most precarious part of his infanthood. And now she could walk outside and let the warmth brew through her! How long it had been since she'd felt really warm!

Rain came and tulips and guests, and at long last, the premier of the Double Violin Concerto. Leopold's Kapelle would be performing the work in the Bach home with the Margrave of Brandenburg attending. The Prince had ordered the Bach's lower floors decked and trimmed until their home looked half a garden and half a colonnade. There were art treasures on the walls, floral silked sofas in the music and sitting rooms, and orange trees in pots everywhere you looked.

On the afternoon of the performance, Barbara stood on the second floor landing listening to the hum of voices swelling and jerking in the hall below. She adjusted her ruby hair combs and checked the train of her burgundy mantua. Sebastian had insisted she have a new dress made for the occasion.

She had selected the mantua style to hide her thinness.

Prince Leopold caught her eye and bounded up the stairs toward her. His face was rosy with excitement. Why did the sight of the Prince's intelligent, eager countenance always depress her these days?

Jealousy, she supposed.

Leopold kissed her hand. "Most lovely lady, we are indebted to you for the use of your home! My confectioner tells me he has taken your advice on the sweetmeats for tonight's table."

She curtsied, forcing herself to smile. "Yes, Your Honor."

"Is every one well? The baby? Sebastian tells me you have had difficulty regaining your strength."

Leopold's concern was genuine, and Barbara felt badly about her ill will. "All is well, Your Excellency."

Leopold offered her his arm and escorted her to the bottom of the stairs where he presented her to the Margrave of Brandenburg. The official's dress was severely military and his Prussian dialect so thick, she could scarcely understand it.

When introductions were accomplished, Barbara found a place on the sofa near the music room door and waited for the concert to begin. Gottfried took his seat at the harpsichord. Then a handful of musicians slotted themselves around him in a horseshoe arrangement of violins, bass viol, cellos and violas. They all wore black frock coats with red vests in a fine brocade the Prince had ordered for the occasion. Prince Leopold and Spiess took the soloists' positions near the harpsichord, and Sebastian strode quickly into place in front of the ensemble. He announced the number, then turned, hands clasped behind him, waiting until the room grew still.

He raised his scrolled baton and gave the downbeat: an ensemble introduction, smooth and running. Herr Spiess entered with the first four notes of his violin solo, brisk and staccato and moving into flowing sixteenths, answered by Prince Leopold; then the two violinists wove their lines together like tapestry, in and out, back and forth, one man tall and regal, the other angular and stooped, but working together as smoothly as hands on a grandfather clock.

The rhythm caught Barbara up. She lived in it, rested in it, was lifted by it. She could see rain beginning out the window, and in a minute, hail. She watched the silver as it pelted into the pink flowering branches of the apple tree. Leopold and Spiess bowed on, against the drama of the bending of the tree and the pelting downward of ice, the soft hail-beat of God's percussion.

Nature is God's instrumental music, Barbara thought. Yes, that's the answer. Sebastian needn't worry about using words in all of his creations. The Supreme Being doesn't.

She watched Sebastian as he conducted. His whole body was alive with the music. In every phrase he was affirming life.

The second movement began a new mood. Spiess' tone shimmered over the beauty of the new theme. The music was quiet, sad and intense with reality. Where did Sebastian get the inspiration for such beauty? she wondered. She wanted to feel every note, live every harmony, stay there forever.

But the melody ended, and the last movement leapt into the air. Every member of the Kapelle joined in like dance, a dance as vigorous and as serious as life. Spiess's first violin entered, yearning; Leopold's second answered, and a soft and rapid conversation commenced between.

Barbara glanced at the Margrave. He was leaning forward, entranced. The orchestra struck up a one-noted theme, with Gottfried's harpsichord continuo solid underneath. Then finally, the whole Kapelle brought the music, resounding, to a close.

No one moved. No one breathed. The moment was timeless.

Finally, the Margrave rose, peeled off his gloves and began clapping. Everyone rose with him.

The applause accelerated. It wouldn't be appeased until Sebastian agreed to perform another of his works.

Barbara was shaken. It had been so long since she'd heard one of Sebastian's compositions in its entirety. She had had no idea how much he had grown.

The rain continued its downpour. It seemed as though the skies were pouring down upon her the truth of who Johann Sebastian Bach was—not just her husband, not just another talented musician in the Bach family who had a vision, but a sage who someday would affect the lives of millions, a genius who had such power in him that the world would one day give him homage—but more than that, a healer, one who would bring the world such solace that his giving to it would always be more than it could ever give him.

Suddenly, Barbara felt very small and unworthy. To speak of oneness with her husband was a farce. Such greatness had little need of someone like her. The gap between them was a universe.

2

Little Leo died that September. Barbara was in the music room listening to Friedemann play his violin when Emmanuel burst in with scared eyes saying Dorothea couldn't get the baby to move.

Another baby held in her arms as cold as ice.

Barbara kissed the tiny nose and long blonde lashes. She sank into the rocking chair with him and softly sang to the back and forth.

The others tiptoed out. Only a month and a half more and Leo would have been a year old. The specter had no mercy.

Two days later, Barbara stood at her baby's graveside with her husband and family. Her breasts throbbed with the milk Leo would never drink. They shouted the unnaturalness of death.

When they returned home, Barbara's sister, Catherina, was standing on their doorstep.

Her ample form was black-bonneted and cloaked, her feet surrounded by bags. With a rush of relief, Barbara ran to embrace her, and for the first time that day, wept without restraint.

The days of Catherina's stay blurred, amorphous, forming and unforming, like a host of gray clouds: spending an afternoon with Sebastian at the castle and fleeing a rehearsal to stumble out into the fog; walking along the edges of the moat and seeing the willows weep with her, bending in a wet and sibilant sobbing; readying the children to leave for the harvest festival with Catherina, and wasting the whole day brooding into the silence with her knitting untouched in her lap.

When Catherina tried to read the Bible to her, Barbara refused to listen. On the last night of Catherina's two-week stay, the Kapelle was practicing in the music room. Barbara crept down to her sewing closet to think. They were rehearsing a concerto Sebastian had written on commission from the Margrave of Brandenburg. Such buoyant music so soon after Leo's death! It seemed almost blasphemous. Had Sebastian mourned his child at all? But that was unfair.

She had seen his tears.

She took the cherub candle stand from her curio cabinet and lit its candle. The reflection of the flame fluttered eerily in the unshuttered glass. Where is Leo now? she wondered. Where are the twins?

Is heaven real? She'd always assumed it was, but now that she was faced with the question in such a personal way, somehow a deeper more urgent way with Leo than any death that had previously touched her, she realized she wasn't at all sure. Maybe it was as the ancient naturalists said: the dead soul resides in the ground—Earth, the Mother of all life—waiting for the cycle to begin again, waiting for reincarnation. Or maybe the soul wandered eternally in a black void? What would it be like to be a spirit without a body? Barbara shivered, drawing her shawl more tightly about her as it began a merciless rain.

Was there an eternal fire for those who didn't believe? Or only nothingness? Was Leo still alive? Oh, how could she bear the thought that he wasn't? No, such an innocent loving soul would be alive somewhere, she was sure of it. And wherever he was, that place was now made near and dear to her because he was there.

"Sister! I thought you were in bed." Catherina's voice startled her.

But then Barbara felt her sister's strong arm wrap its warmth about her shoulders, hugging her the way she used to when they were children and the day had gone wrong. Together they watched the storm.

"The rain will turn to snow tonight, " Barbara said.

They stood that way for a long time, listening to the pounding. Finally, Catherina spoke, "It is better to be in the storm with God than to be in a fastness without Him."

"I am not with God," Barbara said. "I am alone."

Before Catherina left, she reminded Barbara of their father's words: "Whatever the darkness, put your hand to some worthy task. Discipline your mind to it. It will put your fears at bay."

She followed his dictum and by sheer force of will managed an almost normal Christmas celebration for the family. But in January she fell ill. Dorothea nursed her, plying her with dietetic treatments and teas at Barbara's own direction.

Gradually, the violence of her coughing decreased, but the slenderness of her strength remained. She hated the smell of her sick room. It reminded her of her mother's dark, fetid chambers. She must get well!

February arrived, and still she was needing to rest in the middle of the day. One afternoon, she was watching the cat lap up the milk Bernhard was pouring into its saucer. The cat had grown into an exquisite blue-gray creature with a long fluffy tail. It would probably have died if Barbara hadn't taken it in and offered it healing. Why hadn't she been able to keep Leo healthy? Why couldn't she heal herself?

Bernhard left, and a few minutes later, Gottfried burst into the room. He yanked his wig off his red haystack of hair and threw it and his music folio across the floor. "I am vexed beyond endurance. Uncle thinks all there is to life is music: practice, practice, practice, compose, compose. Change this. Improve that. Work harder! You can get it; you're just not practicing enough. Well, that might be all right for him, but for me, there's more to life than music. I have no time to do what *I* want to do, like inviting that girl at the bakeshop to the masquerade, or trying my hand at carving figures from life, not to speak of the footstools I must finish if I am to earn any thalers at the Spring Carnival. Uncle Sebastian has me playing the harpsichord at every single rehearsal and concert he gives, and sometimes he even insists I direct the whole rehearsal so he can go off someplace to write more music that's impossible to learn—cello suites, flute sonatas, harpsichord fugues, more Brandenburgs. The Margrave only commissioned one work. Will Uncle ever be done? And what about the children? He's spent no time with Emmanuel this whole month. Emmanuel told me yesterday he hated his father."

Gottfried dropped into the rocking chair and groaned, "Uncle Sebastian drives too hard, Aunt Barbara. Sometimes I think he's possessed."

Barbara wove her needle into the sock she was mending and stuffed it into her basket. Gottfried was such an amiable and succinct young man that these kinds of outbursts always surprised her.

"It's been three years since you began your apprenticeship," she said. "You need a holiday. Sometimes he forgets everyone else isn't as driven as he."

Gottfried ran a freckled hand through his hair. "It's not that I don't appreciate Uncle Sebastian. I know I'm not a brilliant musician, but he encourages me where I'm strong. 'You can plod,' he says, 'you can persevere. To this I owe all.'"

"He has his moments of humility. I'm sure he will understand your needing some time off. I will speak to him about it."

When Gottfried left, she thought about her own relationship to Sebastian. It was time they talked about it.

Barbara was still awake when Sebastian returned that night. He entered their bedroom balancing a tray. He was wearing the new gold-rimmed glasses Duke Kober had ground for him, and a shirt that was so tight it strained open between every button. He was becoming portly. I must have some new shirts made for him, Barbara thought, and breeches too.

"I've brought you a hefty portion of chocolate torte," he said. He brushed her cheek with his soft lips and scooted a chair up to the bed.

"We play at the castle tomorrow night—the second Brandenburg along with a host of miscellaneous pieces. The orchestral suite in D is a certainty. Leopold says the violin air in the slow movement possesses *Aufschwung* to an unusual degree."[3]

"Flight upward and away? Yes, I agree. How such inspiration comes to you I'll never understand! Friedemann was attempting the air last night, wasn't he?"

"With some success, but of course its intent is beyond Friedemann at his age."

Sebastian rubbed his stockinged feet and stretched his arms. "The commotion at the castle! Nobility from Berlin and Vienna arriving all day! Extra servants bustling about polishing silver and replacing evergreens with ivy, and the culinary chef frantic over all the cake sculptures the Prince has ordered. What with the cotillion tomorrow and all the literary discussions and music the next day, it is as taxing as a festival. Did I tell you the Margrave is coming?"

Barbara pushed her torte about on its plate while Sebastian elucidated detail after detail about the fete.

"You're not eating," he said finally.

"I need to talk to you." Barbara knew what she wanted to say to Sebastian. She'd procrastinated about it far too long. But now that the moment had come, she was fearful. She hated placing her neediness before him. What if he rebuked her? What if he even laughed and made her feel like a child?

She hedged. "I told Gottfried I would speak to you for him. I think he needs a holiday, perhaps even two or three weeks. He works so hard for you at the castle, and then with my being ill, he's been overloaded here too. He needs some time to socialize, to travel about. To go see Maria and Christoph and his brother and sister."

Sebastian frowned. "I need him."

"Couldn't you ask the Prince to plan fewer concerts in March? I'm sure you do more than he expects."

"Perhaps. I will think on it."

"There is something else."

"I am here."

"You might not like what I say."

"Say what you need to," he smiled. "I am yours."

"Are you?"

"You know that."

"No, Sebastian. I don't. I . . ." Lord have mercy, she was going to cry.

She forced herself on: "You've been different since we've been in Cothen, distant, unavailable. It hurts."

He drew back. "I am always available to you. You are imagining things."

"And so you think I'm crazy?"

"Yes. It is all in your imagination. Nothing has changed. I love you, and if you need me, I'm here for you."

"Even during Kapelle rehearsal hours? Even during the Prince's special fetes?"

"If it is urgent. Good musicianship is demanding. Art consumes. It occupies one's every waking hour—if not in the actual doing of it, the thinking out of it. My care for you does not change, but I need you to understand. I've enough to worry about without your dreaming up imaginary torments. Now eat so you can gain back your strength. I have to get to work."

His words came not as from the warm and sensitive man she loved, but as from a stone. He had put her emotions on trial and pronounced them unimportant.

She huddled into herself while he changed into his wrap and didn't meet his eyes when he bid her goodnight and left for his study.

When she could hear his step on the stair no longer, she wrapped her robe about her and ran up the staircase, through Gottfried's room where Friedemann was studying, and out the door to the landing on the outside stairs. It was frigid, but she wanted to feel the ice, the sharpness. There it was in the cold, clear sky: Polaris, at the end of the Little Bear, its tail stretched out because Zeus had pulled the hunter Arcas into the sky. Her father had taught her about the stars, and she had dreamed on Polaris before she was married. Tonight she vowed upon it. "I will never allow myself to be so vulnerable to my husband again. I will make my own life, apart from him. I will find strength elsewhere. I will cease baring my soul." It is the only way, she thought. Openness is too painful. Better to let the barriers grow between us and remain safe.

3

One March day after Kapelle rehearsal, Spiess informed Sebastian that George Frideric Handel was on the Continent on behalf of the English king.

Spiess had come to Sebastian complaining about the way some of the string players abused their instruments. "They let them sit about uncased and bandy them about as though they were toys. You must do something about it."

Sebastian promised to speak to the miscreants, and Spiess nodded, started his ritual casing of his own violin, then turned back suddenly.

"You might be interested to know that Handel is traveling through Germany engaging singers for the Royal Academy's first opera season. His mother lives in Halle, as you probably know, a mere day's ride away. They say Handel is visiting her even now.

"I dare say there will be a battalion of musicians pouring down on him— not me, though. I don't take to his borrowed English ways. A shame, I say, to see a German forsake his country the way he has."

Sebastian listened to the little man's harangue with interest. He didn't commit himself to Spiess on the issue of Handel's citizenship, but he did determine that if at all possible he would make the trip to Halle and at last meet this composer he so deeply admired.

Before he left the castle, he requested a few days leave from Leopold. The Prince agreed it was important he take advantage of this opportunity.

He and Gottfried walked home together, speaking of Handel's accomplishments.

Once at home, they joined Barbara, Dorothea and Emmanuel in the scullery, where they were folding linens.

Sebastian approached the subject of his trip with trepidation. "You know I've wanted to meet Handel for a long time," he said to Barbara. "He and I have so much in common that I'm sure it will be the beginning of a long and important friendship. Yes, an important friendship. There is this hope also: that he will help me publish and disperse my works."

To his surprise, Barbara did not gainsay his proposed trip. "Yes, you must go. You may never again have such a perfect opportunity to meet him."

It was six-year-old Emmanuel who looked up from his numbering of the linens and questioned him. "Why is Herr Handel so important?"

"He is a composer of stature, someone I can talk to about matters of music I am interested in."

Resentment flickered in Emmanuel's black eyes. "Herr Telemann could come to our house to talk to you, and you wouldn't have to go away."

Sebastian raised his eyebrows.

"Handel has great talents, Emmanuel," said Gottfried. "A rare gift for melody."

"Not to mention the dramatic effects in his operas," said Sebastian.

Gottfried dropped his hand on the little boy's shoulder. "Herr Telemann has not had the expanse of training and exposure that Handel has had. Italy, England."

"It is a chance to learn," said Sebastian.

Emmanuel started to say something else; but, Barbara shook her head at him, and the little boy set his quill back to reckoning and said no more.

Sebastian felt his son's resentment like a wall of missed notes between them, dissonant and preventing. Should he discipline him for disrespect? Should he apologize for wanting to travel to Halle? But no, there was no reason to apologize. He must go.

Sebastian sent a messenger to Halle ahead of him, and two mornings later, left Cothen at sunrise.

He traveled in great anticipation, expecting a whole day with Handel and maybe more. They would discuss their noble craft, and their discourse would possess about it a profundity and a spirit of kindredness unparalleled in his experience.

A mile from the university spires of Halle, Sebastian dispatched himself from the post wagon and finished the journey on foot. He blessed aloud the open road and the border of forest. He breathed in the freshness of the spring air. His satchels of music were heavy, but he felt as strong as he had when he trekked the roads to Hamburg in his teens. It was like wine to be in the open and free.

The squirrels were racing up and down the tree trunks on the edge of the road, jerking and darting and swirling after each other.

Striding along at a measured pace, Sebastian thought how nature's noise was so different from man's: the soft scurrying of the squirrels, the wind blowing through the trees, the chirps and twits of birds. All around him and above him spoke a voice profound in its silence.

He remembered what Barbara had told him about the parallel she saw between instrumental music and nature. Yes, her insight was true. Then he thought about how last month when she was still ill, she had said that she would never understand how his inspiration came to him. He should have told her that it was their lovemaking that had inspired the second movement of the Double Violin Concerto. Why had he never told her? Surely he was moving too fast through his days.

Sebastian found a hostel on the edge of the city, a good place, he thought, in which to headquarter during his time with Handel. The innkeeper, however, was anything but hospitable. He wore a black visor crammed so far over his visage that Sebastian could see nothing of his eyes. His jaws had walrus creases, and his tone was hostile. He shoved a pillow at Sebastian. "You will not find Handel pleased to see you."

"Is that so?"

"Handel's been staying at his mother's home now for three weeks, and I've had too many of you musician types staying here. They've trumpeted, and fiddled and drummed all times of the day and night. My wife and I can scarce keep our eyes open for want of sleep. His mother says George Frideric is tired of all of you also. If I were you, I'd turn right around and go back to wherever you came from."

"I've written him of the time of my arrival and must keep the appointment."

The walrus creases shook with the man's "humph" and scowl. "You'll be wanting victuals. Got stew and some wine."

"I'm certain Handel will provide some repast."

Sebastian carried his pillow and satchels up to his bed. There were several other cots in the room. Two of them were occupied by ragged-looking vagabonds who were snoring loudly. He must leave nothing unattended. Quickly he donned his wig and best shoes, then went whistling on his way.

The twilight had deepened into blue-black by the time he reached Handel's home.

He pushed through the well-oiled gate to the door, and thinking to put forth his best appearance, took off his glasses and tapped the brass knocker three times. No answer. All the shutters were closed, and he could see no glimmer of light. He heard an animal shake the bushes, then scurry across the road, but nothing from inside. He knocked again and again until finally the door opened a slit. All he could see was the glow of a candle.

"I am Johann Sebastian Bach, Kapellmeister to Prince Leopold of Cothen,'" he said. "Herr Handel is expecting me."

A quavery voice muttered something he couldn't understand.

He leaned closer. "I came to see George Frideric Handel! Is he at home?"

In the eerie light of the candle he saw a lace cap and a face cobwebbed with wrinkles. "He lives in London now."

The slit in the door narrowed. He moved closer, determined not to let this woman, whom he was sure must be Handel's mother, turn him away.

"Herr Handel is expecting me," he said again.

The woman's voice turned harsh. "He will see no one! I tell you, he's tired of all of you. He left an hour ago. Now go away and let an old woman rest."

She slammed the door so abruptly that Sebastian jerked back, dropped his glasses and stepped on them.

He bent to pick them up, feeling in the darkness. He encountered broken glass. A sliver pierced beneath his thumb nail. Anger rose up with the pain. Handel is probably there, he thought, and that old lady is just jealous of his popularity.

He stood up with a mind to pound upon the door until she was forced to open it again. But then he remembered himself and his dignity and knew he must take Handel's mother at her word. The innkeeper had tried to warn him, and he had been unwilling to hear. Handel had already left on his return journey to England.

Sebastian did his best to sweep the glass off the stoop. He wrapped his handkerchief about the bent gold frames Duke Kober had crafted for him and retreated through the gate and back toward the city.

Did Handel fail to receive my message? he wondered. Or did he receive it, and leave early to avoid me? His head began to ache with the strain to see in the moonless night. His eyes were getting worse.

At last he reached the edge of town where an occasional lantern lit the streets. By the time he reached the hostel, he was hungry and exhausted.

But the innkeeper simply glared at him and said all the victuals were gone.

Sebastian went to bed and fell into strange configurations of dreams: Handel tearing up the Suite in D Sebastian had brought to show him, and Handel's mother laughing at each loud tearing of the manuscript; an avalanche of power proceeding from inside Sebastian and sweeping Handel to his knees to beg forgiveness; and then scene after scene of Sebastian's pouring all he had into his composing for the rest of his life, and door after door being slammed in his face.

He woke sweating. Things were going so well with Prince Leopold. Why had this incident so disturbed him? He prayed, and after a good breakfast, quitted the city. He was eager to get home.

That night Barbara comforted him with honeyed bread and milk and brought him his old pair of glasses, which she'd stored away.

"Tell me everything," she said.

He did, and then confided his fears. "The ride home was one of the most miserable I've ever experienced. I felt joggled and bruised about like a sack of rutabagas. The scenery was like smudges on a painter's palette. The only thing that seemed real to me, Barbara, was the hold fear had upon me, a fear of failure and nothingness; yes, the fear of failure and of being when I died as though I had never been.

"I shape these forms today out of nothingness and wonder if they will ever be seen or heard. Will they be used and deemed strong? Or will they be relegated to some back room and never given a chance? Am I rejected because my works are mediocre, or because they possess a genius few can understand?"

Barbara reminded him that she saw greatness in him. She snuggled close to him and smoothed his aching head with her cool hands. The passion, however, did not leap up in him. He tried to summon it, but could not. Finally, Barbara sighed and turned over. Sebastian was left struggling for sleep.

4

Barbara's strength had rallied over the past few weeks, and she set herself to try to remember the scripture Catherina had read to her after Leo's death. "The God who raises the dead. Put Thou my tears in Thy bottle: are they not in Thy book? I am the Bread of Life." Such phrases came to her with a power she could only call "light."

She wrote to Catherina with a ruthless honesty. "How I hate the way Mother used to blame Providence for her illnesses. I can still hear her. 'I must bear the crosses Providence has willed.' And yet, she did not bear them well. She was constantly complaining and lashing out at Father. She said she was bending to God's hand, but she achieved nothing in her life but bitterness. Does God will infirmity and loss? How can I trust Him if he does?"

The contents of Catherina's answering letter surprised Barbara. "You loved Father so much," Catherina wrote. "What you remember about him is his ability to laugh and to charm. The truth is that though Mother may have been a complainer and caused us misery at times, it was Father who harbored the deepest bitterness. I heard Mother castigate him about it one night. 'How can I maintain any kind of faith during my daily trial if you will not even pray with me. Where else is there to go?'

"Father could not take the Church's criticism of his music. He ended by blaming God. I think that what he needed was some of your Sebastian's perseverance."

Barbara looked up from her reading. Perseverance, yes, my husband has that. His eye is ever on the goal. What might Father have accomplished if he had persevered?

She read on. "Father's bitterness revealed itself in subtle ways, like his ultimate refusal to write any new church music and his silence when men used profanity.

"His unwillingness to explore how God can be Love to us in the presence of suffering weakened Mother's faith. I would not reveal this to you even today, dear sister, but Father confessed to me his deep sorrow that he'd not encouraged you or Mother in the pursuit of God. He told me that some day you would need the strength that only the Supreme Being can provide. 'In that day, Catherina, by your love for me,' he said, 'swear that you will tell her the truth about me. I am deeply flawed.'"

Barbara let the sheet fall to her desk and gazed out the window, unseeing. The letter had reached a place in her where a knot was slowly being untied.

She wrestled for a few weeks, watching Sebastian go through his disappointment with Handel and feeling glad to be able to comfort him a little, but remaining true to her vow. She did not bother him with her own struggles.

Finally, one night in April, she woke with Sebastian breathing deeply beside her. She fought silently for an hour, then knew she could resist no longer. Trembling, she inched out of bed, slipped on her robe and padded downstairs and outside into the spring night.

She spoke to the night sky. Like a womb it seemed to her, like an unthinkable embrace that obliterated and enlarged. The scent of lavender touched her upon a suddenly holy air.

Barbara dropped to her knees. She prayed out loud, "I have thought it was all up to me. I thought if I worked hard enough, I could make everything all right by myself. But I can't, Father."

Release, surprise and joy flamed through her. Never before had she called the Supreme Being "Father." She fell on her face and saw without seeing the triangle of flame that surrounded her obeisance. The Father, the Holy Ghost and the Sin Bearer who was the Son, embraced her with love and provision. She was no longer alone.

In "Regency France and the multitude of petty German courts which aped the French example . . . political, economic, and moral confusion prevailed and reinforced each other. Debauchery and avarice were rampant."[1]

"Alas! yes, it is my duty to act according as I reason! But is action within my power? What aid would I not need in order to forget Manon's charms?"[2]

9

The Spas
1 7 2 0

Sebastian's downheartedness over the Handel affair didn't last very long. As soon as he plunged back into the atmosphere of Leopold's enthusiasm at the making of fine music, he wondered why it had bothered him at all. He wasn't even overly concerned that the Margrave had failed to comment on the concerto he'd written and performed for him in February. Sebastian hadn't finished the collection he had in mind.

He would simply keep composing until he had a compendium of sounds for the orchestra that could not fail to please the Brandenburg noble, or anyone who knew anything about music.

After the May Day celebrations, Leopold asked Sebastian to accompany him to Bohemia as he had the year before.

Sebastian, Spiess, Wideburg, Schmidt and several others from the Kapelle, along with Duke Kober and later Picander, were to be the Prince's guests at the Carlsbad spas. Sebastian had enjoyed the respite so much the summer before that he said yes without even mentioning it to Barbara. He would leave with the Prince on June 1 and be gone for two months.

When the day arrived, Sebastian rolled away in the royal carriage experiencing once more that adventurous feel. Long, white clouds moved above them like wagon trains extending into the blue. They traveled in three carriages. His companions were Prince Leopold, Spiess and Duke Kober. The conversation reminded him of the philosophizing he had enjoyed so much when they'd journeyed to Dresden three years before. Leopold primed them to probe the meaning of art, and Duke Kober challenged them toward thought that was empirically sound. They discussed the requirements for a perfect work of art—"a rigorous technique but also a secret influence from heaven—The artist must have a gift of genius from birth. Or must he?—Perhaps, but a rigorous technique is essential—Music is a science. Or is it?" The new thinkers insisted it was. The rules were to be laid down and followed meticulously. "Can music contain truth even when there are no words? What is truth? Does not all beauty contain truth?" They couldn't come to an agreement on that question, but they did agree that if the poet in words or music portrayed his subject in its simple truth, he would satisfy the highest standard of beauty.

They journeyed southeast to Bohemia, enduring the extremes of temperature with good will and enjoying the beauty of the ascending terrain. Bohemia was known for its proliferation of musicianship, and that in itself would have been sufficient reason for Sebastian to look forward to these summer journeys. Four days into their trip, they stayed the night at their first Bohemian inn. A band of street musicians came to salute them, playing minuets and polonaises upon the harp, violin and horn. The next morning in the marketplace, it was the triangle and the harp, played by school boys hoping to earn a few kreuzers.

Sebastian was waiting in line at the apple cart, listening to the strum and the bell, when the buxom woman in front of him set her child down to hold on to her skirts.

Sebastian glanced at him and gasped. He was staring at a blue-eyed, blond-haired boy who looked exactly like little Leo.

He was about to lift the child into his arms when the mother turned with a cry. Sebastian stammered his apologies, but seeing she would not be calmed, he pivoted, reeling, and stumbled away.

Seeking refuge from the heat and the clamor of the animals and the music and the merchants hawking their wares, he stopped under the eaves of one of the stores. His breath came hard.

Grief seized him—memories, a gap in the circle of space and time where no gap should be. He thought of the day only two weeks before Leo's death when the child had leaned from Barbara's lap to grab at his violin bow. Sebastian had secured his smallest teaching violin and set it on the little boy's shoulder, plucking at it, so that Leo had smiled and whimpered for more.

The cello suite he'd written after the child's death wailed through his mind. It said all the things about his loss he'd never been able to verbalize to anyone. I haven't taken enough time to mourn the child, he thought. He closed his eyes and let the composition sing on. He mourned the presence lost to him.

Then he remembered Barbara's face, the way it had looked the morning he'd left for Carlsbad—translucent and strained. She'd extended her hand for him to kiss, said, "God speed," then turned quickly away.

She had been so withdrawn since Leo's death. The only time he'd noticed that enthusiastic little jerking of her chin was Christmas afternoon when August and Elinor had brought them gifts. Barbara needed to get out more. Leopold's September cotillion would be just the thing. I'll purchase her a bolt of blue silk in Prague, he thought. She can make a new dress.

When Leopold's caravan rolled into Carlsbad several hours later, Sebastian deposited his bags in his attic room, tugged on his boots and an old summer coat, and left through the backdoor. He needed to be out and away from everyone, in order to get perspective on what he'd like to achieve while he was here.

Everything was as he remembered it—the outdoor pool behind the mansion-like building, a dozen or so guests soaking in the pool—mostly old men in degrees of undress—then the trail up the mountain into the pine trees. He plunged into the forest.

The pungent smell of pine reminded him of his boyhood treks in the forests of Thuringia. He was thirty-five years old now, but the vigor of his work and prospects made him feel like a youth.

Up the mountain he continued, passing resting places along the way: a gazebo, a bench, a fountain of spring water funneled through a stone spout.

He bent to drink. The liquid ran down cool, the taste so bitter he grimaced. He bent to drink again. Carlsbad's mineral water was thought to contain traces of arsenic, which, like an inoculation, had the power to cure dyspepsia and all manner of evil humors.

Sebastian continued his climb, noting plumes of steam curling through the trees at each scenic view. Most of the springs lay in sight of snow-covered peaks. He lingered at a particularly wide vista. How small we are, he thought. And how vast is God! One needed a visit to the mountains from time to time to be reminded. Carlsbad was a stopping place for nobles from all over Europe: every part of Germany from Bavaria to Brandenburg, and also Russia, Italy, Poland, Austria, England, France, The Netherlands, and even Sweden. He hoped this time to meet someone who would be impressed enough with his orchestral works to fund their publishing. Leopold had helped him gain the favor of a Leipzig publisher and wanted to help Sebastian further, but his funds were dwindling. It seemed as though some composers were instantly awarded publication, and others had to waste their time ingratiating themselves with publishers and patrons all over Europe before anything was ever seen in print. Nothing in Sebastian's life ever seemed to come easily.

Up the mountain the jet of a geyser shot higher than any of the spouts around it, and then another, even higher. This one could not be more than five hundred feet away. The wind picked up, and Sebastian felt the drizzle about his head and shoulders. Suddenly uneasy, he buttoned his coat tightly at the middle, and plunged back into the woods. The place was beginning to seem more infernal than curative.

2

He saw her for the first time that night.

He was making his way through the lobby when he noticed a young auburn-haired noblewoman helping an old man up the stairs. Servants trailed behind carrying valises and trunks, and Sebastian wondered that the Lady did not ask one of them to help her with her charge. The man was weak and bent, his whole body a tremor. Patiently she guided him into a suite off the first landing. Her pretty face was filled with concern.

Sebastian had made it his habit to quickly quit the premises when he saw a woman to whom he was attracted. His libido was strong. There was a magnetism about this woman, however, that kept him lingering—only to determine if the compassion he'd sensed in her was real, he told himself.

Soon she returned to the lobby. She nodded at Sebastian, then spoke to the clerk behind the marble counter, "My husband requires a map of the baths."

She spoke excellent German, with a trace of French accent.

Sebastian leaned against the marble counter, thinking to request his key. She smiled at him. Her lips were painted deep plum to match her dress, and her amber eyes were huge and merry.

"You are here to take the baths?" she asked. She scanned him from head to foot.

Sebastian felt the heat rise. He hesitated.

"Perhaps you've come for Carlsbad's renowned offerings of drama and music? Or are you seeking games of chance?"

When Sebastian still said nothing, she tilted her head at him, her eyes teasing. "Or yes, you are seeking love?"

"Definitely not that," said Sebastian. "I'm a guest of Prince Leopold, a member of his Kapelle."

"You are not the man they are calling the Prince of Claviers!"

Sebastian bowed. "Guilty. But really, it is quite ridiculous."

"Now why would you say that?" It wasn't an idle question. She was really interested.

They talked a few minutes more, long enough for Sebastian to learn that music was one of her passions.

A rough voice interrupted them in French, "Countess, you are late!"

"Marquis Dubois!" Her tone was gracious. "How good to have found you so soon." She lifted her arm gracefully, and the nobleman bent to kiss her hand.

His wig was black with spiraled curls. Lace drooped from the sleeves of his blue coat, and he wore silk stockings that showed off his calves.

"Marquis Charles Dubois, this is the Prince of Claviers himself."

The Marquis scrutinized Sebastian as though he were a wall hanging.

"Prince Leopold's servant?"

"Really, Charles, he is the best of German musicians."

The wrinkles across the top of the Marquis' aquiline nose deepened. "Then we will be entertained. Get on to your practice, fellow."

Sebastian rooted himself angrily to his place at the counter.

Marquis Dubois shook his head, muttering something about servants not knowing their place anymore. He offered his arm to the countess, and she smiled apologetically over her shoulder as she glided away.

Sebastian stood bemused. There was an inner beauty and a vulnerability in this countess that drew him. He must set his mind to avoid her.

Two hours later, Sebastian and Prince Leopold were discussing the concerts they would be giving in Carlsbad when several women burst into the room. They pounced on the Prince like hungry cats.

"Leopold, you must attend with us / a play based on a work by Cervantes / props like none you've ever seen / the actor a young prodigy / Your predilection for the new will certainly / seats near the stage / You simply must . . ."

The group consisted of a short, fat woman whose fan fluttered as fast as her lips, a lady in navy brocade who was slim and graying, a middle-aged woman bedecked with jewels who was plain as a turnip, and the magnetic young countess herself. It was she who stilled the bedlam.

"Ladies, control yourselves. The Prince will think we are simpletons. My dear Leopold, you simply must accompany us to the Colonnade this evening. Cervantes' *Don Quixote* has never been seen in such a light."

"Why should I be intrigued with other talent when I have the pride of Germany in my own court?" Leopold asked. "Ladies, my Kapellmeister Johann Sebastian Bach. Sebastian, Countess Eugenia Brock, the Marquise Delacroix, Lady . . ."

But Sebastian heard none of the other names.

Eugenia, Eugenia Brock.

The Prince was speaking to him. "What is it we are playing tomorrow night, Kapellmeister? Sebastian!"

"Your pardon, Excellency. The Double Violin Concerto.

Eugenia's amber eyes held a special light in them, an interest beyond that of any of the other ladies. "And improvisations?"

Sebastian bowed. "Whatever my Lady requests."

The ladies left, and immediately the Prince's chamber door once again swung inward.

It was Duke Kober. He stared after the noblewomen, adjusted his monocle and winked at Leopold. "So it is as I predicted. Countess Eugenia is here."

"With her ancient husband."

"He stays in the baths?"

"And Marquis Dubois takes advantage."

"The French aristocracy have an intriguing propensity for affairs."

"I hear the Marquis has quarreled with the beautiful Eugenia."

"Her fortune has brought her only trouble."

Sebastian soon discovered that avoiding Countess Eugenia wasn't going to be easy. She was the first to approach him after his concert. She extended her hand for him to kiss. "Your rendition of my ballade was exquisite. You have the power to make a heavy heart light."

Sebastian was pleased out of all proportion. He told himself every new acquaintance with nobility was important. It was only sensible that he at least show an interest. "And you know this because it is what you experienced?" he asked.

"I found the dialogue in your concerto's slow movement haunting."

"Haunting? Others have found it meditative."

"It had me meditating on the mystery of a good marriage and how your marriage must suit you. My husband has grown old before his time. We do not . . . He can't . . ."

Embarrassed, Sebastian took her arm and moved her away from the crowd. The night was warm, her arm bare and soft, her perfume exotic. He halted when they reached the gardened walk, looked down at her and was surprised to see tears in her eyes.

She brushed her cheek. "I apologize. You Germans must think we are a dissolute people. But it is a part of our culture, part of the way we cope with the uncertainty of our times. Some of your music is so intimate. I thought you would understand."

"I have a good marriage," Sebastian said.

"She is beautiful?"

"She is."

"Ah."

Countess Eugenia fell silent as they strolled on among the flowering plants. Suddenly she pointed toward the sky. "Look."

A fuzzy gold ring was circling a disk of moon and turning across it were the wings of a bird. Silently they watched.

Countess Eugenia's amber eyes shone. When they could see the bird no longer, she spoke, "We have a bird sanctuary at home. The Count has re-planted trees."

They talked for a while of the beauties in nature and the why of art, and when she finally rustled away, Sebastian stood watching after her. His insides were churning. A half-hour more with her and he would have been lost.

He must not forget to whom he belonged.

3

In Cothen several weeks later, Barbara was perusing the calendar Maria had given her.

She found herself increasingly glad for the liturgical year. She'd looked back to Advent and Epiphany, pondering. She'd taken seriously the personal evaluation required at Lent. And Easter, after her God-encounter, had possessed high, new meaning. Life so easily sunk into a senseless round of scrubbing floors, washing clothes and cooking. The liturgical shapings of the year provided a firm path upon which she could walk.

Ever since January she had been using the ample blocks of her calendar for recording important events and thoughts: Friedemann's first harpsichord lesson; Emmanuel's triumph in the arithmetic tournament at the village school; an organ work of Sebastian's accepted by a Leipzig publisher; Sebastian's trip to Halle, then Carlsbad. In the block for today, she penned in "Gottfried leaves for Ohrdruf." Then she gathered up the shirts she'd ironed for Gottfried and took them to his attic room.

He was strapping a gift for his mother, one of his small hand-carved stools, onto his rucksack.

"Are you sure you will be all right?" he asked.

"Sebastian will be home soon, and Dorothea is a great help. I would, however, appreciate a couple of hours in the countryside before you leave."

Gottfried agreed to watch Bernhard and Emmanuel, and soon Barbara was tying on her bonnet and hurrying outside. She walked the dusty trails and hills toward the field of wildflowers she was looking for, then across the field to the brook and the copse of trees. She relaxed in the shade. Ever since Sebastian had left, the emptiness of the house had seemed a monstrous mouth that threatened to swallow her. And without Gottfried, either—

She prayed at the brook, as had been her habit ever since that pivotal April day. She begged God to grant her the grace of His Presence. Sometimes she felt Him so near that she could almost touch Him. In those moments, nothing else mattered.

Today, however, she prayed, she listened, and she waited; but He did not come. He was so elusive. Just when you thought you'd got hold of Him, He disappeared.

Restless, she struck out across the hills. She walked and walked. She ignored the growing pain in her stomach. Then she realized her vision was blurring, and her legs were beginning to shake. The pain in her abdomen increased.

One foot in front of another. "Give me the strength to walk the distance."

Somehow she reached home. Immediately, Gottfried abandoned his plans to leave and helped her upstairs and into bed. When she woke, the pain was gone. She hurried down to the kitchen to begin the evening meal.

Dorothea entered with the sprinkling bucket. "Mama, you're up. I was going to water the flowers."

Yes, the pinks on the sill looked wilted. They had flowered and multiplied far more than she'd expected this last month. They'd even survived a knocking over by Bernhard and an afternoon of wind outdoors.

Today, however, they were like dancers drooping, limp, their heads hung down. Barbara seized the watering can and poured life into them with her will and hand. Strange that after all these days of standing tall to take whatever came, to bloom the more at every onslaught, they would suddenly fail.

The night on the garden walk, when Sebastian realized how vulnerable he was in Eugenia's presence, he set himself a rigid program of reading the catechism and composing. He determined that he would emerge from his studies to perform when Leopold wanted him to, but leave the moment the last note was sounded. He allowed himself several visits to services and concerts at the Church of the Convent of the Holy Cross, and sometimes spent an afternoon in the Spas' expansive library. A volume he found by the French Jesuit Pascal proved profitable. These activities he allowed, but the cotillions and nightly games of cards he avoided. Dramas too, he forswore. The Sclavonian dialect in one play he attended with Schmidt was difficult to understand, but it was so overtly sensuous that he'd left aching with lust.

His resolutions lasted until the last week of their stay.

Picander arrived on Monday. After a morning hour in the baths, Prince Leopold, Spiess, Duke Kober, Picander and Sebastian relaxed on the columned porch. They could see the gabled rooftops of houses below, and above and to the right, the rickrack of snowcapped mountains.

Picander was wearing a gold shift that revealed his muscular legs and biceps. Prince Leopold had thrown on a maroon velvet wrap. His blonde hair was frizzed out, still damp about his face. "And how is France?" he asked Picander.

Picander fingered the wooden cross about his neck and grinned. "Intellectual discourses after every meal and the possibility of love on every corner. Which of course, I had to avoid meticulously as a good Catholic and as a man who wanted to keep his mind clear. It was my intention to learn all I could about Montesquieu before I took up my new post in Leipzig."

He tapped the brochure he'd tossed on the table. "A portion of Montesquieu's *Persian Letters,* to be published within the next year. The French *philosophe* continues in the spirit of Descartes' rationalism, but he is skeptical about the value of the past. He believes institutions must change; the natural in man must be upheld by human law."

Sebastian leaned forward. "And how exactly does Montesquieu define this idea of the natural?"

"Liberty, the pursuit of happiness."

"Not to mention equality."

"An item of no small importance."

"But does man have such rights, in truth?" Sebastian asked. "The right to happiness for instance?"

Leopold's cobalt eyes danced. "Of course he does, *L'Escholles des Filles, amour, vous plazer.* Everything in a man shouts the need for it, the fact that we were made for it. Sebastian, don't tell me you don't wish to be happy."

"Pascal says no matter how much we seek happiness, how much we desire it, it is not possible upon this earth. No, not possible on this earth."

"Besides, there is duty," said Spiess. "A man has things he is bound to do whether they bring him happiness or not. He works hard for his family. It is a thing of pride, of honor, of civility. It is part of being German."

Duke Kober groaned. "I have two uncles whose sole reason for living is duty. The room is a tomb when they dominate it. I look at the Frenchmen here . . . and the French women . . ."

"Ah, the French women. And where is yours this morning?" teased Leopold.

Everyone guffawed. Duke Kober had been seen in the company of a certain French woman almost constantly during their five-week sojourn.

Kober ignored Picander. "Most Germans err in their unabated solemn-mindedness. Despite my own serious interest in science and certain dutiful regimes, I believe laughter and women are necessary for a man's well-being, at least occasionally."

Sebastian thought about how alive he'd felt when he was in Eugenia's presence. It was the kind of aliveness, yes, happiness, that he used to feel with Barbara. Now they went through the motions of love, but only as routine. He'd been so busy the last year that he'd not thought that much about it. But yes, it was true that their passion had lessened considerably. And now he realized he was hungry for that passion. It was a need.

That afternoon when he tried to concentrate on his composing he couldn't. He paced.

His feelings were exacerbated by the atmosphere of the Spas: the feasts, the nightly dancing, the half-exposed bosoms, the perfume. This summer there seemed to be only a handful of Carlsbad guests who were under a doctor's guidance, and a majority who had come for pleasure. He listened to the voices filtering past his room. He strained to hear that one voice.

Music drifted up from the Colonnade. He thought of Duke Kober's description of his uncles, so committed to duty. Deadness could be the result if one never made it a point to enjoy the pleasures God had given. We are instructed to take time off from our labors, Sebastian thought. I'm not accomplishing anything here. Might as well go watch the dancing.

He donned his long blonde wig and an embroidered vest he'd purchased in Prague.

The minute he walked into the Colonnade, he heard her voice.

"Surely, you don't expect . . ."

"I expect you to treat me as something other than a convenience." The voices were coming from a sitting room off the atrium.

"But the Count insists," said Eugenia.

"He's practically on his deathbed. What does it matter? You either come with me right now, or I'll inform the Count you're carrying my child." It was the voice of Marquis Dubois, Sebastian was sure.

"You wouldn't."

"Wouldn't I?"

Their argument continued, the Marquis' tone growing louder.

Then Sebastian heard a slap and a cry. He'd almost reached the door when the Marquis slammed out and down the steps.

Eugenia was standing in the middle of the sitting room with her head bowed, her mauve lips quivering, and a fiery mark on her cheek. Sebastian strode toward her, but when she saw him, she covered her cheek and backed away. "I am ashamed."

"And I am enraged! You must tell me how I can help."

She studied his face a moment, then lifted her chin, threw back her white shoulders, and tucked her hand through his arm. "You can dance with me."

His emotions warred within him. He'd seen her only at a distance for four weeks, and now when she was near and needy, he couldn't abandon her. He would dance with her once.

She danced supplely, effortlessly—an English contre-danse. Then he consented to a minuet. They approached and retreated to the stately music, hand in hand, side by side, now facing, now gliding past one another. It was a dance of courtship, and each time he was forced to change partners, he was less willing to let her go.[3] She was like a willow tree, waving softly to the colors of life, taking in with intense enjoyment whatever pleasing thing offered itself. Fear seemed foreign to her. Was this what it was like to live naturally, seizing life while you can? Was this what it was like to be free, to live unhampered by restrictions? Why couldn't he just let go?

After the minuet, Eugenia invited Prince Leopold to gather his companions. She wanted them to join her and her cortege for a late afternoon picnic.

"I have only arrived," Picander said to Sebastian, "and if you do not join us, I will be deeply offended."

The scriptural warning was like a trumpet in Sebastian's thinking: "Make no provision for the flesh to fulfill the lust thereof." But he muted it. "All right," he said, "but I must return early."

He told himself it was only a picnic, and there would be a large group. He would honor the scriptural injunction by refusing to allow himself to be with Eugenia alone.

They picnicked near a gazebo, outside a walled garden a short distance up the mountain. Afterward, Sebastian could remember nothing of the discussion Picander initiated. Eugenia's presence was all. She wore a loose ankle-length frock the color of roses. Her auburn hair fell in waves down her back, and she wore a gold locket around her neck.

Sebastian feasted on succulent lamb, aware of her every move: the way she nibbled at a peach, dabbing the corners of her mouth daintily with a cloth; the way she played with her locket. She was gracious to everyone, noting everyone's need, filling glasses and plates from her basket and flasks, as though she were the servant instead of the countess. Occasionally she lapsed into quiet.

Was she remembering the threat of the Marquis, Sebastian wondered? Was she really carrying his baby? The man's brutality sickened him. He wished he could show her the gentleness she deserved. With that thought he put down his glass. It was time for him to return.

Just then Prince Leopold announced it was time to leave.

Eugenia touched Sebastian's arm, "Humor me. While they are beginning the trek down, come with my maidservant and me to see the garden. My father contributed to its design."

Sebastian took a deep breath and frowned. "Don't worry," Eugenia laughed. "We will only be five minutes. The Marquis awaits me. Bring Picander if you wish."

Sebastian and Picander followed her and the maid through the gate of the woven wicker fence. Eugenia trailed her hand in a fountained pool. Finches twittered. They passed a trellis of pink roses. Picander commented on their delicacy. The air was heavy with their scent.

Picander lingered by the trellis, and up ahead Sebastian saw Eugenia whispering to her maid. The maid took the right trail, while Eugenia took the left toward an ancient oak. She glanced at Sebastian and beckoned. With a swirl of her rose skirts, she disappeared.

War erupted inside of Sebastian. His desire for Eugenia roared within him, and above the roar, a clash like that of swords.

It was the clarion shout of the Christ within him, calling him to the Eternal, battling against Another who whispered of ecstasy now.

It took every vestige of will power, every iota of spiritual strength within him to turn his face in the opposite direction, stride past Picander, out the wicker gate, past the gazebo and down the mountain.

When he reached the safety of his room, he fell to his knees and wept.

5

The journey home was interminable, a whole week that seemed a month. Sebastian received no letter from Barbara while he was gone, but he'd not written to her either.

The day before their departure from Carlsbad, he'd visited Prague and selected a bolt of blue silk for her and gifts of sweetmeats and baubles for the children. Otherwise, he'd hardly left his room during that last week. Leopold was not pleased, nor Picander. But he couldn't help it. If they were truly his friends, they would at least give him the room of his convictions.

He was eager to see Barbara. The closer the caravan drew to Prince

Leopold's domain, the more impatient Sebastian became with his companions' esoteric wranglings. It wouldn't be long, he knew, until he became hungry again for intellectual stimulation. But two months of abstract thinking with no solutions were enough for a while. He longed for Barbara's uncomplicated practicality.

At last they reached the outskirts of Cothen. The Prince disembarked at the castle, instructing the coachman to drive Sebastian and the others home. Through the side streets Schmidt, Duke Kober and Sebastian rode to Schmidt's house. The cellist's son was out playing a game of chase with a friend. Stopping in the middle of the chase, the boy spoke to Schmidt, and they stood staring after Sebastian as the coach lumbered on.

Through the marketplace the coach clattered, and past the bakery. The baker was washing windows. When Sebastian shouted greetings to him, he looked up, nodded and frowned. No "Best of the day to you!" as usual. Every acquaintance Sebastian saw met his "Good Day," with a nod, a somber face and a growing still. Duke Kober noticed. They shared an uneasy silence.

They drove past the post house and through the orchards that separated the outskirts of Cothen from home. Sebastian caught glimpses of his red-peaked roof. Some weather was building up in the north. It was windy but still warm. The carriage turned the bend in the road, and there it was in full sight. Home, at last. The horses slowed.

Where are the children? Sebastian wondered. Not outside as usual. The pinks Barbara planted in the tulip beds look as though they've not been watered for weeks. Even when Barbara has to be in bed, she makes sure things are kept on schedule. Is one of the children sick? By now someone should have heard the horses and come out to greet me.

Sebastian jumped from the still moving coach and ran toward the door. It was locked. He rattled the knocker. He could hear no music or laughter.

The horses snorted and heaved behind him. Duke Kober got out and began walking up the path. Sebastian looked around. Then he saw it. High above his head, nailed into the lintel, was a black wreath. Frantic, he rattled the knocker again.

At last someone began to open the door. Barbara's sister Catherina stood before him dressed in black. She was holding Emmanuel's hand. For a moment they stared at each other, then Emmanuel bolted back into the house crying.

Sebastian's eyes locked with Catherina's. He mouthed the unthinkable, "Barbara?"

"We buried her two days ago."

Interlude Two

Sebastian's violin wandered heavily through the rooms of space and time, wondering, pleading, weeping—praying even—for death. Catherina was there, and the children, and now Elinor, her small face crumpled under her mourning veil. August sat with him, and Sebastian played on.

He had to find an anchor, an answer to his torment.

He agonized in strings of dissonant lines. He spoke the complexities of his wonderings. Where is she? Is it my fault? Where are you, God? What does a man do when he's lost half of his being? Was it me? Was it here? Was it Carlsbad? Or was it simply Barbara's time?

He stood at her grave with night falling. He heard Dorothea's voice. "Papa, you must come home."

He did not heed. He couldn't leave Barbara alone. He had to know where she was. He must beg her forgiveness. He must make her know the faithfulness of his heart.

He could see her now the way she was the night the twins were born! He'd followed the midwife into their bedroom, and there, like a Rubens painting, night-black hair draped across her shoulders, face shining like a Grecian goddess, Barbara was sitting up in bed, cradling a tiny infant in each arm. He'd thought that to lose *a child was the most piercing hurt, but no, to lose the wife with whom you had been one, that was unbearable.*

How foolish now his drivenness seemed—like striving for the wind when he'd had everything he needed at his side! His dreams, his victories, his needs, his cares, his God-anchoring, his God questions, his old age, all of it he'd planned to share with her. He'd never even told her how she had inspired him. Come, come sweet death. I long to join you.

Emmanuel seldom spoke, but in his darkened eyes, Sebastian saw the blame.

August was there with roses, and the violins sang of Ernst and Ambrosius and Sophie and Christoph and little Leo and Maria Barbara Bach.

He made the weary effort to dance the daily duty. The circles widened and spiraled. The shadow of his lamp spiked larger and more angular than the lamp itself, like the reality beneath his life, large with shadowed extreme. He'd inflated ambition, flaunted freedom and bowed too expansively to the philosophies of men.

Delusion!

Is it all my fault? he asked. Have You cut out my heart because of my sin? Of his encounter with God, Pascal had written "FIRE! God of Abraham, God of Isaac, God of Jacob, not of the philosophers and scholars . . . Jesus Christ. Jesus Christ. I have separated myself from Him. I have fled from Him, denied Him, crucified Him . . . Let me never be separated from him . . . I will not forget Thy words."*

Yes, thought Sebastian. And of a sudden, he saw a shimmer of green. God understood. Even his lust for Eugenia, He understood. She was a passing thought. In the whole of his personhood, she was nothing more than a moment. Jesus Christ was his heart.

The violin began its upward flight. He would have fallen, if God in His persistent mercy had not in the last moment strengthened him. And yet, his passion was so urgent, his imaginings so real! He played on, and he prayed. He must choose to believe again: His God was a god of second chances. In this green and cleansing place he would rest. He would wait on His word.

*Blaise Pascal, Conversions

"There had been edicts since the fifteenth . . . {century} forbidding citizens to allow their pigs to run about the streets . . . but pig-sties {existed} . . . in Berlin 'til nearly the end of the seventeenth century and . . . Weimar still had {its}town herdsman at the end of the eighteenth century."[1]

> *"Come, thou sweet hour of death,*
> *That my soul sups on honey*
> *From the lion's mouth;*
> *Make my departure sweet,*
> *Do not delay, final light. . . ."[2]*

IO

Loss

1 7 2 0

"My word, Sebastian, it's only a little over a month since Barbara died, and you've written all this! I cannot get my fingers around it."

"It will challenge Your Excellency."

"I cannot hear these Partitas, much less play them. I will leave them to Spiess. You must come with us for a drive. They say the leaves are already turning in the hills."

But Sebastian refused the Prince's invitation. Catherina and the children needed him. In the kitchen, Emmanuel was helping his aunt sort through the linens. Black head bent over his work, he sat at the long wooden table, thumbing down stacks of sheets and towels.

"What's the count?" Sebastian asked.

Emmanuel shrugged and continued his work.

Catherina was standing at the kitchen counter sorting stockings and shifts. She was dressed in a shapeless brown worsted, her form as square and solid as hewn rock. Her soft brown eyes looked anxious as she glanced at the six-year-old boy, then up at Sebastian. Her rough hands continued their work. She was as efficient as a machinist in her house-holding.

Sebastian leaned against the door lintel and waited. However urgent he felt his own business to be, it had been his way to let a person finish the task they were doing, whether it be a page that needed reading or a collar that needed ironing, before he intruded.

Catherina set a small basket of stockings in front of Emmanuel. "Number these, then it's up to bed. I suspect we are short."

Emmanuel counted, jotted down his numbers, then flung his arms around Catherina's neck for a kiss and ran out.

Feeling suddenly heavy, Sebastian sank into the rocking chair they'd always kept in the kitchen so he and Barbara could talk.

"I'm sorry," said Catherina. "Emmanuel is not behaving well, but I fear what's going on in his mind. He's as solemn as a forty-year-old."

Hair wisping down from her coronet of brown braids, Catherina wiped up a spill on the floor, dropped an errant spoon in its jug and uncovered the strudel she'd made the day before. Carefully, she sliced two perfect squares and measured a fourth cup of cream over each.

"Canon and counterpoint! You remind me of Barbara."

Catherina poured out two glasses of milk and smiled. "We are as different as the field weed and the primrose."

"You work just as she did. Ah, sister, my thoughts plague me."

"In what way?"

"In many ways. I wonder about the why of Barbara's death. Is the doctor certain about its cause?"

"It is as I told you. The hemorrhaging points to some kind of abnormal pregnancy, also the intensity of the pain. But the doctor said there was no way he could be sure."

The possibility that Sebastian might have precipitated Barbara's death through pregnancy was like a stone he wished he could remove from his load of guilt. He heaped his spoon with strudel. The crust was crisp and flaky in his mouth, the apples lush with cinnamon and nutmeg, and today a touch of orange. When times became difficult, Barbara had always stopped eating, whereas Sebastian was wont to eat more. How many more tragedies? he wondered. Hah! I'll end up large as a house.

As he watched his sister-in-law stretch her generous arms and sit down to her own hefty portion of dessert, he considered whether or not he dared bare his soul to her. Right now, he needed discourse not only with the Almighty but also with a human being who understood something of the creative soul, as well as the eternal verities. Uncle Martin's letters often spoke of Catherina's service in the Arnstadt district. She was known for the way she exercised both exhortation and empathy, even among the degenerate. Sebastian wondered if she could be objective in his situation.

He watched Catherina as she poured more cream over her bowl of strudel, took a heaping mouthful and gave a sigh of appreciation. Catherina loved to eat as much as he did. How often he'd heard her bewail her inability to control her appetite! "Food is such a comfort," she would say. "It is my downfall. I cannot imagine a heaven devoid of the sense of taste."

Perhaps this sensual aspect of Catherina's nature would help her empathize with his near fall. "Do you think Barbara's death could be a punishment from God?" he asked.

"Brother, you've been dancing around this ever since you returned home. What is plaguing you?"

"A woman."

Sebastian told her everything in a rush—how he'd met Eugenia, how he'd avoided her at first, how she'd been in such distress, how he'd almost . . . Finally, he forced himself to look into his sister-in-law's square face. "The thing is, it didn't happen. No, it didn't happen."

Catherina was staring out the window. She fisted the table. She leaned her head into her hand. What was she feeling? She had served them day and night for more than a month, staying up often with Emmanuel, and filling in the gaps when Sebastian felt incapable of facing another guest. She'd not had time to deal with her own grief.

Sebastian shoved up from his chair. "I have spoken at a bad time. I should not have spoken at all."

"There will never be a good time. Sit back down."

Catherina's eyes locked with his.

"You have no idea what Barbara went through this last year, do you?"

"I have been at fault."

"You have been so preoccupied with your pleasures and your prestige that you couldn't even see what was happening in your own home."

"You castigate a soul who has been in torment ever since he returned."

Catherina studied him. "What do you know about Barbara's dealings with the Almighty?"

"That her doubts were many."

"You know nothing of the night of her turning?"

"What?"

Again Catherina looked away. "Barbara felt cut off from you; so we wrote. She wrestled it out for months, and then, of a sudden, beheld Him with faith, saw Him in her heart as Father. I had hoped at least that she had shared something of her experience with you. Your estrangement was more severe than I suspected."

"And more so than I. That she would leave me out of her quest for God wounds me deeply. I don't understand."

"The last time she tried to talk to you about her feelings, you rejected them as figments. You were so cold to the reality of where she was, so caught up in your own affairs, that she made a decision never to bother you with her struggles again."

"That's not true. I never . . ."

"We all deceive ourselves. All any of us needs is opportunity, and we will proceed to do the same things for which we judge others. I am not surprised at what you tell me about what happened in Carlsbad. It should not surprise you."

Catherina continued talking, her tone moving from anger to pensiveness as though she too were searching for the meaning of it all. She related details of Barbara's struggle and her coming to peace, and Sebastian began to remember changes in Barbara he'd given little thought to before: the times she had offered to read the catechism to the children when he was engrossed in composing; the day she asked the rector's wife what spiritual books she enjoyed reading; the luminous look he would see in her eyes after she'd been for a walk.

The more he remembered and the more Catherina told him, the more emotion he felt. At first it was relief. Now he could be sure that Barbara would be waiting to meet him on the other side.

Then it was guilt, the torment of knowing that his distraction had been so complete he'd not even been aware of his wife's spiritual quest. No wonder things had been different between them. Barbara had stopped sharing her deepest questions and fears, and their physical relationship, which in the past had been rich with soul-knowing, had dissipated into nothing but the touch of flesh. He'd been so enamored with his exalted place in Leopold's court that he'd lost the ability to see. And Barbara had lost the will to live.

His throat constricted. His shoulders heaved.

Catherina moved to place her hand on his arm. "Sometimes we have to face things squarely in order to grow, go down through the center of them, feel all the pain. You know now that you do not know. It is a chance at a new beginning."

"How can we speak of new beginnings with my wife in the grave? I see what I am, and I do not like it. How can such a man hope to bring any glory to God?"

Catherina knelt in front of him, "You will get through this, brother. We will plow through it together. Despite your shortcomings as a husband and father, you are still God's man. The only thing you can do to cut yourself off from Him is to refuse to accept His forgiveness."

2

George Phillip Telemann appeared the next day. He'd come from directing a performance of one of his operas in Dresden and stopped to offer his condolences. At first, Sebastian was glad to see him. Telemann's prude of a face was always wrinkling up with some well-placed pun or riddle that made everyone laugh. They could use some cheer. He lodged with them overnight and accompanied them the next morning to see Catherina off at the post house. There they waited for the carriage Sebastian had hired for her the week before. He refused to let Catherina gainsay the expense.

German post wagons possessed no covering against the weather, and no seats except wooden boards. After all she had done for them, he could at least ensure her a comfortable trip home.

Dorothea, Friedemann and Bernhard hugged and clung to her, and she promised to return soon. Emmanuel stood back. Then at the last minute, he raced out to the carriage, screaming Catherina's name. He beat his fists against the door. "You'll never come back. I know you'll never come back."

The driver halted his adjusting of the horses' harnesses, and people about them stared. Sebastian tried to pry Emmanuel away from the carriage, but the boy clung to the window and screamed all the louder. Catherina rounded the other side of the carriage, picked the boy up in her strong arms and stroked his hair. "Shh! I will come back, I promise."

She continued whispering and soothing until finally Emmanuel let her set him down. He waved once as the carriage rolled away, then stood unmoving, plump and straight, forlorn in his black stockings and breeches, tiny and alone.

They walked home in silence. Sebastian carried Bernhard, and Emmanuel trailed behind with Telemann. Once inside, they all clustered in the front hall—like a miniature army, Sebastian thought, seeking to muster strength against the emptiness. The clock upstairs chimed ten. Gottfried had left the week before, taking at last the holiday he'd delayed when Barbara had fallen ill, and now Catherina was gone too.

Bernhard began wailing. Dorothea dabbed her eyes and sniffled, and even Friedemann looked about to cry.

"This will not do!" said Sebastian. "Come!"

He motioned them all into the music room and settled himself on the harpsichord bench with Bernhard beside him. Dorothea moved to stand in the curve of the harpsichord. She wore a black cape around her narrow shoulders, and her light brown hair was bound up with a black hairlace. She looked sixteen instead of twelve. Ten-year-old Friedemann leaned against the other side of the harpsichord, his long fingers clasped, his blue eyes blank in his narrow face.

Phillip Telemann followed Emmanuel to the music stand by the window. The boy began turning the pages on the stand. Sebastian's two oldest boys were so different: Friedemann was detached, an aristocrat observing life from his balcony; Emmanuel, methodical and serious, with an intelligence that brooded. Barbara had often referred to Emmanuel's uncanny powers of memory and observation. He would notice if a button were missing from a court servant's sleeve and note that last year Herr Schmitt had grown cucumbers in the fourth row of his garden and this year he was growing beans. He's like I was, Sebastian thought, playing the harpsichord behind my back because he thinks he's ready when I say he's not, challenging his teachers, and always wanting to do things his way.

Out loud Sebastian said, "We must make our plans. I am preparing a system of music lessons for each of you that will make you as musically adept as you could ever need to be. Each of you will have a musical contribution to make to society and to the cohesiveness of our family. For Friedemann, I've begun a collection of exercises, inventions in two voices."

"I want to play them too!" The flimsy wooden music stand clattered to the floor as Emmanuel jerked the music off of it and raced out of the room.

There was a yelp from the cat, whom no one had noticed, then a gray streak out the door and Bernhard scrambling after.

Telemann was striding out after Emmanuel when Sebastian caught his arm. "Let's wait, Phillip. It's best I attend to it."

He turned back to Dorothea. "We must resume your clavichord lessons, daughter."

Dorothea examined her hands, then hid them behind her. Her fingers were weak and double-jointed, the span of her palm so narrow she couldn't even reach an octave. "It's almost candle-making time," she said, "and there's so much other work to be done. I'd hoped to have time for my drawing. The clavichord is so hard."

Sebastian felt shamed. Every time he'd tried to teach Dorothea anything on the keyboard she'd ended in tears. She was slow, and he was impatient, notoriously impatient from what Gottfried said. He must try harder.

He walked around the harpsichord, took one of her hands, and traced his finger across the back of it. He eyed the distance from the end of her thumb to that of her smallest finger. "I'll write pieces to fit your hand, and we will work on your singing. All Bachs have some music in them." He kissed her cheek, and she managed a timid smile.

"Now, Friedemann, let us play something for our guest."

Sebastian and Friedemann were in the middle of performing a violin and harpsichord fugue for Telemann when they heard a clamor and a yowling. They ran into the hall in time to see Bernhard tumbling down the stairs with the cat twisting out of his arms and Emmanuel right behind them. Emmanuel was clutching a quill and the first page of the *Two-Part Inventions*. It looked as though he had written his name across the page a dozen times.

And someone was banging at the front door.

Telemann let in a crooked-nosed crone dressed in grayish brown. She wore a dirty red kerchief about her head. "You be Johann Sebastian Bach?"

"To my great dismay, I am not," Telemann said. "Here is the man." With a flourish and a look of amusement he directed her toward Sebastian.

She pushed in, dragging a squealing pig behind her. "Came to help you out with your house-holding," she said. "Clam it up, Hildegard. Doesn't like all this traveling around, she doesn't, but I had no choice. Husband gone and got himself conscripted and left me with only a tiny tract of land that the Baron's gone and farmed out from under me, and, of course, this here pig."

With the pig still squealing at the top of her lungs, the crone set down her bulging rucksack and poked her head into Sebastian's study. Then she shoved back through the group of gaping children, dragging the pig along. She stuck her head into the scullery.

Sebastian spoke sternly, "If you please, what is your business here? Surely you are not the hausfrau Catherina hired?"

"Nah, Frau Baker's fell sick, name's Bottenhoffer. I happened to be by her house selling some of my curio bottles and told her I'd drop in and see what I could do for you. I'm a good hand with a stew; can make one out of most anything."

Dorothea looked alarmed. "Frau Baker can come tomorrow?"

"Nope! She's down with the ague, shivering like a stuck pig. Says it comes upon her and lasts for weeks."

"I can do the cooking," Dorothea said. "We only need help with the cleaning. My mother had a method you must follow."

Frau Bottenhoffer eyed Dorothea with contempt. "Don't follow anybody's method, child. Got my own method. Can wash windows like a fiend."

"We will hire you for a week," said Sebastian. "But no more."

"Week's something! But you will see. You will like my stew. You got one of those fancy upstairs kitchens?"

The woman handed the pig's leash to Sebastian, stepped over a wide-eyed Bernhard and labored up the stairs, leaving behind a strong waft of snuff. Friedemann rolled his eyes, while Dorothea hitched up her skirts and ran after the woman.

Telemann chuckled. "Got two weeks' worth of meals on the rein and a nonsensical hausfrau. Looks like your problems are solved, old friend."

"You may have to eat her stew, Phillip, if you don't watch it."

"Now, now. The humorist cares for nothing and possesses everything."

Sebastian was in no mood to philosophize. "Friedemann, tie this animal up in the workroom."

Friedemann made a face, "But Papa, what if it's been rolling in . . ."

"There's lye soap in the basin out there."

Bernhard was whimpering. He had a knot on his forehead. A cold pack? Sebastian wasn't sure.

Dorothea would know what to do.

The squealing grew more distant, and Sebastian turned his attention to Emmanuel. Telemann was sitting with the boy on the bench examining the page of Inventions. "So, godson, I see you've autographed every staff?"

"I want to learn them too; it's not fair for them to be all Friedemann's. You think I'm ready, don't you, Herr Telemann?"

"Merely taught you a simple dance or two. Your father's teaching compositions look difficult."

"Then I want to learn your compositions. You can teach me."

Sebastian interrupted. "Take a walk or something, Phillip."

Telemann threw out his twig-like arms with a shrug. "Cast out of my friend's home? Ah well, it is the way of all friendships. Must not expect more."

"I simply need time to think. You can't imagine the devastation . . ."

"Oh, but I can, old friend, I can. Will take a walk as you suggest. Consider my sins."

Sebastian opened the door for Telemann and lingered, feeling suddenly exhausted. He watched his guest turn from the walk and angle to the side of the house, then down the trail Barbara had taken so often. Telemann was wielding his walking stick like a dandy and whistling.

Sebastian sent Emmanuel to his room. Then he launched Friedemann on a regime of harpsichord practice, thinking that perhaps some music would calm the still-squealing pig. He delivered Bernhard to the kitchen for Dorothea to tend to. Then he ascended the stairs to Emmanuel's room.

Emmanuel was sitting on his bed staring out the window into the back yard. There was youngness in the room. Sebastian felt old. He sat beside Emmanuel, looking to see and feel with his son. The tree limbs framed by the window were black across the gray of the morning.

He reached out to touch Emmanuel. Emmanuel pulled away.

Sebastian cleared his throat. "I believe you have it in you to be an excellent musician. I hear it already in your violin playing."

Emmanuel looked sideways at Sebastian through half-closed lids.

"I've decided to commence your lessons on the harpsichord also."

The boy raised his black eyebrows and hunched into himself.

"We will combine it with your violin lessons, a little at a time."

Still Emmanuel said nothing.

Sebastian could hear the faint sounds of the harpsichord downstairs, and Frau Bottenhoffer's voice rising raspy and loud from the kitchen.

How can I reach my son? Sebastian wondered. What is really wrong? The days of their number games seemed an age ago. They'd not been close for a long time.

Emmanuel always seemed to see more than Sebastian suspected. Perhaps . . . "I am sad too, Emmanuel; I miss your mother more than I ever thought it possible to miss anyone. I weep on my pillow every night, and often I cannot sleep. Sometimes I think I will go mad without her."

Emmanuel stared at him. Never before had Sebastian felt uncomfortable under the eyes of a child. But Emmanuel's black eyes pierced. Finally, he spoke. "You made Mama sad because you were gone too much."

The thrust went home. The child knew. He had known all along. Does he blame me for his mother's death, Sebastian wondered? So much hostility, and so young.

Sebastian took a deep breath. "I was being very selfish. I loved your mother, and I love you, but I wasn't acting like it. I was wrong."

Emmanuel sniffed and drew a chubby hand across his nose.

Sebastian forced himself on. "I'm sorry, son. I need you to forgive me."

Silence again, and then in a wistful voice, half whispered, "I wish Mama could hear me play the harpsichord."

And suddenly Emmanuel was in Sebastian's arms, sobbing. "Why did Mama have to die? She was so nice."

Sebastian felt his son's quivering and the wet of his tears. "I don't know, Emmanuel. I don't know."

3

"Changed all the linens upstairs and sprinkled holy water over all the beds, keeps the fiends away. Always do that for my customers—give 'em spiritual service like a good Christian woman. Scrubbed the utensils in the scullery. Didn't see no reason to swab down the floors. Dust will be there tomorrow, same as today. I'll need a bed tonight."

Frau Bottenhoffer was filling up the kitchen entryway, wiping beads of dirt from her forehead with her kerchief. The rest of them were enjoying Dorothea's tender ragout and fresh biscuits.

"You may wait in the scullery," said Sebastian. "We'll bring you a supper plate and lay you a pallet there."

Friedemann was incensed. "She's not going to stay overnight, is she?"

"Hard to find, good help. Best do her bidding!" Telemann sopped his last bite of biscuit with a grin.

Phillip's glibness was becoming a thorn. When he first arrived, Sebastian had thought that here was the answer to his need for a friend with whom he could discuss every level of life: marriage, loss, meaning, craft, God and how to approach the future. Now he was beginning to wonder.

The ultimate performer when he was on the stage, Emmanuel's godfather seemed to have taken to acting all the time. Telemann's attitude reminded Sebastian of Leopold's tales about donning masks for festivals so he could mingle with commoners and take on different roles. I'll give it one more chance, Sebastian decided, open the bottle of wine I purchased in Prague, and try to get Phillip Telemann to drop his mask.

After dinner they settled down with their pipes. They were both in their undress, Telemann in a loose gray shift, looking as relaxed as a cat in the sun. "Ah, a gracious host! Fine wine, fine tobacco."

Sebastian swirled the red wine appreciatively in his mouth. It was full-bodied with only a touch of sweet. "If one could only live on wine!"

"If one could! Now the Frankfurt Frauenstien Society keeps quite a wine cellar. While August the Strong spends Dresden's money on such ostentations as fireworks displays, existing in a free-trading city such as Frankfurt makes it possible for even a musical society to keep a wine garden thriving most of the time. They tell me the Elector's celebration for the Crown Prince's wedding exhausted all Dresden's wine cellars for two months."

"I heard about the celebration when I was in Carlsbad. Some kind of mythological display."

"Two hours worth of fireworks depicting Jason's struggle for the Golden Fleece—all sorts of allegorical embellishments, even the bestowing of the Order of the Golden Fleece on the Crown Prince."

"Royalty must have its pomp. Reminds themselves and us too, I suppose, of who they are."

As much as Sebastian appreciated Leopold, there had been occasions this last year when he'd wondered at the Prince's pageant-like extravagances. His wage was sometimes as much as a month late.

"I'm growing tired of oppression," Telemann said. "Give me the trading cities. Leipzig and Frankfurt have afforded me more opportunity than I ever experienced in a prince's court."

"And your music? Tell me of your latest work."

"Started and completed an opera, a Mass and ten motets this last month."

"In one month? How did you have time to revise?"

"In a mercantile society, quantity is all. My goal is music for the common man."

"But surely, Phillip, it is difficult to escape triteness, even mediocrity, if that is your only goal."

"A musician's goal must be to please his audience, if he wishes to succeed. But of course, if you have no desire for success . . ."

So much for kindredship in the way we pursue our craft, thought Sebastian. Although, he had to admit that he'd had his moments this last year. He'd given in far too often to the desire to please. "You've mentioned nothing of your family," Sebastian said.

Telemann twisted his hand in a rocking motion and shook his head. "Have two children now, girls both, one three and one not quite a year. Maria Katherina has borne me four children. Only these two, however, survive. The youngest is sickly. I'm afraid the Supreme Being has not seen fit to prosper me as a family man. I've wondered about the Frankfurt air. But then Louise and I fared no better in Eisenach."

He frowned and fell silent.

"Louise was a generous soul, yes, a generous soul, and musical too. You miss her, do you not?"

"I miss her." Telemann gazed at his pipe, and Sebastian waited, hoping he would say more, wanting to say more himself, to ask questions, to speak of his own turmoil.

But Telemann swallowed the last of his wine, set the glass down with a conclusive thump and moved to take up his violin. He tapped the manuscript Sebastian had placed on the stand. "This Partita looks exceedingly difficult. You wrote it for Spiess?"

"It is still in the making, a working out of my grief."

"Play it with me."

Together they played the Chaconne, then the Allemande of the Second Violin Partita.

Telemann stumbled often and skipped many of the double stops. Finally he abandoned the effort entirely and let Sebastian finish by himself.

Sebastian dug deeply into the string, seeking the intense tone this work required. He fell deeply into its agonies and ascendings, asking through his music the questions he still had that would only gradually, he knew, be set aside.

When he finished, he realized Telemann was staring at him with undisguised envy. "I once had a violinist in Eisenach, a master of the first rank. Panteleon Hebenstreit. Every time we were required to play together, I had to lock myself in a room for several days, apply nerve-strengthening salves and practice for hours to half match him. You play as well as he. I am astounded at your facility, on the violin as well as the clavier!"

"My father was a violinist, and a fine one. He drilled me unmercifully from the time I was six."

"And I am self-taught. You are greatly gifted in your family as well as your skill. Emmanuel has intelligence and wit."

"You are gracious. But right now, I'm afraid all I feel about my life and family is monumental loss. I am greatly bereaved."

Telemann placed his hand on Sebastian's shoulder and spoke in earnest tones, "I advise you never to remarry. A second marriage will give you all the more pain, all the more realization of what you have lost. Now, I must to bed. Journey home in the morning."

Sebastian waved Phillip Telemann off at dawn the next morning. When he re-entered the house, he discovered Frau Bottenhoffer in Barbara's sewing closet. She was pocketing Barbara's ruby combs. She said she only wanted to look at them, that she was planning to bring them back, that she liked to gaze at pretty things. If they ever needed any ready money, she said, the mistress's candlesticks, she was sure, would bring twenty thalers.

If Sebastian had had a whip, he would have used it on her. He shouted her out of the house, throwing her rucksack after her with a crash. Then he raced to the workroom, grabbed the pig, hoisted the window and tossed the creature out squealing. He leaned out of the ground story window, shaking his fist, daring the woman to return.

When he could neither see nor hear any trace of the crone or her squealing cohort, he closed the window. He wandered back through the music room, the study and the hall. Then he trudged upstairs to start some coffee. They were alone now, Sebastian and his four children, left with their memories and the future stretching emptily ahead. How many weeks or months or years it would be before the desire for death would leave him, Sebastian had no idea. But he had children to raise. He had no choice but to endure.

BOOK THREE · · · *THE INSPIRATION*

"A great virtuoso . . . presented himself as candidate for organist {at the Jakobkirche in Hamburg} . . . but {someone else} presented himself . . . who was better at preluding with his thalers than with his fingers. . . . The . . . preacher {said} . . . if one of the angels . . . should come down from heaven . . . but had no money, he might just as well fly away again."[1]

"I drove to the Tanglewood Festival from Connecticut to hear Yo-Yo Ma play Bach's Fifth {Cello} Suite, a piece that he described as being about loss and resignation: 'the process you go through when you know you have to give up what's most precious.'"[2]

II

Portents
1 7 2 0 — 1 7 2 1

So began a season in Sebastian's life of getting to know his children. Each morning Dorothea would prepare breakfast, then one of the children would appear in the music room for a lesson. Friedemann began demonstrating a startling facility at the harpsichord, and every hour of concentrated work with Emmanuel seemed to work on the six-year-old like a balm.

Gottfried returned in September to continue his apprenticeship, and Prince Leopold resumed the castle lessons and Saturday evening concerts, often in the Bach home. Two afternoons a week, students filed in from town.

Once again the house was filled with music. From morning to night, dances were fluted, fugues harpsichorded, and airs fiddled. There was even the lilt of a gifted soprano. Leopold had given in to the desire of some of his less scholarly courtiers for a hunt. The soprano he hired for the hunting cantata was of such talent that he asked her to be a permanent part of his Kapelle. Her name was Anna Magdalena Wilcken, and her voice was as light as gossamer.

Nights continued to be difficult. Often Sebastian would wake from a dream about Barbara and lie there aching for a different time, any earlier time when he didn't have to exist like an amputee. He realized now that he'd had misgivings about Barbara's health when she was carrying Leo, but he'd been so distracted that he'd let those thoughts dissipate on the wind of his ambitions, like so much chaff.

Over and over he would review his encounter with Eugenia. His imaginings had been so vivid, his desire for her so intense, that it was almost as if he had done the deed. If he felt such inner disintegration over something that never actually happened, how would he have managed if it had? How can man who speaks the name of God as Father and Redeemer not fail to lose the sense of who he is if he let his emotions control his actions? In matters such as these, reason must surely have sway.

October came, and the oak in the front yard turned as red as the apples that lay upon the ground. The pumpkin-shaped hausfrau, the fourth they'd hired in two months, launched the huge and messy project of preserving fruits and vegetables. Dorothea bustled about trying to keep everything else in order. As hard as she tried, however, the house always seemed to be in a state of uproar.

Everyone was relieved when Frau Baker finally recovered. With the advent of the capable Frau Baker as hausfrau, Dorothea seemed so much more relaxed that Sebastian decided to take a trip to Hamburg. He'd heard about an opening for Hoforganist at the Jakobkirche. He would take Friedemann with him, extend the boy's musical education, and relive some of his own student memories. He might even seriously consider the job.

He would never forget that visit to Hamburg when the great organist J. A. Reincken had surprised him with the offer of lessons. Herr Reincken had had the fiery looks of a pirate—old even in Sebastian's sixteenth year, but a hard, lean old, and fierce almost in his commitment to upgrading the quality of German music. Being in Hamburg would give him a chance to visit the Catherinakirche once more, talk to Reincken, play for him, learn from him!

He and Friedemann left on November 8. They traveled mostly by post wagon, occasionally by boat, and Sebastian's oldest son proved to be an easygoing travel companion. He asked questions from time to time, exhibiting a healthy interest in the vastness of the Thuringian forest and his first glimpse of the Elbe River. But he was not intense like Emmanuel.

Several days into the journey they stopped at the village on the Luneburg heath and ate herring at The Squire's Inn.

"Any ducats, Father?" Friedemann teased.

No ducats today, but the cabbage soup was as good as Sebastian remembered it. He savored the sausage-spiced soup, in silence traveling back to that day. When he discovered the ducats in the fish heads, he had taken it as a sign of provision, of blessing upon his direction. Where was he upon that path now? Was his work with Prince Leopold hindering him from his true calling? Or was the time of uninterrupted artistry and expansion a necessary detour? He wasn't sure.

They reached Hamburg on November 13, and Sebastian took Friedemann on a short tour of the sights. As they skirted the harbor, Sebastian explained what he knew of the city's history. The depth of the Elbe gave Hamburg the best natural harbor on the German North Sea coast. It was Hamburg that first brought the North German plain into touch with England, France and Holland. Because the city had maintained its neutrality during the wars, it had also become a refuge for exiles of all kinds, Jews and Protestants.

Friedemann was fascinated by the spired city with its stock exchange and custom houses. He exclaimed and pointed at this and that. He walked backward to observe a passing Hollander's pantaloons and pointed hat. He asked question after question about the cargoes hauled and lifted from ships in the bay. Sebastian pointed out the famous Dutch bank and told his son that Hamburg was the first city in Germany to open a coffeehouse. "Perhaps we'll have time to visit it later. We must check in at the Jakobkirche."

They arrived at the church, only to be told they must wait. "Clerk Lenk is occupied with important church business," a boy with a broom told them. "You may wait if you wish, but it will be at least an hour."

Friedemann and Sebastian sat on a hard bench with several others outside Clerk Lenk's study. They munched on the cheese and bread they'd purchased at the market. Sebastian used his eating knife to cut Friedemann slices of his onion. Men marched in and out of the study, some who had arrived later than they. It was two hours before Sebastian was finally summoned.

The man who sat behind the desk was dressed in black. He had a whitish blue complexion with shadows that lay upon it in crevices. His desk was long and shining, holding nothing but a pad of paper and an inkstand. Wooden niches lined the wall behind, and rows and rows of business ledgers, all dated.

"State your business," he said.

"I am come to candidate for the post of church organist."

The clerk took a folder from one of the niches and fastened a sheet of paper to it. His eyes darted about like a bird's. Not once did he look straight into Sebastian's eyes. "Fill this out."

Sebastian scanned the form. 1. Name; 2. Current title; 3. Job desired; 4. Amount of money you will contribute to the church funds . . . Sebastian cleared his throat. "Herr Lenk, if you please, what is meant by this fourth item?"

Clerk Lenk didn't look up from his writing. "The wording is clear."

"I will need you to explain."

Herr Lenk twisted his quill in his whitish blue fingers. His eyes flit across Sebastian, then up toward the ceiling. "It is the custom here for a new church organist to prove the purity of his desire to serve by contributing to the church coffers."

"Indeed?!"

"Fill it out." Clerk Lenk snapped. "There is no need for discussion."

Roiling inside, Sebastian dropped into the black leather chair, filled out the form with quick heavy strokes, and left the offensive question blank.

Clerk Lenk lifted a ring from a hook behind him and sent it jangling across the desk.

"A Probe of candidates will be scheduled soon. If you wish to practice on the organ, it is available. I'll summon a bellows boy."

It took all of Sebastian's willpower to reach calmly for the key and walk out the door. He slammed the door behind him. "Blast the man and his know-it-all attitude," he spluttered. "Coffers indeed! Greed, hypocrisy! Still worse in the church than anywhere."

Friedemann jumped to his feet. "What's the matter, Papa?"

"Get your bags," Sebastian ordered. "We're going to the sanctuary."

Sebastian shouldered his rucksack and strode down the hall with Friedemann trying to keep up.

"Papa?"

"Simony's the matter," Sebastian bellowed over his shoulder. "People who think they can buy into spirituality—those who have money being considered worthier of church membership than those who do not. In some churches the rich get the best church posts. I didn't expect it from the Jakobkirche."

"So you're not going to take the job?"

Sebastian didn't answer. He didn't trust himself to answer. He flung open the door to the sanctuary and hurried down the side aisle past the gargantuan stone columns and up the back stairs to the organ.

He jerked the stop to signal the bellows boy. The return signal came instantly. Sebastian yanked out most of the sixty speaking stops, levered open the swell pedals and attacked the keys with a racing counterpoint. His fingers flew from the top of the keyboard to the bottom, the pedals booming under his feet.

The sanctuary shook with the sound of his playing, every alcove filled with his passions: his anger at the failures of men, his anger at himself, and his desperate need to find once and for all a direction and a heart to press on.

When he'd purged himself, Sebastian relocked the organ, descended the stairs and strode toward Friedemann. His son was standing in the middle of the sanctuary, eyes riveted to the ceiling, turning round and round. The boy's narrow face with its sharp chin and blue eyes held light upon it, and awe. "Never have I seen such a place, Papa, and never have I heard you play such music. Someday I'm going to have a position in a great city like this, in a cathedral like this, and I will make the organ come alive like you."

They made one more stop before settling in for the night—the Catherinakirche.

Sebastian was happily greeted and assured that yes, all the plans were made for his concert on Saturday. Herr Reincken, however, was ill, too ill even to entertain visitors. He would probably be unable to attend Sebastian's concert. The Jakobkirche bent on simony and now this! Sebastian began to wonder if he should have come.

In the ensuing days, however, Sebastian's mood changed. November 22 was Friedemann's eleventh birthday. They celebrated it ahead of time by attending the opera, Friedemann's first. Then Sebastian took him to the city's coffee house. During the ten days they were in Hamburg, they visited it again and again. One had only to step inside to be caught up in the atmosphere of important happenings: political, philosophical, scientific and artistic. How alive it made Sebastian feel!

They also found the headquarters of the "Moralische Wochenschriften," a paper he'd seen in Prince Leopold's library. Modeled on the popular English paper *The Spectator,* it was filled with essays dealing with social behavior, love, marriage and literature. He read the copy he bought from cover to cover.

He practiced daily on the Catherinakirche organ, and the practice produced in him a high joy. Ideas for new organ pieces and cantatas came in a flood.

An hour before his Saturday concert, he began dressing—loose undershift, white silk stockings, shirt, black breeches, black silver-buttoned coat, cauliflower wig and his favorite organ shoes. He'd scuffed them about during his hours of practice till they looked like the shoes of a beggar. They were out of shape, cracked, and where he'd torn off the buckles, a bit ragged. Friedemann had worked wonders on them, however, polishing them to a candelabra sheen.

Friedemann was still fretting over his own appearance when it was time to leave. He was wearing a purple velvet vest with his black waistcoat, and he'd tied his light brown hair back in a queue. Standing in front of the glass over the washbowl, he was busying his long fingers about the arrangement of his cravat. It was white silk. Sebastian had purchased it for his birthday and had given it to him that morning. "I need some silver buckles, Papa, for my shoes."

Sebastian shook his head. "Hinders the playing."

"But the way you dress makes a difference in what people think of you. Alfred says if I learn the elegant art of dress, it will help me secure important positions."

Sebastian raised his eyebrows. His son had been keeping company with the children of aristocrats far too long. "Do not let royalty bemuse you, son. Prince Leopold quotes Shakespeare on it, 'Robes and furred gowns hide all. Plate sin with gold.' Fine apparel can hide a soul so mean that any humble peasant might rather stand justified before God."

Friedemann cocked his head at his father and frowned.

"We must go. We'll discuss it later."

Sebastian's audience that afternoon was large. He supposed it had something to do with the posters the church had plastered about town: *"The Prince of Claviers to play at the Catherinakirche on Saturday afternoon."* Friedemann had rolled up an extra poster and stuffed it in his valise as a souvenir.

Playing the organ concert that day was pure joy. He reveled in the power of the organ, in the bending of this king of instruments to his will.

He performed the *Fantasie and Fugue in G Minor*, written in Weimar and neglected since. Then on the chance that Herr Reincken sat in the audience after all, he decided to make a change in his program. He would play a tribute to the North German composers, his own improvisations on Reincken's *AnWasserflussen Babylon*.

After the concert, people filed toward him for the customary greetings. A distinguished-looking gentleman thanked him for a fine performance in the old style. A middle-aged lady with sausage curls gushed over his technique.

He looked about for Herr Reincken but saw no one of his appearance. The sudden weight of his disappointment made him realize how much he'd hoped that some way, somehow, he might yet have a chance to visit with his old mentor.

One by one, the men who would be presiding over the Probe at the Jakobkirche introduced themselves and thanked him, but their expressions were masks. Sebastian heard the word "bombastic" down the line, and some off-the-subject talk of politics. "The Prussian king is improving his roads to facilitate export, they say—Diminishing the power of the trade guilds—Berlin dependent on Hamburg to be its seaport—It's a good thing."

At last Sebastian bowed and nodded a weary "You have my most humble and grateful thanks," to the last person in line. Then he turned to climb the stairs back to the organ.

Friedemann stopped him. "Wait!"

Two figures were moving out of a shadowed side aisle toward them. It was an old man leaning on the arm of a young woman. Sebastian waited. The only sound now was the step and shuffle, step and shuffle of the thin old man and his companion, and from the distance the peal of the four o'clock chime.

Nearer and nearer they came. The man looked up at Sebastian, and Sebastian felt a leap of nerves. Those fierce moon eyes! The once auburn hair was now white, but the eyes were the same, a fieriness of intent that one could not mistake. It was Herr Reincken.

The ancient musician halted an arm's length away from him, and Sebastian bent a low bow. "Most honored sir, I had feared you would not be well enough to come."

Reincken only nodded. He glanced at Friedemann. "Your son?"

Sebastian nodded. "Wilhelm Friedemann."

Friedemann executed a bow not even a prince's tutor could have faulted.

Reincken looked amused. "How old are you, boy?"

"Eleven, sir."

Reincken inched his way forward and put his hands on Sebastian's shoulders. Sebastian could feel the weight of him, and the trembling. The girl stepped back.

"Is your son going to be like you, Bach? I taught you only a few lessons that summer you came from Luneburg, but there was a gleam in your eye I never forgot. Such single-mindedness! Almost as stubborn as myself, I thought at the time!"

Sebastian relaxed. The master remembered him.

"I'm moved by your tribute to North German music," Reincken continued. "We have worked hard."

"I owe you much," said Sebastian.

Reincken closed his eyes, and when he opened them, Sebastian was sure he saw a tear.

The master spoke. "I thought the art of improvisation was dead, but I see it lives in you." He paused and cleared his throat. "You have much to say and the genius with which to say it. The church needs your gift. There is too much mediocrity and too little purity of intent."

That was all. He thumped Sebastian's shoulder several times, then turned and gave the young woman his arm. Sebastian watched his old mentor shuffle away. His first emotion was gratefulness. And his second was hope.

Sebastian had to leave Hamburg without taking the Jakobkirche Probe. They'd scheduled it for November 28, and Prince Leopold wanted him home by then. Not willing to close the door yet on the opportunity of moving to Hamburg, Sebastian let Clerk Lenk know he was still interested in the position. Surely a trial performance was not needed. His concert should suffice.

2

On the afternoon of November 27, Sebastian climbed the winding stairs to the west wing of the Cothen castle. He was greeted at the door of Leopold's study by the new butler, Christian Hahn.

Christian's light green eyes rolled about, and he began pulling at his left ear lobe. "There be a surprise waiting for you in there." Christian was a lively young man whom Sebastian had known as a castle lackey. Now that he had been promoted to butler he lived in a constant strain to maintain the expected reserve. He captured his hands behind him, lifted his chin and continued, "The Prince has got himself a lady. I don't know as I like her much. And I can't see you liking her either."

"I am not so uncongenial. Why would I not like her?"

"They say she's an *amusa*."

"She's opposed to the muses?"

"To serious music at least. Likes light stuff and frivolity."

"Knowing the Prince, I can't see how such a relationship could have any future."

"I don't know; I've got this feeling about it. Oh, bye the bye, I finally did it. I asked Elisa if I could husband her."

Christian set his hands on his hips with a bit of a swagger. "You were onto her all right. She said 'yes' quicker than you can blink an eyelid. We want you to play for the wedding."

"Just tell me when to be at the Agnuskirche."

Sebastian gave Christian a wink, and the butler flung open the study doors.

The furniture had been pushed back against the book-lined walls, and a dark-haired noblewoman with a bosom that seemed to be leading her about was performing the intricate patterns of a dance. Leopold was playing the violin, and Anna Magdalena, the young lady of the lilting soprano voice, was observing from a chair. The dancer's honey-colored dress was collared and edged with lace. She was dancing a minuet, her arms tracing the S-curved embellishments with tutored grace. Not once did she touch her skirts.

Prince Leopold had taken off his coat and rolled up his sleeves. He fiddled quickly to the end of the tune, then lifted his bow in salute. "Ah, Kapellmeister! I have been awaiting you. Cousin Henrietta has convinced me to focus on the dance for my birthday celebration this year. The court will learn all the latest steps."

"Princess Friederica Henrietta of Bernberg, my genius of a Kapellmeister and good friend, Johann Sebastian Bach."

The Princess's crimson mouth puckered into a pout as she eyed Sebastian. She gave him a slight nod, then with a swirl of her skirts turned toward the young soprano. "Anna, come and dance with me, and sing that gavotte you were singing yesterday. Perhaps Bach here can play it for us on the clavichord."

Anna's pale blue dress swished about her rounded figure, as she moved toward the Princess and positioned her hands for the male part of the dance. Henrietta was tall, dark and sophisticated. Anna was short and blonde with a nose that turned up and innocent blue-gray eyes. Her lips were painted pale pink.

She glanced timidly at Sebastian as he moved to the clavichord. He smiled at her, and she lifted her chin and began singing a merry gavotte. Sebastian's fingers picked up the tune, and the women stepped into the elegant movements of the dance.

From tune to tune they sallied: gavotte to minuet to bourree to gavotte. Sometimes Anna initiated the song with Sebastian following, and sometimes Sebastian initiated, with Anna's clear voice joining in.

"Show us the way the Italians used to dance the galliard, Anna," cried Henrietta.

"Anna's father and mother still dance the way their ancestors used to," she told Leopold. "It's the most thrilling thing."

"The heels on my shoes are much too high," Anna protested.

"Take them off, darling. Bach here knows a galliard, I'm sure of it. He studies so much old music."

Sebastian felt the Princess's contemptuous tone entirely uncalled for, but he proceeded to play a galliard he'd learned in Luneburg. Hands on her hips, Anna tapped off the rhythm with her foot. Then she launched into a leaping dance. Every part of her was engaged with the music.

Sebastian increased the volume as much as he could on the sedate instrument, and soon Leopold was attempting the steps. Henrietta joined him, with Anna demonstrating, then coaching. The young soprano's demeanor was no longer shy. It was filled with gaiety, and Sebastian saw that when she smiled, she was beautiful.

Suddenly, Leopold ran into a book ladder and knocked it with a crash to the floor. He fell breathless on the couch, laughing. "C'est fantastique! How good you are for me, Henrietta. And you, Anna! What a find!"

"Yes, and it is time I took her home," said Henrietta. "I would have her in her lodgings before dark. Really, Leopold, can't you find a place for her here?"

"Please, Princess, I do enjoy where I am. It is . . ."

The Princess threw up her hands. "I know. It is a place where you can learn about life, whatever that means. You are too quaint."

Henrietta curtsied to Leopold and bustled Anna out the door.

The study fell quiet. Leopold levered himself up from the couch and walked to place a hand on Sebastian's shoulder. "How I have missed you, *bon ami!* I certainly hope this trip to Hamburg doesn't mean you're going to leave me."

Sebastian told him about the simony involved in the position. "I do not imagine I will take the Hamburg position, even if they offer it, no, not even if they offer it, unless . . ." Sebastian paused, thinking about all he had felt during his hours of working at the Hamburg organs—and with the proper voices in the proper cathedral—Herr Reincken's challenge was still doing its work in him. The need for an excellent liturgical music that would both glorify God and reach people with the truth of the Divine longing was still there.

"You know how much I enjoy working for you, Your Excellency. I doubt I will ever find such support and freedom in any other place. Yet I begin to feel compelled to resume work on my church music."

Leopold sighed. "I'm not surprised. My clericals are fanatical in their close-mindedness when it comes to anything more than psalm-singing in our services. But you can still write your church music and use my Kapelle to perform it at the castle.

"In Anna Magdalena you have, I believe, one of the finest young sopranos in Germany. I commission you to write a sacred air for soprano voice. She shall sing it as the opening petition for my birthday celebration."

3

Anna Magdalena Wilcken heard the word "simony" as she was leaving Prince Leopold's study. She wondered where she had heard it before. What did it mean? Something about money, she thought. How glad she was for the Prince's interest in helping his subjects learn. She could go to the new library he was stocking for his employees and look up the word.

Interesting how whenever she came into contact with Herr Bach, she was stimulated to go beyond what she currently knew and sometimes who she currently was. She still remembered hearing him play when she was growing up. Her father was the principal trumpeter in the Weissenfels court, and every time Herr Bach was scheduled to lead their services, her father had insisted she play the closest attention. "You must hear, Anna, what this Weimar Konzertmeister achieves with the voice."

When she was thirteen, she'd begun voice lessons with her uncle in nearby Zeitz. Certain lessons were inked upon her memory. The day would start out ordinarily enough: the usual household chores—checked by her father, with at least one of them found wanting—the chat with her mother while she assembled Anna's lunch, a good session of vocalizing, then setting off on the two-and-a-half mile walk to Zeitz. When she reached her uncle's house, he would open the door, his voice shaking with excitement, his bald head shining with the special scrubbing he'd given it for the occasion. Without even thinking to offer her a cup of water, he would set her to a study of a new cantata he'd just received from J. S. Bach. And the day would be transformed into something extraordinary. Herr Bach's cantatas stretched her voice and her spirit, and now that she was singing in his Kapelle, she felt more alive than she'd ever felt before. It was for this that she was made.

Engrossed in such thoughts, Anna scarcely heard a word the Princess said as they descended Leopold's winding stair. They emerged into the waning sun with the Princess chattering like a magpie. "I refuse to let you walk. It is not good for your skin, and there are too many knaves lurking about these days. Leopold simply does not monitor his police the way he should. Father says that silly old man who sits council as Leopold's Administrator of Justice does nothing but meet with his watchmen twice a year and throw a drinking party.

"The sanitation is about the only thing they do properly. And can you believe that Leopold only has fifteen men in his infantry and four in his cavalry? He only drills them once a year, and they don't even have uniforms."

"My father used to be fond of singing a song about Lippe-Detmold having an army that consisted of a solitary trooper," Anna said.

"How ridiculous! Princes can borrow from the international bankers if they need to. My father says there is a rising sentiment that Prussia will one day swallow us all. Efficient armies are essential in our time. Leopold's problem is he's far too bookish. The money he spends on his library! Not to speak of his musicians. Fah!"

When they reached the Princess's carriage, Henrietta lifted her golden skirts, placed her hand in the footman's, set her well-shaped foot upon the stoop, then rose gracefully into the carriage. Her movements seemed as effortless as the rippling of water in the nearby moat.

Anna placed her own hand in the footman's warm and ready one. He grinned at her impudently, and before she knew what was happening, she was inside the carriage, sprawling. She gave the Princess a forlorn look.

"Alex, how dare you!" Henrietta scolded. "Father will hear about this."

"He wasn't even trying to help you properly, Anna. Don't worry. You will be my protégé. I will teach you the elegant art of movement. It is the ultimate status symbol, and so often the middle class overdoes it. You can tell immediately who they are. I will teach you, and you will be sought after by higher and higher courts."

Henrietta continued her chatter, and Anna stifled a sigh. She'd been flattered by Henrietta's interest when they'd met two weeks ago, but the Princess could be tiring; and Anna wasn't at all sure she wanted to learn the airs of an aristocrat. She insisted that the Princess let her out when they reached the cross street to her lodging. Henrietta didn't like it, but she agreed.

Anna stepped into the peace of the twilight, enjoying the snap of the cold air upon her face and the warm look of lamps being lit inside the half-timbered houses. When she reached the top of her outside stairs, she began rummaging in her bag for her key. Pain and druthers! Where was it? Her music, her pitch pipe, the bag of pastilles she always kept on hand for her throat, comb, rouge, the set of blocks she'd taken for overseeing Leopold's young cousins, her notepad and pencil, her knitting needles . . .

The key should be right here in this side pocket, she thought, but it's not. She groaned as she extracted a mass of yarn she'd taken with her to practice her knitting. What a mess! Still no key. She tried the door. What's this? It's unlocked! Surely . . . Fearfully she stepped inside. "Is anyone there? Frau Herschel is that you?"

Her landlady was always checking on her. Anna knew Frau Herschel to be genuine in her concern, but sometimes she did wish for a little more privacy. Feet were crossing the floor. "Frau Herschel?"

There was a thud and a crash, and a huge figure lunged out of the bedroom. Anna screamed. Out the door and down the stairs she bolted, shouting for help. Across the street and through the swinging doors of the coffee shop she ran. "There's someone in my rooms!"

Several men jumped to their feet. As they shot past her, Anna saw that one of them was the watchman who frequented the shop. Herr Bach's apprentice Gottfried was another.

Frau Herschel rushed in from the kitchen, a coffee-streaked apron tied about her fence-post figure. Together they waited. Anna couldn't stop trembling.

Fifteen minutes later, the men returned. They reported finding no one, and no sign of mayhem, except an open window from which the intruder must have made his escape. The watchman promised to keep an eye on her place that night, and the men headed toward the back to order fresh coffee and beer.

Gottfried stayed behind. He pressed Anna's key into her hand. "I found it on the floor in the bedroom."

Embarrassment turned Anna's face hot. "I must have left my key in the door again. It's all my fault. I apologize for the trouble."

Gottfried's freckled face was sympathetic. "Nonsense, it could happen to any of us. It's not a good idea for you to stay alone tonight, though. Come home with me. Uncle Sebastian's daughter makes an excellent breakfast. You will be better prepared for our early rehearsal."

Frau Herschel interrupted, "She will stay with me. No use her traipsing all the way across town. She'll be too exhausted to sleep."

"That will be easier," Anna said, "but thank you."

After Gottfried left, Frau Herschel took Anna's arm in a bruising grip and shook a knobby finger in her face. "Well, I certainly hope that a scare like this will knock the forgetting out of you, child. How one intelligent person can be so forgetful of essentials like shutting the windows against the rain and taking her key out of the lock, I'm sure I don't know."

Anna thought nothing of her landlady's scolding. She was so used to it at home. It was Gottfried's understanding that unnerved her.

4

Sebastian fell into a depression after he returned home from Hamburg. At least once a week, mind on something else, he would wander into the kitchen expecting to see Barbara peeling apples or kneading bread. Her absence would strike him again like gunshot.

To be caught up in work and forget his loss, then be reminded of it all over again—these were the hardest times.

The Jakobkirche wrote to Sebastian not long after he returned home and offered him the Hoforganist job. The offer, however, was contingent on his paying a certain amount of thalers "to prove his sincerity."

He didn't even have to think about it, just sat down at his desk and wrote a brisk letter declining the position.

Sometimes he thought of Eugenia and wondered how she fared. He was of a mind to ask Leopold if he'd had any news of her, but the times he and Prince spoke casually to one another were becoming rare. Gottfried's account of Anna Magdalena Wilcken's scare prompted Sebastian to speak to Leopold about a full-time watchman in her part of the town. Leopold had agreed. But when Sebastian mentioned something about how Duke Wilhelm organized his police force, the Prince had cleared his throat and given him a warning look.

It was the first hint of anything from Leopold that had been anything but open and friend to friend. Sebastian suspected Princess Henrietta was behind the change. If Henrietta wasn't visiting Cothen, Leopold was visiting Bernberg. Anna told Gottfried one day that for the Christmas festivities, Henrietta had brought her own tailor to outfit Leopold in the latest style. Seldom now did Sebastian see the Prince in the silver outfit that had been his staple. He seemed to be always wearing a different costume. The latest was a livery suit of gold breeches, black coat with gold trim and studded shoe buckles.

The Prince had begun canceling his harpsichord lessons and now desired serious music only on Saturdays. Sebastian was beginning to feel superfluous. He was glad for the time with his children. The bonds were growing strong, even with Emmanuel. But he missed the intellectual and musical forays at the castle.

The gaps in his schedule threw him into a fit of melancholy. He wrestled with his sense of uselessness and still-poignant grief. He dreamed of both Barbara and Eugenia, agonizing over his strong libido. One day he found himself wondering if flogging himself in the manner of the Catholic saints would be of any avail. The thought jolted him. Such penances were not for a man of his temperament and conviction. If, from his eternal state, the great Martin Luther were privy to the thoughts of his would-be disciple, he would not approve.

Determinedly, Sebastian strode into his study, lit all the lamps Barbara and Gottfried had so carefully placed about the room and surveyed the clutter on his desk. It was chaotic. He shuffled through a stack of papers, sorting and filing until he had all the ideas he'd jotted on scraps of paper in order of priority, then all the bills and practical considerations in separate stacks. He hadn't realized how much he had depended on Barbara to keep him organized. He slid a clean sheet of paper onto the desk and inked his quill.

He spent the next half-hour working on a rigorous list of things he'd like to achieve with his compositions. He felt no inspiration, just the realization that only when he had set his hand to doing something that would consume his mind and his heart, would he ever pull himself out of his abyss. First he would finish writing the Fifth Cello Suite. Then he would renew his work on the teaching pieces for his children. He'd finished the small dances and *Two-Part Inventions*. Next would be a set of *Three-Part Inventions*, and after that, a collection of preludes and fugues. He would take his boys and his students through all the major and minor keys—*The Well-Tempered Clavier*, that's what he would call it.

The new practice of tuning claviers with a slightly impure tuning made it possible to use any note for the beginning of a scale with no need for retuning the instrument. The possibilities of this "well-tempered keyboard" intrigued him. He would explore it to the full.

He would also recommence his work on the Brandenburg Concertos, setting himself a deadline to get them to the Margrave by March. The Kapelle would respond to experimenting with each new movement, even if the Prince wasn't always there. Perhaps the concertos would pave a way for him into another position. Not that he wanted to leave Prince Leopold, but he was restless and not at all sure what the Almighty was doing.

Carefully, he penned "Soli Deo Gloria" at the end of each finished concerto. He must always remember why he composed, never forget to think of each composition as an act of worship.

One Saturday in February, he led the Kapelle in a complete rendition of the fourth Brandenburg for the first time. After the rehearsal Anna Magdalena headed straight for Sebastian's music stand. Her blue earrings were dancing, her blue-gray eyes shining.

In the midst of all the other musicians' chatter and gossip, she seemed of one mind only. She began turning the pages of Sebastian's score, tracing her finger across different sections. She was at least a head shorter than Sebastian and as alert as a linnet in a cherry tree. "The way these lines merge together and the lift right here! Ah. It is brilliant!"

She began humming. "I love your flute lines. You could use this melody for a vocal aria. To what words, do you think?"

He threw back his head and laughed.

Instantly, her eyes clouded. "I am being inexcusably bold," she whispered. "It is just that your music excites me so much. Who am I to tell you what you should do with your melodies? Please forgive me."

Her bottom lip was fuller than the top one, with a tiny dent in the middle. It was trembling.

She thinks I'm laughing at her, Sebastian thought. When will I learn?

She began closing the score, but Sebastian stopped her. He placed his hand gently on top of hers. "Leave it open. We will talk about the passage. When you've music in your bones, it has a way of wrapping you up and carrying you along. You never know where it will take you."

They talked awhile, but she remained subdued. He'd thought to help her recapture her eagerness, but the more he deferred to her obvious musicality, the more diffident she became.

When Spiess approached him about looking at a viola d'amour he'd just purchased and Emmanuel marched in asking for help with his Latin, Anna quickly begged leave.

Sebastian shook his head as he watched Gottfried help her with her coat. What was it that had bothered her so much? he wondered.

Emmanuel was tugging at his sleeve, "Here, Papa, this word here."

But Sebastian was watching Anna rummage in her bag for her mittens. She was laughing at something Gottfried had said. Sebastian didn't want her to be frightened of him. She was so gifted. He wanted to be of help.

"In the early years of his reign the Duke {Karl Eugen of Ludwigsburg}, whose birthday was in the winter, often made magic gardens, to celebrate it, like those we read of in the Arabian Nights."[1]

"{In writing the Two-Part Inventions}, Bach clearly wanted to challenge Wilhelm Freidemann and the rest of his children. . . . Without talking down to them, Bach tried to find a musical language a child could grasp. It's a hard balance to achieve, as writers who have tried their hand at children's fiction well know."[2]

12

A New Love

1 7 2 1

The next day Gottfried received word that his father was dying. He packed and caught the first post wagon to Ohrdruf. While he was gone, Sebastian agonized through the details of his relationship with Christoph again, wishing that somehow there might be restitution, wondering if he should have packed up the children and made the trip with Gottfried. But no, the weather was sub-zero and the danger of catching an inflammatory fever not something he wanted to risk with his children. There would be no use in it anyway. Restitution with his brother was impossible.

He had tried to speak to Christoph not long after his Luneburg schooling. But Christoph had eyed him, his colorless mouth working under his long nose, and then rebuked him in harsh tones, "Leave it alone. It is best to let sleeping dogs lie."

The creatures, however, awoke far too often. Sebastian had tried to forgive his brother. But the months of happy work in the moonlight over that precious manuscript—and the jealousy that had flung it into the fire— were still as real to him as though it had happened yesterday. It had been twenty-two years, and bitterness still knifed up in him when he thought of it. What Christoph had done to him was the epitome of unfairness. It would serve his brother right if he failed to be at his deathbed!

The thought jolted Sebastian. Not very mature! And not a comfortable feeling to realize I've made no progress in my attitude in twenty-two years. It was as though there existed in his spirit a thicket of thorns that bloodied him and separated him from an essential person in his life. What had they missed?

Gottfried returned the first week of March. Dorothea announced his arrival, and Sebastian left Friedemann in the music room practicing a two-part invention. He hurried into the hall to welcome Gottfried home. The aroma of Dorothea's baking bread was strong. She was hanging up Gottfried's traveling cloak and muffler while Gottfried brought in the rest of his bags.

Sebastian rubbed his thumb down the flour smudges on Dorthea's cheek. "The smell of your bread makes my stomach rumble." She gave him a weary smile and trudged back up the stairs to the kitchen. Sebastian could hear Friedemann's harpsichord playing, a slow tinkling of the melody in the right hand, then the left. Then together. Excellent!

The door slammed behind Gottfried. He dropped his dispatch case and rucksack on the floor with a thud.

Sebastian caught him in a bear hug. The boy was shivering.

"Christoph?" Sebastian asked.

Gottfried shook his head. "He died a week ago."

Darkness fell over Sebastian like a veil. Never again would he see his brother. Never again would there be the slightest hope of reconciliation.

"Maria?"

Gottfried ran his hand through his matted red hair. "She's holding everyone else together."

Gottfried crouched to open his rucksack and drew out a square bundle. "Father made me promise to give this to you the moment I returned."

Sebastian took the heavy package and tore open the layers. Underneath the coarse paper was something wrapped in linen—an oversized book with a brown silk binding.

"What is it?" he asked.

Gottfried smiled a little, "Open it."

Sebastian dropped onto the hall bench and slowly opened the book.

The familiar title in script: *Clavier Compositions by the Masters* and at the bottom of the page, "To my brother Johann Sebastian Bach with my regards, Johann Christoph Bach."

Sebastian smoothed his hand across the signature on the fine parchment. He couldn't believe it. Gottfried sat beside him. They were silent for a moment, shoulders touching.

"Father was too proud to face you and admit his wrong," Gottfried said. He was choking back tears. "But when he learned he was going to die, he wanted to make amends. He had the book of compositions you spent so much time copying rebound. It's your legacy."

Sebastian's tears came then, for so many reasons: for the loss of the brother he never really understood, for the reminder that life on earth is short, for the grace that was now eradicating every barrier between them.

Something important was happening. The Divine Will was on the move.

2

On the first evening of the Cothen Spring Festival, Sebastian entered Leopold's vast ballroom and gasped. It looked as though the Prince had brought all of his gardens inside. Flowering bushes in yellows, pinks and lavenders were banked against the wall.

Birds were flying through the air. There were trees with mossy seats in corners and alcoves, ivy-ceilinged vineyards, even a pond with black and gold carp. The chirp of the birds and the splashing of a fountain in the center of the hall made the illusion of being outside complete. So much green! It was as refreshing after the long winter as the breaking of a fast.

Sebastian greeted Christian Hahn, who was presiding at the entrance. His somber, black attire was relieved tonight with lace at the neck and sleeves. The little man tugged at his ear lobe, rolled his light green eyes toward the door, then leaned toward Sebastian confidentially, "Elisa is with child."

Sebastian chuckled, "Quick work!" He clapped Christian on the arm with a nod of approval and proceeded toward the west end of the ballroom. Prince Leopold had decided on a redoubt this year instead of a regular cotillion. Masked nobles dressed in hooded dominos and others dressed as troubadours, knights, gypsies, and even a red, forked devil were gathering in groups near the feasting table, sipping ices and nibbling on honeyed nuts.

The violinists were warming up, the flautists running scales. Most of the seventeen members of the Kapelle were already there. Sebastian was later than usual. It was difficult to be enthusiastic about a whole program of dance music and ballades. He set his violin down, lifted the thick strap of his lute case from his shoulder, then opened the harpsichord bench to look for his scores. Anna brushed by him, smiled at him shyly, then stopped to speak with Christian's wife Elisa. Princess Henrietta had wanted the Kapelle to be fashionable tonight, so both of the singers were wearing white damask dresses with hooped skirts and low necklines. Anna had added dangling pink earrings that sparkled about her face. She was never too timid to add a distinctive touch. Her breasts were full, her waist not as tiny as Barbara's but small enough to be comely.

Muttering to himself about keeping his mind on his job, Sebastian jerked a stack of manuscripts out of the bench and sat to organize his music. When he announced to his musicians his final decision about what they would play that night, Spiess groaned, and Franz, the bassoonist, gave a sigh of relief. Schmidt, however, remained his huge, implacable self. As long as he had a chance to bow a shimmering melody from time to time on his beloved cello, he didn't care what music they played.

Sebastian began the evening's program from the harpsichord: the latest music from Paris, as Princess Henrietta had requested, followed by the dancing—minuets, gavottes, bourrees, a passepied and more minuets.

Then it was time for Anna to sing her solo, but Sebastian had difficulty getting her attention. She was watching someone on the dance floor. Sebastian swiveled to see Leopold and Henrietta, holding each other's gaze in the last deep curtsy of the minuet.

Sebastian sighed, slipped his lute strap over his head and stared in Anna's direction. Everyone else was ready. Elisa nudged her, "Anna." Her whisper was loud.

Anna jumped, looked flustered, then quickly descended to take her place in the curve of the harpsichord. She flipped her music open, studied it for a second, then lifted her blue-gray eyes to Sebastian. He raised his eyebrows. She nodded.

He strummed the first chord. Her silvery voice floated upon the haunting melody. It was as though she were wed to it. An English love ballade, the song was foreign, haunting and ending with death. It was a song for listening, not for dancing. Sebastian was mesmerized.

He let her take the lead instead of directing her. Her musical instincts were superb.

Her last note was a high one. She caught it perfectly, then faded it to nothing. The silence was breathless. And then, the great ballroom exploded. Anna moved toward the applauding crowd, curtsying and bowing again and again. She smiled her radiant smile. Then she glided back to her place in the Kapelle. She'd performed as elegantly as any princess.

The Kapelle played for another hour with Sebastian playing mechanically, thinking about Anna's performance. She had woven a spell that no one could resist, and her technique had been perfection. He decided that during the recess he would escort Anna to procure some refreshment. He wanted both to establish a better rapport and encourage her giftedness.

Leopold took the dais at exactly 8:30 P.M. to announce the first round of feasting. Sebastian recased his lute. Then he adjusted his wig, brushed the powder off his shoulders and buttoned his coat tight at the middle.

He intercepted Anna as she struck out toward the servants' drawing room with Elisa. "Fraulein Wilcken! May I escort you to the drawing room for some refreshment?" He offered his arm.

Anna hesitated.

Sebastian felt a surprising flutter of nerves. He simply must think of a way to bridge the gap between them. He would attack it straight on. He grinned at her. "You do not wish to be escorted by someone who's almost old enough to be your father?"

Anna laughed. "Oh, dear me, no, no, Herr Bach. You are not that old. Unless . . . Exactly how old are you?"

"Well . . ." He wiggled his eyebrows.

She laughed again. "What a presumptuous question! Forgive me. Father always says I never know when to be quiet. Bold, he calls me. Totally inappropriate for a woman. I was just so surprised that you would want to escort me. I am honored, and I am famished."

Sebastian took her arm, and they strolled toward the door. "Knowing you women, you will probably want no more than a minuscule roll and a half a cup of fruit juice."

"Oh no, I love to eat!" That delightful smile again, that eagerness.

"Then we have two things in common—music and the love of good food."

Anna stared up at him. Then she bit her lip and looked down. Out into the broad, carpeted hall he conducted her, to the right, then to the right once more, down a narrow hall and toward the servants' drawing room. Other Kapelle members and servants were swarming along ahead of them, chattering. Her hand was light on his arm. He stole a glance at her. Her pink lips bore the slightest hint of a smile, and the silvery tendrils of her wig bounced with the spring in her step.

They entered the drawing room at the end of the hall. "Oh, my," Anna exclaimed. "Prince Leopold is a gracious Sovereign."

Yes, the Prince had had the servants' drawing room festooned as greenly as the ballroom—a vineyard in the corner, a small pond flanked with flowering bushes, and a long table loaded with bright punches, fowl, fish, pâtés and cakes.

Sebastian found Anna a seat. At the feasting table, he elbowed his way through the hungry servants, piling both their plates with pâtés and biscuits, chocolate confiseuires, a blancmange and gingerbread nuts.

Carefully, he examined all the cups, each different—some porcelain, some glass. He chose the one he thought most beautiful and poured into it a mixture of light wine and fresh orange juice, always available from the Prince's orangeries.

When he returned, he found Gottfried sitting in his place. He and Anna were talking animatedly. Sebastian cleared his throat. Gottfried jumped up, gave Anna's hand a quick squeeze and left.

Anna gulped her drink thirstily.

"My nephew tells me you love books."

"Oh, he sees me in the library here sometimes. What I love is learning. Why, there are worlds in one word: simony, solstice, nefarious, fraternity. My reading skills, well, frankly, I could use a tutor, but with the money I have to send home to father, there just isn't enough left to hire one."

"A fine trumpeter, your father. Is he ill and not able to work?"

"Oh no, he . . ." She looked confused.

Concerned, Sebastian waited.

"He's a very practical man and feels I would not use my money wisely if given too much leeway. He means well."

Sebastian remembered something of Court Trumpeter Wilcken from the times they'd played together in Weissenfels years ago. The man's attitude seemed always brusque and his treatment of women patronizing. He was beginning to understand Anna's diffidence.

"And yet, you are a person in your own right. To honor your father is important. I do not gainsay that. No, I do not gainsay that. Do not, however, let his attitudes bind your soul. There is freedom and kindness in the world. It is yours for the taking."

She tilted her head to gaze up at him. "I am not used to such understanding. Both you and Gottfried have it, and I have not known how to react. It is a man's world, and most men, I'm sorry to say, seem to give little thought to the fact that a woman is a person too."

"Not easy, for a woman with an artist soul. I am afraid I have been remiss in waiting until now to offer you the proper thanks for the fine musicianship you bring to my Kapelle. Your gift is a significant one. You create a mood every time you sing, and that ability is something that cannot be learned. One must be born with it. You also have a gift for performance."

"I have always come alive in front of an audience," Anna said. "I have wondered if it's a wicked streak in me. Isn't it pure vanity to be so eager to parade your talents? Don't they say pride is an abomination to God? Abomination. The sound of it is as horrid as, as . . . why, as horrid as the peacock head on top of that pâté on the confectioner's table."

Sebastian chuckled, "The ability to perform without the kind of fear that paralyzes is as much a gift as the music itself. To sing the way you did tonight is to serve. It is to offer a gift to everyone who hears, to lift them out of themselves."

Anna sipped the last of her drink absently, thinking.

Sebastian jumped up, "I will get you some more."

He returned with the cup so full that she sloshed it on her white dress.

Frantically, she began rubbing at the spreading stain. "Pain and druthers!"

"Do not rub at it. That's the one thing I know about stains."

"I'm forever ruining some piece of clothing by not dealing properly with a stain," Anna said.

"It is my contention that such things are not all that important."

"Really? And so it is mine. I think too much practicality can stifle the joy of making and life. What is more important? That the floor be swept or a dream be dreamed? That a stain be eliminated or a song be sung with the whole of you? I know what the majority of people seem to believe, but I cannot for the life of me embrace it."

Sebastian smiled. "It does make one feel alone. The artist sits dreaming of ways to change the world while everyone else races frantically about hammering nails. Fires to build, dishes to wash, pots to repair, shoes to shine, wigs to powder—they're enmeshed in a daily round of practicalities, and once they're done, the whole round has to be done all over again. I find it very difficult not to become impatient with it all. Earth rent is the way I think of it. Certain things have to be done, so get them done as quickly as possible and get on with changing the world."

Anna was as still and as wide-eyed as the deer he'd seen the other day in the Prince's garden. She said nothing, only nodded and began buttering her roll.

Sebastian stuffed down a chocolate confiseuire appreciatively and downed his own drink. The laughter and talk in the room were growing louder. More servants were entering. Here came Christian with Elisa on his arm, then a lackey hefting a basket filled with flasks of wine. Sebastian hoped his Kapelle would be careful about the wine. They still had two hours of music to play.

He crunched into a pickled herring hors d'oeuvre. "This is unusually fine."

"Herring?"

"Try some."

As Anna took the wafer from him, their fingers touched, lingered. She lifted her eyes to his. The radiance of her! He felt a rush of heat. She was blushing.

Quickly, she turned away.

Suddenly, Sebastian had an overwhelming urge to wrap his arms around Anna's small and rounded frame and kiss her until she swooned. Gottfried stopped in front of them. Sebastian felt as embarrassed as if his nephew had caught them kissing.

"Andrew wants to demonstrate the music his group can make with a card and the edge of a hat," Gottfried said to Anna. "He wants us to demonstrate the galliard."

"Goodness, is there room?"

"If we ask everyone to make it. Have you heard them, Uncle? They can make the sound of almost every wind instrument."

Anna was already taking off her shoes. Sebastian watched as everyone shoved back the chairs. In a moment Anna and Gottfried were leaping about the room to the sound of the makeshift instruments. They sounded uncannily like recorders, oboes and flutes. Everyone was whistling and clapping. When had Anna had a chance to teach Gottfried the galliard, Sebastian wondered. He watched them together, and the excitement within him evaporated. Gottfried and Anna, of course. What had he been thinking?

3

The morning after the ball, Anna woke to the sound of rain. By dawn, there was quiet and then birdsong. She threw on her wrap and padded out the door onto her landing. Every leaf and blade glistened as the sun climbed higher. Water fell from the trees like leftover tears.

She leaned against the rail, searching the branches for the bird. It was one of her private joys that the view from her rooms, unlike most places in the west section of Cothen, included trees. She lived next door to a miniature park, which, now that spring had come, was teeming with all variety of birds.

There, a flick of red near the top of that fir tree! Once again the bird sang out, and another bird answered, and another. Before long the air was alive with clucking and tweeting and chee-ri-o slurring and buzzing, melodious beeps and whines and dip-a-dee's and worry-worries.

The joy in her was like the leaping of the galliard in her spirit, or was it her soul? It was a joy that had a wildness in it she couldn't remember having ever felt before. She thought of Herr Bach's face last night when he'd offered her the herring. His coal eyes had turned deep and shining. And his touch had melted her. She'd never seen the side of him he'd showed her last night: the way he'd teased about his age and taken her arm and strolled jauntily with her into the servants' drawing room. His face had been full of color, not drawn and white the way it had been ever since Frau Bach died. The funny way he wiggled his eyebrows and the way his fluted lips had so readily spread into that great smile last night was . . . well, endearing.

She had revered him, even feared him sometimes, in rehearsals. He was exacting.

But last night, he'd treated her not like just another member of the Kapelle, but like an equal, a person of importance. He was deep, and he listened to her. He valued her musicianship and her ideas. Was she falling in love? Or was it just the infatuation of a student for a teacher, something that would pass when their work together was finished. There was a considerable age difference. She was twenty, and Gottfried had told her last night that Herr Bach was thirty-six.

He was so far above her. And yet, her intuitions about people seldom failed her. The way he'd looked at her last night was the way Leopold looked at Henrietta, the way Christian had looked at Elisa before they were married.

She remembered something her mother told her in one of their many talks about marriage. "When it comes to love, Anna, don't forget that a love which will endure the trials of a life together cannot be recognized in a day or even a month. Every passing day will reveal it. You must be patient."

That afternoon she had to take the post chaise to nearby Wittenburg to sing in the spring festival. It was ten days before she saw Herr Bach again. When she returned, she unpacked and did her washing, then settled into a whole day of teaching. She had ten young voice students, all of whom had missed lessons while she was gone.

Finally, she was free to visit the castle. She wanted to study the Calvinist *Psalter.* She'd been in the castle library for an hour, immersed in the wonderful imagery of the Psalms, when Herr Bach entered.

She felt a fluttering in her stomach. He didn't see her at first. He was carrying a manuscript with him. He strode toward the history bookshelf. She noted his confident stride, his broad back, the cock of his head as he traced a long finger across the titles. How purposeful he always looked!

He settled on a brochure of maps and a thick black book. She could see the title as he turned, Latin it looked like. He opened the book, reading as he strode in her direction. To be able to read in Latin and French! She must think of a way to save more money.

Finally, he glanced up. His broad oval face brightened for a minute, then turned solemn. "Fraulein Wilcken! You are studying again." His tone was business-like.

"The Calvinist *Psalter*," she said. "The Psalms are so beautiful. They speak truly, right to one's core. And there is music in the very words. You are studying also?"

"I'm preparing to send off the Brandenburg manuscripts. I thought I'd familiarize myself with the Margrave's environs, the roads, how long it will take the manuscripts to reach him, how long it will take for him to send word and reimbursement back."

"And this?" Anna touched the thick book, wishing she dared to touch the hand that gripped it.

He drew back. "A little German Catholic history. I'm feeling the need to stretch my mind. Am becoming too self-obsessed these days, yes, too self-obsessed. An old widower like me has to be careful. You can get morose."

As he spoke, his mouth tightened and his winged eyebrows drew together in a frown. His face had that drawn, white look again. Is he ill? she wondered.

She decided to be bold. "With Frau Bach gone, your responsibilities with the children must overwhelm you. It must make it very difficult to guide them in their studies, discipline them, see that they are clothed and well and still get all your work done. Perhaps I could be of service to you as an extra copyist. My father says I have a fine hand."

"At some future date perhaps. There is nothing now, however. I must leave you to your studies." His tone was brusque, dismissive.

He turned at the sound of footsteps. "Ah, Gottfried. You will want to walk Anna home." He wheeled and hurried out the library door.

Anna mumbled a barely audible "good day" to Gottfried. She felt hurt. Today's Herr Bach was a completely different person from the one who'd bantered with her at the ball. He'd hurried away as though demons were pursuing him and relegated her to Gottfried. She must have imagined his interest. He was probably just being kind.

4

Sebastian left the castle feeling frustrated and a little angry. The combination of Anna's girlishness and wisdom was irresistible. She'd been studying the Psalms.

He'd always sensed in her a natural spirituality. The air he'd written for the Prince's birthday cantata about the birth of the Christ child had moved her to tears.

With a great exertion of will, he set thoughts of Anna aside and sped on to the duties of the rest of the day. He entrusted the Brandenburgs to the postmaster, then hurried home for Emmanuel's music lesson. The seven-year-old was so sensitive that Sebastian tried not to be even a minute late. Sometimes he felt the boy ruled him.

After helping the children with lessons that night, he drew a stack of manuscript paper out of his desk drawer and began work on a Passion. He'd decided to write one based on the gospel of John. Spiess said that ever since Barbara's death the sense of suffering in Sebastian's compositions had been unmistakable. "Everyone hears it. You must write a Passion."

Sebastian knew that Christ's abnegation and suffering were so far beyond anything man would suffer that it would be impossible to ever understand it. But his grief did help him to identify with the passion of Christ more than he had in the past. If his difficulties made him a more profound composer, it was worth it, he knew.

The process, however, was not one he wanted to repeat. Perhaps it was better that he not remarry. To care for someone else as deeply as he had cared for Barbara and not only lose her but fail her would be unendurable.

Day after day, Sebastian listened for the pounding hoofs of the *reitende* post, eager to see if he'd heard from the Margrave. The family expenses were ballooning as the children grew. Dorothea was becoming a young woman.

She needed a whole new wardrobe. She was a fine seamstress for her age, but with all the sewing and mending she needed to do for the rest of the family, she had no time to sew for herself.

He needed to hire a needlewoman to create several dresses for Dorothea, and that would be expensive. He was hoping for a significant remuneration from the Margrave. But the days passed and then the weeks, and still there was no word. Sebastian didn't understand.

One May morning, Sebastian was outside questioning the courier when Gottfried and a strange young woman appeared from the trail behind the house and strolled into the yard. She touched Gottfried's arm, and he grabbed her hand as they headed for the oak branch swing. They settled into the swing together. Gottfried wrapped his arm around her shoulders and whispered something in her ear. She giggled.

Sebastian didn't know what to think. His nephew had spent hours the day before repairing the broken slats in the swing. Was it for this unknown girl? What about Anna? He felt angry and hopeful at the same time. The courier promised to keep an eye out for Sebastian's expected letter, clucked to his horse and the horse trotted on, bridle jangling.

Sebastian walked up to the couple. "Nephew, I need to see you inside."

Gottfried looked surprised. "You haven't met Bridget. This is Trumpeter Wideburg's daughter, back just two weeks ago from England."

Sebastian bowed, "Fraulein Wideburg. A moment please, Gottfried."

They hurried inside the house. "Did I not take enough time tuning the harpsichord?" Gottfried asked. "Or is it the hinge on that window upstairs I haven't repaired yet?"

"Neither. It is that I don't understand about this Bridget."

"Sir? Now it is I who don't understand."

"What about Anna?"

"Anna?"

"Yes. Why are you flirting with this Bridget?"

"We met each other in the marketplace last week. Anna introduced us."

"That makes it even worse. Does she know you are with Bridget today?"

"No."

"What about Anna's feelings? I expected better of you. Anna deserves better."

Gottfried's freckled face looked even more bewildered. "I still don't understand."

Sebastian sighed in exasperation. "All that you and Anna have done together, the dancing, the walks home. Anna will be hurt when she finds out you are seeing someone else."

"You thought . . ."

"Well?"

"No, no. Anna and I are friends only. We see each other at the coffee house across from her lodgings. There is always dancing going on there, and she shows me steps. She's easy to talk to. She knows all about Bridget."

Sebastian felt as though he'd been shackled for months, and suddenly the chains had fallen off.

"Besides, Uncle, she's interested in someone else." Gottfried gave him a knowing grin and hurried back outside.

Sebastian stood in the hall for a minute, thinking. Who could Anna be interested in? Do I dare hope it's me? Why did Gottfried grin like that?

He strode through his study and into the music room, eyes half-closed, meditating, wondering. He nearly ran into Dorothea. She was sitting on the floor, dressed in her old brown russet, surrounded by material and old clothes. She had never felt comfortable using Barbara's sewing closet, so Sebastian had given her permission to work in the music room in the mornings. It was difficult to have his music room so often occupied with household matters. But he knew it helped Dorothea, so he tried to be patient about it.

He stepped gingerly over the heaps of cloth, careful not to disturb the piles of pins and spools Dorothea was sorting.

"Papa, how am I ever going to get the boys' summer clothes ready if they won't be still long enough to let me pin? Emmanuel just stepped in the sewing basket and upset everything." She was near tears.

At that moment, Friedemann appeared in the doorway, chomping at a hunk of black bread dripping with cherry preserves. "Are you ready for me, Dorothea?"

Dorothea glared at her brother. "If you keep eating like that, we won't have preserves left to last the week."

Frau Baker had taken ill again, and they had been without a hausfrau for a month. Dorothea told her father that morning that the only vegetables they had left were a few crocks of cabbage and beets. Barbara always had the garden planted by March, and now it was May and they hadn't even cultivated the ground.

A pox on all these practical matters! thought Sebastian. I don't have time for it.

There was a thunder of feet on the stairs. Then Bernhard tore into the room with Emmanuel chasing him. "Bernhard, you give me back that inkpot."

Bernhard was six years old now, as nimble as a squirrel and almost as tall as Emmanuel. His seven-year-old brother was still on the pudgy side.

Quick-witted he might be, but fast he was not. Bernhard was holding Emmanuel's porcelain inkpot, the one Sebastian had brought him from Prague, high above his head. Bernhard swiveled and dodged. Emmanuel jumped and grabbed. And then, Bernhard tripped.

Sebastian watched, horrified, as the black ink streamed over the floor straight toward the silk Dorothea was cutting for Friedemann's new shirt. Sebastian jerked the material off the floor. Too late.

There was a rivulet of ink inching down the length of the expensive material.

Dorothea burst into tears.

Emmanuel began creeping toward the door.

Irritated at the "have to" of the whole situation and angry with the boys for their thoughtlessness, Sebastian shouted at Emmanuel. "Stay right where you are."

The boy stopped dead still. Sebastian turned back to Bernhard. He was fidgeting, staring down at the floor. "Look at me."

Their eyes locked, Bernhard's purple-brown ones bright with animation, his auburn hair falling in a curled lock across his forehead. Small Grecian nose, heavy lashes, he had the good looks of his mother, and more. He possessed an elfish way about him of teasing and cajoling that made him difficult to discipline. But Sebastian refused to succumb.

"Up to your room! No dinner tonight."

"But Emmanuel . . ."

Sebastian pointed toward the door, "Go."

Head down, Bernhard hurried out of the room.

"Emmanuel, go get the hoe and start breaking up the ground in the vegetable garden. No stopping until I say, unless Dorothea calls you for a fitting. And if she does, I don't want to hear anything but a good report. Now, go!"

Friedemann was leaning against the doorpost with his hand over his mouth, trying to smother a laugh.

"And you, Friedemann, I grow tired of your letting Dorothea shoulder all the responsibility. Go find your mother's spot remedy book and help Dorothea salvage this material."

Friedemann started to protest.

"Don't tell me it's women's work. It's work that has to be done."

When the boys were gone, Sebastian dabbed at Dorothea's tears with his handkerchief and gave her flat little nose a kiss.

"I'm so tired, Papa."

"I know; me too."

That night, Sebastian lay awake thinking for a long time. Dorothea was being robbed of the last years of her girlhood. She seldom laughed, and there had appeared on her face this last month a set, worried expression that made her look thirty years old instead of thirteen. And then, there were his own needs, yawning. He needed a companion who believed in him to be there for him each night, someone he could help and love in return.

Anna Magdalena. A rich name for an interesting young woman. He had seen her with the children in the castle, young cousins of Leopold's who needed watching. You could tell she loved children, and she was creative with them. Could it be possible that Anna was interested in him? What would Barbara have thought about her?

Emmanuel would contrive something to not like about Anna, Sebastian was sure. The others? Well, how could he know unless he tried it? Yes, he would walk Anna home after tomorrow's rehearsal and invite her to come to the Bach house for coffee or perhaps for tea.

Between 1721 and 1722 Johann Theodor Jablonski of Danzig published the first short encyclopedia, regular postal services began between London and New England, and Count Zinzendorf founded the first Moravian settlement in Saxony.

"The questions raised by a skeptical generation of musicologists do not destroy the image of Bach as a religious composer . . . they give a fresh picture of him as a human being deeply involved in all aspects of the world around him, as well as of the world to come."[1]

13

The Proper Time
1 7 2 1 — 1 7 2 3

During the six weeks after Anna's encounter with Herr Bach in the library, she alternately languished and scolded herself for being a fool. She tried to recapture the spirit of happy independence she had enjoyed before the redoubt. But she found herself watching Herr Bach during rehearsals and afterward, her heart quickening every time he laughed or his face softened with compassion. She kept hoping he would offer to walk her home. But he always seemed in a hurry.

Sometimes she asked Gottfried questions about Barbara and the children. At one point Gottfried eyed her: "You seem awfully interested in Uncle Sebastian's past these days."

She could feel her face turning hot. She had never been able to wear a mask.

Henrietta continued to be Anna's unofficial patroness. "I enjoy your company, dear; I am surrounded by old biddies."

Anna often accompanied the Prince and the Princess when they took trips together: to Leipzig to take part in the promenade, to Halle for a court festival, and once even to Berlin. When Henrietta began bringing her dancing master to Cothen, she often asked Anna to attend the lessons. Anna would sing with a flautist while Leopold and Henrietta danced. They reminded her of mating birds, swerving, blending, swooping, flinging away, then coming together again, courting. The sight of them set up a longing in her as painful as a wound.

One afternoon in late May, Anna was struggling to get her music into her overstuffed bag after singing in the Kapelle. She was thinking how striking Henrietta had looked today. The Princess's orange and red bodice had drawn attention to her coffee-colored eyes and crimson lips. She'd been bold to not wear a wig, just her own elaborately coifed black hair.

Leopold liked Henrietta's boldness. Anna had heard him say once he'd never met anyone like her. This afternoon he'd toasted the Princess then kissed her in front of everyone. What would it be like to have someone love you like that?

"And where might you be, Miss Wilcken?"

Startled, Anna looked up into Herr Bach's amused black eyes.

She felt embarrassed. "Day dreaming, I'm afraid."

"The imagination of the artist! It does save us at times, does it not?"

"It is a partial saviour."

He raised his eyebrows. "Perhaps we could discuss that further while I walk you home. If, that is, you haven't made other arrangements."

Anna was amazed. He was actually asking to walk her home. "No, I, well . . ."

He looked disappointed, "You do have other plans."

"No, I'm sorry. I didn't mean that. Well, not exactly. I was thinking of riding home with Christian and Elisa. But it is a fine day for a walk."

The set look about Herr Bach's mouth relaxed. A twinkle appeared in his eyes, and he offered his arm with a grin.

She laughed. Quixotic, that was the word that described him. When they were together, she never knew when the solemn Kapellmeister was going to change into a fun-loving galant.

Soon they were strolling through the streets along with other couples out enjoying the spring air. The afternoon was drawing to a close. When they reached the marketplace, the temporary stalls were being disassembled.

Country dwellers were streaming toward the town gates.

"Some nefarious characters lurking about," Herr Bach said. He indicated a couple of big men with scraggly beards. Their expressions were furtive. "Let's hope they're out of the town by the time they close the gates." They edged around the dispersing crowd, the shouts of craftsmen and the loading of carts forbidding much talk. When they'd passed the last stall, Herr Bach spoke.

"What do you think of the descant Henrietta arranged for us tonight ?"

Anna groaned. "Leopold will keep trying, and Henrietta will keep blocking his attempts. I fear she is even more an *amusa* than I thought."

The Kapelle's assignment that day had been to provide music for an early dinner honoring Henrietta and the Prince's closest courtiers. Henrietta had arrived with several spaniels on leash. The dogs sat near her chair at the table and howled every time a violin played in its higher registers. The spaniels were so disruptive that Prince Leopold finally decided to dismiss his musicians early.

Anna walked along with Herr Bach, feeling more and more animated as they discussed the why and how of individuals who did not value high art and the usefulness of the imagination. Herr Bach said that Bernhard had more imagination than any of his other children. Emmanuel was almost as practical as his mother had been. Friedemann was phlegmatic, with a lazy bent that prevented much initiative. And Dorothea? "Well, I'm not sure I understand Dorothea," he said. "No, I do not understand her. She has a talent for drawing, but an anxious streak that seems to forbid invention."

Herr Bach had never mentioned his children to Anna before. He was so open today, she thought, even more than he had been the evening of the redoubt. She glanced up to see the scrolled sign of the coffee house across from her lodgings. The time had passed so quickly. They stopped at the bottom of her stairs.

She smiled up at him, "I thank you for your escort."

Sebastian bowed, but made no move to go. The frown crease deepened between his winged eyebrows. He cleared his throat. "I was wondering if you would have tea with us tomorrow afternoon. Dorothea makes a fine scone."

"You are planning a gathering?"

"No, just you." He looked uncomfortable.

"Just me?"

"And the children. Anna . . ."

The sound of his voice around her first name made Anna feel strangely vulnerable.

"I'll be straightforward with you," he continued. "I admire you. You have depth and winsomeness. I would like to deepen our acquaintance. Actually, well, what I'm wondering is . . . if it is not too sudden . . ." He paused, groping for words. Then he blurted it out, "I would like permission to court you."

The words startled her. She blinked. She felt disoriented. She stammered. "Oh my! I wasn't expecting . . ."

"If you enjoy my company even a little, if you take even half the delight that I do in our conversations, grant me the privilege of a few months to seek to fan that spark into a fire. I will write to your father tomorrow. If, that is, your answer is yes."

Anna didn't know what to say. He must have been thinking about this for a long time. Did she love him? She thought she did. What about the age difference? Was she interested enough to commit herself this soon?

"I'm not asking for a decision about marriage yet," he said. "Just time to engage in different activities together and get to know each other with honor. Yes, to get to know each other with honor, without stirring up gossipers' tongues."

"You are indeed sensitive."

He looked so anxious that she reached out to touch his arm. "Herr Bach . . ."

"Sebastian."

"Yes, Sebastian, my answer is yes."

2

The tea at the Bach home was a little awkward, but she left feeling she had established a rapport with Dorothea. The next weekend, Sebastian invited her to take a ramble in the country with Christian and Elisa. They rattled through the countryside in the old chaise. The meadows were dotted with yellow flowers, and the air smelled fresh and green. She felt so alive. It was a day of laughter and song.

After that, Anna saw Sebastian several times a week. He walked her home from the castle, treated her to coffee and kuchen in the coffee shop, and danced with her when there was a chance. The townspeople still came to feast at the castle on Wednesday nights, but games of hombre and dancing had replaced the scholarly discussions and serious music.

"At least it gives me a chance to dance with you," Sebastian said. "The Kapelle does fine without me."

Sebastian's innate sense of rhythm as experienced upon the dance floor was something Anna never ceased to marvel at. How fun he was, and how perfectly he moved with the music! They danced as one. Every once in a while the Prince dared ask the Kapelle to play a waltz, and even more surprising, Sebastian dared to dance it with her. The waltz was a recent dance popular among the peasants. Many of the aristocracy and churchmen believed it to be profligate. Anna was sure she would have hated the waltz with anyone else. But she found herself longing for the dance when she knew Sebastian would be her partner.

When they danced a waltz together, she felt like a fluff of dandelion floating upon the wind of Sebastian's wishes. She had never experienced anything so powerful. What could this be but love?

The tone of her parents' letters was various. Her father's response to the courtship was proud, her mother's concerned. "I don't want my daughter marrying a man who is only interested in someone to take care of his children and maintain his house. I hope he has eyes to appreciate how unique you are."

But Anna had no worries on that account. Sebastian knew exactly who she was. They seldom talked about practical matters, but about music and excellence and vision and worship. Once Sebastian showed her his accounts. He spoke of how important he felt it was to make the best possible use of the money God had given him. He said Barbara used to keep the household records, but since her death, he'd been keeping them and enjoying it immensely.

Anna was surprised. "And you not a practical man?"

He shrugged his shoulders. "Numbers are one of my passions. They are like notes on a staff. If you have the patience, you can make them do anything you desire."

But Barbara's and Sebastian's figures, so carefully labored over in the account book, were daunting to Anna. Even the figuring she needed to do at the market to assure she was not being cheated was a struggle. She paged through the account book and shook her head. "I would never be able to do this."

Sebastian turned her to him and drew her into a warm hug. "No worries. It will be my responsibility."

Elisa Hahn gave birth to a boy in September, and Sebastian and Anna agreed to be the baby's godparents. Everyone assumed they would soon marry.

Then one November afternoon, Sebastian took Anna into his study. "I want to show you something."

She liked the smells in his study: books, leather and the smell of Sebastian's pipe tobacco.

He pulled two music manuscripts off a shelf and laid one of them open on his desk. From a drawer, he drew out some kind of chart, which he unfolded until it lay in a long strip beneath the open manuscript. Some of the chart's spaces were filled in, but many were left blank.

"It is time I told you about my dream for a well-regulated music for the church. It will be a complete music for the five-year liturgy, something different. Every cantata, every aria, every recitative, every chorus, every Passion, every instrumental prelude, postlude and interlude, like a diamond. But no remote diamond, a diamond to touch, a diamond with intent."

Eagerly, Anna scanned the open manuscript, humming as she turned the pages. It was a cantata for a Sunday in the liturgy that focused on Judgment Day.

"It looks to me like a powerful diamond," Anna said. "And with this instrumentation . . . has it been performed?"

"Once."

"The response?"

"Mixed."

"May I try it?" She moved toward the music room.

Sebastian held up his palms in a gesture that said, "Wait." It was a gesture she was growing familiar with. It meant she was getting ahead of him, and he wanted her to simply listen for a minute.

"My desire," he said, "is to create with music an atmosphere in the worship service that draws people into the ideas. No, that compels people to become involved, that raises them up into the God who became man. To make them feel the power that is already there in the scripture in such a way that they encounter Him."

Sebastian's intensity held her. He was seeking to put words around an idea so important to him, so profound, that his eyes blazed. "The idea is to have new music for all two hundred ninety-five services in the liturgical cycle. Lutheran worshippers throughout Germany will be faced with the have-to of response Sunday after Sunday: with power, with wrath, with compassion, with majesty, with the pathos of the crucified God. The Passions! Some day I must write one that, that . . . I don't know.

"Anna, I'm not sufficient for this work. I have failed miserably during this time in Cothen. But I was twenty when I first felt the summons to it, and now it is coming back to me full force. I have to try."

There was demand in his eyes now. There was something he wanted from her. It frightened her a little. Who was she to be a part of such a heroic undertaking? She smoothed her hand across the chart. "And these are the services you've finished thus far."

"Yes, it is only a beginning. But here is the cantata for Whit-Monday, here's one for Easter Tuesday, here's one dealing with the gospel text about the publican and the Pharisee. This one uses Luther's Litany for the chorale, and then as we meditate on other lessons from Advent to Ascension . . ."

They spent the rest of the afternoon at the harpsichord with Anna singing through some of the cantata arias and Sebastian playing and explaining the effects for which he was aiming. He'd written a whole cantata on the subject of pride and humility: *Wer sich selbst erhohet der soll erniedrigt werden.*

He began it in Carlsbad before Barbara's death. The soprano aria used rising tones for arrogance and low tones for humility. Sebastian sang some of the bass aria for her, apologizing for his raspy tones. But it didn't matter. She loved the verbal imagery that his music so fit: "Thou then bend my heart." The final chorale was a familiar Meistersinger tune that Sebastian's harmonies transformed. "I will gladly dispense with temporal honor, If Thou wilt only grant me the eternal."

As the afternoon passed, Anna felt more and more in awe. She had known Johann Sebastian Bach was a brilliant musician, but only now was she beginning to understand the depths of his faith.

As the sun was setting that evening, Sebastian steered her toward the park near her home. They sat on an off-the-path bench, sheltered under a trellis of thick vines. He took her hand. "I believe we are truly of one heart, one soul and one spirit. I would complete the union, one at last in all ways. Would you marry me?"

Her "yes" came without hesitation, and he kissed her passionately. His kiss stirred her deeply, and he drew back far too soon. His eyes were filled with emotion.

"We had better go. I will pick you up tomorrow afternoon."

The next day she played a game of chase with Bernhard, listened to Friedemann play the harpsichord and helped Dorothea with the dishes. Friedemann kept after her to let him play for her some more. Dorothea talked freely about her mother. Bernhard brought her the wooden soldier Gottfried had made him, and gave her a kiss. Only Emmanuel remained distant.

Anna expressed her concern. "There's an anger in Emmanuel that isn't normal for a boy of his age."

"He will not be easily won," Sebastian said. "He's the only hesitancy I have about our marriage."

She didn't see Sebastian for three days after that, and when she did see him, he was agitated and distant. "When I told the children you and I plan to be married, Emmanuel locked himself in his room. He is refusing to eat anything and says he'll starve himself unless I promise not to marry you."

Anna didn't know what to say. The thought of all their dreams falling apart because of a willful child! But Emmanuel was more than willful. He was hateful, completely different from the other children. She didn't understand.

"I considered disciplining Emmanuel for his stubbornness," Sebastian continued, "but I don't feel comfortable with that solution considering my past failures with him."

Anna waited, but Sebastian didn't explain.

"I think it would be best if we refrain from seeing each other for a while. Perhaps a month. It will give all of us time to think."

He didn't even kiss her before he left.

3

Anna wept a great deal the first week. She walked home alone every evening, feeling as bereft as a bird without wings. She had difficulty sleeping. Sebastian was so far above her, wonderful in faith and brilliant in his art. Why had she believed that their marriage would ever become a reality?

One night she awoke to the sound of scrounging under her window. She sat up, listening. There it was again, a scraping, a thud and scuffing. She thought she heard a man softly swear. Tight with fear, she groped for the club she kept behind her bed. She could hear the watchman tolling the hour, "Three o'clock, and all is well." She tiptoed across the cold floor toward the shuttered window, then she began screaming and banging the club across the window. She heard the shout of the watchman, another low curse, then feet running away. Soon the watchman was at her door with his lantern, asking questions.

When the watchman left, Anna realized she was trembling all over. She lay awake until the sun rose. Then she stoked the wood in her tiny oven and warmed some chocolate. She was due in Wittenburg late that afternoon and needed to go to the market. But she was exhausted and fearful of stepping out the door. She scolded herself. You are independent and capable. It will lift your spirits to be outside.

She slung her bag over her arm and hurried to the marketplace. The happy commotion cheered her. On impulse she bought some sweet bread. Something sweet always lifted her spirits. As she neared home, she decided to take the path through the park.

Stepping gratefully into the shade, she relaxed. A bird was singing, and the rabbits were bold today. One scampered across the lawn in front of her. Another halted, statue-like, near a tree.

She would be in Wittenburg tonight. It would be good to get away, to be with her friends in the Kapelle there. She began singing lightly, swinging her bag at her side, enjoying the late autumn colors: red berries, bronze marigolds, the crimson-leafed oaks.

Suddenly, there was a crashing in the nearby bushes. A huge man leapt onto the path in front of her. He had a scraggly beard and was brandishing a knife. "And now, Missy, I've got you at last. Put that bag down there on the ground."

Terrified, Anna laid the bag on the path in front of her.

"Get out your money and hand it to me, easy-like."

Anna rummaged in her bag. Finally, she put her hand on her indispensable. "There isn't that much in it."

He snarled at her like an animal. "I know your ways. Been watching you for months. Standing out there on your stoop, counting out your money. Always have a few extra thalers with you."

He grabbed the indispensable and unbuttoned it. Anna groaned. She had transferred all of her money for the Wittenburg trip to her indispensable that morning.

The outlaw eyed her triumphantly as he fingered the coins. He motioned with his knife toward the bushes. She stepped back. "Now, now, no further. You just move over there by that tree, and I'll . . ."

The moment he glanced at the tree, Anna whirled and ran in the opposite direction. But he was on her in a second. He jammed his hand over her mouth and wrestled her to the ground. His breath was sour.

His lips drew back in a yellow-toothed leer. He squinted at her, then he dragged her behind the bushes and began tugging at her skirt. Anna struggled. He scraped the tip of his blade under her chin. "Be still or you'll wish you had."

Horrified at the thought of what was coming, Anna was ready to despair. Then she heard men's voices. The outlaw jerked to look, and she screamed. He swore and was gone.

When the men reached her, she told them what had happened and asked them to take her to Frau Herschel's. The good lady put her to bed and sent a message to Sebastian.

Sebastian was there within the hour. "It's all my fault. I am taking you home with me."

Three weeks later they were married.

4

The only regret Sebastian had about marrying Anna in such a rush was the fact that she didn't have much time to prepare for her wedding. But Anna assured him she had no regrets.

They were married in the Bach home on December 3. Anna's mother and oldest sister came a few days early. They helped decorate the house, winding branches of evergreen up the staircase and along the mantles and trimming the Christmas tree with paper roses of pink and gold, Anna's favorite colors.

Their only wedding guests besides the children and Gottfried were the Agnuskirche clerical who married them, Anna's mother, father, and sister, Christian and Elisa Hahn and August. Elinor was not well, and Leopold was in Bernburg preparing for his own wedding.

They barely escaped a chivari, nothing serious, just some of the bachelors from the town determined to keep them awake during their wedding night with bawdy songs and cowbells. "She's too young for you Bach. It's not fair." When he told them what had happened to Anna in the park, they quickly backed away. She didn't need any more trauma.

When the uproar of the wedding and Christmas activities died down, the Bach family schedule smoothed out quickly.

Anna was eager to learn to cook, and she sought out Dorothea's counsel for every kind of household matter. When there was something Anna had to do that she didn't enjoy doing, she sang. Silvery psalms and ballades now laced the air of the Bach home at all kinds of odd moments. Her voice nourished him.

And the nights! They were profound pleasure. They spoke of God when they lay in each other's arms; they spoke of ideas; and Anna moved with a dancer's grace to the rhythms of his body. She made him feel totally loved, and she was so feminine that he wondered if he'd ever experienced femininity before.

5

It was two months after the birth of their first child, Christiana Sophie Henriette, and more than a year after their marriage that Sebastian made his trip to Leipzig to candidate for the position of Cantor at the Thomasschule.

Sebastian's new timepiece said 6:45 A.M. He tiptoed around the edge of the room behind the rows of gray-uniformed boys. A weary-looking school teacher was finishing his inspection of boots. Quickly, Sebastian ducked out of the dormitory room and into the outer hall. The minute he threw open the door, a flurry of snow burst across his face. He dashed across the courtyard to the front door of the Thomaskirche.

The Rector, Johann Heinrich Ernesti, was waiting for him in the narthex. He was dressed in a shabby black coat and leaned with both hands on his cane. With him were six men in full-bottomed wigs, the men who would make the final decision as to whether or not Sebastian would be offered the job.

Rector Ernesti made the introductions in a clear, penetrating voice. Each council member bowed slightly. Their faces were impassive, but not unfriendly—except for one, an old pastor named Kirkman.

He looked Sebastian up and down as if he were a bear about to be baited. Sebastian was sure he'd seen him somewhere before. Pastor Kirkman's face shook with the palsy, but his look was intense. "You have finished the Passion?"

Sebastian nodded and drew the manuscript from his folio. The Thomasschule Council had commissioned a Passion based on the gospel of John for use this Easter. The fact that Sebastian had already begun work on such a Passion seemed an amazing thing to him. But he hadn't progressed very far. He was forced to write the majority of the work in only ten weeks. As a result, he'd written mostly by intuition, not much time to structure or revise. It was more emotional than most of his works, but the Cothen Kapelle's response to it had been enthusiastic. Anna said there was a raw power about it that gripped her.

"And the cantata for today's Probe?" asked Rector Ernesti.

Sebastian presented a copy to each of the men.

"I will be presenting a five-part cantata I've entitled *Jesus Called to Him the Twelve.*"

The men entered the nave of the church together, and immediately Sebastian's morning fog lifted. The Gothic arches, the delicately ribbed vaulting, the columns, the exquisite altar and the light pouring in across the pipes of the organ caused a rush of joy. He'd played the organ yesterday to begin the worship service. Then, with a view to evaluating the acoustics, he sat with the worshipers, marveling at the beautiful soprano of the boys' voices floating through the regal space. If only this Probe would assure him the position—what a miracle to be able to serve daily in such a church!

Leopold had married Henrietta a week after Sebastian married Anna. Since then, music at the Cothen castle had practically come to a standstill. Sebastian saw no sense in remaining in Cothen. He would have applied for the Leipzig job much earlier if Phillip Telemann hadn't been interested in it.

Phillip was offered the Cantorate, but finally turned it down. "My position as Music Director in Hamburg has many advantages," he wrote to Sebastian, "to which now is added a raise in salary, if I will stay. It may be, however, that the Thomasschule Cantorate will suit your purposes well."

The position of Thomasschule Cantor carried with it a great deal of prestige. The school offered musical scholarships to deserving students. In return for their education these students were expected to provide music for the Lutheran churches of the city. The Cantor was in charge of the musical training of these "foundationers." More important to Sebastian, the Cantor was also expected to compose new music for the liturgy on a regular basis.

That, in itself, was enough to appeal to Sebastian, but when he added the fact that the Thomasschule could provide an excellent education for Friedemann, Emmanuel and Bernhard, the job seemed perfect.

This Monday morning in January, the execution of his cantata could either secure the job for him or lose it. Sebastian took the stairs to the organ while the council members filed into a pew on the ground floor.

The four foundationers Sebastian had worked with on Saturday were already there in their gray uniforms, seated in a wooden pew near the organ and shivering with the cold.

He felt sorry for the boys. He'd slept in the dormitory too, in a private room normally assigned to graduate students; but, the walls were thin, and the students had abused the curfew. His room had been so cold this morning that there was a layer of ice on the water in his washbasin. The boys must often fall ill.

He drew his tinderbox out of his coat pocket and bent to light the coals in the brazier.

"We will warm up our voices on the difficult spots," he said, "and perhaps by the time we are ready to perform, your feet will also be warm. Warm feet and warm voices, what else could a man desire on a cold morning, unless it be a tankard of coffee?"

He grinned at them, and the oldest of the boys laughed. His name was Carl Gerlach, blonde hair, thick oval glasses and a fine tenor voice. He was the one who directed the boys' choir yesterday.

When Sebastian was satisfied that the boys were ready, he chose his organ stops, then signaled to the council members who were waiting on the ground floor. The cantata lasted twenty minutes. Sebastian played the orchestral parts on the organ and sang the bass part himself.

When they were finished, the members of the council mumbled among themselves for a long time. Sebastian waited. The work went tolerably well, he thought. It could have been better; but, with only one day to rehearse, yes, it would do. The council members had received an accurate enough rendition to understand his intent.

The boys were growing restless. "My thanks to you," he whispered. "Your voices show much promise." Carl bowed and thanked Sebastian. The others only fidgeted.

At last one of the council members shouted up at him. "We are through with you, Herr Bach. You may go."

Rector Ernesti waited for Sebastian. "To the refectory. They'll still have porridge and coffee."

After breakfast they walked through the halls of the school, past the classrooms, where the Rector introduced Sebastian to the interim Latin teacher and the math teacher.

In the instrument storage room, they encountered a solid-looking man in a shabby russet coat. His hair, light brown with a reddish tint, fell to his shoulders. His large nose fit perfectly in his big square face. He was polishing a coiled trumpet. He tucked the shell-like instrument under his arm and rose to greet them.

"Herr Bach," said Rector Ernesti, "Gottfried Reiche. He is a renowned town musician who volunteers his help from time to time. His virtuosity on the trumpet, especially in the clarion registers, astonishes audiences to the point of whistling and cheering. He's better than a rope dancer."

Sebastian was intrigued. "I am greatly pleased to meet you, Herr Reiche. I fiddle about with inventing instruments and have often thought a trumpet with valves was needed. So few play the present instrument well."

Reiche raised his eyebrows. "And take away the challenge?"

Sebastian chuckled, "I understand."

"Schedules to check and letters to read," said the Rector. "Take care of him, Reiche." Ernesti shuffled away, tapping his cane.

Reiche showed Sebastian the store of battered violins, viols, kettledrums, wooden flutes, oboes and trumpets available to the foundationers.

"I can't come every day. Hopefully, a new Cantor will sharpen the boys up, help them be more responsible with their instruments."

There was something about Reiche Sebastian immediately liked. He was congenial and confident. They fell into easy conversation, ambling back through the school together, past several noisy classrooms, through the refectory and on to the sanctuary. Someone had lit the candles along the walls.

Reiche stopped and gazed up at the ribbed vault. "I come here as often as I can. The beauty helps me worship."

"Ah, worship. How difficult it is to get at!"

Reiche looked up once more, then around at the arches, the pedestals, the far altar, and back at Sebastian. "I believe true worship comes from the release of the creative urge to the greater glory of God."

Sebastian visited Picander before he left Leipzig. The poet had rooms above a bookstore. A manservant took Sebastian's snow-covered tricorner and surtout and led him into the back room. There was a crackling fire in the red-tiled fireplace. Picander was sitting near it reading a book.

"Sebastian!" He rose with a delighted look on his face. "What a surprise to receive your message! And how is that lovely soprano of yours? Her visit to Leipzig with Leopold and Henrietta was a sensation."

Sebastian was struck again by Picander's good looks: tall and broad shouldered, blonde hair, straight nose, high brow and pale brown eyes. The poet was wearing a red silk wrap over a woolen shift. His wooden cross was dangling from his neck.

There was not a vacant space on his walls for tapestries. All were lined with bookcases, and every bookcase was bulging with thick gold-lettered volumes. A green rug with red fringe covered the floor between his floral couch and chair. He was smoking an ivory pipe.

"A sensation, was it? Well, my friend, you are a sensation. This is the first warm room I've been in since I arrived in Leipzig. It looks as though you have done well."

Picander smiled. "The trade routes help. Easy access from Leipzig to Frankfurt and Dresden. I receive many commissions from princes there. I also do some work for the university, teach from time to time and write brochures. I've recently become a civil servant also. Postal Commissioner. Hot mulled wine, Hans, and some of those cheese tarts! So, you are hoping to become the new Thomasschule Cantor? The wage can't be as good as what you are receiving now."

Sebastian dropped onto the couch near Picander. It was as comfortable as a feather bed in a royal house.

"The fees for weddings and funerals should make up the difference. Besides, things with the Prince are not what they used to be."

"Princess Henrietta?"

Sebastian nodded and accepted the manservant's hot cup of wine, warming his hands around it. "It is time for me to move on anyway."

"Still thinking to transform the liturgy of the Lutheran Church?"

"Musically speaking. I can't shake the compulsion. It is the position of Music Director that goes along with the Cantorate job that excites me. Authority over what is played in every Lutheran church in the city. The possibilities!"

"Possibilities, yes, but . . ." Picander took a puff on his pipe, blew circles, thought.

The hickory smell made Sebastian wish for his own pipe. He sipped the hot, spicy drink. How good it was to be with Picander again!

"But?" he asked.

"I must tell you, I do not envy your position under the town, church *and* university councils. If it were only one council, but all three? They will all consider you their servant. Unless you win their good will from the beginning, they will just as soon listen to a merchant about what goes on in church music as the Cantor. And they probably will if he has money. I hate to say this, Sebastian, but the thought of your carrying out your vision in Leipzig puts me in mind of Don Quixote. You've a mission that could be viable in the right place and at the right time, but here and now?" Picander shook his head.

Sebastian had never seen Picander quite so negative. It was a strong statement to be equated with Cervantes' hallucinatory Don Quixote, but he valued Picander's opinion. They spoke a while longer about the city's cultural offerings, the new coffee house, with its jovial owner Herr Zimmermann, and Picander's continued forays into Enlightenment thinking. It was Voltaire now. Sebastian left the poet, feeling both stimulated and sobered.

6

A month after his trip to Leipzig, Sebastian was informed that another man had been chosen for the position of Thomasschule Cantor. His name was Christoph Graupner. Picander wrote seeking to encourage Sebastian. "Graupner's position as Court Kapellmeister in Darmstadt has been one of a metropolitan magnificence and wealth. By comparison, Cothen is an obscure provincial quarter. See what I mean? Politics! That is all it is."

Another month passed before Sebastian learned that Graupner had been persuaded by his employer to stay in Darmstadt. The position of Thomasschule Cantor was still open, and the Council finally wrote and offered the job to Sebastian.

The night after Sebastian received the offer, he was sitting on the box bench at the end of their bed, rereading the letter to Anna while she nursed the baby. He shook his head. "First the Thomasschule wanted Telemann. Then Graupner. And only now do they offer the position to me. Third choice.

"Doesn't do much for the pride. And look at all these papers I have to sign: an agreement not to leave Leipzig without permission from the burgomaster; a list of my school duties, including taking my turn at morning inspections; devotionals; supervising the refectory and teaching Latin. There's even a stipulation that my music not be too long or of such a nature as to have an operatic character."

Anna signaled to him that the baby was asleep. Then she placed five-month-old Sophie in her cradle and tiptoed to sit on the leather stool in front of Sebastian. He began taking down her hair. He smoothed the soft blonde tresses as they fell to her waist.

"A lot of 'have-to's' for a spirit as free as Johann Sebastian Bach's," she whispered.

"There's a certain kind of lowliness that has a freedom about it, if I could ever capture it. I will need to tell Leopold about the offer tomorrow."

Prince Leopold had recommenced his harpsichord lessons. The next afternoon when Sebastian was winding up the castle stairs, he could hear Leopold practicing.

The Prince jumped up when Sebastian entered his chamber. "I have practiced two hours every day this week, some on the larger harpsichord in the orchestral hall. Your three-part inventions do wonders for my facility. Music is a balm."

"The Princess?"

"She has been in bed all week. We are wondering about a baby."

They plunged into music-making, and at the end of two hours, Leopold was laughing and making future plans for the Kapelle.

"I must speak with you, Your Excellency."

"Shall we philosophize? Christian, bring coffee at once, and some of those chocolate confiseruies left over from last night. Henrietta had no appetite even for chocolate. Picander has prevailed upon me to read some of the pamphlets that are filtering out from France by a new *philosophe* named Voltaire. He challenges Pascal's belief that man can only know God by faith. A natural religion of deism in which reason stands supreme is what Voltaire seems to be espousing. These things concern me. And yet I find in Voltaire a charm I do not find in other philosophers."

"I consider Pascal's reasoning that the Christian doctrine is far better suited than any other to explain the ambivalence of human nature and man's sense of being tossed between 'the infinite and nothingness' convincing," said Sebastian. "And I would talk of these things more, but right now . . . canon and counterpoint, this is difficult!"

Leopold's lively eyes were on Sebastian in such an intense way that it made speaking even more difficult. Here Leopold was, longing for good music again, eager, it seemed, to renew all their discussions and goals of the past, and Sebastian was about to destroy his enthusiasm. There was no way to ameliorate the hurt.

He took a deep breath. "I have received a definite offer for the position of Cantor at the Leipzig Thomasschule. I know you understand my need to accept."

Sebastian was appalled to see tears well up in Leopold's eyes. Quickly, the Prince strode to the window overlooking the moat. It had rained so much that week that the moat overflowed its banks. Sebastian could hear the splash of water and the sounds of men moving rocks and trimming trees. The Prince could refuse to release him; Sebastian knew that. But he wouldn't. He had too much respect for the artist's need to continue pressing on into new territory.

When Leopold turned back to him, his normally rosy face was pale. "I understand. When will you be leaving?"

7

The week before the Bach family planned to leave, Leopold scheduled a concert for castle employees and their families that included the Double Violin Concerto and the Fifth Brandenburg. Sebastian was grateful for another chance to perform one of the Brandenburgs. He'd heard nothing from the Margrave concerning them, only a terse letter from the nobleman's secretary acknowledging their receipt.

Leopold had requested that the Kapelle dress in the old-style uniforms of red and black. It was time to begin. Sebastian walked the length of the hall under the chandeliers to take his place at the harpsichord for the last time. The instrument's reddish brown wood gleamed with the polishing it had received that morning. Against the wall behind the harpsichord, two thick, white candles were flickering in tall wooden candlesticks. Sebastian caught a faint strawberry scent. He thought of Barbara. How would she have responded to his leaving Cothen and taking this new job, with all its uncertainties?

He opened the double-manualed harpsichord. It was the instrument he'd purchased for Leopold in Berlin. The sound was as large a sound as you could manage on a harpsichord. It possessed two foot stops.

He doubted he would ever have a harpsichord of this quality in Leipzig. He smoothed his fingers across the cold, black keys and set the levers to the appropriate pitch. Then he looked up at his Kapelle through the prop and lid of the harpsichord. The flautist was tuning his best wooden flute. Standing beside him, violin readied, was Spiess.

The featured soloists for the Fifth Brandenburg were the flute, the violin and the harpsichord, with an emphasis on the virtuosity of the harpsichordist. Several string players provided the background. Leopold was playing the bass viol.

When Sebastian had the Kapelle's attention, he nodded the downbeat, and the buoyant concerto began. The harpsichord solo at the end of the first movement gave Sebastian a little trouble. He hadn't practiced it for a long time. But everything else went well.

Next came the Double Violin Concerto. Would this be the last time he heard Spiess and Leopold play it? Leopold's technique was tolerable tonight, but the zest seemed to have disappeared from his playing. The Prince kept glancing toward the far door.

They had just begun the last movement when Christian Hahn entered the room. He looked upset. The butler approached the Prince and whispered something in his ear. The Prince shoved the violin at Christian and ran out of the room.

All the music stopped. "What is it?" Sebastian asked Christian.

"Princess Henrietta is dead."

Interlude Three

The next phase of Sebastian's life began at that moment.

He moved through the following days so questioning and so certain, so empty and so full, so sorrowful and so rejoicing that afterward he would remember little but the emotions of the time. As he stood with Leopold's courtiers and friends at Henrietta's graveside, the sixteenth-note figure he'd used in his Passion ran over and over in his mind—"a flood of tears."

Mindlessly, he helped Catherina and Gottfried with the organizing for the move, torn and yet knowing he had no choice. It was time to leave. He mourned over the loss of his patron—the sense of support and closeness. He mourned that he must leave Leopold in his time of need.

The look on the Prince's face when Sebastian said his last good-bye was a cry for help. Sebastian promised he would return to play in his Harvest Festival and pressed a copy of his St. John Passion into his hand. Leopold must now find his own strength as Sebastian must be left free to rejoice in his new sense of direction.

He'd made of Leopold an idol and watched it totter and fall during the last three years. It had freed him to go to his Maker only for direction. He had been on scary ground, no visible support, but even now as he walked within this floating time, he felt a clarity he'd not experienced since he'd been in the Weimar jail, alone with the Almighty.

Anna's face, yes, he would always remember the dear freshness of her face during these days, loving and listening, tireless and compassionate, her poignant soprano singing of death and resurrection.

The trip to Leipzig was chaotic with the three boys, baby Sophie, Catherina, Dorothea, Anna and Gottfried in carriages and wagons, packed and bumping over the rough German roads. They were detained for a long time at the customs booth at the Leipzig Gate. Then, finally, they rolled on through the New Town and then the Old Town. So many people, so much noise, so much stench! Catherina and Gottfried helped them move into their quarters next to the dormitory.

Then came Sebastian's own adjustment to the demanding schedule of his new job: responsibility for high services in two churches and low services in two others, and at the Thomasschule, inspections, devotions, refectory duty, attempting to teach Latin classes and then trying to find someone else to teach them for him, scheduling weddings and funerals, overseeing the perambulatory chorus, rehearsing—rehearsing with voices and hands far too young for the complexity he was writing into their music every night.

Excellence, excellence, excellence! He must strive for it.

He could hear it sometimes in the voices of the boy scholars: clear, sweet, high, like bells, four parts weaving, low parts booming, soft like timpani, delicate as a spider gossamer stretching into the apse.

He immersed himself in the Psalms and found himself identifying with King David. David had written psalms of praise, agony, prayer and longing, and he presented them for use in corporate worship. Through the power of who he was, the depth of his experience with God and his high musicianship, David emerged as the Worship Director of his people.

Though the title did not come quickly to Sebastian, as he had thought it would, he knew it must happen because in him there was springing up a creative urge so strong that scripture put to a music was all he could think of day and night. Wherever he was, he filled every extra scrap of paper around him with sketches: images of bare trees and dark rolling clouds, fortresses, architectures he'd like to build with music, arches of emotion and imagined colors, rhythmic motifs, sonorous bass lines and melody after melody.

In circles he jotted possible orchestrations, some of them daring, in an effort to express the moods he experienced as he studied the liturgy of each upcoming Sunday.

Whenever possible, he raced to the organ in the Thomaskirche and filled the cathedral with the vast organ sounds of his thoughts. In the lilt of melody and form, the organ timbre of gedeckt, diapason, nazard and flute, lay a taste of what it meant to be fully human. Music had the power to teach, to stretch people's souls. He would use it to bend emotions to his will—for God.

He went through the motions of teaching, taking care of instruments and meeting with the Church and Town councils, but his mind was practically always somewhere else.

Every night he came home eager to get to his desk. Every mealtime he was careful to listen to his wife and children. Every Thursday Anna became deeply involved in the newest cantata as she helped to copy parts.

Every week for five years, with the brown volume of Christoph's Music by the Masters *on his desk to remind him that in the end diligence will be rewarded, he wrote a new cantata to be sung for the next Sunday or feast day. And now the music flowed from his pen in a storm of inspiration and creativity unlike anything he'd ever experienced. He couldn't commit it to paper fast enough. He had a mission, and that he set his mind to with all the intensity of his intense soul.*

He poured over his Bible.

He prayed.

He confessed; he tried to be faithful in the time that he had.

"Time, so limited; man so fallible; but surely, Father, it is the power of art to lift us out of our finiteness. My wound is to worship with all I am."

BOOK FOUR · · · *THE STORM*

"There is no thrill of mortal danger to surpass that of a lone man trying to create something that never existed before."

—MICHELANGELO IN *THE AGONY AND THE ECSTASY*

One reason music affects us so profoundly is that "by providing the brain with an artificial environment, and forcing it through that environment . . . our brains are thrown into overdrive. . . . Our very existence expands. . . . {We} realize that we can be more than we . . . are and that the world is more than it seems. That is cause enough for ecstasy." A Bach fugue evokes this very response.[1]

14

Rumblings

1 7 2 6

The baby was finally asleep. Anna laid Gottlieb in his cradle by their bed, checked two-year-old Heinrich, who was asleep in Dorothea's room across the hall, and padded downstairs to the kitchen. Sebastian would be home before long. She hoped his Council Meeting was going well.

So many of them didn't. The Council had fought with him over the directorship of the daily services at the university church and paid him fourteen thalers less than the previous Thomasschule Cantor for directing the festal services. These were only two of the many problems Sebastian had had with the Councils of the city. He hated having to waste his energy on such dickering.

Anna entered the kitchen. It still smelled of ginger from the morning's baking.

Unlike the one in Cothen, this kitchen was on the first floor instead of the more fashionable second. It was dark, with only one small window looking out over the courtyard. The oven was brick with a raised hood, a disappointment after the ceramic oven in Cothen.

She'd baked gingerbread nuts today. They were a favorite with the older boys.

Breaded nuts on a platter, pewter mugs from the cabinet. The boys would be home from their classes at the Thomasschule any minute now. She arranged the mugs and a pitcher of milk on a red cloth edged with lace. Barbara had stitched the lace in the beautiful point d'Angleterre pattern. Sebastian said Prince Leopold's sister Elinor taught Barbara the stitch. Elinor was gone now too. She died last summer, and August hadn't stepped outside the Red Castle since.

Anna munched on the spicy nuts thinking she'd finally managed just the right amount of cloves. She began looking for Barbara's calendar. It wasn't filed with her recipes in her cartonnier. Perhaps in the desk drawer. Anna tugged on the cold metal handle. The drawer was so full she could barely get it open.

She maneuvered out a stack of folded cloth and papers and finally found it. She was hoping Barbara had recorded a remedy that would work for a colicky six-month-old. The calendar's records of daily schedules and health remedies had helped Anna a great deal. Gottfried was the one who rescued it when they were packing for the move.

She missed Gottfried. He had been offered a Hoforganist position in Ohrdruf, and Sebastian agreed that it was time. Sebastian now had two new apprentices. Johann Menser lived in the dormitory in the room provided for graduate students, and Carl Gerlach lived in their garret. Sebastian had met Carl on his first visit to the Thomasschule. He was only sixteen.

The front door flew open with a bang. Belt strap of books slung across his shoulder, twelve-year-old Emmanuel raced in. He thumped his books on the table and began drinking straight from the milk pitcher.

Bernhard was right behind him. "Gingerbread nuts!" The eleven-year-old grabbed a handful and scraped back a chair. His auburn hair had escaped from its queue, and his brown eyes were sparkling.

Sixteen-year-old Friedemann, who had managed to make his drab, gray school uniform look elegant with a black silk cravat, lounged in. He eyed the scene with distaste. "They've got the gentility of a couple of oxen," he said to Anna. She couldn't help smiling.

The boys fell to enjoying what Bernhard called "real food." As Anna poured the mugs full of milk, she silently blessed refectory meals. Learning to cook had been a laborious process, but the refectory's bland vegetables and tough meats had helped her meals to shine.

She sipped her own mug of cold milk, running her finger along the squares where Barbara had jotted notes on her calendar. Butterfly weed! Leo had had colic when he was about Gottlieb's age, and Barbara had dosed him with butterfly weed.

"What's that?" asked Emmanuel.

Anna turned the calendar around so Emmanuel could see. "I'm trying to get some ideas from your mother's calendar to help Gottlieb. His tummy has been as tight as a kettledrum all day."

Emmanuel glared at her from under half-closed lids. "What are you doing with my mother's calendar?"

Anna sighed. She hadn't seen that look for quite a while. "Emmanuel, I learn from her calendar."

"You have no right. Give it to me."

"I didn't know it would bother you. I'm sorry."

"Well, it does bother me. It's mine."

He grabbed at the calendar. Anna swept it out of his reach and laid her hand on his arm. "Tell me why it's yours. I don't understand."

Emmanuel jerked back. "I have lessons to do." He grabbed up his books and ran out of the kitchen.

For a minute, no one spoke. The clock chimed four. Anna's throat was constricting, the tears welling up in her eyes.

"Don't mind Emmanuel," Friedemann said. "Sometimes he gets crazy."

But Anna was discouraged. She and Emmanuel had been doing so well. He'd been difficult the first few weeks after the wedding; but she had been careful not to push, and gradually he'd seemed to accept her. She suspected Catherina had interceded for her.

Barbara's sister had visited them twice now. She'd not been able to attend their wedding, but had arrived soon afterward to help with Christmas.

Catherina's help with the Bach holiday traditions were as invaluable to Anna as the things her own mother taught her about taking care of her first baby. From Catherina she'd learned how to make the Advent wreath and the Twelfth Night Christmas cake—dark with fruit and spices and decorated with gold and silver stars. Catherina had also explained the First Day custom. It had come to them from an Hungarian ancestor named Veit Bach. Each year the Bachs saved back several ears of corn and, on New Year's Day, set them out as a feast for the birds. It was a custom she had grown to love.

When they decided to move to Leipzig, Catherina offered to help them with the move. The difficult trip, made even more difficult by the shocking event of Henrietta's death, was facilitated by Catherina's competent presence. During both of Catherina's visits and for weeks afterward, Emmanuel had been more manageable. He even began offering to help her with the repair of broken items: a cracked bowl, the leg of a chair, even the carving of a new handle for a knife. He had learned much from Gottfried.

As recently as last week, Anna thought her relationship with Emmanuel was becoming not only tolerable, but congenial. One of the chores she dreaded most was shopping in the Leipzig marketplace. It was twenty times as big as the one in Cothen, and it was always swarming with foreigners.

Leipzig was one of the most important trade centers in Germany. It was positioned at the meeting point of two important trade routes: an east-west route for the exchange of western manufactures and eastern raw materials and a north-south route connecting Nurnberg to Hamburg on the North Sea. Trade fairs that attracted people from all over the world were held in Leipzig twice a year. But even without the fairs, the city's marketplace seemed always raucous. Anna hated bargaining, and it was essential these days that she secure commodities and food at the lowest prices possible.

Sebastian's salary was quite a bit lower here, and the cost of living higher. When they first arrived, Sebastian had spent hours working on their accounts. He moved groschen, thalers and guilders about, determining how many weddings and funeral engagements he would need to play in order to provide for their needs, and how much money Anna could spend at the market.

Thriftiness, she'd learned, had always been important to Sebastian, but here it was essential. The Thomasschule provided their quarters rent free, but these were old and drafty. The icy winds were high in the winter, and they found themselves burning a great deal of wood. The halls were crooked and dark, requiring many wax candles. The homemade tallow ones were too malodorous. And there was always something needing to be replaced: a hood for the oven, a windowpane, a section of hearth tile. Besides that, the boys were beginning to eat a great deal, and the babies kept coming.

Last Saturday, Sebastian suggested she take Emmanuel with her to the market. Emmanuel had not protested. She'd donned her brown russet, bemoaning the fact that if you wore the bright colors of the aristocracy in Leipzig, people thought you were seeking to rise above your God-ordained *Stand*.

As soon as she was dressed, she hurried downstairs to meet Emmanuel. His black hair was pulled back into a queue, and he'd thrown a black cloak of Friedemann's about his shoulders. Anna suspected Friedemann had not given his permission, but Friedemann was out playing the organ for a funeral Sebastian had not been able to take.

Together, Anna and Emmanuel stepped out into the cobbled streets of the Thomaskirchoff. To their left the sun was shining on the pinnacle of the Thomaskirche making it glisten like water. The windows were shuttered in the school at the far end of the church. No classes today. Stretching behind them was the building that housed the dormitory and their own quarters. To their right was another Thomasschule building consisting of offices and more lodgings. They passed the public water fountains and ambled along beside the stone water trough that stretched down the street. No ice on the water today. It was warm for January.

As they turned into the busy street leading to the market, Anna stumbled over the uneven pavement. A wheelbarrow piled with sacks of wool was clacking toward them. They swerved to avoid it and found themselves headed for a pile of firewood where a man was swinging an ax. Anna halted no more than a foot from its back swing.

The man swore at them. It was incidents like these that made Anna miss the life of a village. She was still feeling shaky when they reached the marketplace.

"Let's start with flour and sugar," she said, "then butter, coffee and some salted fish. I'd like to find a ham for tomorrow also. The apothecary's on my list, the cooper and the hat maker, then some odds and ends." Two hours later they had everything on their list but the ham. Anna only had twenty-five groschen left.

"Let's try old Franz," said Emmanuel.

"He always begins higher than anybody else," said Anna.

Emmanuel's black eyes glittered in his round face, "I can manage him."

A German hausfrau in the usual black cloak and bonnet was leaving the butcher's stall with a string of pigs' feet. She was shaking her head. Old Franz's bulging eyes and thick lips looked triumphant.

When Franz saw Emmanuel, he hailed him. "It's the young Bach! Come to do some business today? I've got some cracklings that fry up so delicious, they melt in your mouth."

They smelled delicious. Franz's wife was frying some over a brazier. They sizzled and spat. The boy scanned the hanging hams. He pointed. "We'd like that one right there."

It was the largest ham of the lot and quite lean.

"That will be seventy groschen."

Emmanuel shoved his fists to his hips. "That's thievery! I'll give you fifteen groschen."

Franz's eyes gleamed. "You can have a ham bone for that, not much more. Sixty-five groschen with some cracklings thrown in."

Emmanuel's eyes held the merchant's. The boy countered in a firm voice. And back and forth it continued. Their voices rising, guffawing, pleading, insulting.

A crowd began gathering to see this sight, a twelve-year-old boy who barely reached the wily Franz's shoulder bargaining better than most men. Emmanuel's skill and eagerness quickened as the crowd grew. Franz's weakened. Finally, after half an hour, Emmanuel succeeded in purchasing the ham for twenty-five groschen, with a bag of cracklings thrown in.

Anna was impressed. "You are a genius."

Emmanuel bowed low with a sweep of his tricorner, "My godfather taught me."

Anna was surprised, but she asked no questions. Emmanuel kept up a running correspondence with his godfather. The boy was possessive of Telemann's letters, even secretive.

The slamming of the front door jerked Anna back to the present.

It was Sebastian. "And what might you be doing my heart?" Sebastian bent to take her face in his cold hands, gave her a kiss and studied her face. She felt the tears coming.

"Problems?"

Anna told him what had happened with Emmanuel, and Sebastian immediately left to speak to him. She followed him up the stairs to check on Gottlieb.

The baby was grizzling at her breast halfheartedly when Frau Klemm lumbered into the room with her arms full of linens. The hausfrau always came to help with the bi-monthly *gross wasche*. She had a wide, flat nose and her black hair was pasted like twilled linen against her ears. When she walked she looked like a great boat rocking from side to side.

"I will need you to draw most of the water tomorrow," said Anna. "I am singing at the town meeting."

"Humph! Gonna leave the baby, are you, and him sick?"

"We need the money, and this is nothing new with Gottlieb. I plan to purchase some butterfly weed while I'm out."

"Butterfly weed is it? Preventive medicine is the best medicine. You should be more careful what you eat. Gallivanting around showing yourself off doesn't help your nerves. Sours your milk. Probably why your first baby died. Should be getting your rest."

Sebastian strode in carrying a tousle-headed Heinrich. "There is no need for censure, Frau Klemm!" His voice was stern. "I encourage my wife's singing. Such a gift should not be wasted."

Frau Klemm waddled out muttering deprecations under her breath.

Anna smiled a thank you at Sebastian, rocking to soothe Gottlieb's whimpering. Sebastian paced back and forth in front of her.

Heinrich was curling a finger in his blonde hair and singing his crooning tune. He loved it when Sebastian walked him.

"Emmanuel will do without dessert for a week," said Sebastian, "and take over Friedemann's chores. Friedemann has several playing engagements."

"Tell me about your Council meeting."

"It's been changed to tomorrow morning at seven."

"Do you think they've received word from the Elector?"

"I hope so. It would be a relief to have this bickering over the University services behind me. Yes, it would be a relief."

Anna shifted Gottlieb's warm little body to her shoulder. It was time to begin dinner. "I finished your socks. A bit crooked, but at least no holes."

She heard Sebastian chuckling as she left, probably looking at the wool socks she'd spent months on. Sometimes she felt intolerably inept. Frau Klemm's criticism today didn't help. It was so like the woman to say everything she was thinking no matter how it might make a person feel. Anna had learned not to blame herself for little Sophie's death. Sebastian had helped her, speaking to her of resurrection. Then his new *Magnificat*, written not long after Sophie's death, had also ministered to her, restored to her the joy of mothering and the surety of design.

As Anna lay out carrots and cabbages for supper, she could hear Friedemann practicing the harpsichord, and in his pauses, the tinkling of the clavichord overhead. Dorothea was practicing too. Anna sighed. She was eager to get to that new minuet in the notebook Sebastian was writing for her: *The Anna Magdelena Notebook*. How special he made her feel!

She marveled that Sebastian could spend a day similar to hers as far as uncongenial work, then at night still have the energy to compose. Night after night, no matter what, he was at his desk, composing the new cantata for the upcoming Sunday. And he continued to study the works of other composers. "There's so much more to learn," he would say.

She'd never known anybody with so much inner motivation. He was highly German, industrious to the bone. These days, however, it was more than raw discipline. His creative energy had the power of the ocean in it, and the ocean had been at full tide for almost three years. He was in the process of achieving his dream.

2

The next morning Sebastian woke up and lay in bed longer than usual. He felt ambivalent about the day. The work had gone so well on the cantata last night that he longed to be able to continue it this morning. There was a place he reached when he sunk himself minute after minute, hour after hour into the creating of phrase after musical phrase that he often forgot about, until he arrived there once again. It was an indentation he settled into like that in his favorite chair, a movement that was effortless when he had been jerking in fits and starts, a sudden discovering himself to be lost on the vitality of the creative sea. And he had been there so often these last three years! He'd finished three *Jahrgangs,* three annual cycles of music of sixty cantatas each, since he'd moved to Leipzig. It was an explosion in his mind.

Buxtehude's bold harmonies, Reincken's large-scale organ applications, the techniques of word-painting—everything merged together and flooded his music staffs with new life. Sometimes when the flow of inspiration was especially strong, he relegated his classes to an assistant and stayed home to compose.

But this morning he had to attend the University Council meeting. How he hated these meetings! There were too many of them, and the wrangling went on and on. He couldn't believe how long it had taken the Council to make a decision which to him was perfectly straightforward. Why did they need to keep hashing it over and over? He'd petitioned the Elector of Saxony concerning what he saw as his rights in the matter. Though Free Towns like Leipzig were ruled in the main by Councils consisting of patricians, guild members and wealthy merchants, the centuries-old practice of relating to the imperial ruler appointed by the Holy Roman Empire remained. For Leipzig the final verdict in legal matters always rested with the Elector of Saxony.

The aroma of coffee and sausages floated up from the kitchen. Anna! She was such an encouragement. Sometimes he felt as though it was she who made it possible for him to write better than he knew how. They talked far more than he and Barbara ever had. Anna was so sensitive to his creative needs that it was seldom a struggle to set aside his work when she needed him. When he returned to his work from time with Anna, it was practically always with some new inspiration she had given him, either by an unusual insight or simply by the nature of who she was. He didn't deserve such a wife, didn't deserve a second chance. How grateful he was for grace!

Sebastian dressed in his camel hair vest and black socks, then hurried up the two flights of stairs to his apprentice's garret room. Carl was a sack of potatoes in the morning, almost impossible to arouse.

Once Friedemann had found him asleep on the *stankgemach.* The privy was in a closet in the corner of the attic.

Sebastian entered the room to find Carl snoring. His long blonde hair had fallen over his face. Sebastian shook him. He turned over and resumed snoring. Sebastian shook him more vigorously. Carl opened his eyes.

"The Council meeting is at seven," Sebastian said. "They will not tolerate tardiness."

Carl nodded, then turned over and went back to sleep. Sebastian hated to do it, but he had no recourse. He took hold of the icy handle of the water pitcher on the night table, lifted it just above Carl's face and poured.

Carl bolted up, gasping.

"University Council meeting, Carl. My apologies."

It took them fifteen minutes to walk from their quarters on the Thomaskirchoff to the Paulinerkirche. The wind was so frigid, Sebastian was forced to hold his muffler over his nose in order to breathe. The naked oak trees that lined the avenue leading to the university church were like ships without sails, their masts stripped and soulless.

"I think that's Hoforganist Gorner behind us," said Carl.

Several yards behind them, a man was hurrying along like an agitated chicken, his folio shielding his powdered wig.

Finally, they reached the church. Reiche and Picander were waiting for them in the vestibule, Reiche square and solid, looking the image of the respectable elder burgher; Picander tall and handsome and carrying a book, as usual. Sebastian didn't know another man of his acquaintance who could look so fine in a cauliflower wig. It showed off Picander's finely chiseled jaw.

How Sebastian appreciated his friends' willingness to give him their support this morning! Reiche had lived so long in Leipzig and had so faithfully provided excellent trumpet music for every kind of affair—church, university and civic—that all thought well of him.

Picander was a strong supporter of Sebastian's music, and a civil servant. Sebastian hoped Picander's support might influence those in the council who made their decisions on the basis of politics.

"Sebastian!" Picander smiled his contagious smile. "And Carl! I see the winter wind has managed to wake you up."

"Everyone is waiting upstairs," said Reiche. "Only Gorner is not here."

There was a rush of cold wind and a banging of the door, and in came Gorner. "Beef and onions! That wind's so furious it could blow a man's ears off."

Picander laughed and greeted the little man. Gorner returned the greeting with a smile. Then his blue-green eyes lit on Sebastian and instantly dropped. He jerked out a handkerchief and blew his nose.

Sebastian felt a rush of dislike for this womanish little man with his misplaced energy. For three years, he and Johann Gottlieb Gorner had been fighting over who would direct the daily and festal services sponsored by the University, and despite Gorner's street quality musicianship, the Council always seemed to favor him. It made no sense to Sebastian.

They climbed the stairs to the Conference Hall to find six council members in cauliflower wigs seated around a long table. They were dressed in black robes trimmed with lace. The paneled room was cold, no fire in the fireplace, only a small brazier in the corner. Dominus Consul Regens, Dr. Lange, presided at the end of the table close to the mullioned windows. His secretary stood behind him in a livery suit of black and gold.

Consul Lange always reminded Sebastian of a bull preparing to charge. His shoulders were as broad as a bedstead, and his neck was so short that the giant lobes of his ears almost touched his robe. Pastor George Adolf Kirkman was there, shaking with the disease age had brought upon him. Why was it he never missed a council meeting?

Kirkman was the familiar-looking man who had helped judge Sebastian's Probe. It turned out that he was a friend of Duke Wilhelm's. He was the very man Sebastian had overheard discussing his Judgment Day Cantata with Wilhelm that May Sunday in 1717.

Kirkman had liked Sebastian's cantata, but when Wilhelm condemned the quality of Sebastian's spiritual life, Kirkman took it as fact. After Sebastian moved to Leipzig, he discovered that it was Pastor Kirkman who had opposed hiring him as Cantor. He had presented Sebastian to the council as arrogant and rebellious, a troublemaker.

The rapping of Consul Lange's gavel brought everyone to silence. He prayed, then requested a review of the case. His secretary stepped forward to read.

"In September of 1723, Thomasschule Cantor Johann Sebastian Bach requested that he, as the Cantor, be given control over the festal services offered to the public by the University in the manner of long-time tradition. Hoforganist Johann Gottlieb Gorner, however, having been accustomed to taking said services when there was no Cantor, requested he be given the privilege of continuing his work uninterrupted, to prevent a break in what he had been trying to achieve."

As the secretary droned on, reviewing matters they had reviewed dozens of times during the last three years, Sebastian wondered what it was that Gorner was trying to achieve. He'd never heard anything from Gorner's Kapelle but derision for the man's music. If the city's worship music was to be improved, a constant outpouring of mediocrity from the institution responsible for training the city's future leaders was not the way to do it.

Consul Lange was speaking. "We will open the floor for further discussion on whether or not the new Cantor of the Thomasschule shall be given the right to the daily services at the University as well as the festal services. Pastor Kirkman!"

The old pastor was standing, one hand on his silver-headed cane and the other on the table for support. "We have given you the festal services, Bach. Why do you continue to insist on the daily services as well? The council has let you know in no uncertain terms that we desire Hoforganist Gorner to continue directing these services. Have you no respect for God-ordained authority?"

Picander stood in a request to speak.

"Commissioner Henrici!"

Sebastian always felt surprised when he heard Picander called by his real name. He'd always known the young poet by his pen name, Picander; but in Leipzig, only those who moved in artistic circles called him Picander. Others knew him as Commissioner Friedrich Henrici.

Anna didn't feel comfortable with Picander. "Who is he, anyway?" she asked one time. "He wins you easily because he guides the conversation in such a way that you think his interests and convictions are the same as yours. But there's always something going on below the surface, something hidden."

"God-ordained authority is not the issue here," Picander was saying. "The issue is education and discernment. I am not a musician. But I've written many librettos, and I've been exposed to enough music to know what is good and what is not. When Bach sets melodies and harmonies to my librettos, the words always gain in power. Always! And that is rare. Having Bach in control of all the university services will give the students quality. Hearing good music daily will train them in taste and discernment. Leipzig University will become a better educational institution because of it."

Pastor Kirkman's age-spotted face was quivering as violently as leaves on a tree in an autumn wind. "I disagree that Bach's submission to authority is not the issue. He has a history of rebellion. If we give in to him on this, what will he insist on next? Besides, birds of a feather flock together, and there are those whose reputation is questionable with whom he is often seen." He glared at Picander.

Kirkman is accusing Picander of something, thought Sebastian. He wondered what it could be.

Herr Zelinski, the mathematics professor, stood up. "We are not a church council here to discipline a church member, but a university council. As such, it is one of our responsibilities to assure that all our university leaders have been properly educated. Herr Gorner has a university degree. Herr Bach does not."

Sebastian was becoming angry. Without waiting for permission to speak, he addressed his adversary. "Tell us, Gorner, what composers you have studied in order to become a better musician, and which ones you are now studying. Have you studied Buxtehude, Reincken, Bohm, Bruhns, Pachelbel, Palestrina and Fischer?"

Gorner's delicate nose quivered. "I have studied Palestrina."

"And what about musica theorica, musica practica and music poetica? Have you explored the treatises of Martin Luther on these techniques? Have you studied the uses of instruments in Vivaldi, Handel, Torelli, Albioni and Schutz?"

"Vivaldi and Handel."

"And that is all?"

"I'm sure there are others. My university years are far behind me."

"I have studied all these and continue to study: French music, Italian music, the great German church music, the English composers. It is all needed if we are ever to create a distinctive German music."

Reiche dropped his hand on Sebastian's arm. Sebastian's head was pounding.

Consul Lange's bull face was red with anger. "I would advise you to wait for permission before you speak, Bach. Trumpeter Reiche?"

"I will vouch for Bach's character. I am often in his home and with him at Zimmerman's Coffee House. His family life is beyond reproach, and his drinking is always moderate."

"I will vouch for the same," Carl said.

Consul Lange rapped his gavel furiously.

Carl stood up and bowed, "Your pardon, Most Honorable Consul."

"Introduce yourself and speak in the proper order!"

Carl bowed again and cleared his throat, "I am Carl Gerlach, music scholar at the Thomasschule and Herr Bach's apprentice. I would like to say that as a senior student at the Thomasschule and one who takes part often in the services at the Thomaskirche and the Nicholaskirche, access to the University musicians is crucial for good performance. Our boy scholars are few in number, and some have sparse musical talent. If Herr Bach is honored with the position of Music Director for all the University services, excellent church performances will be assured."

Consul Lange squinted his eyes. "And so Herr Bach has an ulterior motive!"

Sebastian didn't know if he could stay in his seat one more minute. He wanted to shout them all down, expose this ridiculous farce. Why in the world did a composer have to compliment and grovel and perform all kinds of machinations to ingratiate men who knew nothing about music and would just as soon have a man with a monkey and a hurdy-gurdy play their worship services as have a master at the pipe organ with a contrapuntal Kapelle.

He was saved by a pounding at the door. Everyone fell quiet. The secretary clipped along behind the black-robed council members and opened the door.

"An epistle from the Elector," a bass voice boomed. The secretary returned and lay the letter on the table in front of Consul Lange.

Quickly, Lange slit the letter open, read it silently, then passed it to the council member on his right. "I will not keep you waiting. It is from His Highness August the Strong, the Elector of Saxony, and it concerns these very issues. His Majesty has decided that the festal services will remain in Cantor Bach's hands, and the daily services in Hoforganist Gorner's. There will be no more discussion. The meeting is adjourned."

A pinpoint of blackness began behind Sebastian's eyes, then crept slowly but inexorably through his mind, down to his chest and into his stomach where it bundled into a knot. He had been so sure that when he came to Leipzig he would be moving into the position of Music Director for the whole city. Long-time tradition had granted the Thomasschule Cantor such unhampered influence. He'd hoped to use his new cantatas in the university services as well as the Lutheran churches he was responsible for each Sunday.

But now any such use of his works would require collaboration with Gorner. It was not an appealing prospect.

3

The rest of the day at the Thomasschule was a gauntlet: a morning of singing and instrumental classes, inspection duty in the refectory during the noon hour, a wedding rehearsal in the afternoon, and a three-hour trek through the city with the perambulating choir. Sebastian hated the compulsory nature of these winter serenades. He knew the boys needed the money; but today, half of them had sore throats, and the weather was growing colder.

Sebastian decided to stop at Zimmerman's coffee house before he went home. Down the cobbled streets he hurried to the well-lit establishment in the Catherinenstrasse. He could hear music—woodwinds tonight. A carriage was parked outside. This was not strange. Many aristocrats frequented the coffee house, but this carriage looked unusually familiar. It was a gilt carriage with red velvet curtains. Its horses were festooned with bells and feathers. They were caparisoned in the same manner as the horses that had been one of his first sights the day he was released from prison in Weimar.

And the carriage! It was the very one that had whisked him and Barbara to the Red Castle the night of Duchess Mariana's attempted suicide.

Sebastian saw him the minute he walked into the chandeliered hubbub of the coffee shop. He was dressed in orange and purple, sitting at a square oak table near the musicians. He had gained so much weight he looked like a mountain. It was August.

A few minutes later, Herr Zimmerman, laughing and jesting as usual, guided August and Sebastian across the red and white marble floor to a corner table that had just been vacated.

"I have coffee from the West Indies today, and Alsatian wine. Here you will be able to study my new Greek painting." Zimmerman raised a plump, well-haired arm to indicate the picture on the wall behind them. Hung tastefully above shelves of colorful bottles, it was a view of a gleaming white building with columns and urns, against the purple-blue of the Mediterranean Sea.

August studied it appreciatively while Sebastian ordered, and soon they were laughing over a bottle of Alsatian wine.

"Finished up the estate business I came for," August explained, "and came in for a drink and some good music. Although," he leaned toward Sebastian with the air of a conspirator, "I am wondering what the proprietor had in mind when he invited that oboist."

The ensemble was still playing on the small stage among the tables, the harpsichordist smooth and inventive, the flute, excellent. The oboist, however, who was using the curved oboe da caccia, kept missing notes.

"Herr Zimmerman informed me you usually drop by on your strolling choir days," August said. His pouched face was flushed because of the wine, and there were bags under his eyes.

Sebastian nodded. "I am glad to see you busy and away from home."

"Mother returned home from Italy a couple of weeks ago and badgered me until I got out. Elinor's death has given everything else the color of death. I've not been able to enjoy anything."

August gulped downed the rest of his wine, clunked the goblet on the table and upturned the bottle for a refill. "Tell me about what it is like to be Cantor of this school."

Sebastian told him about his disappointment of the morning, "The Council and I do not get along, I'm afraid."

August grinned at him, "Why am I not surprised?" August cut a piece of the Lowland cheese Zimmerman had brought them.

He looked up suddenly. "Wilhelm has a growth. They say he may not live more than a year."

Sebastian was surprised, "And you will be the Grand Duke!"

"It is my only hope for any cheer in life. I have already begun working on ideas for new buildings and gardens, a decent-sized theater, real festivals with dancing and masquerades. And the court will play cards daily. Quadrille, hombre. I may even set up some skittles lanes. How about a game of quadrille tonight? Have any friends who might be interested?"

"It's possible. Reiche and Picander might be available."

4

After the evening meal with Anna and the children, Sebastian left for the nobleman's quarters on the square where August was staying. Reiche and Picander were already there. They had their foursome.

Halfway into the evening, August insisted on playing for high stakes. Reiche opted out. Their host took his place and kept replenishing their glasses with French brandy. August drank too much and began to cheat. Picander challenged him.

August denied it, and Picander hit him. The evening ended with August nursing a swelling right eye, Sebastian trying to convince Picander it was in his best interest to apologize and Picander stubbornly refusing. He stalked out, swearing noblemen were pigs.

When Sebastian was assured that August was being attended to properly, he and Reiche left. Sebastian was worried. August had gained so much weight he couldn't even begin to defend himself in a fight, and his drinking was out of control.

Before he left the city, August attended the Sunday service at the Thomaskirche and joined them for Sunday dinner. Anna, Sebastian and August relaxed in the upstairs sitting room after the meal. Sebastian was finishing his strudel and cream. It was crusty, with exactly the right touch of spice. "You have conquered it, my dear."

Anna looked pleased. "I thought your cantata especially fine today."

Sebastian smiled. He felt good about today's performance. Reiche had been there to play the trumpet, and the boys had been particularly expressive. "Clergyman Graff told me that one of the visitors said the work gave her new hope."

August shook his head. "The subject bothered me. The devil fighting the archangel and being thrown out of heaven. I can't believe it."

"But the battles of life are real," said Sebastian. "Inner conflict, outer conflict. There are always personal skirmishes in some portion of our lives. I believe the origin is spiritual."

"The tenor aria was my favorite," Anna said. "'Guide me on both sides so that my foot may not slip, teach me to bring thanks to the Highest.'"

"I am weary of hearing that!" August's voice was angry. "Give thanks in all things. Ridiculous! Give thanks for the loss of a reason to live. Give thanks for the anguish someone like my self-righteous uncle has caused. Give thanks that in this world, ruled by this so-called good and omnipotent God, you come home to find your beloved wife dead. It happens over and over to us, and still we think God is good? I will not believe it. I cannot believe it. Man needs something real to hold onto, something that will give him surcease now. Give me power over men and commodities. Give me drink. Give me smells and tastes and the flesh of a woman. It is the only way, the only way."

Suddenly August's voice broke, and his shoulders began to heave. He stumbled out of his chair and left the room.

"Rococo was provocatively secular and a Parisian invention, a reaction against heavy Classicism of Versailles. It drew inspiration from natural objects in which the line wandered freely—shells, flowers, seaweed. . . . (It was a) reaction against academic style."[1]

"The St. Matthew Passion *is a massive and deeply moving work that has no model, no precedent and no equal in the Baroque Era. . . . It is a work at once magnificent and intimate, despairing and filled with faith."[2]*

15

The Passion
1 7 2 6 – 1 7 2 9

Sebastian had never had many friends outside his family. He saw it as something to do with his tendency to seek solitude when he had extra time and then, an inquiring frame of mind, both artistic and spiritual, which few people understood. The close friends he'd had, like Ernst and Leopold, were younger than he. Picander was also younger.

For some time Sebastian had longed for an older friend he could look to for counsel, someone he could depend on to understand his creative workings and offer wisdom in the spiritual realm. Reiche had become that person. Sebastian counted his friendship a gift from God.

Sebastian still considered August a friend, but not an intimate one because they could never discuss without conflict matters like the redemption of tragedy or the reality of divine guidance. Lately, August had even been urging him to abandon his commitment to the old musical styles. "If you desire success in today's musical world, rococo is your only hope."

Sebastian could never abandon the integrity of his music in such a way. The shallowness of the rococo style was as contradictory to who he was as nursery rhymes would have been to Shakespeare.

Such a comparison, he knew, would bring loud guffaws from his enemies, but he was discerning enough to know that his composing skills were becoming formidable. He decided to prove to August that counterpoint could produce a merry heart and appeal to all. He would publish his partitas, harpsichord suites, he had written for his older boys. Even fourteen-year-old Bernhard enjoyed practicing them.

Of all the volumes of works Sebastian had composed—organ works, cantatas, orchestral works, occasional pieces, motets and solo works for violin, cello, lute and flute—he'd only had three pieces published. The printing business in Germany was behind that of England and France. German commerce had still not recovered from the devastation of the Thirty Years' War.

Gradually, however, publishing houses were springing up. One of them, Breitkopf Publishing, was headquartered in Leipzig. When Sebastian first learned this, he was encouraged. Perhaps Breitkopf would be willing to publish most if not all of his works.

But when Sebastian approached him, the bushy-browed publisher shook his head. "German musicians are so prolific these days that I have to be very selective. Even a new work of Telemann's rarely sells more than one hundred copies, and he still maintains a high degree of popularity in Leipzig. Very few people want to spend hard cash on music. They'd rather barter. Cash is what I need."

Sebastian decided he'd have to pay for the publishing himself. Then he remembered Telemann had managed the cost of some of his publishing by learning to make copper engravings. Sebastian asked Emmanuel to write his godfather and ask for a detailed explanation of the process. Telemann responded immediately. Emmanuel and Sebastian studied the process together.

The boy was excited and hoped he could help.

Sebastian, however, was not so excited. The process was complicated: copying out the manuscript on only one side of the paper, soaking the sheets of paper in oil to make them transparent, treating a copper engraving plate with a substance that made the copper impervious to acid, scratching the notes out with a graver on the plates, then using etching acid to deepen the places laid bare.

Sebastian was still writing his worship music. If he interrupted his momentum to concentrate on conquering the engraving process, he feared a sacrifice of quality in his church cycle. And that was something he refused to allow.

Finally, he decided to pay Breitkopf for the publishing of one partita at a time. Sebastian would sell them from his home.

He published the first partita in 1726 and the next in 1727. They both did well. Every time he made a trip to Cothen for a musical foray with Prince Leopold and Leopold's new music-loving wife, the Prince had more orders for him. Sebastian was even receiving orders from England and France.

One rainy summer day in 1728, Friedemann interrupted Sebastian's Friday afternoon rehearsal with a new batch of partitas. The eighteen-year-old clambered noisily up the back gallery stairs of the Thomaskirche and thumped a leather-covered box on the floor beside the organ. "The third suite, Father. We must celebrate!"

For once Sebastian was grateful for the interruption. He'd begun work on a new Passion, and felt it had the potential to be the best work he'd ever written. It was so difficult, however, that he'd decided to start his students on the work early.

But today, even the older students were acting like twelve-year-olds. They'd been poking and elbowing each other and talking so loudly in between choruses that Sebastian could not make himself heard. He decided to dismiss them early and take Friedemann to Zimmerman's to celebrate.

They hurried through the rain to the Catherinenstrasse, black cloaks flying, tricorners dripping rain, carrying the box between them. The bulbous-nosed Zimmerman met them at the door with a grin.

He was wearing a short, embroidered vest that emphasized his balloon of a stomach. "I'd been hoping for some music on this dismal afternoon."

Friedemann nodded toward the open umbrella beside the coat tree. "I see Picander's here."

"In the back. He swears by that contraption. Oilskin repels the rain." Zimmerman hung their cloaks for them and led them toward a back corner table, grabbing a coffee pot and pewter mugs on the way.

Friedemann nudged Sebastian, "Look!"

The bull-like Consul Lange and a slight-figured man who looked like

Gorner from the back were sitting at a table behind a potted orange tree. It must be Gorner. He was the one man Sebastian knew whom you never saw without his cauliflower wig. Sebastian was required to wear one whenever he was on duty at the school, but he always took it off in leisure hours.

Lange glared at Sebastian over his tankard of beer. Sebastian dipped his head slightly and tried not to return the glare. Lange always made him feel like a lackey. Their most recent conflict was only last week. Sebastian hadn't checked with the Council before he granted one of his students permission to leave for the country to see his ailing father. When Lange and Kirkman rebuked him for not applying to the Council first, Sebastian refused to justify himself. To delay letting the boy go until a meeting of the Council might mean the father would die before the boy had a chance to see him. But Sebastian knew there was no reasoning with Council members. Everything was done by the letter of the law. So he'd listened to their rebuke and said nothing.

Sebastian sank into a chair at the table where Zimmerman was describing the day's specialties to Friedemann. Friedemann asked several questions, then ordered the new French pastry—*setewale* Zimmerman called it, uncommonly rich and flavored with ginger. Sebastian decided on a plate of cinnamon cheese tarts. He downed the hot coffee and bit into a pastry. Ah! The crust was cinnamony, the inside creamy and sweet. Zimmerman's robust coffee was the perfect foil.

Now to check the partitas. He'd ordered one hundred of them. Only two errors. He and Friedemann could correct them easily by hand. Quickly, Sebastian began penning in "Soli Deo Gloria" at the end of each partita. For the refreshment of the spirit and the mind, he thought, something with substance like the paintings of Rembrandt.

As the afternoon wore on, the door swung open with increasing frequency, letting in a draft of cool air and a wet and noisy customer.

At Zimmerman's request for some harpsichord music, Friedemann picked up one of the partitas off the stack they were working through, took his seat at the harpsichord and launched into a merry rendition of the third suite.

Sebastian willed himself to shut out everything around him and began scribbling figures on a tablet. He muttered to himself as he worked, "Cost of production, fifty groschen a partita; and if I desire a fifty percent profit . . ."

Someone interrupted him, "I'd make it sixty percent at least, the way your first two suites have sold."

It was Reiche, just come in from the rain. He drew up a chair and confiscated one of Sebastian's tarts.

"Not even you are allowed to steal my sustenance, Reiche. Go get me another."

Reiche's mint green eyes gleamed in his big face. "You could use a tad of dieting, friend."

Sebastian patted his stomach, "How can a man who has had two wives who excel in cooking not stay plump as a Christmas goose? Performance rained out?"

"Correct! And I haven't had anything to eat since breakfast. All that setting up for nothing."

Reiche left to get some coffee, and Sebastian continued working at his figures: multiplying and subtracting, figuring in discounts for those who ordered more than two, projecting into the future—three more partitas, then perhaps selling them as a set.

Someone slapped him on the back. Sebastian swiveled to see Picander's straight nose, high brow and winning smile.

The poet bent to examine a partita, "Breitkopf never fails to do excellent work!" he said.

He sat in Friedemann's chair, chin propped on his hand to look at Sebastian, wooden cross swinging over the printed notes of the partita.

"Everywhere I travel, duchesses and baronesses are saying they must have every one of the Prince of Claviers' partitas."

"Despite their difficulty?" It was Carl. He reached for a partita. His cloak was dripping water across the table.

Sebastian jerked the suite away from him. "You're wet as a fish."

Carl made a face that made him look twelve years old instead of twenty-one, adjusted his thick glasses, then plopped into a chair.

"Just listen to that partita Friedemann's playing," he said. "The complexity, the diversity, but also the unity."

"A perfect example of music as a formula of the wisdom and order of

God," said Reiche.

Carl nodded, "Thou hast ordered all things in measure and number and weight."

Bach gazed at his blonde apprentice for a minute, thinking what an anomaly he was: a child one minute, a philosopher the next. How often he tried Sebastian's patience! His ability as a musician, however, was indisputable. He would make an excellent Hoforganist, or even a Cantor.

"I'm glad to see you taking this initiative in publishing," said Picander. "Our old attitudes of resignation to the fate of our status by birth must be set aside. You are activating the self in the matter of Leibniz's teaching. I commend you."

Reiche leaned forward. "Hard work, fighting for the right, yes, but sometimes we have no choice but to leave matters in the Almighty's hands. I agree, though, that this could be the beginning of great things for Bach."

"I predict that next will come the Court Composer title. Johann Sebastian Bach, Court Composer for the Elector of Saxony," said Picander. "That's where you belong."

Sebastian nodded. Yes, the title did appeal to him. Perhaps it would happen in time.

As the afternoon wore toward evening, the pounding of the rain slowed, and by five o'clock the coffee house was filled, buzzing with the lightheartedness of men finished with their work for another week. Sebastian must leave soon. He always made it a point now to be home for dinner if at all possible.

One of Zimmerman's waiters kept bringing Picander messages from a lady who was waiting outside. Picander swore under his breath at the first note and scribbled a reply. Back and forth the notes went until finally Picander rose from the table apologetically. He smiled, but there was resentment in his voice. "My admirers will not leave me alone. Women think they have rights just because once you showed an interest."

After he left, Sebastian's second apprentice, Johann, joined them, his short frame clad in a brown cloak that was too large for him and his curly black hair still damp from the rain.

He and Carl began spelling Friedemann at the harpsichord. They launched into some preludes and fugues from the *Well-Tempered Clavier,* but returned to the currently published partita again and again. Men began stopping by Sebastian's table to purchase copies of the partitas for their wives and daughters.

Gorner even hurried over in his jerking gait to examine the music. He clinked out eighty groschen.

"My fingers are far too slow and dull-witted. Perhaps some of Bach's lightning facility will rub off on me if I try his partitas." He rubbed at his delicate nose and winked at Sebastian. "At least I've got the Collegium Musicum going with finesse, organized finesse too, if I do say so."

Sebastian felt a flash of envy! Gorner's new Collegium Musicum was a city orchestra composed of serious musicians. In this particular endeavor, Gorner had no church council hovering over him, no Consul Lange commanding him to use some wealthy merchant's son as a soloist to secure the church's finances. Well, Sebastian thought, that is where Gorner is now, but I am somewhere else. I must finish the church cycle with my very best effort, be faithful in my own circumstances. I must persevere.

2

August sent word the next week that Wilhelm had died. Sebastian knew immediately that he must attend the services. There had been funerals of too many others he'd not attended and afterward wished he had. Wilhelm had been an important part of his life for almost ten years. He should at least pay his respects. Anna was busy with their three small children, so he decided to make the trip to Weimar by himself.

Wilhelm's funeral ceremony was well done. There in the green and gold ducal chapel where Sebastian had presided so often at the organ, he listened to music led by a Kapellmeister from Berlin: "Come, Come Sweet Death," and the "Resurrectus" by Palestrina, effortless voices and playing. For the first time in months, Sebastian was able to relax and worship. He didn't have to be responsible for the service. The music was reverent and otherworldly. If only he could achieve this in his own worship services, not with the Renaissance music of composers like Palestrina, but with the passionate music of the Baroque.

A clergyman read a summary of Wilhelm's life and achievements.

Wilhelm had set up an orphanage and a seminary. He had also reinstated confirmation for all children under his rule, making sure every nobleman, burgher and serf in his realm grew up with a knowledge of the Truth. He'd even founded a library.

When the Weimar clergyman finished, Pastor Kirkman, who had also traveled from Leipzig for the services, rose to speak. Sebastian was deep in thought about life and death and accomplishment. He was forty-three now, an age many men never reached. How many more years did he have? Five, ten, twenty? Whenever he had a period of quiet away from the needs of his family, his teaching and his daily composing, he found himself reviewing his life.

He was not proud of his obstinate spirit, and he had been particularly willful under Duke Wilhelm. Barbara had always felt he should have been more willing to give in to Wilhelm. She'd felt that by not doing so, Sebastian had endangered his future in church music. *Was I wrong not to listen to Wilhelm?* Sebastian wondered. He thought about Picander's beliefs about activating the self and remembered with pain how at Carlsbad similar philosophical ideas had caused him to compromise his discipline to the point of almost committing adultery.

Pastor Kirkman read the scripture he had chosen for his old friend. He voiced his remembrances of the Duke. The old man's face and voice quivered, but his eyes were bright. Then his glance crossed Sebastian's. His eyes changed, steeled. Sebastian's mood of regretfulness vanished. *Like Wilhelm, this important member of the Leipzig council would rather have mediocrity and obedience than excellence and passion. I can never submit to such a man,* Sebastian thought. *It is wrong. It is unfair.*

Kirkman sat down, and the music resumed—about judgment and reward and peace. Sebastian's emotions calmed.

Sometimes he and Reiche discussed the fear they couldn't quite shake that they weren't being as useful to others as they should be. Music was so abstract. A trade, something "old" you do with your hands. Reiche longed for it so much that he had recently begun spending a day each week cobbling for the poor of the city. *How will my life be judged?* Sebastian wondered.

The next day he attended August's induction, and afterward, a feast at the Red Castle. He congratulated August and tried to sound enthusiastic about his friend's plans. But Sebastian was concerned. When August began detailing his ideas for landscaped gardens and elaborate new buildings, with no word at all about how he hoped to help the many needy in his kingdom, Sebastian realized for the first time that there could be a problem. He wondered if he'd failed August, if he'd even led him astray.

3

Back at home he concentrated on finishing the *St. Matthew Passion*. In this his last work for his church cycle, he would seek to lead people to a thirst for God, an ability to see the depth of His goodness, but also to understand something of the abyss of His Son's suffering. I must vindicate my craft, he thought, by achieving with it the highest good.

He finished the Passion in January of 1729 and began planning seriously for its performance on Good Friday. First, he petitioned the Council for help in recruiting more musicians. Kirkman's instant response was negative.

"You've had your chance to choose your foundationers for the music scholarship program, and they are under your training. If they are not sufficient, it is not our fault. Hiring town musicians requires money, and neither the Church nor the Town Council has it to spare."

The council members around the long table all nodded. Their faces were hard. The only person in the paneled room who exuded any sympathy was Carl von Kirchbach. He was a university student whose father was a nobleman of considerable wealth.

"You don't understand," Sebastian said. "This work needs two twelve-voice choruses, two seventeen-member orchestras and an extra twelve-voice choir for the chorales. It is to be an intense celebration of the Passion of our Lord. It deserves our best."

The secretary behind Consul Lange was scribbling all this down, but Lange gave him an irritated look and motioned him to stop. Lange slapped his hands on the table and leaned forward with a thrust of his bull head. "Bach, your impertinence will never end, will it? Who do you think you are? That is double the amount of musicians allotted you. Why in the name of God did you write a work that required so many musicians to whom you have no access? Change the orchestration. Rewrite the composition. It's as simple as that."

While Kirkman and another council member were voicing their approval of Consul Lange's ultimatum, Sebastian's impatience was boiling up in him like a pot of scalding milk.

The man has no idea what he is dealing with, Sebastian thought. I did not choose the texture of the work. Its life is its own. Finding fault with it is like finding fault with a tree because it has too many branches. The man is a fool.

He was about to burst out in retort when von Kirchbach stood up. "Councilmen, please. Think." Von Kirchbach was a regular cello player for Sebastian's Kapelle. He was also brilliant.

He argued cogently for Sebastian's request, and the council listened. He affirmed the power of Sebastian's Passion, and the desperate need for more trained musicians. He even hinted at the withdrawal of his father's financial support for certain city projects if they did not help the Cantor of the Thomasschule in this current dilemma.

Reluctantly Consul Lange gave in. "We will grant you a stipend to hire more musicians, but don't expect a continuance."

After the meeting, Sebastian thanked Von Kirchbach for his help, but hurried home with the vestiges of his ire streaming along behind him. This victory, he knew, would make the next battle more difficult. As he strode along, he willed his mind to concentrate on the good of the moment. The stipend would not hire as many musicians as he had hoped, but it would help, and with Friedemann, Emmanuel and Bernhard alternating singing and playing different instruments, the Passion had a chance for a decent performance.

The next evening, Sebastian arrived at the Thomaskirche for the Passion rehearsal in good spirits. He strode through the sanctuary and up the gallery stairs.

What he saw was unbelievable. There amid all the gathering musicians was Gorner, seated on the organ bench. This had to be somebody's idea of a jest.

But Gorner hopped down from the bench and approached Bach with a worried expression. He bowed and blinked his eyes hard.

"My apologies to you, Bach. Markhoffer is seriously ill. The Council elected me to take his place as Hoforganist for the Passion." He shrugged his thin shoulders. "I knew you wouldn't like it. But it is, after all, a fine opportunity for me."

Speechless, Sebastian stared after Gorner as he retreated to the organ, climbed onto the organ bench and began clicking out his stops. A sharp pain shot across Sebastian's forehead, and for a moment, all his enthusiasm for his new work fell into a pit of something that felt like doom. Gorner was a notoriously bad sight reader, and most likely, he'd had no time to study the music. How could this be happening?

Sebastian took a deep breath, adjusted his wig and buttoned his coat tight across the middle. He clapped his hands for attention. The rustling of pages and clattering of instruments quieted.

"Today we will read straight through the first section. No stopping if at all possible. Do your best. Just keep going."

At the first organ entrance, however, Gorner began in the wrong key and became so confused, he ceased playing at all, hunched into himself and peered over his shoulder at Sebastian.

Sebastian continued to wave the scrolled up manuscript he used for a baton, but Gorner couldn't find his place. Sebastian clenched his teeth.

"Back at the organ entrance."

Gorner attempted it again, while von Kirchbach bowed the bass line as loudly as he could on the cello. The dissonances that came from the organ as Gorner dithered about on the keys were so unspeakable that Sebastian didn't think he was going to be able to endure another note. Finally Gorner managed to achieve the proper key.

They stumbled on for an hour with Sebastian trying to focus on the fine timbre of the boy sopranos' voices and the excellent reading of Emmanuel and Friedemann on their solos while Gorner punched at the keys with the finesse of an organ grinder's monkey. Some of the boys began imitating the chicken-like movements of the little organist. Sebastian tried to ignore them. His wig was growing tighter and tighter.

They were in the middle of one of the plaintive "Sacred Head" chorales when Gorner accidentally jerked out the trumpet stop. He was playing a wrong pedal tone, and it blared over everything else and kept blaring. One by one the singers dropped out. The boys started giggling.

The pain in Sebastian's head was intolerable. He couldn't take it any longer. He reached up, clutched at the coarse powdered hair of his wig, jerked it off and hurled it over the boys' heads straight at Gorner.

It struck Gorner smack on the left side of his head, and Gorner was so startled he stood straight up on the pedal keys. The pedals emitted a thunderous roar. Gorner swatted at the wig, which was hanging sideways across his shoulder, knocked it off, then kept swatting at the powder the wig had left on his coat. Everyone in the Kapelle collapsed with laughter.

Gorner jumped down from the organ and wove his way through the violin section toward Sebastian. His delicate nose was quivering.

"Well, Bach, I judge you think your wig might lend me some of your facility. I bow to your supremacy. You play, and I will learn."

Sebastian marched toward the organ, and with a warning look at the tittering boys, slid onto the organ and jerked and pushed at the stops.

"You snapped up that suggestion like a ring neck duck diving for its supper," Gorner whispered from behind him.

Sebastian growled at him under his breath. The man was incorrigible. Sebastian tried to find the place in the organ score, but his vision was blurring. This was happening more and more often now.

He slapped the music shut. "We will commence at the beginning of the chorale."

Sebastian finished the rehearsal from the organ, playing everything from memory.

After the rehearsal, against the noise of music cases slamming and boys racing through the nave and out of the church, Sebastian looked around for Gorner. Finally, he saw him sitting in a front pew whispering to Picander. The poet had told Sebastian he might be attending the rehearsal. He was eager to hear how his libretto was working with the final version of the Passion. Sebastian approached them unseen.

"Bach played the whole last section of the rehearsal," Gorner was saying, "without ever looking at the music, and he directed at the same time."

He sounded defeated.

"His memory is phenomenal," said Picander, "but as he often says, he has worked hard. I challenge you, Gorner, work hard, determine your own fate. Why, who knows, if you apply yourself, you might even capture the position of Court Composer for the Elector of Saxony!"

Sebastian couldn't believe what he was hearing.

"Pshaw," said Gorner. "Don't be ridiculous."

"You have a desire to learn, and you have organizational skills far above those of Bach's."

"Well, perhaps."

The anger Sebastian had only barely corralled by the proper playing of the organ through the rest of the rehearsal erupted. He rounded on Picander. "So, Picander, you will have Gorner in the Court Composer position now. What sloppy reasoning of the modern mind has brought you to this point?"

Gorner flinched. He had a hurt look in his eyes. Sebastian felt a prick of guilt about his attitude. Mediocre musician or not, Gorner was a human being made in the image of God. No such being deserved contempt.

Picander's handsome face looked troubled. "Do not take offense. Who knows what any of us might achieve if we work to our capacity. Leibniz would agree with me. That beating of the wig you inflicted upon Gorner has left him without spirit."

Sebastian sighed. He didn't understand Picander—his secretive relationships with women and the back-clapping word games with which he went about wooing the worst with the best—but he knew he had not been right to treat Gorner the way he had in front of his students. Reluctantly, Sebastian apologized.

He walked out with both of them. "All I seem to receive these days from the authorities is opposition," he said. "I get a pummeled feeling sometimes. Stay more and more out of sorts, yes, out of sorts."

4

Not only was there opposition almost everywhere Sebastian turned. There was also death.

Anna and Sebastian had been married six years, and during that time they had had five children. Three of them died: little Sophie who died their first year in Leipzig; Ernst Andreas, who was born after Gottlieb and lived only a few days; and Gottlieb, who died soon after Wilhelm's funeral. He was three years old.

Then, only a few weeks before the premiere performance of the *St. Matthew Passion,* Sebastian was summoned to Cothen. On the twentieth of March, Anna, Sebastian, Friedemann and Reiche were bumping along the road in a hired carriage. They were going to another funeral ceremony. Prince Leopold—risking, laughing citadel of talent, energy and ideas—had died suddenly: a failure of the heart. He was thirty-three.

Sebastian's shock and grief had been so intense that Anna was troubled. She was glad Reiche had consented to make the journey with them. The solid-looking trumpeter sat across from her in the carriage, his green eyes and hair with its reddish tint set off by a russet cravat. His presence lent stability, a kind of calmness that you experienced around people who spoke little and listened much.

His presence always did that, whether it was at their table in the midst of a lively argument about rococo versus counterpoint, the new English book by William Law that dealt with the devout and holy life or the treaty between Frederick William of Prussia and Emperor Charles VI.

The carriage careened along, the trot of the horses' hooves and the lumbering of the wheels the only sound. Anna could see the sun on the horizon. Everyone else was half-asleep, but Anna's mind was its most alert during the first part of the day. This morning her thoughts twisted and circled and plunged and retreated through tunnels and passages in her mind.

She was concerned about Sebastian's grief; she worried that she'd forgotten to take the oatmeal pot off the stove; and she kept reviewing the argument she and Emmanuel had had yesterday afternoon. Emmanuel had railed at her when he'd learned that Friedemann was being allowed to go to Cothen and he wasn't.

"I am sorry you are disappointed, Emmanuel, but it is your father's decision. I had nothing to do with it."

"You have something to do with everything Father does. Why is it you get to go and I don't? I can help with the music as much as you and

Friedemann."

"Friedemann is nineteen, and you are fifteen. It is important that he begin to meet people, make his talents known."

"That's not it at all. You only use that for an excuse. You hate me, and I hate you, you, you . . . barmaid!"

Anna felt as though Emmanuel had struck her. How could he speak to any adult with such disrespect? She'd not told Sebastian about it yet. He had enough to deal with as it was.

The sun had risen now, but they were all shivering. The horses heaved and jerked, the road, more often than not, being almost impassable with the mud and ice. Anna unwrapped rolls and passed them out, and when they reached a more even stretch, poured coffee from the warming tankard.

Reiche finished his brioche with an appreciative smack and began humming a chorale tune. His eyes rested alternately on Sebastian, then Anna and then on the passing scenery.

"Prince Leopold must have been an extraordinary man," he said suddenly. Sebastian nodded.

"I have heard his musicianship was versatile and engaging. His duo with Spiess on that Double Concerto of yours is often spoken of in musical circles." Sebastian raised his eyebrows in surprise.

"Leopold's first wife was an *amusa*," said Anna, "but even she loved to hear Leopold sing. 'Any song or aria, even something horribly serious,' she once told me, 'is a romance in my Prince's mellow bass voice.'"

"Very gifted," said Sebastian. "Enlightened. He treated me as an equal, introduced me to the ideas of Leibniz and Descartes. Dresden with Leopold was a cultural feast with the best of the aristocrats."

"Perhaps Leopold's son will be like him," said Anna. "His second wife will encourage it, I am sure."

Friedemann rubbed at his sharp chin. "I remember mother saying Prince Leopold had a natural majesty about him that outshone Duke Wilhelm's like silver outshone crockery."

Sebastian chuckled, and Anna smiled at him and placed her hand over his.

"Do you remember Prince Leopold's face when Henrietta's dogs began howling that night during the music?" she asked him. "You could tell Leopold was exasperated. But he managed the situation with the finesse of a prince as well as a romantic. No one thought worse of him, and Henrietta stayed happy."

"And the rift between you and Leopold when you came to Leipzig?" Reiche asked Sebastian.

"Quickly healed. I dedicated my first partita to his son, and we've made music together and philosophized about truth and the new philosophies many times since."

"This death, then, is not like so many others," said Reiche. "No regrets. You can celebrate your friendship and his resurrection?"

Sebastian closed his eyes. Friedemann fiddled with his cravat, glanced at Anna, then Reiche, than back at his father. Reiche's words are never empty, Anna thought. They are truth that comes out of a silence wherein there is healing.

Finally, Sebastian opened his eyes. "The loss is an abyss, but you are right, my friend, I can mourn without regret. We will celebrate the Prince's life."

For the memorial service, Sebastian led the Cothen Kapelle in performing selections from the *St. Matthew Passion*. Friedemann played a strong second violin. Reiche played brilliantly in sections where Sebastian would have liked to have had a trumpet, but couldn't on Good Friday because tradition forbad it.

Anna sang a soprano aria. "Although my heart swims in tears because Jesus takes leave of us, yet His testament makes me glad. . . ."

Sebastian could not look at her as she sang. He maintained his composure throughout the service, but quickly left after the last chorale. He would be letting loose his weeping, Anna thought, giving Leopold up to God in some private place.

When they arrived home several days later, Anna was surprised to see a tall, thin man helping Emmanuel into a coach. The footman strapped Emmanuel's green and silver valise onto the back. In front of the entourage, Frau Klemm paced back and forth in her rocking gait, shaking her finger and scolding. Dorothea was watching from the doorway, alternately twisting her apron and wringing her hands.

"It's Telemann," said Sebastian. He scrambled down from the carriage and ran toward them, with Anna following.

The coach had already begun to move off, but Telemann saw them, shouted to the coachman to halt and hurried down to meet Sebastian. He threw out his twig-thin arms. "How relieved I am you have arrived!"

"What is this, Telemann?" Sebastian demanded. "Emmanuel?"

Emmanuel looked belligerent, but also a little frightened.

"No, no, don't blame the boy," said Telemann. "I insisted. Knew you would understand. Am taking him with me to Dresden. Have a performance there; need some extra violinists. Thought I'd stop by and see if you could spare the boy for a week or two. Found him morose over your trip to Cothen. You really should use him more, Sebastian. If I had a son like him, I'd . . .Well, you don't know how fortunate you are. Take him for granted, that's what you do.

"Emmanuel's violin is quite as excellent as your wife's voice. Why you take her and not him, . . ." Telemann shook his head. "I am convinced the trip is essential for him right now. Will give him the experience he needs and a break from the monotony of Latin and Theology. Have already spoken to the Rector."

Telemann clapped Sebastian on the arm, and without waiting for a reply, strode back toward the coach and signaled to the driver. The clatter of the horses' hooves on the cobblestones drowned out their attempt at goodbyes. Emmanuel didn't even wave.

Anna felt hurt by Telemann's tone toward her and was incredulous that he would be so presumptuous as to whisk Emmanuel off without asking permission. Sebastian was staring after them, his winged eyebrows drawn together, his fluted mouth set.

"You'd think being Emmanuel's godfather gave Telemann the rights of the Almighty," he said. "He could be right, though. A trip to Dresden might help Emmanuel. I certainly don't know what to do with him these days."

Yes, thought Anna, maybe being away from them for a while would help Emmanuel, enable him to see things more clearly. She still hadn't told Sebastian about the boy's outburst before they left for Cothen. Perhaps she wouldn't have to.

By the time Holy Week arrived, Anna realized she had set herself too many tasks, as usual. Friedemann and Carl had helped her finish the part-copying for the Passion a month before. So she'd decided to make an Easter dress and bonnet for herself and her two-and-a half-year-old daughter. Elisabeth Juliana Friederika they had named her, but everyone called her Liesggen.

Anna offered the hospitality of their home to several of their Cothen friends who had expressed a desire to hear the *St. Matthew Passion.* Christian and Elisa would be staying several nights with their seven-year-old son; and Duke Kober, Spiess and the cellist Schmidt and his wife would sup with them at evening meals. She'd extended the invitations before she remembered they would be hosting a traveling physician that week also. They'd engaged him to observe Heinrich. The five-year-old was not developing as he should. He'd always been able to entertain himself for hours at a time, but his relationships to his siblings were almost nihil. It wasn't that he didn't understand what was said to him or what was going on, but he responded like a puppet, straight-faced and with no warmth.

When he spoke, it was usually in parrot-like repetitions of a question someone had asked him or some other word-combination he remembered from long ago. Anna feared he was feeble-minded.

Sebastian was overwrought with constant rehearsing and the frustration of having several key musicians fall ill this last week of rehearsal. But he took time to notice her frenetic activity and gently scolded.

"You are far too generous with your time, sweetheart. And sewing! You know how you hate it. You should have asked Dorothea to do it."

"She works so hard, Sebastian."

"I insist you at least give her the responsibility for Heinrich and Liesggen on Good Friday. Come to the church early. Listen to the rehearsal. The music and the quiet will strengthen you."

On Good Friday, Anna stepped out into the April air just after noon. She was wearing her new bonnet and shiny gray dress. She'd even decided to be daring and wear the pearl drop earrings Sebastian had given her for her birthday. She approached the entrance of the Thomaskirche, stopping to marvel again at the huge chiseled rose above the door and the arches rising to a point above it. She could hear birds singing in the flanking trees. There wasn't much time to listen to birdsong these days.

As she slipped into the church, she heard Sebastian's best boy soprano singing: "I will give my heart to Thee; sink Thyself in it." Then came the recitative and both choirs singing the chorale: "Know me, my keeper, my Shepherd, take me to Thee."

As she moved into the nave, she felt a quietness creep into her. The music captured her. It lifted her weariness. The sanctuary was lit by a few flickering candles, the giant columns shadowing the pews; and on either side of the altar at the far end of the church, glass windows caught the sunlight.

Where she stood too, light flooded in, and to her left the organ pipes ascended, glinting, to the ceiling. She tiptoed up the gallery stairs and seated herself among the musicians, in an empty chair. Sebastian always saved one for her when he thought she would enjoy attending a rehearsal.

The boys' sopranos swirled around her, then the violins. How she loved to be in the midst of the sound! Today the galleries were fuller than she had ever remembered seeing them. There were eighteen singers and twenty instrumentalists—the majority boys—and the rest university players and town musicians. Instrumentalists were arranged along the sides of the organ, the choir in front of the organ and also in a second small loft in the altar wall.

The musicians would be performing for at least four hours. Three and a half of that was the Passion, with a break in the middle for a forty-five-minute sermon. They would also be performing on Sunday, Monday and Tuesday. Even on normal Sundays the students sang two whole services for two different churches, the hours of their labor mounting to ten—warm-up at 6:00 A.M., last chorale at 4:00 P.M. At least her Sundays were usually restful. Sebastian's never were.

She stayed in the gallery for a while, joining in on passages she knew. Sebastian drilled the musicians on weak spots, stopping occasionally to reiterate the meaning of the words to a soloist. "This must have agony in it / think of how Peter would feel / be Judas / emote / think about what you are singing."

Anna could feel Sebastian's tenseness. What hopes he had for this Passion! He had stayed up praying much of the night.

When the worshipers began to trickle in and Sebastian halted the rehearsal to confer with Gorner, Anna left the gallery and took her place in their pew. Her family gathered with their Cothen friends. She saw Reiche and his wife across the way and later Picander, who took a seat beside Reiche. The sanctuary was only two-thirds full. Unusual for Good Friday. She supposed it was because of the Passion being presented at the New Church. That work also was new, by a promising young composer named Frober.

Sebastian began the organ prelude. They sang the opening chorale, *"Da Jesu an dem Kreuze stund,"* and then it was time for the first part of the Passion. "Come, you daughters, help me lament." Quiet, awed, both choirs sang, then the highest boy sopranos joined in with the descant, "O guiltless lamb of God."

At first, Anna was painfully aware of the people around her and how they were responding to the music. Then she became so involved in the message of Sebastian's Passion that she forgot everything else. The high sweet violins. The increasing drama and anger of the crowd. Jesus' agony in the Garden! The pain was written into the music.

No, it was not perfectly performed. Two of the major soloists stumbled a great deal, and Gorner's performance was only fair; but, for the most part, Sebastian's intent came through.

She responded along with the rest of the congregation with the appropriate chorales.

Sebastian had them sing the chorale melody, "O Sacred Head Now Wounded" again and again. Each singing had different words and harmonies expressing perfectly the emotion of that moment in the drama of the last days of Christ.

"What is the cause of all such woes?" the congregation sang. "Ah, my sins have felled Thee. Ah, Lord Jesus, I have deserved this which Thou art suffering!"

Then finally, at the very end, came the lullaby as Jesus was laid in the tomb, infinitely sorrowful and infinitely sweet.

Anna felt within her a deep hush. She didn't want to leave this place. She had encountered God.

During the first half of the 18th century, Europe was engaged in continual power struggles. Frederick Wilhelm I of Prussia was creating a highly efficient army and tightening the administration of his territories. Russia was expanding westward, and France was vying with Saxony for control of Poland. A year after Friedrich Augustus became the Elector of Saxony, Russia decided to back Saxony and help the Elector ascend the Polish throne.

"The further Bach carried his religious work, the more bitter grew the conflicts with the authorities during each of the periods in which he devoted himself to this task."[1]

16

A Royal Ceremony

1 7 2 9 - 1 7 3 4

Sebastian was attending an emergency Council meeting the next Wednesday afternoon when the physician gave Anna his verdict on Heinrich. The spectacled physician stood in their dark hall, black tricorner in hand, shaking his head.

"I have not seen Heinrich relate to anyone in the family with any kind of emotion. His extreme concern over the placement of objects in his room is also worrisome. I have never known a case where these symptoms did not progress to the point of total helplessness. The fact that you tell me he's been hearing voices—well, in my mind, that settles the question of what is to be done. He must be institutionalized."

Anna was shocked. "You can't mean an asylum? Surely there is something we can do for him here. Aren't there things I can learn from what they do in such an institution that I could employ with him? What about my visiting this place that you service and studying children like Heinrich? And what of his musical interest? I believe that developing a musical skill does much for the development of the whole person: discipline, coordination, the joy of creating beauty with your own voice or hands."

"I have seen no evidence of musical interest in Heinrich."

"None at all?"

The physician shook his head. "I realize this week has not been a normal one for this house. But the inability to adjust to routine difficulties is one of the factors that leads me to diagnose your son's condition as severe. As Heinrich grows older, his condition will worsen. He will become more and more dependent. I know of an asylum that has begun experimenting with treatment for such conditions. For the good of all, I advise you to institutionalize him soon."

All Anna could do after the physician left was sit in her bedroom and cry. She'd heard her mother and father talk of a child like this among her cousins. They blamed the parents. The father was too distracted with his work as a master mason and the mother never showed the child enough affection.

It was true that Sebastian was often distracted, but whenever possible, he made it a point to ask Heinrich to join him on the harpsichord bench during practice sessions. Often Heinrich lingered outside the door of the music room when Sebastian was teaching, waiting for his father to invite him in. When he did, the five-year-old would run to take his place on the footstool Sebastian kept beside his teaching chair. Heinrich would sit, unmoving and rapt, straight as a soldier, until the lute or the violin or the harpsichord lesson, or whatever it happened to be, was over. Sometimes he stayed through Sebastian's whole afternoon of teaching.

The sentences Heinrich remembered usually had to do with these times of sharing music with his father. "A sarabande must be played slow as molasses, a gigue quick as a rabbit hops," he would mimic out of the blue. Or, "Hit the right notes at the right time, and the instrument plays itself."

Are Heinrich's problems my fault? Anna wondered. Do I spend too much time trying to win the favor of the older boys? Does Heinrich sense my distraction when Emmanuel is in the room? Surely I have taken the welfare of my own children for granted.

She crossed the hall to see the five-year-old sitting on the floor near the chair where Dorothea was busy mending.

Liessgen was bouncing about in her wooden walker. Sebastian swore Liessgen was going to grow up to look just like her mother: curly blonde hair, big blue-gray eyes. Heinrich's head was cocked, his thin body still except for the movement of his arm. He was placing a block on top of a tower he was building. He was very good at this building. Sometimes you couldn't coax him away from his blocks to eat.

Anna watched him, her love for him and her concern tightening into a pain around her chest. What were they going to do? She heard the front door slam. Heavy steps were coming up the stairs.

It was Sebastian back from the Council meeting. She ran to meet him on the landing, threw her arms around his neck and started sobbing.

They sat on their bed. He held her hand and listened as she poured a whirlpool of thoughts and emotions into his silence. She told him all the physician had said and all her fears about the reasons for Heinrich's problems. And as she did, she suddenly knew what she had to do.

She wiped her tears with the handkerchief Sebastian had given her. "I will write to Catherina," she said. "Working for the orphanage for so many years, she will know of children like this. She will have ideas. The doctor is wrong. Heinrich can be helped. I know it. It will just take more love, more time. We will use music. We can work out a kind of gradual remedy: daily singing lessons at first, working with words; then, perhaps some of the exercises you gave me when I first began playing the clavichord."

As the words tumbled out, she felt more and more sure. "If I have to employ Frau Klemm several days a week, I will give Heinrich the time he needs. He will grow and develop."

By this time she was pacing up and down in front of Sebastian. He was sitting on the bed, watching her.

There was love in his eyes, but his shoulders were hunched, and his graying brown hair looked the way it did after he'd been composing or fretting over something for hours.

She stopped and looked at him more closely. His clothes were disheveled, and his shoes muddy, as though he had been walking the streets.

He looked haggard, old, not like himself at all. She sat beside him, took his broad face in her hands and kissed his soft, full lips.

"It will be all right," she said. "I know it now. Heinrich will be all right."

Sebastian nodded. Then he threw back his head and let out a loud sigh. "I have thought long about Heinrich," he said. "I have not wanted to worry you, but the physician's recommendation does not surprise me. I have feared such an outcome. The doctor's failure to even consider your testimony about Heinrich's musical interest, however, causes me to distrust his decision. I have heard that physicians who work for institutions tend to be prophets of doom concerning these kinds of illnesses."

"So you think he was being too pessimistic?"

"The boy is only five. And his vocabulary is large. If we add to that a growing musical vocabulary, well, with God and a loving family, nothing is impossible. Today I would give anything for Heinrich's simplicity of mind, yes, I would give anything." Elbows on his knees, Sebastian clamped his long fingers to his head and groaned.

"Something else has happened, hasn't it?"

"Baroness Zelenka went to see the pastor Friday night after the performance of the *St. Matthew Passion*. She was so angry she didn't hesitate waking him. He spoke to her in his undress.

"She said she'd heard plenty of Passions in her day but this one was an outrage to decency. The Council quoted her to me. 'God help that man Bach, if he's not produced an opera-comedy!' She threatened to cease her support of the church, and she is a major donor."

"Why in the world would she think it a comedy? The woman has no idea of what she speaks," said Anna.

Sebastian frowned. "I began to wonder. Perhaps the work really is laughable. Perhaps I'm deceiving myself as to its quality."

"Nonsense. It is profoundly moving."

"But what if your love for me keeps you from seeing it clearly?"

Anna shook her head. "My soul could never have been touched so deeply by something that didn't have the hand of God upon it."

Sebastian nodded, then sighed, "Be that as it may, the fact is that the Council has given me an ultimatum."

"What kind?"

She could see tears welling up in his eyes. "I must agree to tone down the dramatic aspects of my works or lose my job. And I am forbidden to ever perform the *St. Matthew Passion* in the Thomaskirche again."

Anna was appalled. "You must petition the Elector. The Court Composer title must be yours."

2

The ban on the *St. Matthew Passion* was a great blow to Sebastian. He had hoped to be able to perform his church cycle, complete with his own Passions, at the Thomaskirche for years. He wanted to let the music grow on the people, deepen in its impact, as all good music does. But now he didn't even have the freedom to perform what he wanted to in his own church.

He had prayed diligently over the Passion and believed that God would use the work as a steppingstone to performances in other churches.

Revelation taught that worshipers in heaven brought golden bowls that contained the prayers of the saints rising like incense to God. If God considers my prayers that precious, Sebastian wondered, why does He not answer? If writing a passionate liturgical music that draws people to God is the work He created me for, why is this happening?

He'd accomplished his goal on paper. He had more than three hundred cantatas, passions, motets, and occasional pieces in his cupboard. But what good did they do anyone if the music stayed on the paper, or if, when it was performed, it was performed poorly? Glory to God? Hardly.

He felt, as Anna did, that receiving the prestigious title of Court Composer for the Elector of Saxony would give him the authority he needed to proceed freely with his vision.

Picander counseled him, however, to wait until the present Elector died. "The Elector's son," he said, "is more interested in the arts than his father. Don't dull your chances by risking a rejection and having that rejection on paper when Frederick Augustus comes to the throne."

Sebastian waited, spending carefully planned time with Heinrich, enjoying the continued work of Gerlach and several other apprentices and working with his older sons. He was seeking to shape them into the best musicians possible. Emmanuel was the best student he'd ever had, and he seemed to have let go of the bitterness he'd held onto for so long about Sebastian's second marriage. Sebastian felt he and Emmanuel worked together extremely well, and that was a great joy.

For now Sebastian tried to focus on the moment, the holy present. It was difficult for him to do, being so driven and so concerned about the future of his sacred music. But Anna was good at it. She encouraged him to stop thinking so much about doing and learn to concentrate on the art of being. He made the effort. He sought to relish the good in each day, whether it was a stimulating discussion with Reiche and Picander over how intimately God is involved in the lives of human beings or a meal of herring, parsleyed potatoes, dill bread and *setewale* that his Anna placed before him with a bottle of Rhine wine. He was gaining weight, but he didn't care. Good food and wine, his pipe and the passion of a good marriage were part of the compensations, he believed, for the troubles inherent in earthly life.

As far as his official work, the next four years were a crazy quilt of blame and affirmation, opposition and acclaim. One of the two Collegium Musicums in Leipzig lost its director and offered Sebastian the position. He accepted eagerly, launching into composing new orchestral works, telling himself that all music done well can glorify God. His secular music was well received. His sacred works, however, were still suppressed. The Council kept his salary at a minimum and even fought with him over the right to choose which musical scholars were given entrance to the school.

The old Rector of the Thomasschule died, and the new Rector immediately began championing Sebastian's cause. "Praising God in music links you with the heavenly choirs," Rector Gesner would tell Sebastian's foundationers. "You should be eager to give your leisure time to practice for any musical performance."

But Sebastian was just beginning to make significant progress in his church performances when he learned that Gesner was leaving. The next Rector would probably be Vice-Principal J. A. Ernesti. He was a nephew of Kirkman's, and he was young, hot-headed and utilitarian. Sebastian had heard him boast about what he would do if he were the Rector. He would direct the balance of studies toward more modern subjects like natural science, grammar, languages, history and the higher mathematics. He considered music unimportant, even outmoded.

The Elector of Saxony died in 1733. "Now, Bach," Picander counseled, "send some of your best work to Frederick Augustus quickly! Observe the period of mourning only. Get your name in front of the new Elector as soon as you can."

Friedemann was offered the position of Hoforganist at the Sophienkirche in Dresden. Sebastian considered this a propitious sign. The Elector of Saxony ruled his realm from Dresden, and if he was amenable to Sebastian's petition, Sebastian could perform music written especially for the ruler in Friedemann's church. Sebastian didn't expect he would be asked to move to Dresden. He felt that Leipzig would be a better place to raise and educate his children in the Lutheran tradition. But Friedemann could act as a go-between, or at least, initiate the use of his complete church cycle in Dresden.

Friedrich Augustus was Catholic, so Sebastian began work on a Mass.

He would have to set aside his great love of Luther's German translation of the Bible and revert to the use of Latin. Sebastian loved using Luther's scripture exactly as the religious pioneer had translated it, when possible. The founder of the Lutheran church had given all he had to his translation, translating it first in the word order of the original, then taking each word separately and gushing forth as many synonyms as possible. Then he would set all that aside in a free rendering to catch the spirit. Finally, he would bring together the meticulous and the free.[2] The process reminded Sebastian of the way he worked to perfect his own music. The more he learned of Martin Luther, the more he identified with him.

Luther's translation, moreover, was profoundly German. A procurator became a burgomaster. The road from Jericho to Jerusalem wound through the Thuringian forest. The great man had personalized scripture for the Germans, made it easier to appropriate. For composers, however, the Latin Mass had for centuries been the highest form of sacred music. It was to this that spiritually minded composers had long aspired: to write one Mass that would truly glorify God.

Sebastian knew that by undertaking the task of writing a Mass, he would invite criticism from narrow-minded Lutherans. But it was something he had to do, a challenge he could not ignore. He took off ten days from work, delegating his rehearsals and services to the capable Gerlach. And once again, he traveled to Dresden, this time alone and incognito, his purpose to attend a Catholic Mass.

Determined not to waste any time, he arrived late Saturday night and went straight to the Elector's own church early Sunday morning.

The incense and icons disturbed him when he first entered, but he sat and waited, willing to learn. As he listened to the chanting and the Latin words set to music, it lifted him out of himself. The remoteness of the language and the way this particular composer had dealt with it caused him to experience God as high and lifted up. It helped him feel the totality of His Otherness. Sebastian rested in the music, praising his Lord for this surcease from dailiness, this glimpse of Majesty, Serenity and Power. As he traveled home, he prayed for the ability to write just such a powerful Mass, something that would lift people out of themselves and into the glory of God. *"Jesu juva!"* he whispered. "Jesus help me."

During the spring of 1733, Sebastian wrote the Kyrie and Gloria of his Mass in B Minor. He returned to Dresden that summer and presented it to Frederick Augustus with a petition over which he'd agonized. He'd used all the skill in civility that he could muster.

"To Frederick Augustus . . . My most Gracious Lord:

"I submit in deepest devotion the present slight labor of that knowledge which I have achieved in musique, with the most wholly submissive prayer that Your Highness . . . (will) deign to take me under Your Most Mighty protection."[3]

Sebastian went ahead to describe the injuries he had suffered in Leipzig and said that if he were granted the position of His Highness's Court Composer, these injuries would disappear. He continued on, promising his "indebted obedience and untiring zeal" in composing any music His Royal Highness needed. He promised his unceasing fidelity and signed himself as a humble and obedient slave.

When Sebastian gave this letter to Anna and Emmanuel to read, they both rolled their eyes. But they knew as well as he, that if you were to gain a powerful ruler's favor, the way you approached him was crucial. You must pave the way with assurances of your fealty and reverence or be turned away.

Sebastian received the Elector's reply several months later.

Anna was picking up Heinrich's blocks in the study while Sebastian worked on accounts. Bernhard was in the music room practicing the harpsichord for the rehearsal at Zimmerman's that night. Emmanuel brought in the mail.

Anna smiled her beautiful smile at Emmanuel, bundled up the blocks in her apron and took the stack. "So much today!"

"Several letters for Friedemann in a feminine hand." Emmanuel sighed and put on a lugubrious face. "The forwarding we do for him! What does he have that I do not?"

Anna sat down on the black leather settee against the wall. It was the one piece of furniture they had room for in the study besides Sebastian's desk and chair.

Emmanuel sat with Anna to help sort the letters. Sebastian watched them. Anna would examine each piece and present it to Emmanuel. Then Emmanuel would quickly scratch a designation on it with his pen and set it on the floor in its appropriate pile.

Later, Emmanuel would carry the correspondence concerning Sebastian's partitas to his own desk to do his part in helping Sebastian with the dissemination of his works. He kept the lists of new orders and counted and recorded incoming money.

"I could wish for your organizational talent!" Anna said to Emmanuel.

"Only the wicked are given such gifts," Emmanuel quipped. "Now you, my dear stepmother, must be exceedingly virtuous."

He said it with good humor, and Anna shrugged and tucked a blonde curl back into her mobcap. Several of the blocks in her lap thumped to the floor. She laughed.

Emmanuel was nineteen now. With more maturity, he'd developed a sense of humor, sarcastic at times, but a good foil for his usual sobriety. He was short and stocky. His clothes never looked as fine on him as they did on Friedemann. Girls did not vie for his attention the way they did for his older brother's. But Emmanuel could be witty and profound. When young women took the time to get to know him, they enjoyed his conversation.

Anna gave a little exclamation. "A letter bearing the Elector's seal!" Her blue-gray eyes were shining as she padded to the desk to give Sebastian the letter. Emmanuel joined her. "I know it will be good news," said Anna.

"I've been praying every night since you began the Mass."

Sebastian turned the envelope over. It was the finest of parchments. His hands were shaking. The message in this letter had the potential to change his life. He found Barbara's letter opener in his desk drawer and carefully slit the envelope.

The message was in an elaborate hand, but it was short and generic. The disappointment was a stone in his stomach.

"I am refused," he said. "No reason given except the usual civilities."

Anna moved behind him and threw her arms around his neck. "How can it be? There isn't, there can't be a more suited candidate."

He took one of her warm hands, trying to calm himself with the reality of her, always there and believing in him.

"He says he is not ready to confer the title on anyone at this time. But it is this time, this month, this year, that I need his authority behind me."

Sebastian sighed and shook his head. "The older I grow, the less my prayers seem to be answered. I prayed more than I've ever prayed over the *St. Matthew Passion,* and it seemed to do no good. I praise God for a supportive new Rector and start to flourish, and the Rector is gone before I can turn around. Rector Gesner told me today he is leaving in January."

"The children and I have been praying every morning for another Rector as fine as he," said Anna.

"The Rector is already chosen. It is definite as of yesterday. Vice-Principal Ernesti."

Emmanuel whistled. "J. A. Ernesti has a deplorable reputation among the university students. Opinionated, stubborn, materialistic, as modern as they come. And you, my good father, are always getting into trouble with fools."

Anna cleared her throat.

"It's the truth! The *zippelfagottist,* the nanny goat bassoonist in Arnstadt," Emmanuel wiggled his black eyebrows. "Duke Wilhelm with all his forbidding of dances and choosing your friends for you. Pastor Kirkman and Consul Lange who would sooner have a mediocre music director with a university degree than good music in the church. The list goes on and on."

"I'll just have to be more aggressive, just be more aggressive. Keep pursuing the Elector with music he needs until he grants me the title."

"Exactly what Uncle Telemann would say!" exclaimed Emmanuel. "You'll have to do something."

"But mightn't we be dealing here with a deeper matter," asked Anna. "With all this trouble over your church music these last ten years, I've been thinking how one learns about a principle like the importance of Sabbath rest, say, and you believe it in your mind, but then suddenly the truth of it drops over you in some unexpected place. And from that point on, you know what God says is reality because it meets a deep hunger in your soul. Illumination, I think it's called. But it never comes when you expect it to. It happens to me unexpectedly, sometimes in a quiet moment after a riotous day—a realization that my soul rides upon easily and truly, like a musician discovering music, or a weary body resting at last in restorative sleep.

"Mightn't there be some greater truth God is seeking to form in you, dear—I don't know, trust, humility, finding your needs met in His Presence alone? I wouldn't deign to say what it might be, but something that God deems more important than recognition of your church works?"

Sebastian felt suddenly impatient, "That doesn't help, not now."

"I'm sorry. Forgive me. I only . . ."

"Stop apologizing, Anna. You don't have to apologize for being who you are. You're probably right. But I must have time to think."

Anna backed away and bent to regather Heinrich's blocks, clunking them into her apron with quick jerky movements.

She walked to the window sill, tucked the violin Heinrich had left there under her arm and picked up a vase of dead flowers. Head down, she hurried out; but the minute she stepped into the hall, the vase slipped from her fingers and crashed to the floor.

Cursing himself for his insensitivity, Sebastian jumped up to help her pick up the shards. He knelt in front of her and took her chin in his big fingers. He raised her face to look at him: the quivering lips, the upturned nose, the big eyes filling with tears. She was so dear and innocent.

A hammering at the front door interrupted them. Anna stood up.

"It's probably Reiche and Picander!" She stumbled away leaving Sebastian holding the sharp pieces of the pink and gold vase. It was the only piece of porcelain they possessed, a wedding gift from Henrietta. He knelt there looking at the fragments. Bernhard's harpsichord music had stopped, and he could hear voices in the hall. The shards were slivers on his palm. They would not be able to salvage the vase, and he hadn't had time to apologize to Anna.

When he descended to meet Reiche and Picander, Bernhard was talking to them. The gray cat, now very fat and very old, but still preferring Bernhard to anyone else, was rubbing against the boy's legs. Reiche wore his usual russet coat, and Picander had a red plume in his tricorner.

"Herr Picander is celebrating," Bernhard said.

"Ah! The red plume."

Picander dipped his head in a mock bow. "Today I received word that Breightkopf is planning to reprint one thousand copies of my collection of *Gravely Droll and Satirical Poems.*"

Sebastian felt amused and jealous at the same time. Why was it he was having to publish his works himself while Picander had publishers fighting over the rights to publish his? The ways of the modern thinker seemed always prosperous.

Anna descended to welcome them. She'd taken off her mobcap, tied her blonde hair back with a pink ribbon and rouged her lips with the slightest pink. Picander bowed with a sweep of his tricorner. Anna curtsied, mumbled the appropriate greetings and glided on into the kitchen.

"It's a perfect evening for one of Sebastian's new keyboard concertos!" Reiche said.

"I could wish I were in Dresden directing the Mass for the Elector instead."

"Why not the Italian Concerto or this new three-harpsichord piece the Bach men are rehearsing tonight?" asked Picander. "I trust you are ready, Bernhard?"

Bernhard tipped his head and grinned. "Is any musician ever ready when he is trying to live up to Papa's standards?"

"I'm afraid I will not be playing anything for the Elector at all," said Sebastian. He told them about today's letter. His friends were surprised. They stood in the hall speculating about why Frederick Augustus would have made such a decision.

In a few minutes, Dorothea was calling them to dinner. They sat at the end of the long table Gottfried had built for them during his visit last Christmas. Sebastian's new apprentice George, Emmanuel, Dorothea, Anna, nine-year-old Heinrich, six-year-old Liesggen and baby Friedrich were already seated, waiting for Sebastian to pronounce the blessing.

Slices of cold ham and mutton were arranged on pewter platters around Anna's usual summer touch of flowers, and there were plenty of cheeses and loaves of black bread and lettuces and carrots from their kitchen garden. Heinrich was sitting near Liesggen, ducking his honey-blonde head in quick, jerking motions. Anna poured his mug full of milk to calm him and captured the spoon two-year-old Friedrich was banging against his bowl.

When everyone was still, Sebastian pronounced the blessing. He tried to speak only what he meant, but it was useless. He must give thanks, and he didn't feel thankful. He felt out of touch with his wife and out of touch with God.

After the prayer, Dorothea rose from her seat beside Anna to finish some preparations. She set a bowl of her hot mustard sauce in front of Sebastian. "Is something wrong, Papa?"

"I received a rejection from the Elector today."

Picander raised his glass to Sebastian, "We will drown our sorrows in your excellent music at Zimmerman's wine gardens tonight. Why you are so bent on sacred music alludes me. Could it not be a phenomena of a faulty thinking instilled in you from your childhood by all this Bible reading and church attending, something entirely within you and not from the outside?"

Emmanuel was sitting next to Picander. "You think Papa's drivenness over this church cycle might not be from God?"

Picander tapped the book in his coat pocket, "Thinkers today are beginning to believe we do not live in an open system, but a closed one. Man has more potential, more resource within himself than we ever realized.

"Why, consider all the recent discoveries and inventions: the flying shuttle loom, the mercury thermometer, the ability to measure the pressure of a man's blood, three-color printing, the ability to prevent smallpox. Do we even need God to help us when He has already gifted us with such mental resources? Armed with reason and inventiveness, we can achieve anything we desire. Think about it. Is it not irreverent to speak of the great spiritual force who pervades all things as a character who purposes and prohibits, who acts into our petty worlds, who fulfills our desires and wants? Why I was with a noblewoman in Paris last month who was actually praying that God would provide a space for her carriage outside the Opera House! Do we not do the Supreme Being a great disservice by bothering him with such trivialities?"

"Now, Picander, you are as faithful a church attender as any of us," said Reiche.

"I attend church for social reasons. It is good for the vocation." Picander tried to make his handsome face look sober, but his pale brown eyes gleamed.

"Counterpoint and canon! You were saying something different last month when your cousin was ill."

"Searching, my good man, searching. And trying to have a modicum of a good time. Being too serious about the Bible takes all the merriment out of living. Sin is an increasingly outmoded idea. Man needs freedom if he is to become all he is meant to be. Which reminds me, I met someone you know the other day."

"In Paris?"

"Countess Eugenia Brock. Now, she is a phenomenal woman!"

Sebastian was taken aback. Doors he'd tried to keep shut for years burst open. Memories and images leapt into his mind.

"Who is Countess Eugenia Brock?" asked Bernhard.

Sebastian was desperately trying to think of a way to change the subject.

"A paragon of beauty!" said Picander. "Now, she is a woman whose philosophy I could embrace."

"What philosophy?" asked Emmanuel.

Anna glanced up from spooning oatmeal into baby Joanna's mouth, "Yes, tell us more."

It was Reiche who saved him. The trumpeter cleared his throat and held up his pocket watch, "Zimmerman will be waiting."

The stroll through the Leipzig streets toward the town gates was rejuvenating. Plates and utensils clinked through open windows. Carriages whisked early theatergoers through the streets, and couples murmured quietly, strolling home from the Promenade outside the Small Thomas Gate. As they drew closer to the wine gardens, Sebastian caught the scent of wet earth and roses. Zimmerman clanged open the iron gate and waved them in. Herr Zimmerman always closed his coffee house during the summer and transferred his business to his wine garden outside the town gates. This was the one day he closed his establishment at night, but he loved opening it for Collegium Musicum rehearsals. Sebastian never grew tired of the ambiance of this place: the trellised roses, the white iron tables, and in the middle of it, the ancient oak spreading its shade. Soon all his musicians arrived, and Sebastian immersed himself in music. It was a joy to play with Emmanuel and Bernhard that night. Zimmerman had actually managed to find him three harpsichords for the rehearsal. They would be ready to perform the work publicly soon.

Bernhard left immediately after the performance, something about a game with some friends. The vagueness of his explanation bothered Sebastian a little, but he fell into deep discussion with Picander on the way home and thought no more about it. Picander said he was certain it wouldn't be long until Frederick Augustus visited Leipzig. "I will do everything within my power to see that you are chosen to direct the music for the event."

Sebastian apologized to Anna that night. She understood.

"It troubles me to think that God might be the author of the obstacles I am encountering," said Sebastian.

"Do you think Picander's reasoning is affecting your faith?"

"It's possible, my dear, it's possible."

3

When Frederick Augustus decided to visit Leipzig, he only gave the Town Council three days notice. Picander kept his word and convinced the council to appoint Sebastian music director for the royal ceremony. The whole city scrambled to prepare. The ruler would stay with a wealthy merchant named Apel, who lived on the marketplace.

There would be a torchlight ceremony at 9:00 P.M., in which nobles, town officials and university students would participate. Everyone expected the vast marketplace to be teeming with people from the outlying villages as well as the city itself.

Ignoring the new rector's command to continue the school schedule as usual, Sebastian canceled all his classes and concentrated on writing a brand new cantata for the ceremony. He only had time for one evening rehearsal with his Collegium Musicum. For this event they were forty musicians strong: instruments of every sort from viola de gamba to oboe da caccia, plenty of kettledrums and trumpets and fifteen fine vocalists. Reiche would be playing all the trumpet solos.

At 5:00 P.M. on the evening of the ceremony, Sebastian summoned Emmanuel to the music room.

They had converted the two second floor rooms, one on either side of the stairwell into space for his music lessons and instruments. They had three harpsichords now, along with Sebastian's lute-harpsichord and two clavichords. Instruments also hung on the walls from pegs: several violins, two lutes, a viola, a violino piccolo, and a violone.

Sebastian sat at the double-manualed harpsichord reviewing the parts of the cantata featuring the strings. Emmanuel would be serving as lead violinist tonight, and Sebastian wanted to make sure his son understood and carried out the intent of the music. The other string players would follow suit.

Emmanuel entered with his violin and a sheaf of music tucked under his arm. "We've found a dozen more music stands. Do you think that will be enough?"

"It will have to do. Have you practiced today?"

"Ran through the cantata once. Not too difficult."

Sebastian took Emmanuel's music and set it on the stand near the harpsichord. "Let's hear it."

Emmanuel began bowing through the soaring lines. Sebastian stopped him and pointed to the second staff, "Right here. Play it again."

Emmanuel repeated the long phrase. Mechanically, it was perfect, but it had no soul. "No, son. Make it speak. Rise up, up, hold, then lean into the next phrase."

Emmanuel played it again.

"Better, but thin. Again."

Emmanuel played the phrase again and kept going, but still the music was dry. The entire string section would sound dead if Emmanuel played this way tonight.

Sebastian grabbed the instrument from him and played the whole first page, digging the bow into the strings, filling the lines with majesty and passion. He thrust the violin back at Emmanuel.

Emmanuel glared at Sebastian from under half-closed lids. He set the instrument to his shoulder and began playing the same way he had before. Sebastian's patience fled.

"Stop this spineless drivel, Emmanuel. Listen to yourself. Emote. Feel the shape, the message. There is no sense in my having to play violin tonight. You can do it as well as I. Think about who you're playing for. Honor the Elector. He is your Sovereign. Play music, not mathematical figures. Clean and penetrating, yes, but make the violin say something."

Emmanuel's face was as red as a Hussar's uniform. He tightened the strings of his bow, adjusted his handkerchief on his shoulder and tore into the music. He played the violin the way Sebastian had always known he could, better than he ever had before. Sebastian tried to tell him how pleased he was, but Emmanuel didn't answer, just slapped the music shut and left the room. Ah well, thought Sebastian. We've had this type of session many times before. He knows it is for his good. He will get over it.

Anna decided not to go to the ceremony that night. Heinrich had been doing unusually well lately, practicing the harpsichord every day and speaking often. He'd even begun to adjust well to minor changes in his routine. But she didn't want to push him too far. There would be a great deal of noise and commotion in the streets and marketplace tonight. Sebastian agreed that it would probably be best if she kept Heinrich, Liessgen and Friedrich at home.

Reiche stopped by the house to walk to the marketplace with Sebastian. He looked tired.

"I don't like the look of you tonight, friend. Are you ill?"

"These days it is difficult to know if I am well or not. So many changes in this old body. Aches upon aches. But what a delight your musical tribute to the Elector has been to me!" Reiche patted the coiled trumpet he carried under his arm. "She thrives on the works you compose for her."

"I am counting on your fine trumpet tonight, and your prayers."

The weather was crisp and clear. It was the best kind of autumn night. They jostled through the streets with a stream of people, all headed for the marketplace and all talking excitedly. When they reached the square, the vast area was already crowded with people. White-belted soldiers with muskets were lined up in rows in front of the residence where the Elector was staying. The six-story mansion had eighty windows, and they were all glowing with light.

Sebastian set up his stand in the space near the soldiers allotted to the musicians. It looked as though everyone, all forty musicians, including Emmanuel, Bernhard and George was already there. He heard the rumblings of the parade. Soon he saw the first torch. Forward they came: six hundred university students marching twelve abreast, each carrying a flaming torch and singing a German anthem. The students wove their way through the swath of street marked off for them. Their lights moved in a river, orange dots and ovals and comets of bright leaping life filling the empty trough. The smoke blew strong and acrid through the air. People began to cough.

The marshals halted the forward march and pivoted toward the mansion. At that moment, the Elector and the Electress appeared. They were standing in the second story balcony. Frederick Augustus was dressed in red and gold. He wore a wide ribbon across his massive chest with the imperial crest dangling over it.

The sword at his hip was covered with gems, and he held the Polish crown under his arm. Today was the anniversary of his accession to the Polish throne. With Russia and Austria's support, Saxony had once again been granted sovereignty. Beside the Elector stood his consort, Maria Josepha. She was dressed in an open court robe of yellow and gold. It glittered with gems.

Sebastian gave Reiche the signal. His brilliant trumpet fanfared through the square. The students sang their prepared salute. A volley of guns exploded.

Then the speeches began. Town officials and trade representatives spoke in lengthy tributes. Everyone was vying for the Elector's favor. At last the Collegium Musicum was given its chance.

Sebastian threw himself into the music, seeking to pull from his musicians a strong, majestic tone that would affect everyone. Emmanuel was doing well. This was the Sovereign that God Himself had placed over Leipzig. To honor him was to honor God. The words Picander had written for his cantata were working well. *Presie dein glucke, gesgnetes Sachsne,* "Praise thy good Fortune, O Saxony." The singers were capturing the magic of the moment, the excitement of having with them their ruler and king.

The Elector had been seated when they began, but not long into the twenty-minute cantata, he and his wife rose. They watched and listened, rapt. Ecstatic that he'd so captured the Elector's attention, Sebastian conducted on: splendors trumpeting, voices chorusing, shapes and sounds of glory lifted up, up into the air and across the multitudes in the square.

After the cantata, there were a few closing words by the Burgomaster, a short response from the Elector and a long prayer. Then the Elector withdrew, the soldiers exited and the crowd began to disperse. Sebastian was gathering his music, when an epauletted messenger clicked his heels in front of him. "From His Most Serene Highness, Prince and Lord, the Elector of Saxony, Frederick Augustus, Royal Prince in Poland and Lithuania." He held out an envelope and bowed.

Sebastian tore it open. "To the Illustrious Cantor of the Thomasschule," he read. "The Electress and I have heard something deeper than honor in your music tonight, something that connects one with the Divine. The late hour has been made worth it because of your fine music. We will plan to reconsider your petition."

Sebastian felt like shouting! Yes, it had all been worth it: the race to write and perfect the music, the risk of bringing down Rector Ernesti's wrath upon him, the difficult session with Emmanuel. The Elector was going to reconsider his petition. *I must tell Reiche,* Sebastian thought. But he didn't see him anywhere—he'd had a spasm of coughing after the cantata. No Emmanuel either, but Bernhard was still there, slinging the strap of his viola case over his shoulder, his auburn curls plastered and sweaty from the wig he'd been wearing.

Sebastian felt like hugging the boy. "You did a fine job tonight. Everyone did." Sebastian showed him the missive, "And—good news from the Elector! Tell Anna and let her know I'm going to walk awhile before I come home."

Sebastian took back paths to avoid the press. He could hear distant songs and laughter from taverns and coffee houses, and above the shadowy buildings there rose a huge harvest moon. He thought how the moon had begun only as an idea in the Creator's mind, then upon the Creator's word it had materialized for all to see. So, Sebastian's idea for tonight's cantata had been nothing but a speck in his mind a few days before. It had been unseeable and unhearable. And tonight it had shouted before the world its reality.

He stopped to gaze at the moon, and he prayed out loud. "The lines have fallen to me in pleasant places. Thank You for this night. What a privilege it is to partake with You in the elixir of creating!"

He walked the rest of the way home in a state of euphoria. His life was taking a turn for the better. The Elector would make him Court Composer of Saxony, and he would be asked to play his cantatas and Passions everywhere. His family was doing well. Heinrich was improving. Friedemann was successfully fulfilling his job as Hoforganist in the capital city of Dresden, and Emmanuel's profound musicality would bind them increasingly together, erasing all the problems of the past.

When he finally arrived home, he entered the empty hallway to hear someone shouting. The music room door burst open, and Emmanuel pounded up the stairs. In a minute, Anna emerged. Bernhard was with her. Sebastian took the stairs two at a time.

Anna was sobbing so violently she couldn't speak.

Bernhard explained, "A university student, a friend Emmanuel was expecting, dropped by to leave a message about a fete Emmanuel was invited to, something about the place being changed. When Anna saw the friend was drunk, she told him in no uncertain terms that Emmanuel would not be coming. The fellow left without telling her where the celebration was to be."

"I didn't know Emmanuel had been hoping for this invitation all week," Anna sobbed.

"Anyway," continued Bernhard, "when Emmanuel got home, Anna told him that she didn't think it was wise for him to associate with such people. Emmanuel was furious. It turns out this friend is a baron. To be invited to his fete means Emmanuel is at last accepted by the highborn students at the university."

"Emmanuel asked me what right I had to make judgments on his friends," said Anna. "He said I'd made his life," she choked, trying to control the sobs, "that I'd made his life a hell."

Sebastian was horrified. He drew her to him, holding her, smoothing her hair.

"That isn't all," said Bernhard. "He went upstairs to pack. He says he's leaving home tomorrow."

During the reign of the Saxon Elector August III (Frederick Augustus), there was a continual struggle between the former great powers France and Austria and the newly emerging powers Russia and Prussia. The Saxon Elector attached "himself to whichever power seemed to be in a commanding position, but he achieved no more than the preservation of the status quo with Saxony remaining as a relatively minor state except in cultural matters."[1]

"{Bach's and Ernesti's quarrel} was one more chapter in the eternal battle between the practical and the creative minds. Ernesti's antagonism should have been no surprise to Bach: there's an Ernesti in every artist's life."[2]

17

A Riot in the Church
1734 – 1737

The next morning Sebastian woke with a foreboding that was more like a premonition, and it was something besides Emmanuel's leaving. It had the feel of death. He climbed the stairs to Emmanuel and Bernhard's room on the top floor. They'd converted the attic into two rooms to give Sebastian's apprentices, as well as their older boys, more privacy. Carl Gerlach had not been living with them the last two years. He'd been serving as Hoforganist at the Neuekirche, but his ambition was to be Cantor. So he had recently returned to live with them and study under Sebastian. When questioned, he would adjust his thick glasses and say, "Herr Bach can teach me more about composing for the church than any pedant in a university."

Both Emmanuel and Bernhard were asleep. Emmanuel lay, arms flung out, black hair tangled, as though he'd been tossing all night. His green and silver valise stood ready by the door, and his trunk stood open between his desk and his bed. It was almost filled with neatly folded linens, music and books. Sebastian tiptoed past the sleeping boys to Emmanuel's desk. A letter marked for the express lay on the blotter. It was to Phillip Telemann. Sebastian dipped Emmanuel's quill into the ink pot and scratched a quick note across the back of an old envelope. "At least delay your departure for a day so we can discuss the matters that lie between us."

Sebastian was due in the dormitory this morning to lead devotions. Attempting to assuage his own anxiety, he led the boys in the reading of several psalms that focused on God's help. Then they sang *A Mighty Fortress.* The morning passed slowly: an hour and a half supervising the boys' morning meal in the refectory, a meeting in the Nicolaikirche across town to help a young man and his intended plan a wedding, back to the Thomasschule for a rudimentary string class, and then the rehearsal with the perambulating choir. Gerlach helped him drill the altos and sopranos in sections. The boys enjoyed Carl. He was twenty-four now, but his ways were still boyish, and he had a rare gift for teaching. He knew how to balance hard work and fun.

Sebastian was standing outside the classroom discussing the day's walking route with Carl when Ernesti pounded down the hall toward them. "Well, Bach, I see you decided to come to work today. Should I be honored? The Council shall hear of your insubordination!"

Carl had substituted for Sebastian during his preparation for the royal ceremony. "How could I have honored our Sovereign properly if I had not delegated my classes?" asked Sebastian. "Only three days to write and rehearse a whole new work. I'm certain Carl did a fine job."

"That is not the issue."

Sebastian looked at the drawstring lips, the bulging forehead and the already receding hairline of the stocky Rector. Ernesti was as stubborn as he, and Sebastian had yet to see any hint of a meeting of minds between them. The new rector's attitude toward the music classes in the school was the exact opposite of what Rector Gesner's had been, no encouragement, no help, only hindrance.

"Did you attend the ceremony last night?" asked Carl.

Ernesti started to answer, then turned to see who was clipping up the stairs into the hall.

It was Gorner. The little man jerked his head about, looking from side to side, then seeing the three of them, hurried toward them. He was out of breath.

"Is Dr. Biedermann in the infirmary? We need him at once. Herr Reiche has collapsed in the street."

By the time they found the physician and raced out to the fountain in front of the school, a crowd had gathered. Dr. Biedermann forced his way through the crowd, sleeves rolled up, black bag in hand. Sebastian was right behind him. Reiche was lying on his side. His tricorner was jammed up against the side of his head, his eyes were closed and one hand was clutched to his chest. A burlap sack lay nearby, its apples spilling out across the cobblestones.

The doctor knelt to feel for his pulse, then lay his head on Reiche's chest. Sebastian held his breath. Everyone else waited. The silence was tense. In a minute, Dr. Biedermann sighed, rolled Reiche on his back and lifted one of the trumpeter's hands, then the other, and placed them across his chest. He rose and shook his head.

Later, Dr. Biederman explained to Sebastian that Reiche's wife had sent for him in the middle of the night because her husband was having trouble breathing. He couldn't stop coughing. "The smoke at the ceremony," said the doctor, "brought on a respiratory attack and probably a failure of the heart. He should never have left the house this morning."

Reiche's wife visited Anna and Sebastian that night with her married daughter. She requested that Sebastian write the commemoration motet for her husband.

Sebastian was so numb with grief that he was having difficulty attending to anything. It required Anna's prompting for him to finally say yes. When Frau Reiche left, he told Anna that his jubilation after the Elector's ceremony the night before seemed like another world, another existence. "Life is a tragic affair," he said, "yes, a tragic affair."

In his prayers that night, he prayed a prayer that he returned to often. "Come, come sweet death. I would like to be safe before God's throne. I would like to have You, Father, unravel the puzzle of life and wipe away the tears. I would like to know peace."

To Sebastian's relief, Emmanuel agreed to stay a while longer to assist him with the funeral service. When they were rehearsing or discussing the motet or the chorales, Emmanuel was amiable enough. But when Sebastian or Anna attempted to urge him into discussion of their conflicts, he grew sullen and walked away.

He had already been planning to leave in January to begin studies at the University of Frankfurt. But now he insisted on leaving by the first of November. He would journey to Hamburg to stay with Telemann until after Christmas.

"Uncle Telemann says his opera personnel are quite adept. The Hamburg opera is a much finer venture than that of Dresden. And you yourself, Father, know how excellent the church music is. I will visit your old mentor's Catherinakirche and many others. I will play in Herr Telemann's Collegium Musicum and travel with them to Berlin. I have not had the advantage of taking such trips with you the way my older brother has. I must make my way on my own."

Emmanuel's words about Sebastian's showing partiality to Friedemann in the matter of musical trips was unfortunately too true. Friedemann had accompanied him to Hamburg right after Barbara's death, to Dresden several times for operas, and twice to Berlin to inspect organs. When Emmanuel had become old enough for such trips, there had never seemed to be enough time.

Sebastian agonized through the preparations for his friend's funeral, then conscientiously led the music and helped with the tributes. Finally, it was over. Two days later, Sebastian and Emmanuel stood at the new post house outside the city walls. They were both wrapped in great coats and mufflers and surrounded by Emmanuel's luggage.

The cold was fiery on their faces, the countryside still covered with snow from the storm two nights before. Only one other passenger waited, a young man hunched against the cold, alert for the sounds of the only coach that would run that day. At least Emmanuel had allowed Sebastian to purchase coach fare for him. It was an inclement time of year to have to travel such a long distance in a post wagon.

Sebastian's nearsighted eyes swept over the blurred stretches of hills lying out from the city. How difficult to lose his friend and his son at the same time! He poured coffee from the warming jug Anna had sent, offered Emmanuel a cup, then poured another for himself. The hot coffee soothed the tightness in his throat. "I'd rather have honesty between us than this wondering," he said. "Help me understand. Anna has always been kind to you. She has tried to serve and understand you."

Emmanuel rolled his black eyes. Sebastian looked down so Emmanuel couldn't see how his disrespect wounded him. He brushed his foot across their tracks in the snow. Emmanuel set his booted foot on one of his trunks, propping his elbow on his stocky leg. His long fingers were ungloved and cupped tightly around his lidded mug. He turned his head to eye his father.

"You ask for honesty. Then you will have to forgive me for speaking bluntly. It has all been very well for you to take up with a woman almost young enough to be your daughter. I am twenty-one years old, and I understand that men have their needs. I have tried not to blame you for it. But try as I might, I have never been able to like Anna. I resent her intrusion into our family life. I resent her trying to take Mother's place. I abhor the fact that she still treats me like a child. That she takes up all your extra time and I receive only the dregs doesn't help. I have feelings too, Papa. I am not a board."

Sebastian reached out to touch him, but Emmanuel threw up his broad palm. "There is nothing you can say. I have not been able to change the way I feel. I don't think I will ever change. Just hope there is never a time when your beloved is thrown on my charity. Toward her I have none."

Emmanuel's round face was filled with contempt.

Sebastian felt ill. "We can work it out."

"Nothing is impossible, right? Forgiveness! Seventy times seven! But it *is* impossible for me. All I know to do is get out of the house and try to forget. I will not speak of it further."

And that was it. Emmanuel would listen to nothing Sebastian said in Anna's defense and nothing about the harm to his own soul of such clutched bitterness.

The carriage arrived. The coachman hefted the two passengers' trunks and valises onto the top of the carriage with a great banging about and cursing, secured them with expert knots and waved the boys to board. Emmanuel bid Sebastian a brisk good-bye, and he was gone.

As Sebastian watched the coach disappear down the white road, with the jingling and the hawing and the puffs and clods of snow and mud shooting back from wheels and hooves, he hurt to the core.

All the years of seeking to help this son accept the mystery of God's ways, and all the love Anna had given him in spite of rebuffs, had accomplished nothing! How he hated to see Emmanuel go with the bitterness still raging. But go he did, leaving a vacuum in Sebastian's life and a fear of some dreadful reckoning in the future.

2

The situation at the Thomasschule grew worse in the days following Emmanuel's departure. Ernesti began to choose favorites from among the students, and as the boys watched the daily wrangles between Ernesti and Sebastian, they began to take sides. One day after classes were over, Sebastian overheard a group of foundationers gathered in the hall to take wagers. The swarthy-faced Krause led out. "I wager fifteen groschen that Herr Bach will start it. It will be fists / Have you ever seen a duel? / That's with guns, isn't it? / Sometimes swords / They say Cantor Bach is an expert fencer / Well, my money's on Rector Ernesti—not quite so much bulk."

Sebastian hurried out the opposite way, undesirous of letting them know he had overheard.

Both Sebastian and Anna still felt that if he became the Court Capelle for the Elector, all his troubles would be over. With the Elector as his patron, supporting him and protecting him, Ernesti and the Council members would be forced to be more reasonable with their Cantor. Surely they would treat his vision and his music with more respect.

As it was, Sebastian had little heart to perform his cantatas very often. Sometimes he would try the judgment cantata or the *Magnificat* or *Jesus Calls the Twelve*, but they were practically always ruined by some squawking instrument or monotone soprano, and he would come away after the Sunday services with an attitude of frustration and anger instead of an attitude of worship. When Rector Gesner had been his champion, the church music had improved in quality; but Gesner's rectorship had been far too short. If the Council wasn't appointing to his Kapelle the very boys Sebastian reported to be without talent—like Krause—they were berating him for presuming to choose the hymns. And that prerogative had always been the Cantor's. It simply wasn't fair.

Sebastian prayed that the Elector would not delay in appointing him

Court Composer. But week after week the post arrived, and Sebastian shuffled through the mail to find nothing that bore the Elector's seal. He began to dread the days the post came. Is the Elector's delay because he is serious in his admiration of my music, he wondered, and wants to wait until he has fully evaluated the cantatas I've been sending him? Perhaps he has to deal with others in his court who have precedence. Or perhaps his strong feelings about the quality of my work were so transitory that he has totally forgotten me.

During that first winter after Reiche's death, Sebastian missed him sorely. His friend had been a balancer for him. It was as though the weight and measure you are accustomed to using every day to calculate your resources was no longer available.

Sebastian always tended toward extremes. Anna was able to help him some, but he wanted her to feel secure. He didn't want to burden her too much with his struggles.

Instead of spending more time in prayer in order to gain perspective, Sebastian spent more time with Picander. The poet's cheery rooms—his blazing fire, brightly colored rugs and walls of books—always welcomed him. With Picander's civic responsibilities, commissions for librettos and active, though sometimes secretive, social life, Picander was a busy man. But he always seemed to have time for Sebastian. He truly valued Sebastian's mind. Such a friend was rare.

One January afternoon before Sebastian returned home for Anna's evening meal, he decided to have a smoke with Picander. The poet got out his ivory pipe, and Sebastian helped himself to the poet's supply of Turkish tobacco, tamped it down in the old pipe he'd brought with him and lit it for the first draw. They commiserated over the loss of their friend Reiche.

"I will miss him," said Picander, "but you! His grasp of scripture meant a great deal to you, didn't it?"

Sebastian puffed on his pipe. "I need Reiche more now than ever before. Emmanuel has not written us one word; the Thomasschule furor escalates; the Elector does not write. Reiche's words of wisdom are sorely needed, but"—he blew a smoke ring and watched it for moment—"what God does, He does rightly."

They sat in silence for a few minutes, savoring the rich aroma of the tobacco, listening to the popping of the fire. Then Picander spoke. "I would like us to think on the theology you have just espoused. If God is a God of love, how can He be the author of such losses?"

Picander fingered the wooden cross he still wore around his neck. "We need to use our minds, be rational about everything, not just accept all the old ways of belief. We need to forge thinking conclusions of His reality. Consider this. Reiche died of a combination of the smoke, his age and over-exertion. God had nothing to do with it. It was a series of natural happenings. It was cause and effect. If he had not played at the ceremony, he would still be with us—or even if he'd been wise enough to stay home the next morning. No, I do not believe God deliberately chose to allow these two great losses you have had so close together. If God is a God of love, everything must happen in a closed system. He does not reach in to change things. He expects us to learn and grow and right matters ourselves. How else can you explain all the evil in the world?"

They discussed freewill versus sovereignty and God's power versus His love, and at first Sebastian felt comforted by Picander's conclusions. He didn't feel quite so guilty over Emmanuel's departure or quite so much in agony over the why of Reiche's death at this particular time.

Ernesti continued his changes at the school. The language teachers were ordered to replace their French and English paintings with charts and conjugations, and to delete their lectures on art. The natural science teacher was to enroll in a university science class and extend his teaching hours.

One Friday Sebastian was in the basement checking to see if any of the school instruments needed to be repaired when Krause brought him word that the Rector wanted to speak to him. Krause and Sebastian had never gotten along. He was a fourth-year musical scholar who was convinced that because his grandfather had been a noted singer, he too had the gift. But he didn't. His voice was nasal and limited in range, and he had the rhythm of a three-footed cow.

Krause left, and Sebastian clipped the length of the basement to Ernesti's office, knocked at the door with its bottle glass window and entered at Ernesti's command. The Rector was dressed in black as usual, but today he wore a double-rectangled collar of a transparent white material. His bulging forehead was scored with lines of concentration. As he looked up to see Sebastian, his eyes turned cold. "It has traditionally been the responsibility of the Cantor to teach Latin, Bach. I will expect you to do so starting next week."

Sebastian buttoned his coat decisively across his bulging stomach. "I do not have the time to teach a Latin class. And I do not have enough enthusiasm or skill to do so. It was the subject I abhorred the most, yes, abhorred the most when I was in school. Herr Pezold has always instructed the subject for me. I pay him from my salary."

"Pezold is going to be teaching English. He is quite busy studying to prepare for it. You will decrease the length of your string classes from two hours a day to one and begin teaching Latin next month."

There was a sharp knock at the door.

"Enter!"

Consul Lange flung open the door, then frowned when he saw Sebastian. "I hope I'm not too early."

"Certainly not. We were just finishing." Ernesti gave Sebastian a dismissive nod. "Next month, Bach!"

Sebastian marched out and slammed the door behind him, muttering to himself as he stalked down the echoing corridor. "Cut my string classes to an hour and half! I'm having enough difficulty readying my students to give some semblance of worship at four different churches on Sundays as it is. It is a foolish and vindictive ultimatum, and I will not obey it."

The next Monday was the rainiest day they had had all spring. The downpour began before dawn, and at 2 P.M., it was still raining.

Sebastian gathered the twelve carefully picked boys who were scheduled to make the rounds of the city. They huddled in their thin coats. Several of them were coughing. The Church Council had always been insistent that the perambulating choir sing the Monday tours in all weather. Important patrons expected their anniversary serenades. Sebastian looked at the boys' miserable faces. He could not do this. "We will not sing today, boys. Go to your rooms and spend the time resting or studying."

Before he could don his oilskin to brave the weather once again, Ernesti was upon him. "What's this Krause is telling me about a cancellation of the perambulating choir?"

Struggling to suppress his annoyance that Ernesti had evidently set Krause to spying on him, Sebastian's words were short. "Unlike others around here, I was trying to think of the boys. I fear for their health."

"We will have no cancellation."

Had the man no compassion at all? Ernesti's world was nothing but a plethora of jots and tittles. "It is too late, Herr Rector. The boys are gone."

He left the school with Ernesti yelling after him like a fractious wife. Sebastian went straight to Zimmerman's. Picander was there, sitting at a back table alone, with a warming tankard of coffee and a beaker of brandy. His handsome face brightened when he saw Sebastian. He stashed the papers he was working on in a leather folio, then poured two brandies. Sebastian passed the brandy snifter under his nose. Ah! Just what he needed on such a miserable day.

Zimmerman offered them cheese and onion rolls, and they shared a companionable silence over their repast, commenting occasionally on the music of the young lutanist who was entertaining. The hum of men's conversation and the music and the brandy revived Sebastian. He told Picander about Ernesti's new demands.

Picander asked him if he thought he would lose his position if he didn't comply. Sebastian shrugged. "I'm beginning to wonder if I would even care."

They discussed utilitarianism and how, if one could look at the situation objectively, Ernesti had to be admired. "Ernesti is a single-minded man," said Picander. "He throws everything into achieving the goals important to him. He is determined to do all within his power to create a system for himself that will run smoothly. Having you in his system may not be part of his plan."

Sebastian and Anna had discussed the possibility of trying to find a different position. But Sebastian had petitioned a friend in Russia several years ago about a Cantor position, and there had been little interest. Sebastian was fifty years old now, and most churches would not want to hire a new Cantor or Hoforganist as old as he. He needed to be able to keep this position, make it workable and receive assurances that his family would be taken care of when he died.

The one small victory Sebastian won against Ernesti during the next month was the Council's decision not to force him to teach Latin. Gorner, now a member of the Town Council, had spoken in his defense. The little man never ceased to surprise Sebastian.

Sebastian kept pleading with God to turn the heart of the Elector of Saxony toward him or bring some change into his circumstances that would enable him to begin performing his whole church cycle with beauty and effectiveness. The attempt to perform his new *Christmas Oratorio* at the Nicolaikirche in December was disastrous.

By the time the fall term of 1736 arrived, Sebastian had abandoned all hope of ever becoming the Court Composer of Saxony. For the first time in his life, he began skipping his daily time of private prayer. God was remote, the scriptures stale.

He began to wonder if God had ever really been there for him. Perhaps his plans and dreams and sense of the presence of God and greater eternal glories had only been a figment, a wish. Perhaps, it was, as Picander said, that the God who created the universe with all its immensities was not a God who reached down into time to help man with his individual troubles.

Anna brought him Martin Luther's translation of the Bible with the Calov commentary that had meant so much to him in the past. But he leafed through the Psalms, noted his underlining and notes—his identification with King David as the Worship Director of his people, David's access to three hundred fine musicians, and his own access to only thirty—many incompetent—and found that the commentary only made him feel worse.

He immersed himself in composing new orchestral, and he indulged increasingly in drink and in lengthy musical nights and discussions with Picander. He would come home after these sessions with a desperate kind of longing, take Anna in his arms and lose himself in the touch of her body. But the next day, all his turmoil would return.

The fall term arrived with a fresh group of music scholars Sebastian had some hope for. Then Ernesti informed him that it now belonged to the Rector to decide who would be Prefect. The Prefect served as assistant conductor for the Thomaskirche and the Nicolaikirche church services. This student would conduct when Sebastian needed to play the more difficult parts on the organ or the lead violin. The wrong Prefect would assure a deplorable performance no matter how well the musicians were prepared, and besides, it had always been the right of the Cantor to choose the Prefect. Ernesti didn't care about music or worship. He only wanted to establish the supremacy of his power in all areas of his institution.

Then one Friday in November, Sebastian was giving his new apprentice Franz a harpsichord lesson when he heard the rumble of a carriage outside. He scrambled to the window.

Four magnificent white horses were pulling a carriage to a halt in front of their door. The carriage bore the Elector's crest. A footman dressed in red and gold jumped down to open the carriage door. The man who stepped out wore a red frock coat elaborate with gold braid. It was one of the Elector's secretaries. Sebastian remembered seeing him at the torch-light ceremony.

Sebastian rushed up to his bedroom to swoop up his coat and wig. Frantically, he jerked on the black velvet coat, fumbling with the silver buttons. He struggled with his cauliflower wig. It was abominably tight and impossible to get on straight the first time. Brushing the powder off his shoulders, he took a deep breath and descended the stairs.

The Royal Secretary stood just inside the open front door talking to Anna. He was clutching a parchment scroll.

Twelve-year-old Heinrich and his four-year-old brother Friedrich were crouching behind the door, peering around it to see, then jerking back and giggling. Liesggen was standing in the kitchen doorway, blonde hair in a knot on top of her head like her mother's, with Dorothea behind her.

Anna smiled up at Sebastian, "Herr Bach! We have a royal envoy, one of the Elector's own secretaries."

As Sebastian reached the ground floor and bowed low, he saw his white knee socks were sagging. He stood up quickly hoping the official wouldn't notice. "Your Magnificence. You honor our humble home."

The official raised his blonde eyebrows and smiled a little. "I will not keep you in suspense," he said. Carefully, he unrolled the scroll and began reading. "Whereas His Royal Majesty in Poland and Serene Electoral Highness of Saxony, etc., has most graciously conferred upon Johann Sebastian

Bach, upon the latter's most humble entreaty and because of his ability, the style of Composer to the Court Capelle, . . ."[2]

He read on—but Sebastian was so excited he barely heard—something about this certificate bearing upon it the imprint of the royal seal and his Majesty's august signature.

When he finished, the official rolled the certificate back up and presented it to Sebastian. "His Majesty has instructed me to tell you that you have sent him music worthy of the gods, and he regrets that the conferment of the title has tarried. He expects a personal performance in Dresden as soon as you are able."

Once more the official bowed. Then he pivoted and left. The minute the coach was out of sight, there was a whooping and a hollering that Sebastian thought surely must bring neighbors out and into the streets. He wanted to share his news with everyone.

"We will embark upon a promenade," he said. "All the family will go. Franz, go find Carl. You must both come with us. Anna, we'll take the perambulator for Christian."

They shared the news with every friend they saw that afternoon, and they bought food in the stalls and went home to spend the evening dancing and singing. Sebastian and Anna sang and played together that night with wholeheartedness and cheer. Anna's voice lilted through the house, and Heinrich played every dance he had ever heard, first on the harpsichord and then the clavichord. There might be much Heinrich didn't understand, Sebastian thought, but he did understand when things were joyous or sad in the hearts of those he cared about. At such times, he contributed something invaluable to their home.

4

Sebastian entered the school the next day confident that, with the way news tended to spread in the city, almost everyone in the school would know about his royal title. Perhaps Ernesti would do something to honor him in front of the students. Perhaps this would be the end of all their animosities.

Sebastian walked into his classroom to find not a congratulations committee but an abomination. Krause was warming up the Sunday Kapelle. Carl was sitting at the harpsichord looking defeated.

The expression on Krause's face was smug. "Cantor Bach! I have begun the warming exercises for you."

"What do you think you are doing? We have spoken of this enough. Gerlach is my choice for Prefect this year."

Krause dipped his head in a mock bow. "And Carl is a worthy choice. But I am Rector Ernesti's choice. He told me this morning to take the position with confidence. He wants me to assist you in leading the worship service tomorrow. At least someone recognizes my qualities."

Incredulous, Sebastian marched out to find Ernesti. The school was empty today, except for the Sunday Kapelle and a few teachers who had come to work in their classrooms in quiet. Ernesti was in his study with the door open. He raised an eyebrow and gave Sebastian his drawstring smile— more a smirk, thought Sebastian—and today a hint of malice.

"It is a breach of the Cantor's contract for the Rector to appoint the Prefect, Ernesti. You know that. I am Court Capelle now, under the Elector's protection. I will appeal to him if you do not allow me the right to appoint my own Prefect, and you will pay the penalty. Gerlach has been working with the boys for several weeks on the pre-Advent cantata we plan to present this Sunday. I expect the performance to be unusually fine. An inept conductor will ruin it."

Ernesti slapped his hands on his desk, rose to his feet and leaned toward Sebastian. His eyes narrowed. "You think this Court Composer appointment will change things," he asked, "give you the power to move me around like some chess pawn? Well, you underestimate me. I would not be so arrogant about this title if I were you. It is a formality, an effort by the Elector to get you off his back. And how I wish I could do the same! Oh yes, I know how you've pestered the Elector these last two years with cantata after unwanted cantata. He must be sick to death of your unwanted gifts. As I am sick to death of having you forever in my way. Court Composer!" He spat out the word like profanity.

The words were a slap in the face. Sebastian had never dreamed that Ernesti wouldn't change his tone the minute he had a royal title. He should have known that, modernist that Ernesti was, he would downplay the authority of the distant Elector.

Ernesti flung his arm, pointing, toward the door. "Out of my sight Bach. There will be no more discussion about this Prefect issue. Krause, it is. Now out!"

Sebastian raged out, stalked down the hall, past his now empty classroom, through the refectory and on into the back gallery of the Thomaskirche where Krause had taken the boys to work with the organ. He vaulted up the stairs, pounded into the gallery and did the thing that came most naturally. He seized Krause by the collar, wrestled him down the stairs and then out of the church. He would at least have a decent rehearsal today.

Sebastian sought out Picander after the rehearsal. He had been so sure that being awarded the Court Composer title would be the answer to all his problems. He thought it would gain him the respect he needed to press forward with his vision for his worship music.

Where was God in all this debacle?

Picander's manservant informed Sebastian his employer wouldn't be home for another hour.

Sebastian replied he would wait. He headed for Picander's library and began flipping through the books: Descartes, Leibniz, with sections underlined about monads. He read that monads were a microcosm of the universe, characterized by the same dynamism and self-sufficiency that was characteristic of nature as a whole. The monad was completely self-determining. Nothing acted on it from the outside. Souls were the prime example of a monad. Each monad strove for self-realization through acts of individuation.[1]

Sebastian glanced at a pamphlet by Montesquieu, then drew a book by Voltaire off the shelf. The young Frenchman's works were increasing. Voltaire had a quarrel with the seventeenth-century thinker Pascal. Sebastian leafed through the volume until he came to a heavily underlined page. Picander was no sterile bibliophile. He believed in using his books.

Voltaire, it seemed, considered Pascal a "sublime misanthrope." Voltaire believed that belief in God was feasible only as an inference from the observable realm of nature, where alone, he believed, God was manifest to man. Such belief, then, was an act of reason, not of faith.

The front door slammed, and Picander strode in, "Sebastian! I could use an ear today."

"As could I!"

Picander shot straight to the liquor cupboard. "I recommend that today we abscond with our rule not to drink before 4 P.M. You look as if you need it, and I know I do."

He offered Sebastian a short tumbler of brandy, downed his own in one swift gulp and sat staring into the empty fireplace. "I've another woman problem. This time I'm afraid I have a pregnancy on my hands. The woman wants me to marry her."

Sebastian was taken aback. This was the first time Picander had ever volunteered any information about his social life. Sebastian had had his suspicions about Picander's morality, but this sudden confession left him shocked.

"So would you say, Sebastian, that my sins have caught up with me? My mother used to frighten me with that proverb, something about your sins being sure to find you out."

"So what will you do?"

"Try to convince her to get rid of the pregnancy. I know a village barber who takes care of women for hire and has good success without complications."

Again Sebastian was shocked. He downed his brandy and moved to pour another. "But the commandment not to take another's life?"

"Every situation has its unique exigencies. The woman does not want the child. And to marry me would be a comedown in her station. She doesn't love me. She simply does not know what else to do. And to live my life with her? She is ugly and stupid, despite her status. Her only good feature is her bosom. What kind of life would we have? And who knows when life begins? I maintain the spirit enters the child at birth."

"How can you be so confident?"

Picander relaxed and grinned, "A gift from the gods."

"If I lived such a life, I would be paralyzed with guilt."

"When you know that the only happiness in life is what you wrest from it for yourself, what you find in those glimpses of heaven with a woman or over a glass of wine or a good meal, then you find courage to really live."

"But what of peace and the fulfillment of the presence of God?"

"The Cosmic Clockmaker? I need a truth I can see and touch."

"Then you do not believe at all?"

"Of course I believe. But it is simply not reasonable to believe that the great Being who created the vast expanses of the universe would be concerned with tiny man. You have it all symbolized in Galileo's discovery that the earth circles around the sun and not vice versa."

"And the Bible, the death of God's Son for man's sins? How much more concerned and personal can a God be than One who is willing to experience an agonizing death in order to bring us to Himself?"

"It is myth, Sebastian. Don't you see? Truth, yes, but allegorical, symbols only. Now there is where the fascination lies, to calculate what the Crucifixion means on a deeper level. Something to do with patterns that repeat themselves throughout history, I think. Fascinating to surmise."

Sebastian's mind was reeling, and somehow, he couldn't bring himself to tell Picander what had happened to him at the Thomasschule. Did Picander even know about his new title? What did it matter? What did anything matter? He must get out of this place.

He mumbled some excuse and exited, returning automatically to the Thomaskirche. He would practice the organ.

But try as he could, he couldn't concentrate on the music for tomorrow. He would go to Zimmerman's. He entered the afternoon hubbub and was immediately hailed and feted for his new title. He stayed there for a long time, feasting with friends and laughing and drinking.

Then Gorner sat down at his table and eyed him as Sebastian poured yet another drink. "Court Composer Bach has troubles? Drink is a cheat they say, as is all worldly acclaim. It turns on you. Ah, the pain!"

He said it with merriment, but it struck too close to home. Gorner had a way of seeing through much, like a jester, Sebastian thought, or a prophet.

He got up from the table and stumbled out into the street.

Sebastian wove his way home with a turmoil in him that was worse than any turmoil he could ever remember. The sky was starless, mirroring his own inner darkness. It was as though he were falling weightless through the black abyss Galileo had unstopped. This was worse than any rejection he'd ever had from any family member or noble or church official, worse than any abyss of failure or worldly loss. He was suffocating in a bog of fear. He was losing his faith in God.

5

Sebastian woke Sunday morning with a headache that made his whole body feel like one searing pain. How would he ever be able to carry out his church duties today? He drank several cups of coffee and dragged himself to the church. Carl was already there helping each boy tune his instrument as he arrived. There were eight singers and ten instrumentalists today: strings, oboe and flute. The boys' voices sounded clear and strong, and the instrumentalists were playing with unusual confidence. This Sunday there might well be a good presentation of his cantata.

Early comers began entering the church for the worship service. The candles were lit. The musicians were reviewing the closing chorale, a working out of *A Mighty Fortress*. Gerlach was directing and Sebastian played the organ.

Suddenly, Krause appeared at the top of the gallery stairs, marched over to the conductor's stand and shoved Carl aside. He swooped up the rolled manuscript Carl had dropped and proceeded to direct. The boys' voices quavered. Livid, Sebastian jumped down to wrest the scroll out of Krause's hand. He jerked Krause's arm behind him, wrenching it upward. "Step aside, you swine."

Krause stumbled back, swearing. Sebastian motioned Carl to take his place, then returned to the organ. Carl began directing, but the boys' voices were tentative. Sebastian watched in the mirror above his music. Krause was standing behind Carl, his fists clenching and unclenching.

Then Ernesti appeared at the top of the stairs with several rough-looking boys. They were boys Sebastian had seen with Krause in the halls many times. Krause glanced at Ernesti. Ernesti nodded, and to Sebastian's horror, Krause seized Carl by the shoulder, turned him and plunged his fist toward his face. Carl dodged just in time, and Krause's fist hit the stand. It went crashing to the floor.

Sebastian could hear voices below. The church was almost full, and people were turning to stare up at the west gallery. That Ernesti would encourage a student to fight in a church service was something Sebastian could not comprehend. What kind of a man was he?

It was time to start the prelude for the service. Sebastian snapped for his musicians' attention and signaled for everyone to sit down. He began playing the organ, filling the Gothic spaces of the church with the *Fantasie in G Minor*. It wasn't the work he had planned to play, but at least it should be complex enough to cover any vestiges of turmoil. Surely, once the pastor had pronounced the invocation, this nightmare would end.

Ernesti was whispering something to the first violinist. He was a red-haired boy with freckles who always reminded Sebastian of Gottfried. The boy bent to whisper into the ear of the musician next to him, and so on through the whole Kapelle.

During the invocation, Carl crept to the organ. There was a smudge on his thick glasses. "Rector Ernesti says no one is to sing or play except when Krause directs. He is threatening punishment if anyone disobeys."

"Do as he says," said Sebastian.

With a sneer, Krause took the rolled-up manuscript from Carl and prepared to direct the first chorale. The eight vocalists stood. Sebastian's head began to pound. *The one Sunday in weeks when I thought the boys were ready to perform my cantata,* he thought, *and now this has to happen.*

He weathered it out for a while, wincing when Krause brought the instrumentalists in too soon on the first chorale, and gritting his teeth when he confused the boys later by beating the music in the wrong meter. It was almost time for the cantata. He could not allow this farce to continue.

When the vice-pastor began announcing the charitable opportunities for the week, Sebastian signaled to Carl to take his place at the organ. Ignoring Ernesti's warning look, Sebastian strode toward Krause, wrested the baton from him and planted himself firmly in front of the conductor's stand.

Sebastian kept his eyes on the music and focused on preparing mentally for the cantata. Then he began beating out the tempo to assure the strings didn't begin too slowly. The four violinists and violists lifted their instruments, and then suddenly, Krause grabbed Sebastian's arm and crashed his fist into his jaw.

Sebastian's reflexes took over. He returned the blow. Krause tumbled to the floor. Then everything was chaos. The ruffians flung themselves into the Kapelle, strewing music everywhere. There was a bass-reeded discord from the organ; a front-row musician falling on the back of two scuffling figures with a cry; another ruffian knocking a violin to the floor; then Ernesti joining in, shoving and yelling. Enraged with the stupidity of the man, Sebastian jerked him around and shook him. Ernesti plunged a fist into Sebastian's nose. Instruments and chairs crashed to the floor. Boys and men groaned and shouted, and the noise from the congregation began to rival that in the gallery.

Sebastian was trying to defend one of the younger boys when the town bailiff hefted his burly body into the scuffle and shouted to everyone to cease or be thrown in jail. When everyone quieted, the bailiff ordered Sebastian to the organ to restore some semblance of worship and marched the ruffians and Ernesti down the gallery stairs and out of the church.

Mindlessly, Sebastian began playing the cantata, and gradually the Kapelle joined in. His vision was so blurred he could scarcely see anything. His nose was bleeding onto the keys. How had he come to such a pass?

6

Anna found him wandering aimlessly in the park behind the church. The trees stood gnarled and upflung in their November nakedness, their shadows lying before her in the near-winter sun.

She loved this park, strolling here often with the children and sometimes by herself to watch and listen to the birds. The only birds today were a few crows. They rose from the chalk-white branches of a birch tree with a flapping and cawing and flew to take perches on the steeple and the peaked roof of the church. Of all the birds she had seen, crows were the ones she liked the least. It seemed to her that they were the harbingers of darkness.

She overtook him as he trailed off the path onto the brown grass. He was hunched like an old man. His wig was askew, his broad face pale and he squinted his eyes at her as if he couldn't see her for the pain. She reached for his cold hand and folded it in both of her own.

"I am a scourge," he said.

"It wasn't your fault."

He shook his head, and she took his arm and led him home. That day she had herring for dinner. Sebastian stared at it, picked at it a little, then put his fork down.

Heinrich, who was sitting next to his father, cocked his head up at him. Sebastian patted his hand, and Heinrich lay down his fork too. Neither of them ate another bite. When Sebastian folded his napkin and pushed back his chair to leave, Heinrich folded his also and left with him.

Anna hoisted little Christian to her shoulder and watched the two climb the stairs together. At the second floor landing, Heinrich took his father's hand and tugged him into the music room.

Soon she heard the twelve-year-old's inimitable music: "Jesu, Joy of Man's Desiring," and his own improvisation on the Air from the *Suite in D.* The harpsichord music continued for a long time. Heinrich embellished each harpsichord piece with beautiful trills and turns. His musical intuition was faultless.

After she and Dorothea had finished the dishes, Anna took Christian and Friedrich upstairs for their naps.

She peeked into the music room to see Sebastian leaning back in his chair with his eyes closed and his face peaceful. Sebastian was no longer King David, the Worship Director, but King Saul, tortured in spirit; and his son Heinrich, so overlooked and insignificant in the world's view, was his David.

Anna ached with her husband during the next few days. He would go nowhere and he would eat almost nothing. When she realized how bad his vision was, she sent for Dr. Biedermann. It was the worst of news: cataracts. She watched Sebastian listen to the physician's verdict, his face falling, his shoulders heaving in silent agony over the prognosis of certain blindness.

During that first week, Anna spent much of her time with Sebastian, listening as he lay on his bed and tried to explain to her the depth of his torment. He said he was confused about everything. He thought it had been God's will for him to defend the rights of his office.

"But," he said, "if defending it can propel me into such a sorry situation, I must have been wrong. I have profaned the house of God. Surely God is punishing me for my pride and presumption."

His anxiety was welling to the point of chaos, drowning his hope, destroying even his desire to compose.

"There is nothing clear," he said, "nothing rational, nothing certain in all the world. Picander's thinking, the thinking of the finest of the minds in all Europe, has led me unwittingly to the place of doubting everything I've staked my soul on since before I can remember."

His past decisions, his current desires, the value of his work before God had, in his mind, all come into question. He felt as if demons were possessing and beating and battering his mind and emotions.

"If I really love God, how could I have ever let myself profane His place of worship. I want death to come, Anna. It would be sweet. I no longer want to live."

Anna listened and listened as he poured it all out. She feared belittling the complexity of his search by pasting catechism answers on his life. So she said nothing.

She wanted to tell him that she still believed God's hand was on his music; that she saw greatness in him; that no one who labored in the work of the Lord would ever labor in vain; that he simply needed to confess his sin, and the Father would restore him to continue steadfast in the work which yet remained. Someday, some way, his striving for excellence in a worship music that would glorify God would be rewarded. She was sure of it. But he needed a passionate patience, and so did she.

When he had talked it all out, she left him, thinking that this mood would not last long. But it did. It stretched into the next month and through Christmas and on into the beginning of the New Year. His eyes were better. The doctor had prescribed some drops and a darker lens for his glasses, assuring him that he could have five to ten more years of adequate vision. But still Sebastian refused to go to the school or the church to fulfill his duties. He delegated it all to Carl, closeted himself in his study and took long aimless walks. Ernesti was threatening to dismiss him.

Finally, Anna wrote Catherina. She didn't know what else to do. Barbara had noted on her calendar, which Anna still referred to often, how her sister could speak to Sebastian about spiritual things more forthrightly and effectively than anyone else.

When Catherina arrived, large and motherly looking with gray in her coroneted hair and certitude in her brown eyes, Anna felt an instant relief. Catherina stayed for a week, closeted with Sebastian for several hours a day. They talked and read the Bible, and after dinner she listened to family performances of some of Sebastian's new church music. Anna, Liesggen and Dorothea sang while Heinrich played the harpsichord. Sometimes, at Catherina's insistence, Sebastian would join them on the violin.

Heinrich spent his day trailing Catherina about the house. When she was with Sebastian in the study, he sat patiently outside the door until she appeared. She would act surprised when she found him waiting. "What would you like to do today, Heinrich?"

He would look off, then down at his hands and off again. "Hit the right keys at the right time and the music plays itself."

"What about a game of backgammon?"

"Plays itself, plays itself."

She would extend her hand, and he would take it and they would go off to learn another rule of backgammon or a new Bible verse. Anna was amazed at how much Catherina was able to help him in such a short time.

One day Catherina left after the noon meal, wearing her black lace bonnet. She returned with a brand new volume of a work by Pascal. "I think this godly man's thinking will be able to speak to where Sebastian is right now in a way no one else can."

The one discussion Anna overheard between Catherina and her husband had something to do with the meaning of *Soli Deo Gloria*.

"Perhaps, my brother, your problem is as simple as this. You have written at the end of your works, 'To God alone be the glory.' But you have been seeking your own glory, along with God's. In such a quest, you will never find fulfillment or peace."

Interlude Four

Late into the night, he sat in the music room struggling to read Pascal by candlelight. "What will become of you, O man, who try by your reason to discover what is your true condition? . . .Know then, proud creature, what a paradox you are to yourself. . . . Be humble, impotent reason; . . . learn from your Master of our true condition. . . . Hearken unto God."[1]

He blew out the candles and sat in the darkness, thinking for a long time. Finally, he fell to his knees beside the harpsichord bench and began praying. "Father, I abhor myself. No matter where I go, I cannot get away from what I have become. You are determined to reveal to me the reality of my nakedness, the ugliness of all my striving, striving, seeking to control, to achieve. And how small my success in spite of all my strivings!

"I am struck down, a broken clay pot. I have indulged in wine, piling on sensation, numbing my soul, accepting as truth the reasonings of men. Gone are the halcyon days when I shot the spirit arrows of truth and, despite my bondage, stood free. I have missed too many communions. I have failed to take the time to humble myself before You.

"I have wanted to glorify You with my music. But what can I ever do with *intent pure enough to fitly meet, much less glorify, a holy God? What can anyone ever do? Who has ever done it well? Men paint unholy decisions holy 'for the glory of God,' ruffians decree riots, kings butcher nations 'for the glory of God.' Glorifying You? Luther did it by a holy rebellion, but mine has not been holy. I have lost all sense of proportion.*

"Can You redeem me, Lord, from this self? Will You? You have renewed me after worse fallings. You have turned curses into blessings. You have filled me to compose for You, and I have known You were writing through me. I have known with a faith beyond reason that art has the power to lift into the infinite. And You, Father, who know all things, know that my deepest heart's desire is still the same. I want to worship You with all that I am. I want to live and create for Your glory alone. Have mercy upon me.

"I repent of my abominable pride. I choose to daily seek to remember the real truth about who I am and who You are. I would learn to live repenting daily of the uselessness of relying on myself for the propagation of my works.

"I will wait on the unfolding of Your purposes, flowing steadily from Your initiative. I will do only what is put before me with humility and faithfulness.

"Teach me to live out of the still quiet place within, where You dwell. If I am to be Worship Director of Your church, then, Father, You create that reality in Your time. I bow at Your feet, oh Lord. There is the highest place."

BOOK FIVE · · · *THE REFUGE*

When Frederick the Great became King of Prussia in 1740, he had the fourth largest army in Europe. In quality it was the finest. His "attack on Silesia (an extremely important province on account of its agriculture and production of textiles) in 1740" began the wars which led to the breaking up of the Holy Roman Empire.[1]

{The Canonic Variations } "record the master {Bach} old, wise, and experienced almost beyond belief, whose art was Miltonic in majesty, ease, and certainty, and uniquely inexhaustible."[2]

18

Resurrrection

1 7 3 9 — 1 7 5 0

Anna sat at the kitchen table copying parts for Sebastian's newly revised *St. Matthew Passion.* The finished parts were stacked neatly in the middle of the table with a paperweight on top of them. Fresh manuscript paper, some they had bought already lined and some she would need to line herself, lay waiting in two not-so-neat piles, and in a pot standing beside an inkwell were several quills of different widths and two quill knives.

Everyone said her hand was so much like Sebastian's that they couldn't tell which manuscripts were his and which were hers. His diminishing eyesight made it ever more imperative that he have competent musicians who could copy parts for him, and even take musical dictation.

Anna put her whole heart into this work, seldom tiring of it because it was such a tangible way of supporting her husband. Her careful copying of his music was a labor of love. She finished the last pages that had been damaged. She'd had to redo the right half of several pages and draw in her own lines. She pressed on to the next section where Sebastian had roughed in a few edits. Only three harmonic changes, it looked like. The main change was the words. Picander's original libretto read, "Lord, my heart is open to Thee. Ah! Thou within it. Love, faith, endurance, hope shall be Thy bed of rest." She copied in Sebastian's words above the proper notes: "Mouth and heart are open to Thee, all highest, sink therein! I in Thee and Thou in me: Faith, love, endurance, hope, shall be my bed of rest."[3]

Two-year-old Carolina squealed happily as she mowed down the blocks she'd been stacking.

Carrots, cabbages and onions were piled into the cooking pot on the stove ready for slicing for tonight's stew.

The family Bible lay open at the end of the long kitchen table. Sebastian never skipped family devotions these days. He would read a chapter from Martin Luther's translation of the Bible, and they would pray and sing a hymn or chorale; and if he were home at noon, he would read a proverb and engage the children in a discussion of its practical meaning for the day.

Except for the worry over Bernhard—they hadn't heard from him in months— the last two years had been good ones. Sebastian had resumed his story-telling: God's provision through the herrings, the bassoonist, the story of Handel's old mother, the sudden appearance of his moon-eyed mentor in Hamburg, the tale of his and Anna's courtship and how he had been convinced she was in love with his nephew Gottfried. He had even taken to narrating the story of how he'd thrown his wig at Gorner. The younger boys liked to take turns throwing the wig. The fun-loving Sebastian she had so enjoyed in their courtship and early years of marriage had resurfaced.

Not long after the riot in the service, Sebastian had appealed to the Elector for help. The Elector had responded, and from that point on, Sebastian had had no problem securing the Council's support in appointing his own Prefect or choosing his own hymns. They even consented to his hiring members of the Collegium Musicum for the festal services, if he felt it was needed. But Ernesti still acted the adversary, and Sebastian told Anna he had grown weary of the conflict. He began to withdraw from both the school and the church, performing only the duties he couldn't delegate.

Instead of throwing all his energies into performing his church cycle, Sebastian began to approach Sundays as a day when he, first and foremost, sought to enter the presence of God. He said he was seeking simplicity in his personal worship. Often he delegated the service to Carl or a promising apprentice and sat with his family in the back of the Thomaskirche or even took them to the Neuekirche or St. Peter's. A simple chorale would sometimes fling him into joy. His black eyes would shine, and he would walk home wrapped in silence. Later he would tell Anna what had happened. It would always have something to do with a dovetailing of a poetic or musical phrase or a pastor's text with something that had already been happening deep in his spirit.

Anna had experiences like that occasionally. Hers came in the form of explosions of joy, so deep and so unexpected that she told Sebastian they were what made her know God was real.

Carolina suddenly shrieked. She flailed at the blocks she'd been lining end to end around her and threw one that hit Anna sharply on the foot.

The baby began crying at the top of her lungs. Anna got up and knelt in front of her. Instantly the two-year-old quieted and raised her arms. "You must play by yourself a little longer. Here! You can measure out beans like Mama."

Anna dipped a big tin cup into the sack of beans under the sink and set it front of Carolina with a string of spoons and a big bowl. Carolina flung her hand against the cup and scattered the beans across the floor.

"Stop it, Carolina."

Carolina wailed.

Anna sighed. This little girl was the most spirited baby she had ever had, and that was saying something. She had borne twelve children. She wouldn't mind one more child, perhaps another girl. If the baby were healthy, she would have three boys—Heinrich, Friedrich and Christian—and three girls—Liesggen, Carolina and the new baby to watch grow into maturity. A nice balance. Not any more after that, she told herself. She yearned to have time to practice and to work on her reading skills. She'd had little time to pursue reading and felt impoverished because of it.

The beans and blocks were still sliding and thudding all over the kitchen floor.

Anna picked up Carolina's well-packed little body. She would have to discipline her. As she was laboring up the stairs to find the wooden paddle, the front door flew open. It was Sebastian. His face was ashen. He was holding a letter in his hand, and she could see the remnants of a black seal. Fear fell over her. She hurried into their bedroom to put Carolina in her crib, then ran back down to Sebastian. "What is it?"

He tried to tell her, but his voice broke. He began sobbing. She took the letter. Who did they know in Jena? Bernhard! He'd been studying at the University since January, it said. She gasped, and her tears welled. Bernhard had died of a fever the day before.

That night their house was filled with sounds of weeping and moaning and short gasping questions and prayers.

Bernhard had been only twenty-four. He would never have a family of his own now or a chance of accomplishing anything significant on earth. Of all Barbara's children, Anna had loved Bernhard best. She remembered how the little boy had warmed to her from the beginning. She had gone to the Bach house nervous, and, auburn curls bobbing and face filled with mischief, he had urged her into a game of chase. Before the afternoon was over, he had entrusted her with the wooden soldier Gottfried had carved for him. His attachment to the gray cat, his love for all animals and his sensitivity had caused her to feel increasingly close to Bernhard as the years passed. This was impossible to bear.

They brought his body the ten miles from Jena and held a memorial service at the Thomaskirche a week later. There was a huge attendance of family and friends. The neighbors brought hams and roasts and vegetables and sweets, and after the burial, family members gathered around their table.

"What was he doing in Jena?" asked Gottfried.

Gottfried was sitting across from Anna with his mother Maria on one side and his wife and two children on the other. Anna thought how mature Gottfried looked. His freckled face was filled out, and his red hair was combed back neatly into a pigtail.

"Attending the university, evidently. He ran up debts when he was Hoforganist at Muhlhausen. Gambling. Sebastian paid the debts for him, and we were sure that Bernhard had changed."

"Bernhard always managed to make you think things were better than fine with him."

"Didn't he? What a charmer!" The tears came again. Anna had wept all through the service.

"Always thought he had a bit too much tomfoolery about him, though."
It was Emmanuel. He drew up his chair to sit beside Maria.

"There you are, you scoundrel!" Gottfried reached across the table to
grip Emmanuel's hand. "*Accompagnist* to the Prussian Crown Prince! And I
was there to hear your first harpsichord lesson."

"I've had to work hard," said Emmanuel with a grin.

Gottfried chuckled. He turned back to Anna, "So, Bernhard had ceased
to write you?"

Anna nodded, "It was difficult. Sebastian convinced some church officials in Sangerhausen to give Bernhard a second chance as Hoforganist.
But they wrote last summer that Bernhard had failed to pay for choir
items they had already given him the money for. They were hoping we
knew where he was."

"Bernhard left Sangerhausen without even writing you about it?" It
was Anna's sister. She and her father were sitting next to Gottfried's wife.

"I suppose he was ashamed."

"Now it appears he was trying for a law degree in Jena," said Emmanuel.
"He developed an acute fever."

"How far medicine has to go!" Anna's father was seventy years old now.
His voice was raspy and his body prone to all kinds of ailments. It meant a
great deal to Anna that he would make the journey to attend the service.
"Got any of your mother's cure-all tea around?" he asked. "It's the only
thing that seems to help my gout."

"I'm sorry, Father. I don't."

"Your mother always kept it on hand."

"I know I should be more efficient."

Before Anna's father could respond, Sebastian walked up behind Anna
and put his big hands on her shoulders. "Anna is the perfect wife, Herr
Wilcken. She is exactly what I need."

Anna started to say she didn't deserve such a compliment, but she had
apologized enough already. Being around her father always made her revert
to old habits.

"Is there no one else around here who could use a little sustenance?"

cried Friedemann. He was the most fashionably dressed person at the table. His coat had the new boot cuff, and he'd been wearing skintight gloves that he took off only to eat.

Sebastian sat in the big chair at the end of the table and bowed his head. Everyone immediately fell silent. He prayed, a long, somber prayer, commending Bernhard once again to God. But as soon as he pronounced the "Amen," the chatter resumed.

"Uncle Telemann sends his sympathy," said Emmanuel as he forked up a thick piece of ham. "He was in Berlin last week and made me promise to convey his deep regrets that he could not be present today."

"And how is Phillip Telemann?" asked Sebastian. "Still tossing out dry jokes and writing reams of music?"

"Yes, reams of music. And more laughter these days than bitterness."

"I think your friendship has helped him."

As Anna buttered Carolina's bread she thought how strange it was that, in the midst of such grief, they could speak of normal things. Funerals always seemed to further family unity. Catherina was here, and Maria's daughter Judith. Dorothea spent almost the whole dinner hour hovering over everyone, making sure the children were being taken care of, keeping an eye on the men's beer mugs and brewing more strong coffee. Dorothea was thirty years old now and still had no desire to leave home. Her heart was pure servant.

When dinner was over and everyone was settled for the night, Anna slipped into her chemise and sat in the rocking chair to thumb through the new moral weekly her sister had brought her. Sebastian drew his pipe out of the drawer in the bed table and quoted the poem he'd written in her little clavier book more than ten years ago:

"Whene'er I take my pipe and stuff it
And smoke to pass the time away,
My thoughts, as I sit there and puff it,
Dwell on a picture sad and gray:
It teaches me that very like
Am I myself unto my pipe."[4]

He grinned at her as he stuffed his pipe, "Terrible poetry!"

"But fun!" she said. She watched him light the old pipe, then take a draw. She closed her eyes for a minute and relished the hickory smell. Sebastian's mind was definitely set on things above these days, but it did not keep him from enjoying the earthly pleasures allowed. Somehow it made her love him even more.

"Did you see Picander today at the service?" she asked.

"Picander!"

"I saw him when I took Carolina out to the narthex. He left in the middle of the sermon."

"I miss him."

"With every year it seems we collect more holes in our lives, by death or misunderstanding."

"Reiche would have understood why the riot in the church affected me so adversely. But Picander didn't. I tried to be diplomatic, but evidently I went too far when I told him I feared he might have crossed a line that would one day destroy him."

"You said he thought you were being judgmental."

Sebastian stretched his legs out on the bed and adjusted the pillows behind him. He began blowing smoke rings.

"Every day there is something in my speech or thinking I have to repent."

He looked at her with humility and tenderness in his black eyes. What a refuge he had become!

Impulsively, she lay down beside him and threw her arm over his big body. She hugged him and snuggled close. He set his pipe aside and turned to take her in his arms. That night they comforted each other with their love.

2

With the new freedom Sebastian now possessed to manage his responsibilities at the school and church however he desired, he increased the hours he stayed home to compose. Anna would scold him a little about the strain on his eyes. But he felt driven to write and perfect as much as possible before he lost his eyesight, and who knew exactly when that would be?

His plan was to finish all the compendiums he had in mind and then to start back with his earliest organ and church works and revise until each work was as perfect as he could possibly make it.

He thought of the *Mass in B Minor*, not only as a work to help people encounter God, but also as a compendium for all the vocal styles he knew. The *Orgelbuchlein* would be organ preludes for an entire church year, the *Brandenburg Concertos* a compendium of orchestration techniques, and the *Goldberg Variations,* commissioned by a Count he'd met in Dresden, a compendium of his variation techniques. He even planned to write a work presenting every one of his counterpoint techniques. He would call it *The Art of the Fugue.*

Would these works ever receive more than a smattering of performances? He believed that, in their own way, each of the compendiums worked in the hearer a cleansing, a refreshing of the spirit. He hoped they would gain a wide hearing. But he was learning to be content with the knowledge that God could hear his choruses and trumpets and recitatives and deep alto arias and fugues as though they were being played by the finest Kapelle in the world.

All the intricate weavings of melodies and textures done to the highest apex of his ability he daily offered to God as worship. God heard and saw, and that was all that mattered.

One day, ten-year-old Christian came running up to the study. "Mama says to tell you you have a guest, Papa, a musician from England."

"Another one?"

"He says he is doing the Grand Tour, and that he has been told he must not neglect to stop by to see the great organist Johann Sebastian Bach."

The man was already in the music room listening to Friedrich play a three-part invention. He looked to be in his mid-twenties, had a florid complexion and wore a monocle, a long gray vest and a gray coat with sleeves that were several inches too short. He carried a bulging rucksack.

When he saw Sebastian at the door, he jumped to his feet and lifted his tricorner. He spoke in halting German.

"Lord Low from London. You must be the great man."

Sebastian returned the bow, feeling pleased in spite of himself. He didn't mind the occasional salute to his accomplishments.

"I have heard you are an experienced composer as well as a virtuosic clavier player," said Lord Low. "I too am a serious composer and thought since I was in Leipzig, I should stop in and meet you."

"I am honored," said Sebastian. "We can talk techniques and have some music if you wish."

Friedrich, who was thirteen now and was looking more like Emmanuel every day, closed his music and started to leave.

Lord Low held up his hand. "Please stay. I teach also."

"Me too? Can I stay?" Christian's face was eager.

Lord Low dipped his head.

"Well!" said Sebastian. "You must tell me if you've heard any of Handel's concerts."

"I possess the best seats in the house. Was there for the premiere of *Messiah* four years ago."

"Now that is a work I would like to hear." Sebastian's old desire to meet Handel reappeared. He had tried to arrange a meeting with Handel not long after the Leipzig move, but again he'd been disappointed.

"I was advised, Herr Bach, to give you a theme and ask you to improvise on it."

Lord Low played a theme that had possibilities. Sebastian took his seat at the double-manualed harpsichord and set his fingers to work on the smooth keys.

He played with the theme's motifs, inverting them, transposing them and creating new rhythmic patterns. Soon he had everyone tapping their foot and laughing at his tricks with rhythms and trills. Anna and Liesggen were standing in the doorway now, and Heinrich had crept in to sit on his footstool.

When Sebastian finished, everyone applauded.

Lord Low clapped gratuitously. "Your impromptu composing is quite nice. Permit me to show you a little something I composed impromptu for one of my students."

He reached into his bag and selected a manuscript.

"I will show you boys something every harpsichord pupil needs to know."

The Englishman began playing a study piece presenting various kinds of trills. Friedrich and Christian rolled their eyes at Sebastian. They had both learned these techniques in their first year of study. Sebastian placed a finger on his lips and shook his head.

Lord Low played on and on, stopping often to explain and not pausing for comment.

Anna signaled it was time for dinner, but as soon as Lord Low finished one piece, he drew another from his bag, keeping up a running explanation and commencing again to play. The aroma of bread just out of the oven was almost too tantalizing to bear, but Sebastian forced himself to patience.

Finally, Lord Low swiveled to face them. He adjusted his monocle with a self-satisfied smile. "I could go on and on. With the help of God, I have become quite prolific. But—" he checked his pocket watch, shut it with a click, then stood up. "I'm, sorry to say I have another appointment."

He bowed, "Thank you for playing for me, Herr Bach. I hope the time has been profitable for you also."

"You will not stay to supper?"

"I have an appointment, as I said. With a publisher, as a matter of fact. One cannot always be thinking of one's stomach."

He bowed and clattered down the stairs and out the door.

Friedrich's black eyes were sparking fire.

"How could you abide such arrogance, Papa? The man is a fool."

Sebastian felt the same. But he saw too much of himself in the Englishman. "Lord Low is young. He may have to go through difficult times, but he will learn."

3

A young man who was a member of Sebastian's Collegium Musicum and who desired to find a mathematical and philosophical basis for music had established a society in Leipzig. The Mizler Society was composed of a select group of musicians who were exploring the idea of music as "sounding mathematics." Sebastian was considering joining the society, and that required a portrait.

He had had Anna's portrait painted a year before and had watched the process with pleasure. Her beauty increased as she grew older. Her blonde hair had silvered, and there were wrinkles at the corners of her blue-gray eyes. But there was a shining about her, a fragility that made none of that matter. Who she was was beautiful. A good marriage was a priceless gift! Yes, having Anna's portrait painted had been pure pleasure. But having his own portrait painted was another matter. Anna and Dorothea worked for weeks sewing a new black velvet coat that would fit his growing bulk.

"Remember," Sebastian had told Dorothea as she pinned up the hem of the coat, "there must be fourteen buttons that can be shown in the portrait."

Dorothea sounded exasperated, "Yes, Papa, I know. Fourteen. The number for the name Bach. How could I forget?"

He found himself more and more intrigued with numbers these days. Some of it was a game for him, like the puzzle canons he and Emmanuel sent each other to solve. And some of it was a challenge he set for himself: a determination to use a certain number of measures in a work or to utilize a musical figure a specific number of times. It was the kind of thing a poet did when he limited himself to a certain number of syllables or a rigid form of rhyme.

When he donned the coat the day of his first sitting and tried to button it, he couldn't. Anna and Dorothea had been so careful when they measured. Had he gained that much in a month? It put him in a bad mood. He supposed he could meditate a long time on the fact that there was too much of him.

Anna ushered the painter in. Elias Gottlob Haussman lived in Leipzig and had gained quite a following as a portrait painter. He was teasing Anna. "You are, Frau Bach, the perfect subject. The crones, the stern-faced matriarchs, the courtesans who always try to seduce me: how to give them some hint of beauty or take out of their eyes that lecherous stare, ah, it is a difficult task. But you! How rare it is to be able to paint someone just as they are and never have a complaint. You must sit for me again."

Anna looked pleased, but a little embarrassed. "I believe one portrait of Anna Bach is quite enough. My stepson Emmanuel thinks it is too much." A sad look crossed her face. Sebastian felt a rush of anger toward Emmanuel.

When Emmanuel had seen Anna's portrait at Christmas, he had sworn and challenged Sebastian, "Why is it you never had mother's picture painted?" He had stalked out of the house and hadn't returned until after midnight.

Anna was searching her pockets. "I have those regulations for the portrait somewhere. The composition Herr Bach is submitting for his entrance to the society must be somewhere in the picture, in his right hand, I think."

Sebastian crossed the room to meet them. "I have it, dear. Found it on the harpsichord this morning."

The painter read the instructions and spent a great deal of time eyeing all the corners of the room, moving instruments and chairs about and finally maneuvering Sebastian into the position he desired.

"There, the composition, in your right hand. Turn it upside down so we can see the title. Let's see: *Canonic Variations in 6 Voices*. Now turn your head this way. You really must button your coat."

Sebastian frowned. "I can't."

"Try it."

Irritated, Sebastian struggled until he managed to button two of the buttons. He sat there for a few minutes feeling as though he were wearing a stomacher. Suddenly, one of the buttons popped off.

"Confound it!" Sebastian scrambled to find it. A long thread was dangling from his coat. "See what you've made me do."

Haussman looked cross. He mumbled something under his breath.

"Never mind. Make yourself as comfortable as you can, and I will try to capture you with the properly formal look."

Sebastian thought that the sittings would never end.

Never had playing with Carolina and her little sister Susanna seemed so appealing. Anna scolded him because he kept allowing them to interrupt his pose. The painter had to return every day for two weeks instead of the usual six days. The result was an expression on Sebastian's face that was more severe than pleased him. But what did it matter? He'd now fulfilled all the requirements for joining the Mizler Society, and he could enjoy their company regularly to discuss the intricacies of his art without reserve.

One of the works Sebastian spent a great deal of time perfecting was the *Mass in B Minor*. Toward the end of the fifth movement, the *Crucifixus,* he wrote the vocal and instrumental lines so they sank quietly into their lowest registers. Thus, he depicted Jesus being musically lowered into the tomb.

The *Et Resurrexit* immediately followed in an explosion of blazing glory. Sebastian believed this juxtaposition to be particularly effective. It said all he felt about the glorious hope of the Resurrection, something that was impossible for him to express in words.

To his mind, the most important revision of the Mass was what he did with the Credo: "I believe in one God, the Father Almighty . . . and in one Lord Jesus Christ, the only-begotten Son of God. . . ." He took the numbers normally assigned to the alphabet and added up the numbers for J. S. Bach. The sum was 41. The sum of the numbers for the Credo was 43. The two numbers added together came to 84. He began working at the music so that his Credo would consist of exactly eighty-four measures. At the bottom of the movement he penned in the number 84. That was all. But what it mean to him was, "Bach believes." It was an act of worship—like the craftsman of old who spent as much time carving the inside of a church pillar as he did the outside—for the eyes of God alone. "Your servant Bach believes."

4

Sebastian was sixty-two years old when he saw August for the last time.

The new Prussian king Frederick the Great declared war against Silesia a year after he took the throne. Saxony had vacillated in its allegiance, and as a result, travel had not been safe for several years. Finally, the Peace of Dresden was declared, and in 1745, the roads became passable once more.

Sebastian's eyes were growing so dim that he didn't know if he would have many more chances to travel. When the Elector summoned him to perform his Mass in Dresden, Sebastian decided to take a detour and visit August. He hadn't been to Weimar in years.

The moment August received word Sebastian and Anna had arrived, he invited them into his state bedchamber where he was breakfasting in bed. He was wearing a purple silk bed jacket protected by a linen napkin and was in the middle of shoveling in a platter of sausages when he waved them in.

He instructed his chambermaid to prepare some ham and fruit for them from the loaded breakfast table. "And some wine, pour wine all around. You have stayed away too long, Sebastian. Anna, well!" He looked her up and down, a bit too interestedly, Sebastian thought. "What maturity has done for you, my girl! I could wish my ladies-in-waiting would mature so well. I have to have a turn over in them every two or three years. They start to sag. Brioches, preserves? And coffee, of course. Sebastian Bach must have his coffee. Go find some, Hannah." He smacked the chambermaid's backside, and she rushed away giggling.

"You must stay the day. After breakfast you can hear reports from my gardeners and architects with me. I will dismiss my ministers so we can make music. State business can always wait."

Sebastian and Anna remained as long as they could bear it. But dinner began at two P.M. and dragged on until six P.M., and August's jokes were growing bawdier. When he invited them to an evening of playing quadrille with him and his ladies-in-waiting, Sebastian declined.

"If we are to reach Dresden on time, we must leave at dawn. My old bones need rest."

The next morning they rode through the Weimar land, noting run-down mills and beggars along the way. August was not the person he had been. There had been a time when his sensitivity had given Sebastian the hope that someday he would become a servant of his people. But August had struggled with the difficulties of life and lost. Now he lived only to eat, drink and be merry. "There may not be a tomorrow," he said.

Sebastian understood how he felt. Yes, tomorrow any one of them might die. "Nevertheless," he said to Anna, "I am glad Barbara did not live to see what August has become."

The Dresden performance for the Elector was a success, as was their visit to one of Friedemann's services at the Sophienkirche. When Sebastian told Friedemann that, as *Accompagnist* for Frederick the Great, Emmanuel had invited him to attend one of the Prussian king's musical soirees, Friedemann offered to travel with him to Potsdam. "We will finally have a chance to meet Emmanuel's wife and see his son."

They made the trip in the spring of 1747. It was late afternoon when they arrived. They had just alighted from their coach at Emmanuel's residence when a courier from the king arrived to escort them to the palace. Sebastian immediately turned to follow him.

"You must change, Papa. You can't enter the presence of a king looking like that."

Sebastian surveyed his black coat and breeches. The coat was the one Anna and Dorothea had made for his portrait. It was a little dusty, but a good brushing would probably take care of it. "Punctuality is more important," he said and followed the courier to the chaise with Friedemann straggling behind.

When they arrived at the castle, the doorman hurried Sebastian up a winding staircase and across a marble floor to the *Stadtschloss*. The music room was said to be the Prussian king's favorite room in the new palace. Frederick was an accomplished flautist and a genuine connoisseur of chamber music.

When Sebastian entered the room, his first impression was that of stark contrast. The room had green walls and gilded wood carvings, and the women in the audience wore brocade skirts that billowed out from their waists like umbrellas. But the King was in simple military dress. He wore a red waistcoat with black breeches, high boots and a pigtail.

He was standing in front of a stand holding his flute, his musicians arranged in a semicircle in front of him with the audience behind.

Emmanuel, who was wearing a white periwig like the King's, was seated at a Silbermann piano. Sebastian knew Silbermann and had suggested some improvements to his piano to improve the action and tone. He was interested to see what the quality of this one was like. The piano had such potential.

The doorman whispered the news of Bach's arrival to the King, and the King immediately raised both arms for silence.

"Gentleman," he said, "old Bach is come!"

Everyone turned in his direction and began a polite applause. Surprised that the King would take this much notice of him, he bowed and then with Friedemann's help, wound his way through the people to the King. Frederick the Great's presence was overpowering. His bearing was so authoritative that when Sebastian found himself face to face with him, he felt like falling to his knees. Instead, he bowed again, as deeply as he could manage, and apologized for his appearance.

"We are here for music, not dress," Frederick said, and then he smiled at Sebastian.

"Your skills at the keyboard are legendary, and I have an intense interest in musical puzzles. I have a theme for you."

The King strode to the piano. Emmanuel slid off the bench, and the king played his theme.

Immediately, Sebastian was intrigued. The theme had a long descending figure of chromatic notes that would be difficult to transform into a fugue, but he lived for such challenges. He forgot everything but the music he already heard in his head. He sat down at the piano.

He played the theme first in a two-part, then a three-part fugue. Then he elongated it, inverted it, embellished it and tried a canon. When he finished, everyone applauded enthusiastically. He felt he could have treated the theme more masterfully if he'd had more time, but the king seemed pleased. Frederick set him other puzzles and asked him to play some original works. Then he paraded him through the castle, ferreting out every harpsichord and Silbermann piano so that Sebastian could pronounce his verdict on each instrument and bring out its greatest powers. He even asked Sebastian to accompany him on a tour of the organs of Potsdam during the next few days to judge the organs of the city. It was a wonderful time in every part, except that it was exhausting.

Sebastian traveled home with Friedemann, feeling grateful for the easiness of his son's presence. He could be silent with Friedemann. He could think. Being feted by such a ruler as Frederick the Great had been exciting. It was something he had not expected.

He must remember that his rule for living ever since the riot in the church was to daily repent and so to cultivate humility. Despite the counsel of others to give in and write rococo music in order to gain more popularity, he had years ago decided to stay within the boundaries of the old music. To him it was far more than a stand for the traditional. It was a stand against a music that had no depth. He would work with Frederick the Great's theme and create something masterful. He would write it for the glory of God and to honor the king, and he would call it the *Musical Offering*.

5

Sebastian remained vigorous for the next two years of his life, except for his deteriorating eyesight. By January of 1750 he could see nothing but blurred shapes of light and dark. It was agony not to be able to see to compose. He decided to risk a cataract operation. Dr. Beidermann contacted a peripatetic oculist from England for him, and the operation was set for March 20.

The procedure was done in Sebastian's home, and when the doctor removed the bandages a few days after the operation, Sebastian could see. Certain that this was a new lease on life and eager to finish his *Art of the Fugue,* Sebastian left his bed too soon. There were complications, and the doctor had to operate again several days later.

This time when the bandages were removed, Sebastian could see nothing at all. The world was black as the densest ink.

The days passed with Sebastian so weak he couldn't leave his room, and the school began to advertise for another Cantor. But in spite of his condition, he continued his work, dictating more revisions to Anna or to his son-in-law. Liessgen had married a young man named Altnikol, who had worked for some time as a bass singer and string player for Sebastian.

Never did Sebastian let up in his determination to leave nothing mediocre behind. His legacy would be one of excellence for the greater glory of God. Had his life counted? he wondered. What would happen to his work? In his mind he saw his church cycles carefully stacked and marked so anyone could find a specific Sunday's music with ease. "These, Lord," he prayed, "these, especially, are my gift to You."

He thought of all the agonies of soul he had experienced in his sixty-five years of life: the battle with Duke Wilhelm, his friendship with August, his setting up Prince Leopold as an idol, his failure with Barbara during the last years of their marriage, his folly at Carlsbad, and all his pride over his work in Leipzig and the temptation toward raw rationalism that had caused him to profane the house of God. The thinking of the philosophers had begun to reach into the mind of the common man, even here in Germany. Sebastian wondered what such thinking would lead to: the age of man, the triumph of reason without revelation? Sebastian was convinced that no one could imagine the scope of the Eternal Verities. Man needed revelation. He prayed that his music would give to those who heard it a holy rest and a belief in God's Word.

One morning he was praying, and the sounds in the house faded. Suddenly he felt as though he were on a different plane. He walked the seven steps to the chair in front of the window where Anna always laid out his clothes. He was praying, communing, his spirit reaching, longing with an unutterable longing for a more intimate experience with the only Other in the universe who could satisfy all his desires. My aims have been high in this life, he thought, and the cost dear. But if my struggles and sacrifices have in any way pleased my God, it will have all been worth it.

As he stood facing the window, enjoying the warmth of the sun on his face, its light seemed to flow into him and grow and shimmer and color. As suddenly as the crash of cymbals in the midst of a long solitude, the view from the window burst upon him. There before him was the high summer green of the park, pierced with beams of light and dots of yellow and red, and blue above it—strong bright blue, eternity reaching, wooing him up and on. He could see!

Afterword
N o v e m b e r   1 0 ,   1 7 5 0

Why do you sing, O bird concealed in a tree?
Has Sol's raised head beguiled you this November day?
You trill as though your heart could never be free
Of joy. You lilt, you pause, you burst again
Into sentences long of worshiped praise.
And already the wind chills.
Are you mocked by the Daystar? Or do you know?
Wiser than we, do you leap to rejoice the moment there's chance?
Do you seize it, feel it, speak the joy to the corners of its fullness
So I can know it and wrap it in my memory—
For when the darkness comes?

It was several months after Sebastian's sight had returned, and Anna sat
at the kitchen table, attempting to write in a journal. The poem had come
easily, but as she tried to write about the events of the last several months,
she scratched out words and agonized over spellings. It was hard to see the
reality of her loss on paper. Sebastian's absence was a stone in her very soul,

and the written word seemed only to make it worse. The doctor had insisted, however, and she had never been one to ignore the advice of those she trusted. Finally, she asked her son-in-law to help her with the details:

> *"Sebastian was so excited that day his sight was restored that he shouted like a boy. He wondered what his sudden sight could mean. But only a few hours later he was seized by a stroke and then a burning fever that laid him to bed, never to get up again. We lost him on the evening of July 28, 1750. He was in his sixty-sixth year, a long life for our day, but the length comforts me little. The heartbeat of my life has gone.*
>
> *"We buried him in the Thomaskirche burial grounds. The funeral service was well attended. All the family was there, and all Sebastian's Leipzig friends and many of his pupils.*
>
> *"Telemann came with Emmanuel, and Picander arrived early and stayed late, weeping much and speaking to me of how he had missed Sebastian, and how he was once again seeking God. The greatest surprise, however, was Gorner. Not only did he play the organ for the service beautifully, he came to the house every day for a month afterward, helping us with whatever we needed. And now he has offered the girls and me financial help, which I fear we shall greatly need. Liessgen and her husband are taking Heinrich, and Emmanuel has consented to take Christian. Emmanuel is the only son with adequate finances to support all of us, but he has let us know in no uncertain terms that the girls and I are on our own. I do not know what will happen to us.*
>
> *"Every now and then, when I am unable to sleep, I pause on my way to the kitchen at Sebastian's study door. And I imagine I see him the way I so often did, sitting there thick and energetic in his black leather chair, candles flickering in his brass candelabra. He is humming and tapping his foot, his ears are privy to sounds and realities no one else can hear. He was an oasis, a miraculous clearing in the forest, a place of beauty that outer chaos could never destroy.*
>
> *"I have always believed that because Sebastian used his gift with excellence for the glory of God he would be rewarded. We are promised blessings pressed down, shaken together and running over. Now that Sebastian is gone, I do not see how such a promise can ever be fulfilled. But we see through a glass darkly. We have no choice but to trust."*

Postlude

The story of the life of Johann Sebastian Bach is not complete until it tells in a few bold strokes how his works were resurrected. That story is a drama in itself.

After Sebastian died, his works sank into oblivion. They were outdated before they were completed. In the last half of the eighteenth century, the name Bach meant either Carl Phillip Emmanuel Bach (Emmanuel) or Johann Christian Bach (Christian).

Sebastian's works were remembered only by connoisseurs and a handful of faithful students and followers. Most of his cantatas, passions, oratorios and motets lay hidden in the Thomaskirche library. The *Art of the Fugue* sold no more than thirty copies, and Friedemann and Emmanuel were far from meticulous about guarding their father's original manuscripts. Friedemann gained notoriety for his indiscriminate selling of his father's manuscripts in order to turn a penny.

Then in 1789 a young musician named Wolfgang Amadeus Mozart set out to visit Berlin. En route, he stopped at the Leipzig Thomaskirche and played Sebastian's old organ. The current Cantor, a former pupil of Sebastian's, was so pleased that he surprised Mozart with a performance of Sebastian's motet, *Sing unto the Lord a New Song*. According to an eyewitness, the choir had only sung a few measures when "Mozart sat up, startled; a few more measures and he called out, 'What is this?'"

When the motet was finished, he exclaimed in a kind of rapture, "Now there is something one can learn from!"

Upon his request to see the score, the Cantor explained they had no conductor's score, only parts. Mozart said that then he must see the parts. When Mozart received them, he sat down "with all the parts around him—in both hands, on his knees, and on the chairs next to him—and, forgetting everything else, did not get up again until he had looked through everything of Sebastian Bach's that was there."[1] After that incident Mozart's compositions exhibited a sense of counterpoint and complexity that had been absent before.

In 1802 Johann Nicolaus Forkel published the first official biography of Johann Sebastian Bach. Much of it was based on information from Friedemann and Emmanuel.

Samuel Wesley, nephew of John Wesley and a brilliant organist, promoted the cause of Sebastian's music in England. Wesley considered Bach's works a musical Bible and would often exclaim when practicing one of Sebastian's organ chorales or fugues, "I am sure that none but a good man could have written this."[2]

Some years later, Ludwig van Beethoven devoted the proceeds of a concert to Sebastian's only surviving daughter, Regina Susannah. She was living in poverty. Beethoven called Sebastian the "Father of Harmony."

It was the year 1829, however, that saw the true revival of Johann Sebastian Bach. A twenty-year-old genius named Felix Mendelssohn took a risk "for the honor of God and Johann Sebastian Bach." At this time, great musicians and connoisseurs were recognizing Sebastian's genius and were encouraging increased publication of his works, but the public still considered his music unmelodious, mathematical and unintelligible.

Under the tutelage of Carl Friederich Zelter, who was a leading personality in the musical life of Berlin, Mendelssohn had come to know and love Sebastian's vocal works, particularly the *St. Matthew Passion*. Urged on by a few Bach enthusiasts, he began rehearsals for what may have been the first public performance of the *St. Matthew Passion* since its Thomas-kirche premier.

The young Mendelssohn had entered the project with a great deal of apprehension. Audiences were accustomed to hearing a Bach piece or two performed as a part of a many-composered program—but a whole evening of nothing but Sebastian Bach? It could be a disastrous failure. Mendelssohn's friend Eduard Devrient, who would be singing the part of Christ, encouraged him: "The *St. Matthew Passion* (is) the greatest and most important of German musical works. (It is) our duty, not to rest until we (have) brought it to life again so that once more it might edify man's spirits."[3]

As the Berlin singers and instrumentalists rehearsed over a period of weeks under Mendelssohn's artful direction, their enthusiasm grew. They were amazed at the Passion's architectonic grandeur, its abundance of melody, wealth of expression and powerful dramatic effects.

Mendelssohn knew that nothing less than instant success was needed, and that is exactly what God gave him.

Every obstacle vanished. When Devrient wrote his account of the March 11, 1829 performance, he said, "Never before have I felt a holier solemnity vested in a congregation than in the performers and audience that evening."[4]

A second and third performance were demanded. The second took place ten days later and was crowded like the first. The third was presented a month later under the direction of Zelter.

The sensation in educated circles of Berlin was extraordinary. Everyone felt this revival of the popularity of a half-forgotten genius was of profound importance. Rehearsals sprang up in other cities, and other works of Sebastian's were performed, notably his *St. John Passion* and his instrumental works.

The Bach revival had begun.

In 1843, at the urging of Mendelssohn and Robert Schumann, the people of Leipzig erected a monument to Sebastian Bach at the Thomaskirche. He had been buried there in an insignificant grave.

In 1850 the *Bach Gesellschaft* was founded for the purpose of publishing a complete edition of Sebastian's compositions. As they worked, music scholars came to the conclusion that it was doubtful whether anyone in the world of music had matched Johann Sebastian Bach's industriousness. When his scores were finally collected and published, the completed edition filled sixty huge volumes.

In 1888 a Bach Choir was established in Bethlehem, Pennsylvania, a Moravian center with strong ties to Germany—musical as well as religious. Their programs typically include major choral works of Bach's with leisurely intermissions and the playing of chorales by a brass quintet. During the progress of the sacred works, the congregation stands to sing the chorales.

In 1950 the Lutheran Bach Society was formed to encourage the use of Sebastian's church cycle as part of the Lutheran liturgy.

Toward the end of the twentieth century we can read about a Bach performance somewhere almost every day. Dance companies choreograph works like the *Musical Offering* and the *Goldberg Variations*. Virtuosic pianists consider even his simpler works such as the *Two-and Three-Part Inventions* worth recording. The prestigious boys' choir at the Thomaskirche in Leipzig considers itself Bach's Choir. The famous cellist Yo-Yo Ma invites a landscape artist, a kabuki performer, a choreographer, an architect, a film maker and an ice dancer duo to help him design videos to accompany his rendition of Bach's six cello suites. A New York chorus celebrates its twenty-fifth anniversary by performing twenty-five Bach cantatas. The conductor says, "The cantatas are the most important body of church music ever written."[5]

Charles Marie Widor, French organist, composer and teacher of Albert Schweitzer, summarized Sebastian's music legacy with these words: "Bach is . . . the most universal of artists. What speaks through his works is pure religious emotion. . . . For me, Bach is the greatest of preachers. His cantatas and Passions tune the soul to a state in which we can grasp the truth . . . and rise above everything . . . paltry, everything that divides us."[6]

A Word from the Author

Many who read this record of Bach's life ask me, "Was it really this way? Did this really happen?" I wish I could sit down with each of you and answer your specific questions about which events are history and which were invented to fill in the gaps. It may be helpful for you to know that every chapter of *Bach's Passion* is based on at least one historical event in his life. And, yes, the herring story is true! After his death, Bach's sons jested about how their father was forever retelling the story of the herrings at the dinner table. As regards the rest of the book, I have sought to remain true to every date to which we have access. Each of the major characters is real. Only Eugenia and a handful of minor personages are fictional. It has been a special joy to me to bring to life Bach's wives and children.

Glossary

Adonis wig. Man's wig made of fine hair; very fashionable and very expensive. "a fine flowing adonis or white periwig."[1]

Allemande. A simple, rather heavy dance in moderate duple time, first appearing about 1550. In the seventeenth century it became a stylized dance type used as the first movement of the suite.

Amusa. A term used for someone who had little or no interest in music.

Appoggiatura. An ornamental note that is connected melodically with the following main note. It is sung in the same breath.

Aria. A melody in an opera, cantata or oratorio for solo voice with instrumental accompaniment.

Badinerie. A dance-like piece of humorous character which appears in some eighteenth-century suites.

Ballade. In German usage, a poem derived from the English ballads but of greater poetic refinement. The ballade dealt with historical or fanciful matters, usually medieval, and was often set to music.

Bard. An ancient poet and singer of epic poems who accompanied himself on an instrument.

Baroque Era. A period of history (approximately 1550 to 1750) when the style of art and architecture was characterized by curved rather than straight lines and much ornamentation. The music consisted of highly embellished melodies and fugal or contrapuntal forms.

Bass viol. The chief instrument of the string family in the Baroque Era, also called viola da gamba, possessing six and or seven strings.

Blancmange. A sweet, molded jelly-like dessert made with milk, flavoring and starch or gelatin.

Bourree. A seventeenth-century French dance in quick duple meter with a single upbeat.

Brioche. A light, rich yeast roll made with flour, butter and eggs, shaped like a fat bun with a topknot.

Burgher. One of the conservative middle class.

Canon. A type of composition in which a melody introduced in one voice is restated in other voices that overlap the first and successive voices in strict imitation.

Cantata. A composite vocal form of the Baroque Period, consisting usually of a number of movements such as arias, recitatives, duets and choruses based upon a continuous narrative text.

Cantor. The director of music in the German Protestant Church.

Caparison. An ornamented covering for a horse.

Cartel clock. A clock (usually a wall clock) that has a cartel or decorative point at the bottom of its case.

Cartesianism. The philosophical or mathematical ideas of René Descartes.

Cartonneir. A wooden organizer used for filing papers.

Catherinakir che. The church in Hamburg where Johann Adam Reincken served as composer and organist from 1663 to his death in 1722. His work in this position won him a considerable reputation in North Germany.

Cauliflower wig. A bob-wig that is closely curled.

Chemise. Shirt-like undergarment, generally of linen.

Chaconne. A form of baroque music characterized by continuous variation in moderately slow triple meter.

Chaise. Lightweight carriage with two or four wheels, drawn by one or two horses. Some have collapsible tops.

Chorales. The hymn tunes of the German Lutheran Church. Martin Luther, who was an accomplished musician himself, considered the chorale an important pillar of his reform movement. He preferred vernacular texts and simple, tuneful melodies, and he worked diligently to build up a repertoire of suitable texts and melodies.

Chur ch music cycle. Music written for the five-year-cycle of a church's authorized liturgy.

Clarino r egister. The highest notes on the valveless trumpet of the seventeenth and eighteenth centuries. Trumpeters in Bach's time were trained to play a continuous scale from the third octave upward (without valves!). The most outstanding trumpet virtuosos of modern times find the high, rapid passages of the Bach epoch baffling.

Clavichord. The earliest type of stringed keyboard instrument, consisting of a wooden oblong box, sometimes portable, sometimes resting on legs. The strings are set in vibration by tangents, small brass wedges that are fastened to the rear of the lever.

Clavier . Any keyboard, including an organ.

Collegium Musicum. Musical association connected with a university.

Compendium. Concise but comprehensive treatise.

Concerto. A musical composition for one, two or three solo instruments and an orchestra.

Confiseuires. French pastries.

Contredanse. A dance in which two couples face each other and move against each other in a variety of steps and movements.

Continuo. The bass part of baroque composers' scores. Played by harpsichord or organ along with viola da gamba or cello.

Cotillion. A formal ball.

Counterpoint. The art of adding related but independent melodies to a basic melody in accordance with fixed rules of harmony.

Cravat. Neckerchief or scarf.

Descant. A florid melody sung by a few treble voices as a harmonic addition to the main melody.

Diapason. In medieval musical theory, the octave. Derived meaning: the flue-pipe work of the organ which forms the backbone of each keyboard. The diapason tone does not exist in any other instrument. It is characteristic of the organ.

Domino. Loose robe or cloak with wide sleeves and hood, worn at masquerades with a mask.

Ducat. Term used for a gold piece in eighteenth-century Austria, Bavaria and Germany.

Duke. A prince who rules an independent duchy. In eighteenth-century Germany, the terms Prince, Duke, and Margrave were often used interchangeably.

Empiricism. The search for knowledge by experiment and observation.

Epaulette. An ornament for the shoulder of certain uniforms.

Flautist. A person who plays the flute.

Fop. A vain, affected man who is too enamored with his clothes and appearance.

Fowling piece. Type of shotgun used for hunting wild fowl.

French overture. The first standard type of overture. It consists of a slow introduction followed by a lively piece in imitative style.

Fugue. The latest form of imitative counterpoint, brought to its highest perfection by J. S. Bach. Always written in contrapuntal style, it is based on a short melody called a subject or a theme, which is stated at the beginning in one voice and is imitated by other voices in close succession. It continues to reap-- pear throughout the entire piece in different places and in all voices.

Galliard. A sixteenth-century dance in moderately quick triple time. It was danced with exaggerated leaps.

Garret. The space or rooms just below the sloping roof of a house.

Gavotte. A French dance of the seventeenth century in moderate 4/4 time. Bach frequently used the stylized gavotte in his instrumental suites.

Gedackt. A term used for an organ register consisting of stopped pipes (pipes plugged at the top to produce a tone an octave lower).

Gigue. One of four dance movements in the suites written between 1650 and 1750. It is characterized by dotted rhythms and is written in either 6/8 or 6/4 time.

Grenadier. An infantry solider who is a member of a regiment attached to a royal household.

Groschen. A coin probably comparable to the American nickel.

Gross untersat. One of the stops (the handle by which the organist draws on or shuts off different registers) on Bach's Weimar organ.

Harpsichord. A keyboard instrument of the sixteenth to the eighteenth centuries; similar in shape to the modern grand piano, but differing from it in the pro- duction of sound. The strings are plucked mechanically by a plectrum instead of being struck by a hammer. The greatest deficiency of the harpsichord is its inability to produce gradations of sounds by a stronger or lighter touch.

Heath. A tract of open wasteland covered with low shrubs and heather.

Herr. In German, a man or a gentleman. Also used as a title corresponding to *Mr.*

Hessian. Any of the mercenaries from the western central region of Germany called Hesse. These mercenaries fought in America on the side of the British in the Revolutionary War.

Hoforganist. The organist in an eighteenth-century German church, sometimes responsible for writing the music and directing the choir.

Hombre. A card game played by three players with forty cards, popular in the seventeenth and eighteenth centuries.

Hurdy gurdy. An early instrument shaped like a lute or a viol, played by turning a crank attached to a wheel.

Improvisation. The act of composing, or simultaneously composing and perform- ing, on the spur of the moment and without any preparation.

Kapelle. Private or small orchestra, often including voices.

Kapellmeister . The director and supervisor of all the music and musicians in a court.

Kreuzer. The term used for groschen in South German territories.

Konzertmeister. Choirmaster responsible for directing Kapelle and sometimes composing music.

Laudanum. Any of certain opium preparations used as treatment for an assortment of ills in the seventeenth and eighteenth centuries.

Librettist. A writer of the words or text of an opera, oratorio or other long choral work.

Lipizzaner. Imported into Austria from Spain and Italy in the mid-1500s, these beautiful show horses have strong bones, short legs and thick, arched necks. Most of them turn white when they mature. The best known Lipizzans in modern times are those trained in Vienna at the Spanish Riding School. They perform graceful jumping and dancing feats.

Liturgy. The prescribed form of ritual for public worship in any of various religions or churches.

Lute. An old stringed instrument related to the guitar. Its body is shaped like half a pear. It possesses six to thirteen strings stretched along a fretted neck, which is often bent into a sharp angle. Some of the strings are tuned in unison or in the octave for a louder sound. These strings are called courses.

Lutanist. A lute player.

Lute-harpsichord. An invention of Johann Sebastian Bach's that sounded like a lute, but was played like a harpsichord.

Mantua. Loose gown possessing an unboned bodice. It was joined to an overskirt with a long train and worn open in front to expose a decorative underskirt.

Margrave. See Duke.

Michelsschule. St. Michael's School in Luneburg, Germany, affiliated with St. Michael's Church. In Bach's time this "Latin school" possessed a famous choir school that offered scholarships to talented students.

Minuet. 1. A slow, stately dance of French rustic origin. Introduced at the court of Louis XIV around 1650, it soon became a favorite dance all over Europe. 2. A movement in a baroque suite written in 3/4 time, to be played at a very moderate tempo.

Monad. In philosophy an elementary being thought of as an ultimate unit.

Motet. A contrapuntal song of a sacred nature, usually unaccompanied.

Musica theorica. An ancient interpretation of music that considers "music in its measured arrangement as an image of the perfect cosmos, rationally ordered by God according to measure and number."[2]

Musica practica. Based on "the model of that Father of the church, Augustine," this is the idea that "music is the praise of God, and its effect on men the renewal of the heart, in the sense of cleansing from evil, and 'all music' has this effect, not only church music."[3]

Narthex. The church vestibule leading to the nave. In early Christian churches a porch at the west end for penitents.

Nazar d. A mutation stop on the organ used with a unison or octave rank to change the character of the tone by focusing on a certain overtone.

Oboe da caccia. Possibly a Leipzig innovation of the oboe. Curved tenor oboe covered with leather.

Ordres. F. Couperin's name for his collections of pieces in the same key. An ordre usually begins with pieces in the allemande, courante and sarabande style, but also includes other pieces with fanciful titles.

Overture. Instrumental music used as an introduction to an opera, oratorio or other
similar work.

Partita. A musical term used in the seventeenth and eighteenth centuries for either a suite or a series of variations.

Passepied. A dance of a spirited character in 3/8 or 6/8 meter.

Passion. A musical setting of the text of the Passion (the sufferings from Gethsemane to the cross) of Christ. Bach uses the biblical text as basic narrative and poetic texts for arias and large choruses. His form is a succession of cantatas, each concluding with a chorale.

Pastille. Originally a French term for a flavored lozenge containing medicine.

Pianofor te. Term used for the piano by its inventor because of the new instrument's gradation of tone in contrast with the harpsichord. Invented by Bartolommeo Cristofori of Florence and experimented with by the most famous of early piano makers, Gottfried Silbermann.

Plectrum. A small piece of horn, tortoise-shell, wood, ivory or metal used for the playing of certain stringed instruments. A harpsichord's quills are a mechanized form of plectrum.

Point d'Angleterre lace. A bobbin lace, wherein you use a small notched piece of wood, bone or ivory called a bobbin.

Polonaise. A Polish dance of festive and stately character that developed from courtly ceremonies and processions.

Polyphony . Music written as a combination of several simultaneous voices, each having some degree of individuality. Counterpoint.

Posaune. An organ stop that sounds like a trombone.

Postilion. One who rides the left-hand horse of a two-horse carriage when there is no driver.

Prefect. In some private schools, an older student with disciplinary authority.

Prince. See Duke.

Probe. Term used for the audition given to eighteenth-century musicians when applying for a church job.

Quadrille. 1. Names of dance figures. 2. Pieces of a march-like character which are played during the entry of dancing groups or of important personages. 3. The name of a four-player card game popular in the eighteenth century.

Quodlibet. A humorous form of music characterized by quotations of well-known melodies or texts combined in an illogical manner.

Ragout. Highly seasoned stew of meat and vegetables.

Rathaus. Town hall.

Refector y. Dining hall in a school, monastery or convent.

Resolution. The passing of a dissonant chord or tone in a chord to a consonant chord (or tone). The moving from the discordant to the harmonious.

Rood. Large crucifix at the entrance to the chancel of a medieval church, often supported by a rood screen.

Rococo. In the fine arts and applied arts, a designation for the eighteenth-century style that was characterized by an abundance of merely decorative scroll and shell work and by a tendency toward hedonism and frivolity. In music, the rococo style exhibits the same tendencies with an emphasis on pleasantness and prettiness. The wholehearted adoption of the rococo style resulted in a deterioration of artistic standards under certain musicians.

Rucksack. A type of knapsack strapped across the shoulders.

Sarabande. A seventeenth- and eighteenth-century dance of dignified character, written in slow triple meter. The sarabande from Bach's sixth partita shows the dance in its final stage of artistic idealization.

Semiquaver . Sixteenth note.

Savoir -fair e. On-hand knowledge of what to do or say.

Ser f. A person in servitude, bound to his master's land and transferred with it to any new owner.

Sculler y. A room not far from the kitchen where pots and pans are cleaned and stored, where the rougher, dirtier kitchen work is done.

Sforzando. Forcing with a sudden and strong accent on a note or chord.

Sonata. Today, a composition for one or two instruments, usually consisting of several movements. Originally, an instrumental composition as opposed to a cantata (something sung).

Sprezzatura. The nonchalant attitude that was supposed to be a habitual part of the aristocrat's bearing in the eighteenth century.

Stankgemach. German word for privy. In eighteenth-century cities it was often built into a closet in the corner of the attic.

Suite. An important form of instrumental baroque music consisting of a number of movements all in the same key. Each movement possessed the character of a dance.

Staccato. Sharp, distinct breaks between successive tones.

Surtout. Loose, long overcoat with one or more spreading collars. It was worn by men in the latter half of the seventeenth century and on into the nineteenth century.

Thaler. Comparable to the American dollar or the English pound.

Thomaskir che. St. Thomas' Church in Leipzig, Germany.

Thomasschule. St. Thomas' School, affiliated with St. Thomas' Church.

Timbr e. The quality of sound that distinguishes one voice or instrument from another.

Toccata. An organ or harpsichord composition in free, idiomatic keyboard style, employing chords and running passages; usually quite virtuosic.

Tricor ner. A hat with the brim folded up against the crown to create three sides.

Trills. 1. A rapid alternation of a musical tone with the tone above it. 2. the warbling sound made by some birds.

Valise. A piece of old-fashioned hand luggage.

Viola da gamba. See bass viol.

Viola d'amour . A member of the viol family, all lacking the brilliance of the modern violins. The viola d'amour was distinctive in that it possessed sympathetic strings made from thin wire stretched behind the bowed strings. This produced a silvery resonance.

Wilhelmsbur g. The larger castle on the Weimar royal grounds, the dwelling of the Grand Duke of Weimar.

Notes

CHAPTER 3

1. Maurice Ashley, *The Golden Century*, (New York: Frederick A. Praeger Publishers, 1969), p. 213.
2. W. Murray Young, *The Cantatas of J. S. Bach* (Jefferson, North Carolina: McFarland and Company, Inc., Publishers, 1989), p. 21.

CHAPTER 4

1. Johann Friedrich Reichardt, "Bach Judged at the Distance of Half a Century" [quoted by Hans T. David, Arthur Mendel, eds., *The Bach Reader* (New York: W.W. Norton and Company, 1966), p. 265.]

CHAPTER 5

1. W. H. Bruford , *Germany in the Eighteenth Century: The Social Background of the Literary Revival* (London: Cambridge, At the University Press, 1935), p.18.
2. Herbert Kupferberg, *Basically Bach* (New York: McGraw-Hill Book Company, 1984), p. 54.

CHAPTER 7

1. Romain Rolland, *Jean-Christophe in Paris* (quoted in *Basically Bach* by Herbert Kupferberg), p. 173.

CHAPTER 8

1. Jacques Gelis, "The Child: From Anonymity to Individuality," from *A History*

of Private Life III, Roger Chartier, ed., (Cambridge, Massachusetts: The Belknap Press of Harvard University Press, 1989), p. 315.

2. David Ewen, *Musical Masterworks,* 1944.
3. This movement is known today as the "Air on the G String."

CHAPTER 9

1. Robert Anchor, *The Enlightenment Tradition* (New York: Harper & Row, 1967), p. 36.
2. Antoine-Francois Prevost, *Manon Lescaut,* quoted by Robert Anchor in *The Enlightenment Tradition* (New York: Harper & Row Publishers, 1967), p. 56.
3. Robert Dumm, "The Play of Courtship," *Clavier* (Evanston, IL: The Instrumentalist Co., March–April, 1966), p. 41.

INTERLUDE TWO

1. Blaise Pascal, *Conversions* (Grand Rapids, MI: Eerdmans Publishing Co., 1983).

CHAPTER 10

1. W. H. Bruford, *Germany in the Eighteenth Century: The Social Background of the Literary Revival* (London: Cambridge, At the University Press, 1935), p. 113.
2. Salomon Franck, Cantata Text quoted in *J. S. Bach, Life: Times, Influence* (New Haven and London: Yale University Press, 1984), p. 25.

CHAPTER 11

1. Johann Mattheson, Hans T. David and Arthur Mendel, eds., *The Bach Reader* (New York, NY: W. W. Norton and Company, 1966) page 81.
2. Mark Salzman, "Exploring Bach All Over Again with the Help of His Friends," *New York Times,* September 7, 1997, H-79.

CHAPTER 12

1. Justinus Kerner, quoted by W. H. Bruford, *Germany in the Eighteenth Century: The Social Background of the Literary Revival* (London: Cambridge, At the University Press, 1935), p. 100.

2. Anthony Tommasini, "Complex Uses of Simplicity," *New York Times,* September 1, 1997, A-13.

CHAPTER 13

1. Kupferberg, Herbert, *Basically Bach,* (New York: McGraw-Hill Book Company, 1984), p. 82.

CHAPTER 14

1. Robert Jourdain, *Music, the Brain and Ecstasy* (William Morrow & Company, 1997), quoted by Christopher Lehman-Haupt in a New York Times newspaper article, "How Does Mozart Chill the Spine?"

CHAPTER 15

1. Kenneth Clark, *Civilisation,* (New York: Harper & Row, 1969), p. 231.
2. Greenberg, Robert, "Bach and the High Baroque," *Greatest Lectures by America's Superstar Teachers,* (Fall Catalog, 1996), p. 21.

CHAPTER 16

1. Leo Schrade, *Bach, The Conflict between the Sacred and the Secular* (NY: Da Capo Press, 1973), p. 88.
2. Roland, H. Bainton, *Here I Stand* (New York: Meridian, 1950), pp. 255, 257.
3. Hans T. David, Arthur Mendel, Editors, *The Bach Reader* (New York: W.W. Norton & Company, 1966) pp. 128, 129.

CHAPTER 17

1. Barbara Schwendowius and Wolfgang Domling, eds., *Johann Sebastian Bach: Life, Times, Influence* (New Haven and London: Yale University Press, 1984), p. 13.
2. Herbert Kupferberg, *Basically Bach* (New York: McGraw-Hill Book Company, 1984), p. 65.

INTERLUDE FOUR

* Blaise Pascal quoted by Robert Anchor in *The Enlightenment Tradition* (New

York: Harper & Row, 1967), p. 60.

CHAPTER 18

1. Barbara Schwendowius and Wolfgang Domling, *Johann Sebastian Bach: Life, Times, Influence* (New Haven and London: Yale University Press, 1984), p. 13
2. Eva Mary Grew and Sydney Grew, *Bach* (New York: Collier Books, 1962), p. 153.
3. Barbara Schwendowius and Wolfgang Domling, *Johann Sebastian Bach: Life, Times, Influence* (New Haven and London: Yale University Press, 1984), p. 29.
4. Hans T. David, Arthur Mendel, eds., *The Bach Reader* (New York: W.W. Norton & Company, 1966), p. 97.

POSTLUDE

1. Hans T. David, Arthur Mendel, eds., *The Bach Reader,* (New York: W.W. Norton & Company, 1966), p. 360.
2. *Ibid.*, p. 366.
3. *Ibid.,* p. 379.
4. *Ibid.,* p. 385.
5. Harold Rosenbaum quoted by James R. Oestreich, "An All-Bach Program that, the Fact Is, Isn't Quite," The *New York Times*, November 21, 1997.
6. Charles Widor, quoted by Albert Schweitzer, translated by Ernest Newman, *J. S. Bach* (Boston: Bruce Humphries Publishers, 1911), xii.

GLOSSARY

1. Edward Maeder, Editor, *An Elegant Art* (New York: Harry N. Abrams, Inc. Publishers, 1983), p. 221.
2. Barbara Schwendowius and Wolfgang Domling, Editors, *Johann Sebastian Bach: Life, Times, Influence* (New Haven and London: Yale University press, 1984), p. 97.
3. Ibid., p. 97.

Selected Bibliography

Anchor, Robert. *The Enlightenment Tradition.* New York: Harper & Row, 1967.

Apel, Willi. *Harvard Dictionary of Music* . Cambridge, Massachusetts: Harvard University Press, 1960.

Apel, Willi. *Masters of the Keyboard.* Cambridge, Massachusetts: Harvard University Press, 1947.

Ashley, Maurice. *The Golden Century.* New York: Frederick A. Praeger Publishers, 1969.

Bainton, Roland H. *Here I Stand.* New York: Meridian, 1977.

Boorstin, Daniel J. *The Creators.* New York: Random House, 1992.

Boyd, Malcolm. *Bach.* New York: Vintage Books, 1983.

Bruford, W. H. *Germany in the Eighteenth Century: The Social Background of the Literary Revival.* London: Cambridge: At the University Press, 1935.

Burney, Francis. *Continental Travels of Dr. Francis Burney,* 1770.

Chartier, Robert, ed. *A History of Private Life: Passions of the Renaissance.* Cambridge, Massachusetts: Harvard University Press, 1989.

Clark, Kenneth. *Civilisation.* New York: Harper & Row, 1969.

Cumming, Valerie. *A Visual History of Costume: The Seventeenth Century.* New York: Drama Book Publishers, 1984.

David, Hans T.; Mendel, Arthur, eds. *The Bach Reader.* New York: W W. Norton & Company, 1966.

Dowley, Tim. *Bach.* London: Omnibus Press, 1981.

Ewen, David, ed. *Great Composers, 1300–1900.* New York: H. W. Wilson Co., 1966.

Grew, Eva Maria and Syndey. *Bach.* New York: Collier Books, 1947.

Harman, Carter. *A Popular History of Music.* New York: Dell Publishing, 1956.

Hook, Judith. "Religion in the Age of the Baroque." *The Christian World: A Social and Cultural History.* Edited by Geoffrey Barraclough. New York: Harry N. Abrams, Inc., 1981.

Hutcheson, Ernest. *The Literature of the Piano.* New York: Alfred. A. Knopf, 1964.

Kupferberg, Herbert. *Basically Bach*. New York: McGraw-Hill Book Company, 1984.

Leaver, Robin A. *J. S. Bach and Scripture: Glosses from the Calov Bible Commentary*. St. Louis: Concordia Publishing House, 1985.

Lindsay, J. O., ed. *The New Cambridge Modern History: Volume VII, The Old Regime (1713–63)*. London: Cambridge University Press, 1957.

Machlis, Joseph. *The Enjoyment of Music*. New York: W. W. Norton & Co, 1957.

Maeder, Edward, ed. *An Elegant Art*. New York: Harry N. Abrams, Inc. Publishers, 1983.

Marly, Diana de. *An Illustrated History*. New York: Holmes and Meier Publishers, Inc., 1985.

Melton, James Van Horn. *Absolutism and the 18th Century Origins of Compulsory Schooling in Prussia and Austria*. Cambridge: Cambridge University Press, 1988.

Pirro, Andre. *J.S. Bach*. New York: The Orion Press, 1957.

Schrade, Leo. *Bach, The Conflict between the Sacred and the Secular*. New York: Da Capo Press, 1973.

Schweitzer, Albert. *J. S.. Bach*. Boston: Bruce Humphries Publishers, 1911.

Schwendowius, Barbara and Domling, Wolfgang, ed., *J. S. Bach: Times and Influence*. New Haven and London: Yale University, 1984.

Sheehan, James J. *German History: 1770–1866*. Oxford: Clarendon Press, 1989.

Winternitz, Emanuel. *Musical Autographs*. New York: Dover Publications, Inc., 1965.

Young, W. Murray. *The Cantatas of J. S. Bach*. Jefferson, North Carolina: MacFarland and Company, Inc., Publishers, 1989.

To order additional copies of

Bach's Passion

send $16.99 plus $3.95 shipping and handling to

Books Etc.
PO Box 4888
Seattle, WA 98104

or have your credit card ready and call

(800) 917-BOOK